FAIR GAME

Titles by Patricia Briggs

The Mercy Thompson Novels
MOON CALLED
BLOOD BOUND
IRON KISSED
BONE CROSSED
SILVER BORNE
RIVER MARKED

The Alpha and Omega Novels
ON THE PROWL
(with Eileen Wilks, Karen Chance, and Sunny)
CRY WOLF
HUNTING GROUND
FAIR GAME

MASQUES
WOLFSBANE
STEAL THE DRAGON
WHEN DEMONS WALK

THE HOB'S BARGAIN

DRAGON BONES
DRAGON BLOOD

RAVEN'S SHADOW
RAVEN'S STRIKE

FAIR GAME

AN ALPHA AND OMEGA NOVEL

PATRICIA BRIGGS

ACE BOOKS, NEW YORK

THE BERKLEY PUBLISHING GROUP
Published by the Penguin Group
Penguin Group (USA) Inc.
375 Hudson Street, New York, New York 10014, USA
Penguin Group (Canada), 90 Eglinton Avenue East, Suite 700, Toronto, Ontario M4P 2Y3, Canada
(a division of Pearson Penguin Canada Inc.) • Penguin Books Ltd., 80 Strand, London WC2R 0RL,
England • Penguin Group Ireland, 25 St. Stephen's Green, Dublin 2, Ireland (a division of Penguin
Books Ltd.) • Penguin Group (Australia), 250 Camberwell Road, Camberwell, Victoria 3124, Australia
(a division of Pearson Australia Group Pty. Ltd.) • Penguin Books India Pvt. Ltd., 11 Community
Centre, Panchsheel Park, New Delhi—110 017, India • Penguin Group (NZ), 67 Apollo Drive,
Rosedale, Auckland 0632, New Zealand (a division of Pearson New Zealand Ltd.) • Penguin Books
(South Africa) (Pty.) Ltd., 24 Sturdee Avenue, Rosebank, Johannesburg 2196, South Africa

Penguin Books Ltd., Registered Offices: 80 Strand, London WC2R 0RL, England

This is an original publication of The Berkley Publishing Group.

This is a work of fiction. Names, characters, places, and incidents either are the product of the author's
imagination or are used fictitiously, and any resemblance to actual persons, living or dead, business
establishments, events, or locales is entirely coincidental. The publisher does not have any control over
and does not assume any responsibility for author or third-party websites or their content.

FIRST EDITION: March 2012

Library of Congress Cataloging-in-Publication Data

Briggs, Patricia.
Fair game : an Alpha and Omega novel / Patricia Briggs.—1st ed.
p. cm.—(Alpha and Omega ; 3)
ISBN 978-0-441-02003-4 (hardback)
1. Werewolves—Fiction. 2. Serial murderers—Fiction. I. Title.
PS3602.R53165F35 2012
813'.6—dc23
2011047724

PRINTED IN THE UNITED STATES OF AMERICA

10 9 8 7 6 5 4 3 2 1

To all those who live in the dark fighting monsters
so the rest of us stay safe

ACKNOWLEDGMENTS

No story is written alone. I'd like to thank the usual suspects as well as Supervisory Special Agent Randy Jarvis, Public Affairs Specialist Katherine Gulotta, and Special Agent Greg Comcowich of the Boston FBI for the time and effort they spent so I had a chance at getting things right. Thanks also go to the fine people of the Ghosts & Gravestones Tour of Boston. You rock. Though I have to say, if I never hear the phrase "Boston Molassacre" again, it will be too soon. Brenda Wahler sent critical information at just the right moment. Thank you.

As always, if this book is enjoyable, it is their fault—all mistakes are mine.

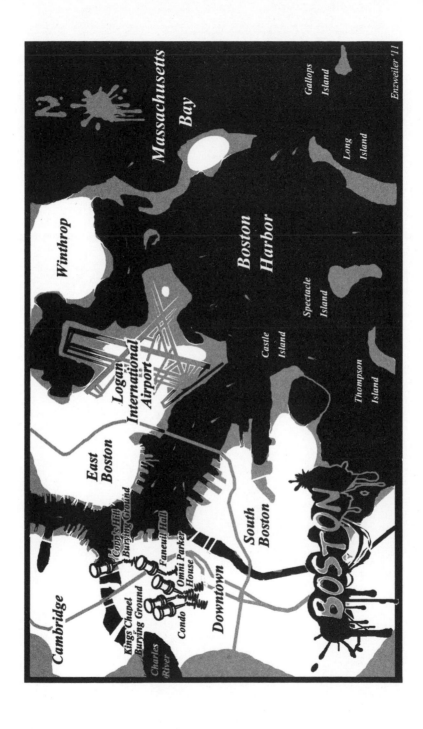

A Fairy Tale

Once upon a time, there was a little girl named Leslie.

The year she turned eight, two things happened: her mother left Leslie and her father to move to California with a stockbroker; and, in the middle of a sensational murder trial, the fae of story and song admitted to their existence. Leslie never heard from her mother again, but the fairies were another matter.

When she was nine, her father took a job in a strange city, moving them from the house she'd grown up in to an apartment in Boston where they were the only black people in an all-white neighborhood. Their apartment encompassed the upper floor of a narrow house owned by their downstairs neighbor, Mrs. Cullinan. Mrs. Cullinan kept an eye on Leslie while her dad was at work, and by her silent championship eased Leslie's way into the society of the neighborhood kids who casually dropped by for cookies or lemonade. In Mrs. Cullinan's capable hands, Leslie learned to crochet, knit, sew, and cook while her dad kept the old woman's house and lawn in top shape.

Even as an adult, Leslie wasn't sure if her dad had paid the old woman or if she'd just taken over without consulting him. It was the kind of thing Mrs. Cullinan would have done.

When Leslie was in third grade, one of the kindergarten boys went missing. In fourth grade, one of her classmates, a girl by the name of Mandy, disappeared. There were also, throughout the same time period, a lot of missing pets—mostly kittens and young dogs. Nothing that would have attracted her attention if it weren't for Mrs. Cullinan. On their daily walks (Mrs. Cullinan called them "busybody strolls," to see what people in their neighborhood were up to), the old woman began stopping at missing-pet notices taped in store windows and taking out a little notebook and writing all the information in it.

"Are we looking for lost animals?" Leslie asked finally. She mostly learned from observation rather than by asking questions because, in her experience, people lied better with their lips than they did with their actions. But she hadn't come up with a good explanation for the missing-pet list and she was forced, at last, to resort to words.

"It's always good to keep an eye out." It was a not-quite answer, but Mrs. Cullinan sounded troubled, so Leslie didn't ask her again.

When Leslie's new birthday puppy—a mutt with brown eyes and big feet—went missing, Mrs. Cullinan had gotten tight-lipped and said, "It is time to put a stop to this." Leslie was pretty sure her landlady hadn't known anyone was listening to her.

Leslie, her father, and Mrs. Cullinan were eating dinner a few days after her puppy's disappearance when a fancy limousine pulled up in front of Miss Nellie Michaelson's house. Out of the dark depths of the shiny vehicle emerged two men in suits and a woman in a white flowery dress that looked too summery and airy to be a good match for the men's attire. They were dressed for a funeral and she for a picnic in the nearby park.

Unabashedly spying, Leslie's father and Mrs. Cullinan left the table to stare out the window as the three people entered Miss Nellie's house without knocking.

"What are they . . . ?" The expression on Leslie's father's face changed from curious (no one ever visited Miss Nellie) to grim in a heartbeat, and he grabbed his service revolver and his badge. Mrs. Cullinan caught him on the front porch.

"No, Wes," she said in a strange, fierce voice. "No. They are fae and it's a fae mess they've come to clean up. You let them do what they need to."

Leslie, peering around the adults, finally saw what had gotten everyone in a tizzy. The two men were carrying Nellie out of her house. Nellie was struggling, her mouth wide-open as if she were screaming, but not a sound came out.

Leslie had always thought that Nellie looked as though she should be a model or a movie star, with her sad blue eyes and downturned soft mouth. But she didn't appear so pretty right then. She didn't look frightened—she looked enraged. Her beautiful face was twisted, ugly, and, at the same time, breath-stealingly scary in a way that would haunt Leslie's dreams even as an adult.

The woman, the one in the airy-fairy dress who'd come with the men, exited the house about the same time the men finished stuffing Nellie in the backseat of the car. She locked the door of Nellie's house behind her, and when she was finished she looked up and saw the three of them watching. After a pause, she strolled across the street and down the sidewalk to them. The woman didn't appear to be walking fast, but she was opening the front gate almost before Leslie realized that she was heading for them.

"And what do you think you're looking at?" she said mildly, in a voice that had Leslie's father thumbing the snap that held his gun in the holster.

Mrs. Cullinan stepped forward, her jaw set like it had been the day that she'd faced down a couple of young toughs who'd decided an old woman was fair game. "Justice," she said with the same soft menace that had sent the boys after easier prey. "And don't get uppity with me. I know what you are and I'm not afraid of you."

The strange woman's head lowered aggressively and her shoulders got tight. Leslie took a step behind her father. But Mrs. Cullinan's retort had drawn the attention of the men by the limousine.

"Eve," said one of the men mildly, his hand on the open car door. His voice was mellow and rich, as thick with Ireland as Mrs. Cullinan's own, and it carried across the street and down the block as if there were no city sounds to muffle it. "Come to the car and keep Gordie company, would you?" Even Leslie knew it wasn't a request.

The woman stiffened and narrowed her eyes, but she turned and walked away from them. When she had taken his place at the car, the man approached them.

"You'd be Mrs. Cullinan," he said, as soon as he was on their side of the street and close enough for quiet conversation. He had one of those mildly good-looking faces that didn't stand out in a crowd—except for his eyes. No matter how she tried, Leslie could never remember what color his eyes were, only that they were odd and strange and beautiful.

"You know I am," Mrs. Cullinan said stiffly.

"We appreciate you calling us on this and I would like to leave you with a reward." He held a business card out to her. "A favor when you need it most."

"If the children are safe to play in their yards, that is reward enough." She dried her hands on her hips and made no move to take the card from him.

He smiled and did not put down his hand. "I will not leave indebted to you, Mrs. Cullinan."

"And I know better than to accept a gift from the fairies," she snapped.

"Onetime reward," he said. "A little thing. I promise that no intentional harm will come to you or yours from this as long as I am alive." Then, in a coaxing voice, he said, "Come, now. I cannot lie. This is a different age, when your kind and ours needs must learn to live together. You could have called the police with your suspicions—which were correct. Had you done so, she would not have gone without killing a great many more than the children she has already taken." He sighed and glanced back at the car's darkened windows. "It is difficult to change when you are so old, and she was always in the habit of eating small things, was our Nellie."

"Which is why I called you," Mrs. Cullinan said stoutly. "I didn't know who it was taking the little ones until I saw Nellie over by our backyard two nights ago and this child's puppy was missing in the morning."

The fae looked at Leslie for the first time, but Leslie was too upset to read his face. "Eating small things," the man had said. Puppies were small things.

"Ah," he said after a long moment. "Child, you may take what comfort you can that your puppy's death meant that no more would die from that one's misdeeds. Hardly fair recompense, I know, but it is something."

"Give it to her," Mrs. Cullinan said suddenly. "Her puppy's dead. Give her your reward. I'm an old woman with cancer; I won't live out the year. Give it to her."

The fae man looked at Mrs. Cullinan, then knelt on one knee before Leslie, who was holding very tightly to her father's hand. She didn't know if she was crying for her puppy, the old woman who was more her mother than her mother had ever been—or for herself.

"A gift for a loss," he said. "Take this and use it when you most need it."

Leslie put her free hand behind her back. He was trying to make up for her puppy's death with a present, just like people had tried to do after her mom had left. Presents didn't make things better. Quite the opposite, in her experience. The giant teddy bear her mama had given her the night she left was buried in the back of the closet. Although Leslie couldn't stand to get rid of it, she also couldn't look at it without feeling sick.

"With this you could get a car or a house," the man said. "Money for an education." He smiled, quite kindly—and it made him look totally different, more real, somehow, as he said, "Or save some other puppy from monsters. All you have to do is wish hard and tear up the card."

"Any wish?" Leslie asked warily, taking the card, more because she didn't want to be the focus of this man's attention any longer than because she wanted the card. "I want my puppy back."

"I can't bring anyone or anything back to life," he told her sadly. "I would that I could. But outside of that, almost anything."

She stared at the card in her hand. It had one word written across it: GIFT.

He stood up. Then he smiled—an expression as merry and light as anything she'd ever seen. "And, Miss Leslie," he said, when he shouldn't have known her name at all, "no wishing for more wishes. It doesn't work like that."

She'd just been wondering . . .

The strange man turned to Mrs. Cullinan and took her hand in his and kissed it. "You are a lady of rare beauty, quick wits, and generous spirit."

"I'm a nosy, interfering old woman," she responded, but Leslie could see that she was pleased.

As an adult, Leslie kept the card the fairy man had given her tucked behind her driver's license. It looked as clean and fresh as it had the day she'd agreed to take it. To the shock of her doctors, Mrs. Cullinan's cancer mysteriously disappeared and she'd died in her bed twenty years later at the age of ninety-four. Leslie still missed her.

Leslie learned two valuable things about the fae that day. They were powerful and charming—and they ate children and puppies.

CHAPTER

1

ASPEN CREEK, MONTANA

"Go home," Bran Cornick growled at Anna.

No one who saw him like this would ever forget what lurked behind the Marrok's mild-mannered facade. But only people who were stupid—or desperate—would risk raising his ire to reveal the monster behind the nice-guy mask. Anna was desperate.

"When you tell me you will quit calling on my husband to kill people," Anna told him doggedly. She didn't yell, she didn't shout, but she wasn't going to give up easily.

Clearly, she'd finally pushed him out to the very narrow edges of his last shred of civilized behavior. He closed his eyes, turned his head away from her, and said, in a very gentle voice, "Anna. Go home and cool off." Go home until *he* cooled off was what he meant. Bran was Anna's father-in-law, her Alpha, and also the Marrok who ruled all the werewolf packs in his part of the world by the sheer force of his will.

"Bran—"

His power unleashed with his temper, and the five other wolves, not counting Anna, who were in the living room of his house dropped to the floor, even his mate, Leah. They bowed their heads and tipped them slightly to the side to expose their throats.

Though he made no outward move, the speed of their surrender testified to Bran's anger and his dominance—and only Anna, somewhat to her surprise at her own temerity, stayed on her feet. When Anna had first come to Aspen Creek, beaten and abused as she'd been, if anyone had yelled at her, she'd have hidden in a corner and not come out for a week.

She met Bran's eyes and bared her teeth at him as the wave of his power brushed past her like a spring breeze. Not that she wasn't properly terrified, but not of Bran. Bran, she knew, would not really hurt her if he could help it, no matter what her hindbrain tried to tell her.

She was terrified for her mate. "You are wrong," Anna told him. "Wrong. Wrong. Wrong. And you are determined not to see it until he is broken beyond repair."

"Grow up, little girl," Bran snarled, and now his eyes—bright gold leaching out his usual hazel—were focused on her instead of the fireplace in the wall. "Life isn't a bed of roses and people have to do hard jobs. You knew what Charles was when you married him and when you took him as your mate."

He was trying to make this about her, because then he wouldn't have to listen to her. He couldn't be that blind, just too stubborn. So his attempt to alter the argument—when there should be no argument at all—enraged her.

"Someone in here is acting like a child, and it isn't me," she growled right back at him.

Bran's return snarl was wordless.

"Anna, *shut up*," Tag whispered urgently, his big body limp on the floor where his orange dreadlocks clashed with the maroon of the Persian rug. He was her friend and she trusted the berserker's judgment on most things. Under other circumstances she'd have listened to him, but right now she had Bran so angry he couldn't speak—so she could get a few words in past his stubborn, inflexible mind.

"I know my mate," she told her father by marriage. "Better than you do. He will *break* before he disappoints you or fails to do his duty. *You* have to stop this because he can't."

When Bran spoke, his voice was a toneless whisper. "My son will not bend or break. He has done his job for a century before you were even born, and he'll be doing it a century from now."

"His job was to dispense *justice*," she said. "Even if it meant killing people, he could do it. Now he is merely an assassin. His prey cling to his feet repentant and redeemable. They weep and beg for mercy that he can't give. It is destroying him," she said starkly. "And I'm the only one who sees it."

Bran flinched. And for the first time, she realized that Charles wasn't the only one suffering under the new, harsher rules the werewolves had to live by.

"Desperate times," he said grimly, and Anna hoped that she'd broken through. But he shook off the momentary softness and said, "Charles is stronger than you give him credit for. You are a stupid little girl who doesn't know as much as she thinks she does. Go home before I do something I'll regret later. Please."

It was that brief break that told her this was useless. He did know. He did understand, and he was hoping against hope that Charles could hold out. Her anger fled and left . . . despair.

She met her Alpha's eyes for a long moment before acknowledging her failure.

ANNA KNEW EXACTLY when Charles drove up, newly returned from Minnesota where he'd gone to take care of a problem the Minnesota

11

pack leader would not. If she'd been deaf to the sound of the truck or the front door, she'd have known Charles was home by the magic that tied wolf to mate. That was all the bond told her outright, though—his side of their bond was as opaque as he could manage, and that told her a whole lot more about his state of mind than he probably intended.

From the way he let nothing leak through to her, she knew it had been another bad trip, one that had left too many people dead, probably people he hadn't wanted to kill.

Lately, they had all been bad trips.

At first she'd been able to help, but when the rules changed, when the werewolves had admitted their existence to the rest of the world, the new public scrutiny meant that second chances for the wolves who broke Bran's laws were offered only in extraordinary circumstances. She'd kept going with him on these trips because she refused to let Charles suffer alone. But when Anna started having nightmares about the man who'd fallen to his knees in front of her in mute entreaty before his execution, Charles had quit letting her go.

She was strong-willed and she liked to think of herself as tough. She could have made him change his mind or followed him anyway. But Anna hadn't fought his edict because she realized she was only making his job harder to bear. He saw himself as a monster and couldn't believe she didn't also when she witnessed the death he brought.

So Charles went out hunting alone—as he had for a hundred years or more, just as his father had said. His hunt was always successful— and, at the same time, a failure. He was dominant; he had a compulsory need to protect the weak, including, paradoxically, the wolves he was there to kill. When the wolves he executed died, so did a part of Charles.

Before Bran had brought them out to the public, the new wolves, those who had been Changed for less than ten years, would have been given several chances if their transgression came from loss of control. Conditions could have been taken into account that would lessen the punishment of others. But the public knew about them now, and they couldn't allow everyone to know just how dangerous werewolves really were.

It was up to the pack Alpha to take care of dispensing commonplace justice. Previously, Charles had only had to go out a few times a year to take care of bigger or more unusual problems. But many of the Alphas were unhappy with the new harshness of the laws, and somehow more and more of the enforcement fell to Bran and thus to Charles. He was going out two or three times a month and it was wearing on him.

She could feel him standing just inside the house, so she put a little more passion into her music, calling him to her with the sweet-voiced cello that had been his first Christmas gift to her.

If she went upstairs, he'd greet her gravely, tell her he had to go talk to his father, and leave. He'd come back in a day or so after running as a wolf in the mountains. But Charles never quite came back all the way anymore.

It had been a month since he'd last touched her. Six weeks and four days since he'd made love to her, not since they'd come back from the last trip she'd accompanied him on. She'd have said that to Bran if he hadn't made that "Grow up, little girl" comment. Probably she should have told Bran anyway, but she'd given up making him see reason.

She'd decided to try something else.

She stayed in the music room Charles had built in the basement while he stood upstairs. Instead of using words, she let her cello speak for her. Rich and true, the notes slid from her bow and up the stairway. After a moment she heard the stairs squeak under the weight of his feet and let out a breath of relief. Music was something they shared.

Her fingers sang to him, coaxing him to her, but he stopped in the doorway. She could feel his eyes on her, but he didn't say anything.

Anna knew that when she played on her cello, her face was peaceful and distant—a product of much coaching from an early teacher who told her that biting her lip and grimacing was a dead giveaway to any judge that she was having trouble. Her features weren't regular enough for true beauty, but she wasn't ugly, either, and today she'd used some makeup tricks that softened her freckles and emphasized her eyes.

She glanced at him briefly. His Salish heritage gave him lovely dark skin and exotic (to her) features, his father's Welsh blood apparent only in subtle ways: the shape of his mouth, the angle of his chin. It was his job, not his lineage, that froze his features into an unemotional mask and left his eyes cold and hard. His duties had eaten away at him until he was nothing but muscle, bone, and tension.

Anna's fingers touched the strings and rocked, softening the cello's song with a vibrato on the longer notes. She'd begun with a bit of *Pachelbel's Canon in D*, which she generally used as a warm-up or when she wasn't sure what she wanted to play. She considered moving to something more challenging, but she was too distracted by Charles. Besides, she wasn't trying to impress him, but to seduce him into letting her help. So, Anna needed a song that she could play while thinking of Charles.

If she couldn't get Bran to quit sending her mate out to kill, maybe she could get Charles to let her help with the aftermath. It might buy him a little time until she could find the right baseball bat—or rolling pin—to beat some clarity into his father's head.

She deserted Pachelbel for an improvised bridge that shifted the key from D to G and then let her music flow into the prelude of Bach's *Cello Suite No. 1*. Not that that music was easy, but it had been her high school concert piece so she could practically play it in her sleep.

Her fingers moving, she didn't allow herself to look at him again, no matter how hungry she was for the sight of him. She stared at an oil painting of a sleeping bobcat while Charles stood at the door and watched her. If she could get him to approach her, to quit trying to protect her from his job . . .

And then she screwed up.

She was an Omega wolf. That meant that not only was she the only person on the continent whose wolf would allow her to face down the Marrok when he was in a rage, but also that she had a magical talent for soothing wolfish tempers regardless of whether or not they wanted to be soothed. It felt wrong to impose her will on others, and she tried not to do it unless the need was dire. Over the past couple of years, Anna had learned when and how to best use her ability. But her need to see Charles happy slipped over the barrier of her hard-won control as if it wasn't there at all.

One moment she was playing to him with her whole self, focused solely on him—and the next her wolf reached out and calmed Charles's wolf, sent him to sleep, leaving only his human half behind . . . Charles turned and walked purposefully away from her without a word. He, who ran from nothing and no one, exited their house by the back door.

Anna set down her bow and returned her cello to its stand. He wouldn't come back for hours now, maybe not even for a couple of days. Music hadn't worked if the only thing holding Charles in its spell was his wolf.

She left the house, too. The need to do something was so strong it had her moving without a real destination. It was that or cry, and she refused to cry. Maybe she could go to Bran one more time. But when the turnoff for his house appeared, she drove past it.

Like as not Charles was headed to Bran's to tell his father what he'd done for the wolves of the world—and it would be . . . awkward to follow him, as if she were chasing him. Besides, she'd already talked to Bran. He knew what was happening to his son; she knew he did. But, like Charles, he weighed the lives of all of their kind against the possibility that Charles would break under the strain of what was necessary, and thought the risk acceptable.

So Anna drove through town, arriving at a large greenhouse in the woods on the other side. She pulled over and parked next to a battered Willys Jeep and went in search of help.

A lot of wolves called him the Moor—which he disliked, saying that it was a vampire kind of thing to do, take a part of who a person was and reduce him to it with a capital letter or two. His features and skin showed traces of Arabia by way of North Africa, but Anna agreed that certainly wasn't the sum total of who he was. He was very beautiful, very old, extremely deadly—and right now he was transplanting geraniums.

"Asil," she began.

"Hush," he said. "Don't disturb my plants with your troubles until they are safe in their new houses. Make yourself useful and deadhead the roses along the wall."

She snagged a basket and started picking dead flowers off Asil's rosebushes. There would be no talking to him until he'd accomplished what he intended, whether that was to calm her down before they talked, get some free labor, or merely keep the silence while he tended his plants. Knowing Asil, it could be all three.

She worked for about ten minutes before she got impatient and reached for a rosebud, knowing that he always kept an eye on anyone working with his precious flowers.

"Remember the story of Beauty and the Beast?" remarked Asil gently. "Go ahead. Take that little bloom. See what happens."

" 'Beauty and the Beast' is a French fairy tale and you are a mere Spaniard," Anna told him, but she took her fingers off the bud. Beauty's father had stolen a flower at great cost. "And in no way are you an enchanted prince."

He dusted off his hands and turned to her, smiling a little. "Actually, I am. For some definitions of 'prince.' "

"Hah," said Anna. "Poor Belle would find herself kissing your handsome face and then, poof, there would be the frog."

"I think you are mixing your fairy tales," Asil told her. "But even as a frog I would not disappoint. You came to talk fairy tales, *querida*?"

"No." She sighed, hopping up to sit on a convenient flat table next to a bunch of small pots that held a single pea-sized leaf each. "I'm here to get advice about beasts. Specifically, information about the beast who rules us all. Naturally I sought you out. Bran has to quit sending Charles out to kill. It is destroying him."

He sat on the table opposite hers and looked at her with the space of the narrow aisle between them. "You do know that Charles lived nearly two hundred years without you to take care of him, yes? He is not a fragile rosebud who needs your tender touch to survive."

"He's not a killer, either," Anna snapped.

"I beg to differ." Asil spread his hands peaceably when she snarled at him. "The results speak for themselves. I doubt that there are any other wolves with so many werewolf kills under their belt outside of present company." He indicated himself with a modest air that was a tribute to his acting skills, since he didn't have a modest bone in his body.

Anna shook her head at him, her hands curling into fists of frustration. "He isn't. Killing *hurts* him. But he sees it as necessary—"

"Which it is," murmured Asil, clearly patronizing her.

"Fine," she agreed sharply, hearing the growl in her voice but unable to keep it down. Failing so spectacularly with Bran had taught her she needed to keep her own temper in check if she wanted to convince old dominant wolves of anything. "I know that it is necessary. Of course it is necessary. Charles wouldn't kill anyone if he didn't see that it was *necessary*. And Charles is the only one dominant enough to do the job who is also not an Alpha, since that would cause trouble with the Alpha of the territories he must enter. Fine. It doesn't mean that he can continue like this. Necessary does not mean possible."

Asil sighed. "Women." He sighed again, theatrically. "Peace, child.

I *do* understand. You are Omega and Omegas are worse than Alphas about protecting their mates. But your mate is very strong." He grimaced as he said it, as if tasting something bitter. Anna knew that he didn't always get along with Charles, but dominant wolves often had that problem with one another. "You just have to have a little faith in him."

Anna met his gaze and held it. "He doesn't bring me with him anymore when he goes. When he came home this afternoon, I used my magic to send his wolf to sleep, and as soon as the wolf was quiet he left without a word."

"You expected living with a werewolf to be easy?" Asil frowned at her. "You can't fix everyone. I told you that. Being Omega doesn't make you Allah." Asil's long-dead mate had been an Omega. Asil had taught Anna all that she knew about it, which he seemed to believe gave him some sort of in loco parentis status. Or maybe he just patronized everyone. "Omega doesn't mean power without end. Charles is a stone-cold killer—ask him yourself. And you knew it when you married him. You should quit worrying about him and start worrying about how *you* are going to deal with accepting the situation you got yourself into."

Anna stared at him. She knew that he and Charles weren't bosom buddies or anything. She hadn't realized that he didn't know Charles at all, that Asil saw only the front he put on for everyone else.

Asil had been her last, forlorn hope. Anna levered herself off the table. She turned her back on Asil and strode to the door, feeling the heavy weight of despair. She didn't know how to make him, to make *Bran*, see how bad things were. Bran was the one who counted. Only he could keep Charles home. She had failed to persuade her father-in-law. She'd been hoping that Asil might help.

It was still light out and would be for a few more hours, but the air was already stirring with the weight of the waxing moon. She held the door open and turned back to Asil. "You are all wrong about him. You and Bran and everyone else. He *is* strong, but no one is that strong. He hasn't picked up an instrument, hasn't even sung a note for months."

Asil's head came up and he stared at her a moment, proving that he knew something about her husband after all.

"Perhaps," he said slowly with a frown, rising to his feet. "Perhaps you are right. His father and I should speak."

ASIL LET HIMSELF into the Marrok's house without knocking. Bran had never objected, and another wolf might think he just never noticed. Asil knew that Bran noticed everything and had chosen to allow Asil's subtle defiance for his own reasons. And *that* was almost enough to make Asil knock on the door and wait for an invitation to enter. Almost.

Leah was on the living room couch, watching something on the big TV. She looked up as he passed by and didn't bother smiling, while a woman screamed shrilly from the surround-sound speakers. When Asil had come to Montana, Leah'd flirted with him—his Alpha's mate, who should know better. He'd allowed her the first one, but the second time he'd taught her not to play her games with him.

So she sat on the couch, glanced up at him and then away, as if he bored her. But they both knew that he scared her. Asil was slightly ashamed of that, only because he knew his mate, dead but still beloved, would be disappointed in him. Teaching Leah to be afraid of him had been easier and more satisfactory than just letting her know that her flirtations were unwelcome and would not gain her whatever it was that she wished.

Had he not expected the Marrok to execute him in short order— which was the reason he'd come to the Montana pack—he might not have done such a thorough job of it. But he was not unhappy that Leah ignored him as much as possible—and less unhappy that the Marrok would not kill him than he had expected to be. Asil found that life still had the power to surprise him, so he was willing to stick around for a little while longer.

He followed the sound of quiet voices to the Marrok's study, pausing in the hallway to wait when he realized the man talking to the Marrok was Charles. Had it been anyone else, he'd have intruded, expecting the lesser wolf—and they were all lesser wolves—to give way.

Asil frowned, trying to decide if what he had to say would play better with Charles in the room or not. Strategy would be important. A dominant wolf, such as him or Bran, could not be compelled, only persuaded.

In the end he decided on a private talk and continued on to the library, where he found a copy of *Ivanhoe* and reread the first few chapters.

"Romantic claptrap," said Bran from the doorway. Doubtless he'd scented Asil as soon as Asil had walked by the study earlier. "As well as historically full of holes."

"Is there something wrong with that?" asked Asil. "Romance is good for the soul. Heroic deeds, sacrifice, and hope." He paused. "The need for two dissimilar people to become one. Scott wasn't trying for historical accuracy."

"Good thing," grunted Bran, sitting down on the chair opposite the love seat Asil had claimed. "Because he didn't manage it."

Asil went back to reading his book. It was an interrogation technique he'd seen Bran use a lot and he figured the old wolf would recognize it.

Bran snorted in amusement and gave in by beginning the conversation. "So what brings you out here this afternoon? I trust it wasn't a sudden desire to read Sir Walter's dashing romance."

Asil closed the book and gave his Alpha a look under his lashes. "No. But it is about romance, sacrifice, and hope."

Bran threw his head back and groaned. "You've been talking to Anna. If I'd known what a pain in the ass it would be to have an Omega who doesn't back down in my pack, I'd have—"

"Beaten her into submission?" Asil murmured slyly. "Starved and abused her and treated her like dirt so she would never understand what she was?"

The silence became heavy.

Asil gave Bran a malicious smile. "I know better than that. You'd have asked her to come here twice as fast. It's good for you to have someone around who doesn't back down. Ah, the frustrating joy of having an Omega around. I remember it well." He smiled more broadly when he realized he'd once thought he'd never smile at the memory of his mate again. "Irritating as hell, but good for you. She's good for Charles, too."

Bran's face hardened.

"Anna came to see me," Asil continued, watching Bran carefully. "I told her she needed to grow up. She signed on for the hard times as well as the good. She needs to realize that Charles's job is tough and that sometimes he's going to need time to deal with it." That was not exactly what he'd said, but he'd have bet it was what Bran had told her. His Alpha's blank face told him he was right on target.

"I told her that there was a larger picture that she wasn't looking at," Asil continued with false earnestness. "Charles is the only one who can do his job—and that it has never been more necessary than it is now, with the eyes of the world on us. It's not easy covering up the deaths with stories of wild dogs or scavenger animals eating someone's body after they died from something else, not anymore. Police are looking for signs that their killers might be werewolves, and we can't afford that. I told her she needed to grow up and deal with reality."

The muscle on Bran's jaw tightened because Asil had always had a talent for imitation—he thought he'd gotten Bran's voice just about perfect on the last few sentences.

"So she gave up on me," Asil said, back in his own voice. "She was leaving while I sat content in the smug knowledge that she was a weak female who was more concerned with her mate than with the good of the whole. Which is only what a woman should be like, after all. It really isn't fair to blame them for it when it inconveniences us."

Bran looked at him coolly, so Asil knew he'd hit hard with that last remark.

Asil smiled ruefully and caressed the book he held. "Then she told me that it's been months since he's made any music, *viejito*. When was the last time that one went more than a day without humming something or playing that guitar of his?"

Bran's eyes were shocked. He hadn't known. He rose to his feet and began pacing.

"It is a *necessity*," Bran said at last. "If I don't send him, then who goes? Are you volunteering?"

It would be impossible; they both knew it. One kill, or maybe as many as three or four, and his control would be gone. Asil was too old, too fragile, to be sent out hunting werewolves. He would enjoy it entirely too much. He could feel the wild spirit of his wolf leap at the chance of such a hunt, the chance of a real fight and the blood of a strong opponent between his fangs.

Bran was still ranting. "I *cannot* send an Alpha into another pack's territory without it becoming a challenge that will spawn even more bloodshed. I cannot send *you*. I cannot send Samuel because my oldest son is even more at risk than you are. I cannot go because I'd have to kill every damned Alpha—and I have no desire to take every werewolf into my personal pack. If not Charles, then who do I send?"

Asil bowed his head to Bran's anger. "That's why *you* are the Alpha and *I* will do anything I can to never be Alpha again." He stood up, head still lowered. He caressed the fabric cover of the book and set it down on the table. "I don't think I really need to read this book again. I have always thought Ivanhoe should have married Rebecca, who was smart and strong, instead of choosing Rowena and what he thought was right and proper."

Asil left Bran alone with his thoughts then, because if he stayed, Bran would argue with him. This way, Bran would have no one to argue with but himself. And Asil had always credited Bran with the ability to be persuasive.

BRAN STARED AT *Ivanhoe*. Its cover was a dull blue gray, the weave of the cloth a visible sign of its age. He ran his fingers over the indentations that were the title and the line drawing of a knight wearing sixteenth-century armor. The book had once had a paper cover with an even less appropriate picture on the front. He knew that inside, on the flyleaf, there was an inscription, but he didn't open the book to find it. He was pretty sure Asil had been here long enough to go through the whole damned library to find this book. Charles had given it to him, maybe seventy years ago.

Merry Christmas, it said. *You've probably read this book a dozen times before. I read it for the first time a couple of months ago and thought that you might take comfort in this tale of the possibility that two dissimilar people might learn to live together—a good story is worth revisiting.*

It was a good story, even if it was historically inaccurate and romantic.

Bran took the book and replaced it gently on the bookshelf before he gave in to his impulse to rip it into small pieces, because then he wouldn't stop until there was nothing left to destroy—and no one could manage him if that happened. He needed Charles to be something he was not, and his son would kill himself trying to be what his father needed.

How long had he lied to himself that Charles would be fine? How long had he known that Anna was right to object? There were many reasons, good, sound reasons, for Bran not to be the one doing the killing. He'd given Asil one of them. But his real reason, his true reason, was more like Asil's, though that one was more honest about it. How long would it be until Bran started to enjoy the pleading, the suffering, before the kill? He didn't remember much about the time he let his wolf take charge, though the world still had record of it and it had happened more than ten centuries ago. But some of the memories he did retain were of his terrified victims and the satisfaction their cries had brought him.

Charles would never do that, would never glory in the fear others felt of him. He would never do more than what was needed. A paradox, then. Bran needed Charles to be just what he was—and Charles needed to be the monster his father was to survive it.

The phone rang, saving Bran from his thoughts. Hopefully it was a different problem he could sink his teeth into. Something with a solution.

"I WON'T DO it," Adam Hauptman said when Bran called.

Bran paused.

It had surprised him no end when Adam, of all his Alphas, had been the one best suited to deal with the feds. Adam had a terrible temper and not as tight a leash on it as was prudent. For that reason, Bran had kept him back, out of the limelight, for all of Adam's looks and charisma. But his experience in the military and his contacts, as well as an unexpectedly good understanding of politics and political blackmail, had turned him gradually into Bran's most useful political chessman.

It was unlike Adam to refuse.

"It's not a difficult assignment," Bran murmured into the phone, holding back the wolf who wanted to insist on instant obedience. "Just an exchange of information. We've lost three people in Boston and the FBI thinks it's connected to a larger case and want a werewolf to consult with. The local Alpha isn't qualified—and he's too young to be good at diplomacy when his own people are dying."

"If they want to fly out here, that will be fine," Adam said. "But Mercy's legs aren't healed and she can't get around in the wheelchair without help because her hands were burned."

"Your pack won't help her?" Icy rage froze his voice. Mercy might be mated to Adam, but to his wolf she would always belong to Bran. Would always be his little coyote, who was tough and defiant, raised by a good friend because Bran couldn't trust his mate with someone he cared about who was more fragile than his grown sons.

Adam gave a huff of laughter that eased Bran's ire. "It's not that. She's grumpy and embarrassed at being helpless. I had to leave last week on business. By the time I got back, the vampire had to come take care of her because she'd driven everyone else off. *I* don't have to listen when she tells *me* to leave her alone, but everyone else does."

Pleased at the thought of Mercy ordering around a bunch of werewolves, Bran settled back in his chair.

"Bran? Are you all right?"

"Don't worry," Bran said. "I'll get David Christiansen to do it. The FBI will just have to wait a week or so until he gets back from Burma."

"That's not what I was asking," Adam said. "'Volatile' is not a word I'd normally apply to you—but you aren't yourself today. Are you all right?"

Bran pinched his nose. He should just keep it to himself. But Adam . . . He couldn't talk to Samuel about this; the only thing that would do would be to make his oldest son feel guilty.

Adam knew all the players and he was an Alpha; he'd understand without Bran having to explain everything.

Adam listened without comment—except a snort when he heard how neatly Asil had turned the tables on Bran.

"You need to keep Asil around," he said. "The rest of them are too intimidated to play games with you—and you need that now and again to keep you sharp."

"Yes," said Bran. "And the rest?"

"You have to back off on the death sentences," Adam said with certainty. "I heard about Minnesota. Three wolves took out a pedophile stalking a third grader with a rope in his hand and a stun gun in his pocket."

Bran growled. "I wouldn't have objected except they got carried away and then left his half-eaten body to be discovered the next day before they told their Alpha what happened. If they'd just snapped his neck, I could have let it go." He pinched his nose again. "As it is, the coroner is speculating all over the papers."

"If you backed off, Charles wouldn't have to go out and kill so often, because you wouldn't have so many Alphas refusing to take care of discipline."

"I can't," Bran said tiredly. "Have you seen the new commercials Bright Future has sponsored? The endangered species hearings are beginning next month. If they classify us as animals, it won't be just the problem wolves being hunted."

"We are what we are, Bran. We're not civilized or tame, and if you force that upon us, it won't be only Charles who loses it." Adam let out a breath and in a less passionate voice he said, "In any case, maybe giving Charles a break on other fronts will give him more rest."

"I've freed him entirely from his business obligations," said Bran. "It hasn't worked."

There was a pause. "What?" said Adam carefully. "The business? You've turned pack finances over to someone else?"

"He'd already backed away from most of the daily chores of running the corporation, put it in the hands of five or six different people, only one of whom knows that it's owned by Charles's family. He does that every twenty years or so, to keep people from noticing that he doesn't age. I brought in a finance firm to take over the pack's other holdings, and what they aren't handling, Leah is."

"So Charles is doing nothing at all except going out and killing? Nothing to distract him, nothing to dilute the impact. I know I just said he might need a break, but that's almost the opposite. Do you really think that's a good idea? He enjoys making money—it's like an infinitely complicated game of chess for him. He told me once it was even better than hunting because no one dies."

He'd told Bran that, too. Maybe he should have listened more carefully.

"I can't give him the finances back," Bran said. "He's not . . . I can't give him the finances back." Not until Charles was functioning better, because the money the pack controlled was enough to mean power. His reluctance to trust Charles, who had engendered it, made Bran admit, at least to himself, that he'd noticed that Charles was in trouble a while ago.

"I have an idea," said Adam slowly. "About that task you had for me—"

"I'm not sending him to deal with the FBI," said Bran, appalled. "Even before . . . this, Charles would not be the right person to send."

"He's not a people person," agreed Adam, sounding amused. "I imagine the last year and more hasn't helped that any. No. Send Anna. Those FBI agents won't know what hit them—and with Anna as a cushion, Charles may actually do them some good. Send them in to help as well as consult. One of us can tell the cops a lot about a crime scene that forensics can't. Give Charles something to do where he can be the good guy instead of the executioner."

Let him be a hero, thought Bran, his eyes on the *Ivanhoe* in his bookshelf as he hung up the phone. Asil had been right to point out that there was nothing wrong with a little bit of romance to cushion the harsh realities of life. Adam might have given him the Band-Aid he needed to help his youngest son. He devoutly hoped so.

2

Special Agent Leslie Fisher stared out of the window that looked out over downtown Boston. From her vantage point she had a lovely, very-early-morning view. Traffic was still light, and though it would get a lot heavier as people came to work, lack of parking kept the streets from being as crazy as Los Angeles, the last place she'd been assigned. In the FBI, she got to move every few years whether she wanted to or not, but she'd always thought of Boston as home.

The hotel was old and expensively elegant. Tasteful, striped, satiny paper covered the walls of the meeting room in authentic Victorian style. The smallish room was dominated by the large mahogany table with padded chairs that looked more like they belonged in a dining room than a boardroom. It *was* a hotel, though, no matter how well decorated, and it lacked even the hint of personalization that managed to break through the government drab in her own office cubicle.

She was here to meet a consultant. Though there was the occasional perfectly innocent computer geek or accountant, in her experience, consultants were quite often bad guys who had made deals so that the good guys could catch bigger bad guys: rewarding the smaller evil so that the big monsters got stopped.

Five people dead in the last month: an old woman, two tourists, a businessman, and an eight-year-old boy. A serial killer was hunting. She'd seen the boy's body, and to catch his killer, she'd have met with Satan himself.

In her time in the FBI, she'd dealt with former drug dealers, an assassin already serving a life sentence in jail, and any number of politicians (some of whom *should* have been serving life sentences in jail). Once, she'd even consulted a self-proclaimed witch. In retrospect, Leslie hadn't been nearly as afraid of the witch as she should have been.

Today she was talking to werewolves. To her knowledge, she'd never met a werewolf before, so it should be interesting.

She considered the table they'd all be sitting around. The FBI offices or a police station would have given her side the home advantage—her side being those who fought for law and order. Meeting with people on their own turf, in their offices or homes, lost her that advantage, but sometimes she'd used it to get information she wouldn't have gotten if the people she was interviewing hadn't felt comfortable and safe. Prisons, oddly enough, gave the home-court advantage to the prisoner, especially if she brought a nervous greenie along with her.

Hotels were neutral territory—which was why they were meeting here instead of the office.

"Why me?" she'd asked her boss yesterday when he told her she was going alone. "I thought the whole team was going to talk to him?"

Nick Salvador had grimaced and stretched his large self uncomfortably behind his desk—a space where he spent as little time as possible. He preferred being in the field. "FUBAR ahead," he said, which was his code for politics. When Leslie had come into the Boston office, the previous person who'd had her desk had taped a list of Nick-speak to the bottom of her drawer with a note that said he'd had it faxed from Denver, where Nick had last been posted. There was a full page of swearwords, and "FUBAR ahead" had been first on the list. It wasn't that Nick couldn't dance gracefully with the powers that be if necessary; it was that he didn't like doing it.

"I put in the request and word was we were going to talk to Adam Hauptman. He's done a lot of consults—been guest speaker at Quantico a couple of times. Thought we could get information to help us with the case and pick up a bit besides." He twisted his chair around and his knee hit the canvas side of one of his go-bags. He had a number of them stashed around his office. Leslie had three herself—each packed for different jobs. Hers were color-coded; Nick's were numbered. Which made sense—there were more numbers than guy colors (his bags were khaki, khaki, and that other khaki) and he needed more go-bags than she did because his job was broader reaching. She didn't have to keep a suit on hand, for instance, because she was unlikely to get called upon for television interviews or congressional hearings.

"Hauptman has a good rep," Leslie said. "I have a friend who sat in on one of his lectures, said it was informative and pretty entertaining. So what happened to that plan?"

"Got a call yesterday morning. Hauptman's not available—you remember that monster they found in the Columbia River last month? Turns out it was Hauptman and his wife who killed it, mostly his wife—that's for our information only." Not classified, but not to be advertised, either. "She apparently got busted up pretty badly and he can't fly out. Hauptman found us a replacement, someone higher up. But no more than five people can come to the meet—and we have to hold it in neutral territory. No name, no further official information." He pursed his mouth unhappily.

Nick Salvador could play poker with the best of them, but with people he trusted, every last thing he thought bloomed on his face.

Leslie liked that, liked working with him because he was smart—and never, ever treated her like the token black female.

"That's not FUBAR," she said.

"FUBAR is hearing that the werewolf consultant is 'higher up'— makes it all sorts of interesting to a lot of people other than the FBI," he said.

"Hauptman is Alpha of some pack in Washington, right?" Leslie pursed her lips. "I didn't know there was a higher-up than an Alpha."

"Neither did anyone else," agreed Nick. "I don't know what the deal is, but I've been informed that two Trippers are coming to the party."

Trippers, in Nick-speak, were agents from CNTRP. The acronym stood for Combined Nonhuman and Transhuman Relations Provisors, the new agency formed specifically to deal with the various preternaturals. They pronounced it "Cantrip." Nick called them Trippers because whenever they involved themselves in an investigation he was in, he tripped all over them.

"They wanted to send two Homeland Security agents, too, but I put my foot down." Nick scowled at the phone as if it were to blame for annoying him. "Special Agent Craig Goldstein, who was involved in three earlier cases with this same killer, finished the most urgent of his cases and so is breaking loose from Tennessee to come help us." She'd never met Goldstein, but knew that Nick had, and that he liked him—which was enough of a recommendation for her. "I want him to talk to our werewolf. I wanted two of my agents in there with him—but I got outvoted. Two Trippers, one Homeland Security agent"—his voice dropped coldly—"who has no business whatsoever in this case. And Craig and you."

"Why me?" she asked. "Len could go. That way you could include the police." Len was the local Boston PD officer who worked on their task force. "Or Christine—she's done a few more serial murder cases than I have."

Nick sat back and stilled, pulling all his energy in the way he did when they got a good lead on someone they'd been looking for. "A friend of mine called me and gave me a heads-up. He knows Hauptman—more importantly, Hauptman knows he is a friend of mine. Hauptman called him to give me some more background."

Leslie's eyebrows went up. "Interesting."

"Isn't it?" Nick smiled. "My friend told me that Hauptman said I might want to be careful who I sent. Someone low-key, good with body language, and absolutely not aggressive."

He looked at her and she nodded. "Not Len, not Christine." Len was smart, but hardly low-key, and Christine had a competitive streak a mile wide. Leslie could hold her own, but she didn't need to rub people's noses in it.

"That lets me out, too," Nick admitted. "Angel and you are probably the best fit, and Angel is just a little too green to send out on his own against the bad guys just yet." Angel was fresh out of Quantico.

"I'll take good notes," she promised.

"Do that," Nick said. His fingers were doing the little impatient dance they did when he was thinking among friends—like he was conducting invisible music.

Leslie waited, but he didn't say anything.

"So why are we making this extra effort to get along with the were-wolf?" she asked.

Nick smiled. "My friend told me that Hauptman said that the people we'd be meeting might be persuaded to give us a little more concrete help if the person we sent was someone they felt they could trust."

"People?" Leslie leaned forward. "There's more than one?"

"Hauptman said 'people.' That didn't come through official channels so I saw no reason to pass it on."

Nick was very good at cooperating. Cooperation solved crimes, put the bad guys behind bars. Cooperation was the new byword—and it worked. However, put Nick's back up, and cooperation might mean something . . . a little less cooperative. He might disparage the Trippers in private, but it didn't hinder him at all in the field. Homeland Security, on the other hand, tended to set his back up rather more forcibly because they liked to forget that the FBI had jurisdiction on all terrorist activity on US soil. Nick reminded them of that whenever necessary and with great pleasure.

"I would very much appreciate," Nick said, "if we could use our consultant or consultants in the field."

"It would be interesting to see what a werewolf could do at a crime scene," Leslie said, considering it. From what little she knew about werewolves, it might be like having a bloodhound who could talk— instant forensics.

Nick showed his even white teeth in a heartfelt grimace. "I don't ever want to see another waterlogged child's body with a livestock tag in his ear. If a werewolf might make a difference, get them on board, please."

"On it."

LESLIE PUT HER hands flat on the hotel conference table. Her nails were short, manicured, and polished with a clear coat that matched the sheen of the wood she claimed under her hands. Territorial rights were important. She had a degree in psychology and another in anthropology, but she'd understood it since Miss Nellie Michaelson had gone puppy-hunting in Mrs. Cullinan's backyard.

She'd come early because that was a way to turn neutral territory into hers. It was one of the things that made her a good agent—she paid attention to the details, details like gaining the home-court advantage when dealing with monsters—especially ones with big, sharp teeth.

She'd done a boatload of studying since Nick dropped this on her yesterday.

Werewolves were supposed to be poor, downtrodden victims of a disease, people who used the abilities their misfortune granted them to help others. David Christiansen, the first person to admit to being a werewolf, was a specialist in extracting terrorist hostages. She was sure that his being incredibly photogenic had not been an accident. Leslie's oldest daughter had a poster up on her bedroom door of that famous photo of David holding the child he'd rescued. Other wolves who had admitted what they were tended to be firemen, policemen, and military: the good guys one and all.

She could have smelled the spin-doctoring from orbit. Spin-doctoring wasn't lying, not precisely. David Christiansen's little group of mercenaries had a very good reputation among the people Leslie had talked to. They got the job done with minimal casualties on all sides and they were good at what they did. They didn't take jobs from the bad guys. Because of that, Leslie was keeping an open mind—but because she was naturally cautious, she also was keeping a pair of silver bullets (hastily purchased) loaded in her carry gun.

The door opened behind her and she turned to see a young woman enter the room who looked like she should still be going to high school. Leslie felt that way all too often when she met the new recruits fresh from Quantico. The girl's light reddish brown hair was braided severely in an attempt to make her look older, but the effect wasn't enough to offset the freckles that burst across her pale cheeks or the innocent honey brown eyes.

"Oh, hi," the girl said brightly, her voice touched just a little with a Chicago accent. "I thought I'd be the first one here. It's a bit early."

"I like to get the lay of the land," said Leslie, and the younger woman laughed.

"Oh, I get that," she said, grinning. "Charles is like that."

Charles would be her partner, Leslie thought. They must be from Cantrip. This child wouldn't be a werewolf—there were supposed to be a few female werewolves, Leslie knew, thanks to her Internet crash course, but they were protective of them. They'd never have sent this one out among the feds. Come to think of it, she wouldn't have left the girl alone, either.

"So why isn't your Charles here, then?" He'd abandoned her to the wolves. It made her want to blister his hide—and she hadn't even met him. What if it had been the werewolf awaiting the girl here rather than an FBI agent?

Leslie received a slow grin that took in her private censure and found it amusing. "He lost a bet and had to bring coffee for everyone. He's not happy about it, either. I probably shouldn't enjoy it so much, but sometimes I take great pleasure in sending a man off in a snit; don't you?"

She surprised a laugh out of Leslie. "Don't I just," she agreed before taking a wary breath. This one was getting to her—*she* never laughed while she was working. She reassessed the other woman. She looked like a teenager dressed in a tailor-made, gray pin-striped suit-dress that somehow appeared to be a costume she was wearing rather than real clothing.

"I bet," Leslie said, testing an idea, "that dangerous men stumble all over themselves to make sure you don't stub your toe."

She knew she was right when, instead of looking flustered, the woman just smiled archly. "And I make sure they apologize when they bump into each other doing it."

"Ha," Leslie said triumphantly. "I thought even Cantrip had more sense than to toss a tender morsel to the wolves. I'm Special Agent Leslie Fisher, FBI Violent Crimes Unit."

"I'm Anna Smith, today." The girl gave her a rueful smile. "Not Cantrip. One of the wolves, I'm afraid. And even worse, Smith isn't my real name. I told them it was a silly one, but Charles said it was better to be obvious about it or you or Homeland Security would find some poor Charles and Anna Washington, Adams, or Jefferson to harass."

THE FBI AGENT wasn't exactly what Anna had expected, but she wasn't different, either. Smart, well dressed, confident—that, the TV shows, the movies, had gotten right. Anna had become very good at judging people since she'd been Changed. Body language, scent, those didn't lie. She'd surprised the agent with her revelation, but not frightened her, which boded well for their chances of working together.

The fine lines around bitter-chocolate eyes deepened, and for a moment Special Agent Leslie Fisher looked exactly as dominant as she was. She might be in her mid-forties, but the well-cut suit jacket she wore covered muscle.

Her eyes said she was tough. Tough like a junkyard dog—and not just physically. If she were a wolf—and male—she'd be second or third in a pack, Anna judged. Not Alpha, she didn't have the underlying aggressive territoriality that pushed dominant to the head of the pack, but near that. How many people had the FBI agent fooled with that cool exterior?

The frown in Special Agent Fisher's eyes extended to her full lips as she said, "We are having this meeting here, with as few people as possible, because the man who set it up said it wouldn't be smart to upset the werewolf." She lifted a well-groomed eyebrow. "You don't look easily upset."

Scolded. Anna fought not to grin in satisfaction. Now. How to tell her what she needed to know without scaring her. "They're not worried about upsetting *me*. It's my husband who's the problem werewolf."

The other woman frowned. "So there *is* another werewolf coming here. Your husband?" She sounded faintly incredulous. That Anna was married? That her spouse was a werewolf? That there were two of them? If Fisher knew werewolves well, she'd be most incredulous that Charles had left her alone.

Anna was a bit incredulous about that herself—and it gave her a smidgen of hope that Bran was on the right track with this business. She hadn't been as certain as he and Asil that it would be good for Charles to hunt down a serial killer rather than hunt down misbehaving wolves, but Charles had agreed and so it was done.

"Yes." Anna nodded. "I'm a werewolf. I'm married. And my husband is a werewolf, too."

Fisher's frown deepened. "The word is that whoever we're supposed to meet is up the line from Hauptman, who's the Alpha of a full pack of wolves."

"Is that what the word is?" murmured Anna as she wondered who'd let the word out and if Bran knew about it—or if he'd engineered it. If she kept wondering about how much of her life Bran engineered, she'd end up in a funny farm knitting caps for ducks.

"You are barely old enough to be out on your own and your husband is higher up in the werewolf power structure than Hauptman," said Agent Fisher. "What did they do? Make you marry him when you were twelve?"

Anna blinked at her. In her little world built of religiously watched TV shows and movies, FBI agents would never have said something that personal to a person they had just met. They'd work up to it gradually—or insinuate something carefully. By the suddenly appalled look on Agent Fisher's face, it was the same in her little world.

An Omega makes everyone a bit more protective, Asil had told her a while ago. Anna hadn't really connected it to the human world.

Anna grinned and hid her sympathy. "No. They didn't tie up poor, weak, innocent, little old me and force me to marry him." She considered it. "He's not weak or innocent, but if I'd had to, I might have tied *him* up and forced *him* to marry me. Thankfully, it wasn't necessary."

The other woman had recovered herself. "You said that he is the reason we couldn't bring in more people?"

"Right," Anna said. "But if you wait a moment, I'd rather just explain it once, and I think that—"

She let her voice linger while she timed the footsteps (not Charles's) that she heard outside the conference room door. It might have been some hotel guest wandering the halls, but there were two men walking with purposeful speed that was just a little too fast to be comfortable, the way men who are competing with each other sometimes do.

The door popped open. Leslie's attention diverted from listening to Anna to watching the new additions to the room. She took a couple of steps forward until she stood between Anna and the newcomers, putting Anna at her back. Which made Anna and the FBI agent a team facing the pair of Cantrip people—at least, that was who Anna assumed they were because there were two of them. Two Cantrip, two FBI, and one Homeland Security was what Charles had told her. She found it more than a little interesting that the FBI agent saw them as opponents— and Anna as an ally.

"Jim. So they're letting you out with the big boys now?" Leslie's tone was dry. Anna thought that the two men who came in took that as an amiable comment, one of those digs friends might make. But watching the other woman's body language carefully told Anna that Leslie was very guarded, more so than she'd been around Anna after the first few minutes.

"Leslie!" the younger man exclaimed with a real smile. His body language said he liked the FBI agent, whatever she thought of him. "Special Agent Fisher," he corrected himself. "Good to see you. I am one of the big boys and have been for a long time. This is Dr. Steve Singh."

Leslie reached out and shook the hands that were offered her. "And what does Homeland Security want with a serial killer? That's for the local cops. The only reason this one is FBI is because our killer's been traveling across state lines for years."

Homeland Security. There was supposed to be only one person from Homeland Security. Anna frowned. Charles wasn't going to be happy about that. He didn't like surprises. He probably had a file on everyone who was coming to this shindig.

Singh didn't say anything, just studied the FBI agent's face before moving on to Anna's. She stared back at him, just to see what he'd do. He frowned at her and tried to get her to look away, but even Bran couldn't do that if she didn't allow it, and he was nowhere near as dominant as Bran—or even Agent Fisher, for that matter. But Anna dropped her eyes anyway. There was no sense starting a fight until it was important.

"We heard that there was going to be someone higher up speaking for the werewolves on this," answered Jim Nolastname, apparently oblivious to the staring contest his partner had engaged in with Anna. "We decided that it would be a good idea if we knew who he was and what he had to say."

Only a subtle tightening in the FBI agent's back told Anna that the unconscious arrogance in the man's voice had ticked her off.

"And why are there two of you?" Fisher asked. "The request was for no more than five people. Two of us, two from Cantrip, and one of you."

The FBI agent had known why Homeland Security was checking out the werewolf, Anna thought. She hadn't been surprised that there were two of them—but she was making a point of it for Anna's sake. By not introducing Anna first, she was leading them to think Anna was the other FBI agent and letting them spill their agenda in front of the enemy.

"We leaned on Cantrip a little," said Jim. "They owed us."

It shouldn't really matter that Fisher had made this an us-against-them kind of thing. They were all on the same side in the end—catching the villain. It might have been something as simple as departmental rivalry: FBI versus Homeland Security. Anna narrowed her eyes and considered it. It might have been a little of that—and Fisher definitely didn't like Jim. But Anna thought it was a show aimed at her. Anna was patient; she'd see what the FBI agent wanted from her. In the meantime, she needed to get a handle on the other people in the room.

Jim had a freshness about him that gave him some charm. Anna didn't miss the brains behind the shiny front. Dr. Singh, the older man, was reserved in a manner that reminded her of some of the Alpha wolves she'd met over the past few years.

He was one of the ones who sat in the back and watched their packs, letting matters work out as they would until they veered too far from where he wished. Then he'd pounce with a brutal efficiency that meant he wouldn't have to move again for a while. He'd noticed what Fisher had done, all right, but his relaxed shoulders told Anna that he hadn't yet realized just who and what Anna was.

The door opened abruptly and another man came in. Anna started a little. She wasn't as good at multitasking as she could have been. If she'd been paying attention, she would have heard him approach, but she'd been engrossed in the power play and had missed the sound of his footsteps.

Slight and almost frail in appearance, the newcomer glanced at them all with cool gray eyes. His suit was off the rack and looked a little wrinkled, but its blue gray color matched his eyes and complemented the fringe of trimmed dark hair that narrowly circled the top of his head.

His eyes looked older than his body, and if he was more than five feet tall, it wasn't by much. The paleness of his skin added to the effect, but he moved easily, like a runner.

He frowned at the two men. "Homeland," he said in a neutral tone, then looked at Leslie. "You must be Special Agent Fisher. I'm Special Agent Craig Goldstein. Introduce me, please."

She did, starting with the Homeland Security team. Jim Nolast-name, Anna discovered, was Jim Pierce.

"And this," said Agent Fisher with only a hint of mischief, "is Anna Smith, our werewolf consultant. Anna, this is Special Agent Craig Goldstein. He's our expert on this case."

Goldstein looked . . . stunned, which she was pretty sure was an unusual happening. The Homeland Security duo looked just as surprised. Singh, recovering first, gave Fisher a sharp look.

Anna smiled warmly and reached out to shake the hand that Goldstein had automatically extended at the start of the introductions.

"Hello, Special Agent Goldstein," she said earnestly. "I know that I'm not what you were planning on, but I'll do my best. We're waiting on the Cantrip people and my husband, who has gone out to get coffee."

Charles would be here soon. She'd hoped to wait until the Cantrip people came, but she'd have to take what she could get. If Charles got here before she explained the rules, it might be disastrous.

Anna glanced at them all and blew out a breath. "Listen, there isn't much time. We'll help you. But there are some things you should know. We all need to be sitting down when my husband arrives. Don't look him in the eye. If you do, please, blink or look away if he meets your gaze. Don't touch me, not even casually. I'm going to sit with an empty chair between me and anyone else." Bran had cautioned her before they'd left. In Aspen Creek, in the pack, Charles would be confident in her safety. That could change in a moment out of his territory. Anna was pretty sure he'd be fine. It wasn't Brother Wolf who was in trouble; it was Charles. But she'd promised Bran she'd do what she could to avoid trouble.

Goldstein's face tightened, but it was Singh who asked, "Is he dangerous?"

Anna snorted. "Of course he is. I'm dangerous and I'd bet that you're pretty dangerous, too. This isn't about who is the most dangerous; it's about being smart and keeping everything low-key."

"Are you playing good cop, bad cop with *us*?" asked Jim Pierce.

"Dominant werewolves don't mix well with others," Anna told them. "If you play my game, we'll all be a little happier." She gave Singh, who looked the least happy, a stern look. "If you were meeting a Chinese foreign minster, wouldn't you listen to someone giving you a few pointers in Chinese manners? Think of it like that."

CHAPTER

3

Charles held two of the awkward drink carriers and strode through the crowded hotel lobby. In his hurry, it didn't dawn on him that there was anything unusual about the way his path cleared, or the empty elevator that took him to the third floor where their meeting with the feds was to take place. Not until the man waiting for the elevator when it opened on the third floor backed up three paces and, keeping a wary eye on Charles, broke for the stairs, did it strike him that people's reactions had been a little unusual.

He was a big man and Indian. (He'd been Indian for more than a century and only occasionally thought of himself as Native American. When he paid any attention at all, he might consider himself half-breed Salish or Flathead.) The combination of size and ethnicity usually had people avoiding him, especially in places where Indians weren't as commonplace. Not their fault; it was in the nature of man to find the unknown intimidating, especially when it came in the shape of a big predator. His da dismissed it, but Charles was pretty sure that somewhere in their hindbrain most people knew a predator when they met one.

His brother maintained that what sent people backing away was neither his size nor his mother's blood, but solely the expression on his face. To test Samuel's theory, Charles had tried smiling—and then solemnly reported to Samuel that he had been mistaken. When Charles smiled, he told Samuel, people just ran faster.

The only one who appreciated his sense of humor was Anna.

People didn't retreat from him when Anna was beside him. But even without Anna's presence, having a person he wasn't even looking at backing away from him as if he held a loaded gun instead of a bunch of espressos and lattes in a pair of flimsy cardboard drink carriers was a little excessive. He stepped out of the elevator and moved slowly so the man didn't think he was giving chase.

Brother Wolf thought it might be fun and sent him a picture of the man running terror-stricken through the lobby as Charles loped behind him—still carrying the silly drinks. Because Anna had specified hot drinks for all, and he would never welsh on a bet.

So he walked with deliberate slowness down the hall instead of chasing, instead of rending and tearing sweet, metallic, blood-drenched meat between his teeth, just as he'd taken the elevator instead of running up the narrow stairs where someone might bump into him and spill the drinks.

Da had been crazy to send him on such a mission when he was so close to losing it that even a clueless human could tell there was something wrong with him. Charles had known there was something up when he'd arrived for lunch as requested and it had been only his father who awaited him, cooking BLTs in the big house's kitchen.

Da had eaten his own lunch and waited until Charles had finished his before leading the way to the study. His father shut the door, sat behind his desk, and pursed his lips, giving Charles his "I have a job for you and you aren't going to be happy with me" look. Father-son meals often included that expression on his father's face. When Da wanted to talk to him alone, it was seldom a happy talk.

Charles waited, standing, to hear what his father had to say. His wolf was agitated, unhappy—and that meant he could not sit on the chair provided and hinder his ability to move.

"Asil has been nagging at me about you," Da said.

"Asil?" Asil didn't particularly like him—and Charles hadn't so much as seen Asil for a couple of weeks. Which, come to think on it, was a little odd in a town so small someone might sneeze twice and never notice they'd driven all the way through it.

"Anna, of course, goes without saying," Da continued.

Charles braced himself. She knew why someone had to keep order; she knew why it had to be him—she just thought he was more important. Anna was wrong, but it warmed him that she thought so. If her opinion had made his father decide to send someone else, though, it was something that had to be dealt with. Charles, as the Marrok's son and longtime troubleshooter, was the only option for keeping the violence down to unnoticeable-by-the-public standards. His reputation— and who his father was—kept the packs from going to war to protect their own when someone needed to die.

"I know what she had to say. But Anna is wrong. Brother Wolf is not ready to break loose."

"No," agreed his father softly. "But your grandfather would tell you that you need to cleanse yourself of all those ghosts you carry with you."

Charles flinched. He should have known that his da would understand what was happening to him. Da wasn't a spiritual man, not that Charles could tell, anyway. He was pretty sure that his father couldn't see the ghosts the way that his grandfather would have. But his da had a way of seeing right to the heart of things when he wanted to.

"I have tried," Charles said, feeling about thirteen. "Fasting and sweat lodge haven't worked. Running. Swimming."

"You hold on to them because you do not feel that their deaths were just."

Charles turned his head away slightly and angled his eyes down but not so far that he couldn't see Da's face. "It is not for me to determine the law, only to carry it out."

Da frowned at him, not like he was displeased, just thoughtful. "I had a talk with Adam Hauptman."

Charles raised his eyebrows and found a dry voice to say, "Adam is worried about me, too?"

"Adam is worried about his mate, who is injured, cranky, and obstreperous," replied his father. "So he's not available to take on a rather tricky situation."

Charles didn't follow where this conversation was going, so he adopted silence as a strategy. Da liked to hear himself talk anyway.

The old lobo sighed, stretched, and put his feet up on his desk—a sign that Charles was talking to his *father* and not just the Marrok. "I've been racking my brain—not to mention Asil's brain—with how to make your job easier."

He spoke as if Adam's situation had some bearing on Charles's, though he couldn't see how. "You have."

His father frowned at him. "No. It's becoming painfully obvious that nothing I've done has helped you."

Bran didn't say what it was for a few moments, just studied Charles's face as if it were not the face he'd worn every day since he became an adult nearly two centuries before.

"I cannot send anyone else to enforce the rules—but I am, as of this moment, relaxing the penalties for many transgressions in the hope that it will allow the Alpha wolves to need less . . . *help* enforcing them." He held up a hand and Charles bit back his protests. "You are the only one I can send out, yes. But if you falter, there will be no one but me—and I do not trust myself. So it is necessary that you not break. Anyone who has been Changed less than five years gets one warning. Asil is as frightening as you—and he also is not an Alpha right now. He has volunteered to go out and scare the bejeebers out of young idiots who break the rules the first time."

Charles knew it was wrong. His father had weighed and assessed the needs for the wolves' survival and had made the necessary changes in the laws of the packs. But it wasn't shame, but rather relief, that made him drop his eyes.

"I have failed you," he said.

"No, son," said Da. "I nearly failed you. You are, as Asil has reminded me, one of my pack and I am responsible for your well-being." His tone turned wry.

"Asil has appointed himself my guardian?" asked Charles softly. Asil was overstepping himself.

"He was bored, he told me," said his father. He gave Charles a small smile. "I have given him a job so he doesn't get bored again."

Da rocked back in his chair and studied the ceiling as if it were interesting for a moment, before turning his yellow eyes back to Charles. "Asil scaring the britches off our young wolves won't be enough. I . . . We will still need you to kill. However, Adam thought that maybe doing other things, too, might . . . dilute the effect. Maybe if every trip you take isn't to go kill some more old friends and acquaintances—" Charles hid a wince, or tried to. "Maybe it will help. So. I have a call from some of my contacts in the government that they need to consult with one of us about a possible serial killer."

His father saw his face and smiled without humor. "Not one of us. One of the killers they've been tracking awhile seems to have changed his victim of choice. At least three of his kills in Boston have been werewolves."

"Three? And we didn't know?"

"I knew three had died," said Da. "From three different packs, but someone did not see fit to tell me that they were probably connected. I'll deal with that part."

Some heads would roll—probably not literally. "There is only one pack in Boston." It wasn't quite a question, but Da should have started asking questions if three wolves from the same pack had died in a short period of time.

"One tourist from a Vermont pack and another from Seattle. Only one from the Boston pack. The FBI is interested in anything we can add to the investigation."

"You're sending me?" People instinctively wanted to please Adam. Charles was better at the destroy-and-subdue, not so good at the coax-and-charm.

"No," said his da. "That would be dumb. I'm sending Anna. You are going as her guard. I've sent the particulars of what I know to your e-mail and to hers."

AND THUS CHARLES found himself wandering around a hotel, trailing a pair of federal agents as he held a cardboard coffee cup holder in each hand, instead of out killing misbehaving werewolves. He knew they were federal agents because only men who were partners moved that closely together. Body language said they weren't in a relationship, so that meant military, feds, or cops. Since they were headed the same direction he was, Charles surmised that he'd happened upon two of the feds they were supposed to meet with.

The thought came to him suddenly that he was enjoying himself, stalking feds through the halls of the old elegant hotel, especially because they had no inkling that he was doing it. It amused him.

If he hadn't lost the bet to Anna, he'd never have gotten the chance.

Who'd have thought that the security people at SeaTac would be so worried about him that they'd miss Anna smuggling a bottle of water through the checkpoint? His bet should have been a safe one—and the worst that would happen to Anna was that they would throw out her water bottle.

It was his fault he'd lost the bet.

Maybe Samuel was on to something when he'd told Charles that his expression put people off, because one of the hotel workers who'd been giving him a worried look suddenly relaxed and gave him a cheery grin.

He could have beaten Anna. He hadn't needed to let out a subvocal growl at exactly the right moment to distract everyone when Anna threw the plastic bottle over the scanners and onto someone else's pack on the other side of the machines. No one heard him, not really, just felt the hairs on the backs of their necks crawl while Brother Wolf laughed at their mate's audacity.

Not only had Anna made it through unscathed; she'd distracted *him* while they patted her down and ran her through the scanners. Which had probably been her intent in the first place. Smart woman, his Anna—but she hadn't let him off from paying up on the bet.

When the TSA finally let him through security—because being scary wasn't really enough to keep him off an airplane—Anna had been waiting for him comfortably curled up on one of the little benches where people sat to put on their shoes. She'd raised her blue food-colored water in a triumphant toast and then drank it down to the last drop. It had been Anna's idea, not his, to dye the water so she couldn't just play sleight of hand—she would never cheat on a bet with him.

Watching her throat as she downed the liquid was a strangely erotic thing—erotic and magical, something that couldn't exist in the same universe as the deaths that haunted him. So the ghosts retreated, not a permanent thing, but it was more freedom than he'd had for a while, and it was good.

Charles didn't mind losing to his mate, though leaving Anna alone to deal with the feds while he fetched for her didn't make his wolf happy. But he knew that Anna could charm the birds out of the trees, and a few feds who needed their help weren't going to give her any trouble. No one was going to try to hurt her. Not yet, not before they involved themselves in the FBI's hunt.

Da thought it would be good for Charles to hunt something other than a werewolf, something truly evil. He hoped that his father was right—and empirical evidence tended to support his hope, as his da was frequently correct.

So Charles followed the pair of feds down the hallway to the room where they were meeting his mate and a small group of others. These weren't FBI field agents, he decided, because neither of them noticed him, even though he wasn't making any particular effort to avoid detection. Homeland Security and Cantrip tended to have more chair sitters than the FBI did. They were speaking quietly enough that it would have taken a werewolf's ears to hear them. Unabashedly, he listened in.

"Are you sure this is safe?" asked the blond man of the federal pair nervously. He looked fresh out of college, not yet twenty-five. "I mean, *werewolves*, Pat. Plural."

"They're cooperating with us," said Pat, the older man. Charles pinned his accent as New England native softened a little by a stint somewhere in the South. He was in his early forties and walked like someone who'd done a lot of it. "They'll behave themselves because they have to."

"You don't think they'll be mad because I tagged along? It was supposed to be just you. Five people. Two FBI, two Homeland Security, and one of us."

They must be Cantrip, then, thought Charles. According to Da, there should have been two of them and one Homeland Security. Someone had been flexing their muscles. Several someones. Brother Wolf decided that Charles was feeling too relaxed to teach them to mind their manners better.

"Easier to ask forgiveness than permission," said Pat as he opened the door to the room that they were meeting in. "Isn't that right, Leslie?"

"One of you can leave," said a woman's voice coldly. "Just because you aren't in the FBI anymore, Pat, shouldn't mean you forgot how to count. Five. It's easy. You can cheat and count your fingers if you have to."

"Ha-ha," said Pat, pulling the door shut behind him. Charles stopped to listen before going in. "Bet you that no one really cares. When is the werewolf showing up? I thought the memo said eight straight up."

"Six people is fine," said Anna, and Brother Wolf relaxed further at the amusement in his mate's voice. "Five was just to keep the numbers down."

He'd known she was safe. She was a werewolf, and if the training he'd been giving her didn't make her safe in a room full of humans, he'd been doing it wrong. But still, Brother Wolf was happier listening to the relaxed tones of her voice.

Charles looked at the door and realized that it would be tough to open with both hands full. He might have managed it, but there was another way.

He knew better, knew that the ghosts weren't gone. But the temptation was too great. It had been so long since he'd touched her, and Brother Wolf was so hungry. Almost as hungry as he was.

So he opened the bonds that tied wolf to mate and said, as mildly as he could manage, *Open the door, please—and someone is going to have to drink hotel coffee since I only brought enough for five federal agents.*

The door snapped open and she looked up at him, her face entirely serious and her eyes bright with tears.

You talked to me. But more than words traveled along their bond from her side; she was always generous in sharing her feelings with him. She gave him a rush of relief that almost hid the deep-seated sorrow and pain of abandonment. He'd done that to her; he'd known he was doing it—and still knew that it was the lesser of two evils. He had to protect her from what was happening to him. Knowing he was right didn't mean he wasn't torn, that he didn't regret hurting her.

"I don't mind hotel coffee," she said aloud, her voice a little foggy.

He was afraid that he was going to hurt her much worse before this was all over.

Charles bent his head down and touched his nose to hers, closing his eyes to hide the effect of the knowledge of what he'd been doing to her—and the effect of feeling her, skin on skin, once more. Brother Wolf wanted to drag her away from all of these strangers and find the nearest empty room so he could wrap himself around her and never let go. Charles wanted to say, "I'm sorry for hurting you," but that implied that he would do something differently if he had to do it again. He would never allow the ugliness of his life to stain her, not if he could help it.

So he said something stupid instead. "My wife is drinking the cocoa I brought her." He looked past her and into the room. Except for the two men he'd followed, everyone was sitting down around the table. It must have been her suggestion, because all of them looked tense and uncomfortable. Being seated when someone else is standing can be a position of power—a way of saying, "I am so confident that I can take you that I won't bother getting up." But when a monster comes into the room, everyone wants to be on their feet. Charles was a big monster.

Proof that Anna had been smart to do it, though, was the level of his irritation with the two men still standing behind Anna.

He met the younger Cantrip agent's eyes. The human dropped his gaze and stepped back involuntarily, pleasing Brother Wolf. Charles smiled at the agent with his teeth. "You invited yourself where you weren't asked. You can drink hotel coffee."

And now they'd think he really was stupid, because most humans wouldn't understand that he'd needed to establish who was in charge so that Brother Wolf would know that Anna was safe. Giving an order that they would obey had established the pecking order. It was okay they would think him stupid, he decided. He and Anna could engage in a little smart cop, dumb cop if they needed to. And playing with the federal agents was so much easier than trying to deal with what he was doing to Anna.

She should have picked someone else. Asil. Someone. But the thought of Anna with someone else sent Brother Wolf into a fit of jealous rage.

There is no one for me except you. Anna's quick response reminded him that he'd chosen to leave the bond between them open. He didn't know how much she was picking up, but it was more than time to control himself.

Charles moved past Anna and set the carriers down on the table. Pulling out the single non-coffee for Anna, he handed it to her as he watched everyone sit perfectly still and drop their eyes except for the Cantrip agents: Anna had been educating them.

Anna moved around to the back of the table, taking a chair with no one sitting next to her. The Cantrip agents took empty chairs on the other side of the table after he warned the younger one away from Anna with a lifted eyebrow. Charles stood behind Anna's chair.

"This is my husband, Charles," Anna told them, her hands folded.

"Perhaps it would be a good thing to introduce ourselves again, now that we are all here. I'm Anna."

"Special Agent Leslie Fisher," said the other female in the room, a black woman with intelligent eyes and a firm voice. "Violent Crimes Unit, FBI."

"Special Agent Craig Goldstein," said a slender man in his fifties. "On assignment to the Boston Violent Crimes Unit because I have a background with this serial killer."

Charles nodded to the FBI agents. Fisher's background he knew, because he'd done background checks on all of the Boston VCU. Goldstein he'd find out more about.

"Jim Pierce," said the only man in the room who was smiling. He aimed it at Charles. "Homeland Security. They send me out to gather information."

He'd had a pretty good idea whom they'd send in from Homeland Security because they had only eight people specializing in preternatural matters, and he had files on them all.

Political climber, he told Anna silently, returning Pierce's smile. Pierce's face became a lot less happy and he pushed his chair back a few inches. *On his way to public office. Do you think I should work on my smile?*

Anna glanced back at him and frowned. *Behave,* said his mate, seriously enough. But he read her amusement in the little upturn of her lips.

"Dr. Steven Singh," said the second Homeland agent.

An old-fashioned patriot, Charles informed Anna after exchanging martial arts–style nods with the doctor. *He's on record as personally classifying the fae and werewolves as domestic terrorists.* Charles tended to agree with him. *Neither is here because they desire to help catch a serial killer. Pierce won't have anything to add. Singh is smart enough that he might be of use, even though he doesn't care about the crime.*

The Cantrip agents were more interesting. He didn't know as much about Cantrip, as it was an even newer agency than Homeland Security, having come into being when the werewolves outed themselves. Though funded and authorized by the government, their role was "to collect and share information about nonhuman and altered-human groups and individuals," which left them a lot of leeway. They had two main offices, one on either coast, and otherwise seemed to travel around the country to concern themselves mostly in criminal cases that involved fae, werewolves, or anything else that looked odd to them.

His father tended to dismiss the Cantrip agents as harmless, since they had no authority to arrest or detain anyone. Charles was less sanguine, as they were one of the government agencies required to go armed at all times—and they carried guns with silver bullets. He had files on a lot of their people, but had decided to see who they sent before refreshing his memory.

The older of the two Cantrip agents tried (and failed) to meet his eyes, then stared rather intently at Anna, which caused Charles's hackles to rise—and Brother Wolf didn't like him much, either.

"Patrick Morris," he said. "Cantrip, special agent."

"Formerly of the FBI," said Ms. Fisher with a cool disapproval that said anyone who chose to leave the FBI was a fool.

"Les Heuter," said the younger man, and abruptly became more interesting.

Heuter is a poster child for Cantrip, Charles told Anna. *His father is a senator from Texas. If someone from Cantrip is interviewed in the press, three times out of four it is Heuter.* Which was one of the reasons, Charles thought, that people tended not to take Cantrip more seriously.

He should have recognized Heuter right away, but he looked different in person, not as stalwart, impressive, or pretty, but more earnest and likable. He smelled eager, like a hunting dog waiting for the scent.

Charles wondered if it was the werewolves or the serial killer that caused the young man's adrenaline rush.

He had a good poker face, though. Charles doubted any of the humans in the room would detect how excited Les Heuter was to be here. Charles had never been human, but he decided it must be like walking around with earplugs and nose plugs in all the time.

Goldstein looked around. "People, let's get the ball rolling." He looked at Charles. "The man who set this meeting up tells me that three werewolves weren't likely to be victims by happenstance. According to him, there just aren't that many werewolves out and about. He speculated that three victims has to mean that our killer is targeting werewolves and suggested we lay out all the victims from the beginning for you, Mr. Smith, and see what you think before I start asking questions. In that light, I'll tell you what we know about this one, and would appreciate anything you can give us."

Charles folded his arms and leaned against the wall, his attention on Anna, telegraphing as loudly as body language could that Anna was in charge.

This was Anna's job—if Charles had to deal with them, they'd likely run scared and start shooting werewolves themselves.

"Who *did* set this up?" asked Heuter abruptly.

Goldstein turned to look at the younger man and said blandly, "I have no idea. The man who called me didn't identify himself beyond that, just suggested I take notes and his advice. As most of it seemed common sense, I did so."

Bran, thought Anna.

Probably, agreed Charles. *Or Adam Hauptman.*

Anna met Heuter's gaze and shrugged. "I know who set up our end. I have no idea who set up yours."

Goldstein had taken out his laptop and hooked it up to the video system in the room. He cleared his throat. "Agent Fisher, would you secure the door, please? Some of these images are graphic and I would rather not startle some poor maid."

The door was locked and Goldstein took his glasses off and cleaned them as Agent Fisher turned off the lights. When he put the glasses back on, he donned with them the mantle of authority; the faint air of weakness, of age and harmlessness, vanished. For just an instant, Agent Goldstein was a man who hunted other men, then the aura of weakness returned like another man might don a comfortable old shirt.

"We call our UNSUB—" He paused. "That's FBI-speak for 'unknown subject,' which seems a little more professional and less hysterical than 'killer' and more grown-up than 'bad guy.' This UNSUB is known as the Big Game Hunter, because for the first two decades all the kills took place during the traditional hunting season. The first kill we know of was in 1975, though, given the sophistication of the killings, it is likely that he killed earlier than that." He looked at Anna, who must have changed expression, and said, "Yes. We are absolutely certain this killer is a man."

He hit a button and two pictures came up on the big TV screen, side by side. The first was a school photo of a teenage Asian girl—Chinese, Charles thought. She was smiling gamely at the photographer and there was a bright orange headband in her hair. The second photo was very grainy and showed a naked body, head shrouded in shadows and a white sheet or blanket flung over her hips.

"Karen Yun-Hao was fourteen. She was abducted from her bedroom on . . ."

Charles let the man's voice drift; he'd remember what Agent Goldstein said later if he needed to. For now he concentrated on the faces, looking for clues, for people he had known, for victims who were pack.

The first year their killer took four girls, each a week apart. Asian and young, none over sixteen or under twelve. He kept them and raped and tortured them until he was ready to take the next victim. The FBI thought he killed one victim just before he took the next—though there was some possible overlap. As soon as hunting season was over, he stopped. The first year was Vermont, the second was Maine, where he stayed for a few years, then Michigan, Texas, and Oklahoma.

Organized, thought Brother Wolf, ratcheting up for the chase. A good hunter took only what he needed when he needed it, and their prey was a good hunter. The killer's victims changed gradually through the years, Asian girls and women and then, in Texas, a teenaged boy who was also Asian. The boy was the first victim who was sodomized, but after him they all were, male and female alike. The next year after that his prey was split two and two, women and boys. Then only boys. After that he added a black teenaged girl.

"It's like he's searching for the perfect meal," said Anna softly—and got an appalled glance from Dr. Singh that Charles didn't think she saw; her attention was fixed on the screen. "He started in 'seventy-five. Maybe he was a Vietnam vet?"

"The Asian victims, yes," said the senior FBI agent, looking even more frail than before. "They weren't all Vietnamese, or even mostly. But some people can't see the difference, or don't care. The police already had that theory before the first time the FBI was brought into it in the early eighties. The UNSUB wouldn't be the only one to come out of that mess with a need to kill."

"'These are the times that try men's souls,'" quoted Anna in a soft voice, and Charles knew she was remembering another veteran warrior.

"It took more than five years for the FBI to get involved?" asked Heuter.

Goldstein gave the Cantrip agent a patient look. "Nearer to ten. First, it took a while for the police to figure out they had a serial killer, communication being what it was. Second, the FBI is not in charge of serial-killer cases. We are support staff, not primary." He hit a button and a new photo came up.

"Here's where we came in, the FBI—it was before my time. I first hit this case as a rookie in 2000. In 1984, the Big Game Hunter was back in Maine. This is the first victim that year, Melissa Snow, age eighteen."

Charles recognized her—and she hadn't been eighteen. The next victim was a black boy, a stranger. He didn't know the third victim, another Asian girl. This one was ten.

Brother Wolf decided, looking at the delicate joyful face, that they would find the killer and destroy him. Children should be protected. Charles agreed, and the ghosts of the unjustly executed who haunted him withdrew further.

"Those were the only three victims that we found that year, and after this year the number of bodies we found started to vary. In 1986 and '87, we found three bodies. In 1989, there were two. In 1990, three bodies again, and so on until 2000, when several things changed, but I'll get there in a minute. We don't think that he's changed how he kills. That one week interval between the first victim and the next seems pretty set. So we think he began putting the bodies in less accessible places."

In the next year's group of victims, Charles recognized two of the three. He also noted that the crime scene photos were of better quality—a sign of the FBI bringing in a better photographer, he thought, or just a combination of the advance of technology and the way time degraded color film.

Goldstein commented, "In 1984, two of the victims matched our UNSUB's previous victim choice. From 1985 on out, there are no apparent patterns to the victims. Men and women, young and old. He's still kidnapping, raping, and torturing them for a week before going after the next victim." He took his time, showing them each victim's face. Charles noticed that Goldstein never had to consult his notes for the names, and that when he did go to his notes, it was usually to confirm something he'd just said. "The next year he started in September."

Charles knew three of the victims in 1985 and all of the bodies found in 1986.

Stop him, he told Anna, deciding that the killer's victimology was no coincidence. *This is important. Go back to that first year, the one the FBI joined in the hunt.*

"Wait," Anna said, glancing down at her notes. "Can you go back to the victims in 1984?"

The fae came out about that time, Charles told Anna. *Melissa Snow was fae and as close to eighteen as my father is. She wasn't out then, I don't think, but she was fae.*

Maybe it was an accident? Anna thought as Melissa's face, shining and happy in a family-type snapshot, appeared on the monitor next to her gray and lifeless face. *The fae aren't exactly everywhere, but it is reasonable that he picked one up by mistake.*

She wasn't a half-breed, he told her. *If someone picked her up thinking they were getting a teenaged human, they'd never have been able to keep her. She wasn't powerful, but she could defend herself better than a human would have.*

Can I tell them that?

Absolutely. Then have them go to the next year. Some fae have no bodies when they die. That could be why there is no fourth victim.

Goldstein watched Anna with sharp eyes. "Was she a werewolf?"

"No," Anna said. "Fae." And then she told the feds what Charles had told her.

"Fae." Singh frowned. "How do you know?"

"I'm one of the monsters, Dr. Singh," Anna said without a pause.

"We tend to know each other." It wasn't quite a lie. "The question is, how would the—what did you call him? The Big Game Hunter? How would he know what she was? If he attacked her thinking she was human, she'd have escaped."

"I knew the agent who worked this case," said Goldstein. "Melissa had parents and two siblings who were ten and seven at the time. He talked to them. She was eighteen years old."

No parents, Charles told Anna. *Or maybe they were fae as well. Or she could have taken her appearance from a dead girl. Hard to say. But I knew her . . . not well, but well enough to say that she was not eighteen.*

Could the victim have been the real Melissa Snow and the fae took her identity after she died?

Anna was just covering all the bases, but it was a good question. When had he met Melissa? Years tended to blend into one another . . . *I knew her during Prohibition, she was working at a speakeasy in Michigan—Detroit, I think—but long before the eighties.*

"She was fae," Anna said. "If she had parents and siblings, I suspect they were also fae. They know how to blend with society, Agent Goldstein. Apparent age has very little to do with reality when you're dealing with the fae."

"The other two?" Goldstein asked, though he didn't sound convinced.

"I'm not an expert on fae," Anna said. "It's just chance that I recognized Melissa. But there are fae among the victims every year from here on out."

Goldstein asked, "Every year?"

That would account for the lack of bodies, Charles told her. *Some of the fae just fade away when they die. If the fae lost his glamour, the other fae would make sure the body never came to light.*

"That I've seen."

There was a growing tightness in Goldstein's shoulders, and an eagerness in his scent that told Brother Wolf that Goldstein was thinking, adding this to all of the bits and pieces he knew about the killer, trying to see how this changed the big picture.

Charles considered the repercussions of a serial killer who hunted fae. Surely the Gray Lords would have noticed that someone was killing their people? But they were not Bran, who protected and loved his wolves. If a fae who was not powerful and kept his head down for safety died, would the Gray Lords who ruled the fae even notice? And if they did notice, would they do anything?

"Could the killer be a fae?" That was from Pat, the Cantrip agent. "If he's been killing since 1975 and he was human, he'd be using a wheelchair by now."

Agent Fisher frowned. "I know an eighty-year-old man who could take you with one arm tied behind his back, Pat. And if this guy was eighteen at the end of the Vietnam War, he'd be a lot younger than eighty. But most serial killers don't last this long. They devolve or start making mistakes."

"The Green River Killer hunted for over twenty years," offered Pat. "And when they finally found him, he was a churchgoing married man with two kids and a stable job he'd had for over thirty years."

Goldstein hadn't been listening; he'd been staring at Anna without really looking at her. Thinking.

"I don't think he's fae," he said. "Not our original killer. Why else would he have waited until the fae came out to start killing them?"

Not our original killer, thought Charles to himself.

"I don't know all of the fae personally," said Anna dryly. "Maybe they've been fae all along."

Goldstein shook his head, and Charles agreed with him when he said, "No. This is an escalation of the type of prey the killer hunts."

He's on the scent, said Brother Wolf, watching the older FBI agent with interest.

"Hunting the enemy," said Singh unexpectedly. "Say he's a Vietnam vet. He goes home and sees Vietnamese—or Asian, which is close enough for him—on his territory. So he goes hunting, just like he did in the war. He switches to boys. Maybe it's because he likes sex with boys better—but let's say that it is because he finds them tougher, better hunting. And then he finds the fae—and decides they are more worthy opponents. And, like his original victims, in his eyes they are invaders."

"He's good and he's smart if he's killed this many fae," said Anna. "They tend to be harder to kill than humans. Too bad he didn't pick the wrong one; we'd never find the pieces of his body. I wonder how he managed that."

"He's killed werewolves," said Heuter, unexpectedly. Charles had quit paying attention to the Cantrip spokesperson, dismissing him. "Aren't they harder to kill than the fae?"

Anna shrugged. "I don't run around killing fae, myself. But anything as old as some of them are have a few tricks up their sleeves."

"Melissa Snow died before you were born," said Pat. "How did you know she was fae?" It wasn't what he said, but rather the aggression in his voice, that caused Brother Wolf to take notice that the tenor of the meeting had changed.

"Family photos," Anna shot back, curling her lip. "Or maybe I'm older than I look. Does it matter?"

"You are twenty-five," said Heuter. "Got your photo on my phone and sent it to home base. They got a hit about two minutes ago. Anna Latham from Chicago, mother deceased, father's a hotshot lawyer."

"So how does *he* know?" murmured Singh, ignoring the Cantrip agent's attack on Anna. "How does he know they aren't human? If they'd been out, someone would have noticed he was killing fae."

A werewolf could scent the fae, most of the time.

"Maybe he had some way of watching while his potential victims touched iron. My Scottish grandmother swore that there were herbal salves you could rub on your eyes to see the fairies," continued Singh, who didn't look as though he could possibly have a Scottish grandmother, though Charles could hardly talk because Charles didn't look very Welsh, either.

"Turning your clothes inside out or wearing cold iron is supposed to work, too," said Fisher, who'd been pretty quiet up to this point. Charles rather thought that she was making sure that the Cantrip agents didn't take control of the meeting again, as she'd spoken just as Heuter opened his mouth to say something else.

"You said 'original killer,'" said Anna to Goldstein, and Charles had to fight to hide his smile. He'd thought she'd missed it, but she was just waiting for the right time to spring it on them. "You don't think we're still dealing with the same man?"

"Right," Goldstein agreed, completely ignoring the Cantrip agents and Singh to focus on the murders. "We noticed some differences in the UNSUB's killings starting about 1995 that seemed to indicate he'd acquired a partner. Then in 2000 the killings took place over six weeks. Though we—2000 is the first year I caught this case—only found five bodies, the timeline indicated that there might be six victims. As there were six the next year, and every year thereafter his killing window has been six weeks instead of four, we're pretty sure that there were six victims in 2000 as well."

"If the MO didn't match, how did you know they were still the Big Game Hunter's victims and not some other killer's?" Singh asked. He was caught up in the hunt for their killer—even though *his* hunt had started with an entirely different prey: the werewolves. Brother Wolf agreed with Charles's assessment of Singh: smart and distractible if something more interesting than his current prey ran in front of him.

Goldstein reached into his briefcase and pulled out . . . a bright yellow ear tag. The kind ranchers staple to their livestock. "He tags his kills. In 'seventy-five he used hunting tags for deer, stolen from a hunting supply store. In 'eighty-two, he switched to this. The current batch can be purchased on the Internet in bags of twenty-five for a buck each."

His prey were things to him, thought Charles. *Livestock.*

Or he was trying to turn them into things, said Anna. "Let's keep going through the victims and see if we notice anything more that we can help you with."

Goldstein continued his slide show. As forensics had developed, the killer's methods of dealing with the bodies changed. Instead of leaving them to be found in some out-of-the-way place, he put them in water. Rivers, lakes, swamps—and here, in Boston, the Atlantic, trusting the water to wash away his sins, which were many.

"There have been several changes besides his choice and number of victims," said Goldstein. "1991 had several. The torture was more ritualized, and he seemed to place more importance on it. The killings also started to move back a month. From 1975 until 1990, all of the murders happened in November. In 1991, he moved to October. And each year after that, he moved back a month until 1995, when he started killing the first of June—where he is now."

"If you'll give me a list—with photos—of the victims," said Anna, when Goldstein was through, "I'll do my best to see if we can't sort the fae out of the rest. I believe that the first werewolf victims were the ones here in Boston, but I'll be able to tell you that for sure after I make a few calls."

Charles was fairly sure the wolves killed this year were the only ones, but it wouldn't hurt to be certain. Besides, with a list of the victims, he could send them out to a couple of fae he knew who might be able to come up with more information on the fae victims, maybe ID a few more.

"All right," agreed Goldstein. "We can do that."

Anna frowned, one hand rubbing lightly on her chin as she stared at the collage of photos of the current year's victims—five so far. The last one was a school photo of a little boy. One more victim to go before the Big Game Hunter moved on until next year.

"I'm not an expert on the fae," Anna said. "But I know wolves. For a normal man, or even a pair of normal men, to take on a werewolf—that's pretty ambitious. Predators usually pick victims that aren't likely to leave them dead."

Heuter frowned. "He didn't seem to have much trouble with these. Three wolves, right? And no one saw a thing. I don't think it's as hard as you say. Otherwise someone would have noticed."

Anna tipped her head back, meeting Charles's eyes. *We're here to advise. To give them information. Should we show them?*

Charles moved from behind her to the end of the heavy conference table where no one was sitting. He glanced under it to make sure it wasn't anchored to the floor, then lifted it to his chest height while making sure it stayed level so none of Goldstein's expensive electronics fell off. He set it down.

"Just killing us," Anna said. "That's tough, but it's not impossible. But holding a werewolf while you torture him . . ."

"Magic?" asked Singh. The Homeland Security agent had totally forgotten that his first intention had been to find out more about the werewolves. Charles found that he liked him—and he hadn't expected to.

Anna shrugged. "That or extremely good planning. It's not just strength—we metabolize very quickly. Drugging or incapacitating one of us for long without killing us is extremely difficult."

"Holy water," said Pat the former FBI and now Cantrip agent.

Anna didn't roll her eyes but she let Charles feel her exasperation.

"I could drink it every day for a week—and do it while living in the Sistine Chapel."

"Silver?" That was Heuter, again.

"Are there black marks where they've been restrained?" Anna asked. "Silver burns us like fire or acid."

They didn't answer her question. Charles had noticed that from the 1990s victims on, the photos of the now-dead people were from the neck down, and sometimes there were no crime scene photos at all. He was pretty certain that the lack wasn't an oversight.

"And how," Anna continued, "did he know they were werewolves? Only one of them, the local wolf, had come out publicly."

There was some more discussion, but Charles let Brother Wolf assimilate it while he observed the room. Agent Fisher was watching Anna with the same look that Asil got when he found a rose that he wanted for his greenhouse, sort of greedy and satisfied.

We're not going to have to talk our way into helping with this case, he told Anna. *Agent Fisher wants us for her very own.*

Brother Wolf brought his attention back to the room, where the other Homeland Security agent, Jim Pierce, was speaking. "What if the killer *was* a werewolf?"

Anna shook her head. "Then you wouldn't be finding tagged bodies; you'd be finding body parts."

"Werewolves eat people?" asked Heuter, coming alert like a hound. "That killing in Minnesota—that was werewolves?"

Anna snorted and lied like a politician. "Look. Becoming a werewolf doesn't make you a serial killer—and it doesn't make you a superhero, either. Whoever you were, that's who you are. If a bad guy gets Changed, he's still a bad guy. However, we police our own and we're pretty good at it. Mostly we're just ordinary people who turn into a wolf during the full moon and go out and hunt rabbits."

Being Changed turned everyone into killers. Werewolves weren't timber wolves or red wolves who hunted only when they were hungry. Werewolves were killers—and the ones who couldn't control it sometimes took a lot of people with them before they died.

No one looking at his mate's earnest freckled face would ever hear the lie—unless they were a werewolf, too. His da would be proud.

CHAPTER

4

Anna followed Charles out of the hotel, trying to figure out what had happened with him and why so she could decide how to proceed.

Charles led the way out of the hotel and turned in the direction of the condo where they were staying. Charles, the Aspen Creek Pack, and the pack's corporation had condos all over the place. The one in Boston belonged to the corporation. It made travel more discreet, no hotel charges, no strangers coming in to clean every day.

"Wait a minute," she said.

Charles turned back. The expression on his face was exactly the same as the one he'd had when they left their house yesterday, heading for the airport so he could fly them to Seattle, where they had caught the commercial flight. But he felt so different.

When Charles had chosen to frighten all those poor people at the airport so she'd win her bet, she'd thought she'd detected mischief in his eyes. But it had been so long since he'd laughed—or teased her with his sneaky sense of humor—that she'd been afraid to hope. After all, they *had* been patting him down pretty thoroughly, something that could have ticked him off enough to growl, and the timing *could* have been accidental.

And even the meeting . . . it had been necessary, if the feds were to believe she was the one with the information, for him to feed it to her. And the best way to do that was for him to open the bond between them. Bran didn't want the feds scared of werewolves, and Charles, especially the past few months, was really scary.

If he were just doing it for business's sake, he would have closed their link down when they left the hotel, but he hadn't. And he'd touched her.

Bran, it seemed, had indeed found a cure—or at least a bandage—for his son.

"What?" Charles asked. Evidently she'd been staring at him too long. He reached up and tucked a flyaway piece of her hair behind her ear.

She wanted to grab his hand and hold it to her, wanted to climb into his arms and feel them close around her. But she was afraid if she drew his attention to it, he'd close her off again. So she kept her hands to herself and bounced up and down on the balls of her feet a couple of times instead. She needed to keep him off his game, keep him thinking about other things—and she had just the thing to do it with.

"Let's go exploring." She pulled the city map she'd taken from the hotel's lobby this morning out of her pocket and opened it up.

"I know Boston," said Charles, with a slightly pained look around to see if anyone had noticed the map. It was bright orange and highly unlikely to evade even the most casual glance.

"But I don't," she told him, enjoying the expression on his face. Being mated to a wolf two hundred years her elder meant that she seldom got to see him disconcerted. "And since *I* want to do the exploring . . ."

He would take her to interesting places, she knew. Tomorrow that would be good, and doubtless she'd enjoy it more than anything she found herself. But today she wanted to be more . . . spontaneous.

"If you run around with that bright orange map in your hand," Charles told her, "everyone will think you're a tourist."

"When was the last time you were a tourist?" she asked archly.

He just looked at her. Charles, she had to agree, was not tourist material.

"Right," Anna told him. "Buck up. You might even enjoy it."

"You might as well have 'hapless victim' tattooed across your forehead," he muttered.

She grabbed his hand and pulled him across the street to King's Chapel and the oldest graveyard in Boston—according to her map.

TWO HOURS LATER, she was vying for food in the North Market building of Faneuil Hall Marketplace with what felt like four hundred tourist groups while Charles waited nearby with his back against the wall. The three feet of empty space around him was probably the only space open in the whole place—but that was Charles; people just didn't crowd him. Smart people.

Since most of the tourists in front of the booth where she'd chosen to grab lunch came all the way to Anna's waist, she was pretty sure she was in no danger, but you couldn't tell it by the focused attention her mate aimed at the children.

If you can't tell that I'm looking at something on you that is precisely on level with the little ones' heads—his voice in her head had a rough purr—*then you need your eyes checked.*

Her jaw dropped. Was he flirting with her? Anna turned her head to meet his gaze, which dropped immediately to her rear end. She jerked her head back before he saw her smirk—or her red cheeks. He *had been* checking out the crowd. She'd seen him do it, seen him take a good long look at each of the kids.

But Charles certainly wasn't lying to her, either, so all the rest had been automatic, but checking her out had been on purpose. She smiled and felt her wolf relax into the rightness of flirting with her mate.

She had plenty of time for her cheeks to cool. It took a while before she managed to order food—mostly because she took pity on an overwhelmed teacher who seemed to be in charge of a million kids all by herself. Anna escaped at last with a pair of sandwiches and a couple of bottles of water and let Charles escort her outside the building to hunt for someplace to sit and eat.

"We could have gone into a real restaurant," Charles said, taking a bottle of water she handed him. "Or waited for the starving hordes to disperse before joining the fray." He sounded serious, as always, but she knew better, knew because their bond conveyed his amusement.

"They were all of seven years old. I was confident that I was unlikely to end up on their plate when there were hot dogs and ice cream to be had."

"If they weren't predatory, you shouldn't have had to manhandle them," he said, making tracks toward an unoccupied seating area. Anna saw at least one other person start for the same place, then notice Charles and turn away, but at least he didn't look panicked.

"They couldn't see over the counter to the food," she told him. "We had a deal. They didn't bite me and I'd lift them up so they could see." She'd expected them to be shyer, but they'd really seemed to have had fun. Maybe they'd been too young to be worried about strangers. The teacher had been too busy lifting up her half of the class to worry about Anna. Apparently the mothers who were supposed to be helping had wandered off to the ladies' room.

"All of the children?"

"Half. One at a time. It's not like they weighed very much. And I had help."

"Hmm." Charles raised an eyebrow. "There was some pretty intense jockeying for position considering that the prize was hot dogs and sandwiches and not priceless art treasures. I saw you elbow that woman."

"She cut in front of a seven-year-old little boy," Anna told him indignantly. "Who *does* that?"

"Ladies wearing four thousand dollars in diamonds, apparently." He cleared the table of the remains of someone else's meal and tossed it in a nearby trash can.

"*I* don't cut in front of children and I *have* four thousand dollars' worth of diamonds." She plopped on a narrow bench and put her food on the minuscule table, hoping it wouldn't wobble and dump everything on the ground.

"Do you?" Charles asked mildly, taking a seat on the other side. The one-person benches, unlike the table, looked sturdy enough and didn't creak beneath his weight, though she saw him rock a little to make sure it would hold. "Except for your ring, you don't wear them. And the ring is not worth four thousand."

"That one necklace, right? Wearing it wouldn't make me cut in front of some poor, hungry kid." He was playing with her, he was, teasing her because she was afraid to wear the jewelry his father had given her when they were married. Her wolf wanted to wiggle in joy and go hunt something to celebrate. Anna took a bite of sandwich. "Though maybe I'd have to put on the bracelet, too."

"No," he said. "Just the bracelet would do. But you don't wear them."

Her necklace was covered in at least twice the number of diamonds and several larger stones. She absorbed the idea of the bracelet itself being worth more than four thousand dollars, and was doubly grateful that she hadn't worn them. She tended to play with anything hanging around her neck—what if she broke the necklace?

"There's a time and place for stuff like that." Anna tried not to show him how appalled she was at the value of the jewelry. She preferred to downplay the material changes in her life since she'd met and mated with Charles. They weren't the important changes—if occasionally she found them more difficult than the real ways her life had altered. "When you're going shopping isn't a good time for jewels, especially if that makes you think that pushing around little kids is okay."

He raised his eyebrows. "Oh? When *were* you planning on wearing your diamonds?" Charles sounded amused. He knew that she was planning on never wearing them now that she knew what they were worth.

"Maybe if we were meeting the Queen of England." She thought about it for a moment. "Or if I really needed to outshine someone I didn't like." She took a few more bites of a sandwich that needed a little something . . . onion or radish, maybe. Something with a bite.

She really couldn't imagine a situation dire enough to risk wearing something like that set, especially not if the *bracelet* was worth four thousand dollars. What if the clasp gave way?

"Ah. That would be never?" It didn't seem to bother him one way or the other.

Anna thought about it seriously. "Maybe if I needed to intimidate someone—like if my brother decided to remarry and my dad told me he didn't like her so I had to fly to Chicago and drive her off. I would even cut *her* in line for a hot dog while I was wearing them. But she wouldn't be seven, either."

Charles smiled. It wasn't a laugh or a grin. But it wasn't his you're-going-to-die-before-you-breathe-your-next-gulp-of-air smile, either, which was as close to a real smile as she'd seen on his face for a while.

She gave a contented sigh and tapped the toe of her boot against the leg of his suit. They'd have been more comfortable in casual clothes, but then they'd have had to go change. And she was afraid that going back to the condo would give him an excuse to shut down again.

"It's all right," he said. "We can go change and do some more touristy stuff."

He was reading her through their bond. Hiding the warm fuzzies *that* gave her behind a distrustful look, Anna took a bite of her sandwich and then said, "Okay. But only if you'll agree to do this with me." She took her now-bedraggled map out of her pocket and tapped a finger on an advertisement.

Charles looked, heaved a long sigh. "I should have known we wouldn't get out of here without doing the imitation trolley car cemetery tour complete with costumed ghouls."

"*Not* in my territory," snarled someone behind her.

As it seemed an unlikely response to Charles's pseudo-reluctant agreement, Anna initially assumed it was directed at someone else. But Charles tilted his head and lowered his eyelids, the muscles tightening subtly in his shoulders, so Anna turned around in her seat to see who had spoken.

In rows along the outdoor marketplace were dozens of dark green wagons, resembling nothing so much as the covered wagons in her father's beloved old Western movies. The wagons served as kiosks where people sold T-shirts, purses, or other small portable goods. Standing on the top of the one nearest them was a young-looking black man, fine-boned and slight, watching them—watching Charles, anyway—with yellow eyes as the strings of beading supplies hanging from hooks all over the wagon swayed unsteadily.

From photos, she recognized him as Isaac Owens, the Alpha of the Olde Towne Pack—Boston being the Olde Towne, complete with the final *Es*. He wasn't in the habit of running around on the tops of unlikely perches or he'd have been in the local paper a lot more than he already was.

"You're attracting attention," said Charles in a conversational tone designed not to carry to human ears. Isaac, being a werewolf, would hear him just fine despite being a dozen yards away. "Do you really want that?"

"I'm out. They know who I am." Projecting his voice to anyone who cared to listen—and people were starting to pause what they were doing to listen—Isaac raised his chin aggressively. "What about you?"

Charles shrugged. "In, out, it doesn't matter." He leaned forward and lowered his voice. "No more does your declaration. You lost control of the situation that brings me here when you chose not to report the deaths in your territory. You have no say over what I do or don't do."

"We didn't kill anyone," Isaac declared, and pointed at Charles. "And you will have to go through me to take any of my pack."

Isaac was new, Anna remembered. New at his job, new at being a wolf—and, like her, he'd been a college student when he'd been Changed. Normally it would have been years before he was Alpha, no matter how much potential dominance he had. But the Olde Towne Pack had lost its Alpha last year in a freak sailing accident and Isaac, who had been second, had stepped in to do the job. *His* second was an old wolf who probably didn't know anything at all about this stunt.

The woman who was working the kiosk—her body bestrewn with hand-beaded jewelry and tattoos in a bewildering mixture of color and texture—was backing slowly away, trying not to draw attention to herself. Not a bad strategy for someone caught between predators, though less glittery jewelry might have helped—another reason for Anna not to wear the diamonds.

"If no laws were broken, no one is at risk," said Charles, and Isaac sneered.

"Get off the stupid wagon before that poor lady calls nine-one-one," Anna said, exasperated. "Come introduce yourself, Isaac, and see what happens." She said it loud enough that she was clearly audible to the crowd of people that was forming a ring around them—close enough to see what was going on, not so close as to get involved. That meant she was speaking almost as loudly as Isaac had been.

The local Alpha looked at her for the first time and frowned. His nostrils flared as he tried to catch her scent—which would have been impossible to filter from the rest of the people nearby except that she smelled like an Omega wolf.

After a rather long pause, Isaac shrugged his shoulders to loosen the muscles and walked off the end of the wagon—a good nine- or ten-foot drop. He landed with flexed knees and turned to the proprietor of the shop, who'd stopped when Anna had drawn attention to her.

"My apologies," he told her. "I didn't mean to scare *you*." He smiled and handed her a card. "A friend of mine runs a pub—stop by and have a meal on us."

The woman took the card with a rather shaky hand that steadied as Isaac's smile warmed. She glanced down and her eyebrows rose. "I've eaten there. Good fish and chips."

"I think so, too," he said, gave her a wink, and strolled over to where Anna and Charles sat.

"Nice PR," Anna said. "Though considering what went before, I'm not inclined to give you an A for it."

He studied her, ignoring Charles's brooding presence. "Ayah, nah," he said, exaggerating his Boston accent into incomprehensible nasal sounds before he dropped most of it to continue more clearly. "What in the hell are you?"

"Good to meet you, too," Anna said. "I bet that card was your second's idea, wasn't it? To make up for your lack of manners?" She dropped her voice and added a touch of Boston to it. "Oops—sorry I destroyed your car. Here, have a meal on me. Was that *your* dog I ate? Oh, sorry. Have a drink at my friend's pub and forget all about it."

Isaac grinned, a sudden, charming expression that showed white, white teeth in his blue-black face. "Caught me, darling. But you didn't answer my question."

"She is *mine*," said Charles. His aggressive answer didn't show up in his voice, which was low and calm. "We have a meeting scheduled tomorrow, with you and your pack. There was no need for this . . ." He glanced around. People were still watching them, but they were pretending not to. "Theater," he finished.

"This is Boston, hoss." Isaac bent his knees and squatted, putting his head on a level with theirs. "That's 'thee-ah-tah.' We're all about theater here." He pronounced the second "theater" just as Charles had. He wasn't native to Boston, she remembered. She thought he was from Michigan or Pennsylvania.

Anna gave him a gimlet eye and spoke to Charles. "He was probably walking by and spotted us. Decided he couldn't wait until tomorrow to throw a hissy fit."

"And aren't you one to burst everyone's posturing?" Isaac's dark eyes considered her. Then, in a more down-to-earth tone, he looked at Charles and said, "As a matter of fact, she's right." Then his face and his voice went very, very serious. "I meant what I said. To get to my wolves, you'll have to go over my dead body."

"If you do your job, he'll never have to do his." Bitterness made Anna's tone sharper than she meant it to be.

"She make all of your words, *kemosabe*?" Isaac asked Charles.

Charles raised his eyebrows in an exaggerated fashion and pointed his chin at Anna as if waiting for her to answer for him. He never used his fingers to point. It was, he'd told her, very bad manners among his mother's people.

Speaking of bad manners . . . "Where's our card for a free meal?" Anna demanded. "I think you owe us one. *Cogita ante salis,* my father would tell you. You should think before you leap."

Charles murmured, "Before you depart. Sally forth. Close enough."

Anna was never sure how many of the Latin phrases she knew were right, and how much her father simply had made up on the spot. She'd quit speaking it in front of Bran because he'd get this pained look on his face. Charles seemed mostly to find it funny, a joke they shared. He claimed not to speak Latin, but apparently Spanish and French were close enough to allow him to comment.

"Charles is not here to enforce justice, at least not on you or yours." She nodded at Isaac. "We were coming to you to ask for information. There are dead werewolves and the FBI and police apparently don't have anything but bodies. We were sent here to help them. We were coming to ask you the questions the FBI probably already have in the hopes you could answer differently for us. How were our people taken and killed? Where were they taken from?"

"Information on the dead guys?" Isaac raised his chin and met her eyes. He waited for her to drop hers—and when that didn't happen, he frowned thoughtfully. Likely he'd never met a wolf before that he couldn't either stare down, or felt driven to bow before.

The Omega part tended to confuse a lot of wolves who were used to immediately sizing up others when they first met them. *Is this wolf more dominant or less? Will she do as I ask, or do I have to do what she tells me? Are we close enough in rank that I have to worry about a fight to determine who rules and who is ruled, who protects and who is protected?* Anna didn't register at all on the obey-or-be-obeyed scale—and she apparently came with something that made all the dominant wolves need to protect her.

Finally Isaac shook his head. "My take is that it is some seriously powerful fae, vampire, or something of that ilk. I don't know about the other two—I can give you the addresses of their hotels and their stated businesses. But they've been here before, lots of times. Neither was in the habit of causing trouble, so I don't have them shadowed anymore. But my boy, Otten, he was taken right while he was out jogging along the Charles River about five in the morning."

Isaac glanced over his shoulder as if he could see the river from where they sat, though it wasn't possible. "That's early; I know that's early. But there are other people, and *damn*, he's a werewolf, right?" And Anna realized he'd turned his head so they couldn't see the expression on his face. "Still, no one saw *anything*. No sign of a struggle—and Otten, he's pretty old, right? Old, tough, and a fine scrapper in wolf or human form. He knew how to watch his back. Not someone to be surprised. Pack bonds hit me hard about three hours later, dropped me right down and out—he was hurt that badly. But there was so much static I couldn't get a fix on him when I woke up."

He focused on Charles, meeting his gaze for longer than she'd ever seen anyone outside of his father. "They cut him. Raped him and killed him while they cut into him." His voice was raw with rage, and golden embers sparked in his dark eyes despite the tears on his cheek.

"They," said Charles intently. "How many?"

Isaac looked startled at the question, and then surprise jerked his head up and he frowned. "Two? Two . . . is wrong; there was a third. I just got impressions. Mostly pain. Didn't think the shadows I got were important. Let me think." He closed his eyes and tilted his head, a wolflike motion that was familiar. They all did it, now and again. If Anna's nose quit working, she'd still know a werewolf when she met him, just from that motion.

Isaac frowned and shook his head.

They cut him, Isaac had said. The FBI had shown them only select views of the later victims, as if to hide damage that had some significance they hadn't wanted to share. Or else they were trying not to shock a civilian consultant who might pay so much attention to the dead body, he failed to see anything else. But cutting . . . She knew a kind of creature who might cut up a werewolf before killing him.

"Were the cuts random?" asked Anna. "Or were they in a deliberate pattern?"

Isaac caught on to where she was going. "Witches? You think witches are behind this?"

Charles shrugged. "This is the beginning of our hunt, Isaac. I try not to think anything at this point."

Isaac nodded and looked at Anna. "Could be the cuts were deliberate. Or it could just have been someone playing, like a cat with a mouse—they seemed to enjoy it. The bond between an Alpha and his wolves isn't a mating bond—I just caught the worst of what he was experiencing here and there." Something unhappy grew in his face, and his eyes widened as he kept the tears in. "He wasn't scared, you know? Even when the pain was bad. Otten was a cool one, just waiting for his chance—but they didn't give him one."

"I knew him," said Charles, and his voice said a lot more than the words. It acknowledged and agreed with Isaac's assessment of the man and told Anna—and Isaac—that the dead man had been someone Charles respected and liked. "Thank you for talking to us, Isaac. You've helped. We'll stop them, and when we do, you'll know that you helped."

"You find those bastards"—it came out in a low growl from Isaac's belly, a command by one who was used to giving orders—"who killed Otten . . ." He sucked in his breath and looked abruptly away and down. Anna glanced at Charles but she couldn't see the expression on his face that Isaac had responded to; it was already gone.

When the Boston Alpha spoke again, the command was gone from his voice. "You find them, and I would take it as a personal favor if you called me for backup."

He handed Anna a card. It had only a phone number below his

name, so she put out her empty hand demandingly. He lowered his lids and stared at her as she met his gaze unflinchingly—then wiggled her fingers. "Gimme."

He laughed, wiped the tears from his face with both hands, and looked at Charles. "*What* is she?" But without waiting for a reply—that wasn't forthcoming anyway—he handed Anna a pair of cards that had *The Irish Wolfhound* embossed on them. "Don't bend 'em all up. We reuse them."

Anna snorted as he popped up to his feet and jumped on top of the wagon he'd been on before in an easy leap. With a half wave of his hand, he took off, moving fast without giving the appearance of fleeing. He lightly hopped from one kiosk to the next, rocking them but not enough that anything fell off the shelves.

Charles rose unhurriedly, but without any wasted motions, either, and gathered the debris of their meal. "Let's go while he's still distracting everyone."

THEY WALKED BY the Old State House on their way to the condo. It was sitting right in the middle of a bunch of skyscrapers, looking like a bright gold and white anachronism in the middle of all the dark glass and chrome of its near neighbors. Boston . . . Anna'd been expecting something like Seattle, since so many people compared the two. And there were some things that reminded her quite strongly of the Emerald City—the ocean, for instance—and the whole educated-and-liberal feel to the place. But Boston was different, at least the part of it that she had seen.

It wasn't just older; it *felt* older—and somehow still fresh and brash and still moving on. New World–ish, maybe. Built by people unsatisfied with their lives who crossed an ocean, risking and giving their lives for a new start, right here.

There was the architecture, too. So many buildings here had historic import; they'd been left where they were, no matter how inconvenient. Barricaded on the left and right by busy roads and huge modern buildings, the Old State House was polished and painted and cared for in a way it probably hadn't been back in the colonial days when Crispus Attucks and four other men were shot on the street next to it in the Boston Massacre.

Little narrow colonial roads had mostly disappeared into the wide modern streets, but still popped up here and there—holding such treasures as antique stores and old bookshops. The end effect of massive steel and glass buildings standing guard over their smaller and more delicately built forerunners was eclectic and charming.

"Do you think the killers are werewolves?" Anna asked as they briskly walked back to their condo.

"Werewolves?" Charles considered it and shook his head. "No. Isaac would have known if Otten had been hunted down by werewolves."

They walked about half a block in silence; then Charles shook his head again. "Maybe . . . maybe Isaac wouldn't have picked up on it if the killers had been werewolves. He's young. But the hunt is wrong for werewolves. No one is eating these victims. A werewolf who is hunting like that . . . Other werewolves could smell the sickness of spirit on them." He paused. "*I* could smell it on them. There is no wolf in the country who was alive forty years ago that I have not met since the time the killings began. But it could be vampires—or witches."

"Five thirty this time of year is pretty light for a vampire," Anna said. "But if he's been hunting this long, successfully killing fae and werewolves alike, he's got to be some kind of supernatural, doesn't he? I can't imagine that a vampire wouldn't also drink from the victims— and if that was the case, no one is telling us."

Charles shrugged, dodging around a small tour being led by a man in a powdered wig wearing Revolutionary fashion and carrying an unlit lantern on a stick. Anna dodged the other way and caught a bit of the tour guide's spiel.

"*Revere did not ride alone that night, nor was he, in his own time, famous for the act. Paul Revere is famous because his name is the one Longfellow, nearly a hundred years later, chose to use in his famous poem instead of my good friend William Dawes, who was the other rider out warning of the British invasion.*" Before his voice was drowned in the sounds of a busy city at midday, Anna noted that he had a fruity British accent pasted over a Southern drawl: not a Boston native.

Charles continued their conversation as if he'd never paused at all. "It could be an organization of people who hate the fae and werewolves— like Bright Future or the John Lauren Society. Or a bunch of hunters who see us as a challenge."

"Or a group of black witches, if there was more than one killer."

"Right," agreed Charles. "I don't know enough yet. The FBI were pretty careful about what information they gave us."

"I noticed none of the later victims' crime scene photos show their faces," Anna said thoughtfully. "We saw enough of them that the over-sight couldn't have been an accident."

"No faces, no uncovered front torsos or backs, either. Also no means of murder. Were they strangled? Stabbed? I should have asked Isaac."

"You think the FBI will call us in to help?" She thought so, but was afraid to trust her judgment when she wanted in as badly as she did. The eyes of the victims stayed with her.

Charles shrugged. "Yes. Fisher looked at us like we were candy. But it doesn't matter. If they don't, we'll involve ourselves. It'll be easier if they ask."

They walked awhile in silence. Well, Charles was silent. Anna's shoes made a brisk click-click-click on the sidewalk. She could have walked more quietly, but she liked the way the noise she made blended with the sounds of the city, almost like music.

She bumped Charles as a pretty woman in a business suit and torturously high heels walked past them. "Did you see that? Look at her legs. Look at all the women who are wearing dresses—and look at their legs. Their calves are all bigger around than their thighs."

"They call Boston 'the walking city' for a reason." Charles rumbled as he opened the door to the building of their condo. As soon as he was inside, the faint aura of danger he emitted eased down. Evidently Charles had been in this building often enough that he didn't view it as enemy territory.

"How soon do you suppose the FBI will be calling us?" Anna asked. "If they decide to call us."

"Bored?" He took them to the stairs and, after her previous ride in the slick, modern, very slow elevator, Anna was happy to trot after him.

"Nope. I just want to make sure we have time to do the haunted tour tonight."

He gave her a look and Anna grinned, happily sinking into the warm, safe relationship that had somehow been restored after better than a year of fragmentation. It was too easy; she knew it. But she was going to enjoy it while she could.

"Maybe the FBI will call," he said hopefully. She wasn't buying it; he'd have as much fun running around old cemeteries as she would—he just wouldn't admit it.

"I've got my cell phone," she pointed out. "You've got yours. Get changed and let's go."

He growled.

AFTER THE MEETING with the werewolves, Leslie ate an early lunch at a nearby soup and bread place before walking the rest of the block or so between the hotel and her office. She used the time to mentally process what she'd seen and heard so she could give a coherent, organized version of the highlights for Nick. She finished the last little bit as she rode the elevator up so she was ready before she hit the office.

The office watchdog, known only to Leslie's group as the Gatekeeper, nodded at Leslie and buzzed her in. Leslie headed to her desk but a sharp whistle from her boss's office changed her trajectory.

Nick looked tired. They'd been chasing after two different bank robbers and something that might be a terrorist cell—or might just be a bunch of broke students rooming together—before this serial-killer thing hit their radar. The terrorist cell had top priority over everything. However, one of the bank robbers had been doing his best to put himself on the top of the list. He wore a distinctive motorcycle helmet with a small sticker on top that had given him the nickname the Smiley Bandit. Lately he'd begun working with another faceless, helmeted man who liked to carry a gun and shoot it at lights and cameras after aiming it at people. One of these days really soon now he was going to start shooting people. Their team was short a few since Joe and Turk had been transferred out. The job got done, but all of them were a little light on sleep.

"How'd it go?" Nick asked after she closed the door behind her.

Leslie thought about it. "Interesting on many levels."

He gave an impatient snort. "Share. Please."

She started with a rundown on who was there. Nick grunted when she told him Heuter had come. It was a grunt she couldn't interpret. She couldn't tell if he liked Heuter or disliked him—or if he was just acknowledging that Cantrip had sent in their golden boy.

Leslie told him about the biggest revelation. "Our UNSUB has been killing mostly fae—we think for the past twenty-five-odd years—and no one noticed until a werewolf told us, a werewolf who wasn't even born when the first murders began. Cantrip claims she is Anna Latham.

I'll run the name and see if I agree with them on her identity, but she didn't deny it."

"There have been rumors, if you know where to listen, that werewolves may share a trait or two with the fae. That their ability to heal damned near anything also keeps them from aging."

Leslie absorbed that. "If that's so, I peg our Anna at sixteen and her husband at ten thousand and change."

Nick laughed. "Impressed by him, were you? Craig was, too. He gave me a call as soon as the meeting was over to tell me that he was headed over to see Kip at the Boston PD. He was hoping the police might have someone familiar with the fae they can take the photos to, so we can get a confirmation."

"If you talked to Craig already, why have me do a basic report?" she asked, a little annoyed.

"He said he'd leave the briefing for you to deliver, as he was the senior field agent," said her boss equitably, and then got back to the business at hand. "If it's true, that so many of the victims have been fae, why didn't anyone in the fae communities say anything?"

Leslie shrugged. "Why do the fae do anything, Nick? Maybe they don't want to draw attention or encourage a copycat. Maybe they didn't notice."

"So the killer was out shooting fae and decided to hit a couple of werewolves, too."

"That's the latest theory Craig and I subscribe to."

"What about the werewolves? Will they help us? Do we want their help?"

Leslie tapped the side of her foot on the floor. "The guy is Native American and big. He stood back and didn't say a word he didn't have to. All of us in that room were doing everything we could not to pay attention to him because he was that scary."

"Scary how? Cold? Crazy?"

Leslie frowned at her boss. "Like you get when you are trying to intimidate someone we're questioning—only not so deliberate."

"Thousand-yard stare?"

"Yeah," Leslie agreed. "He's seen some blood somewhere." And the thing that had been bothering her about the pair of werewolves coalesced. "The girl who is his wife, she looks so sweet she ought to be attracting honeybees. Innocent. Even Jim Pierce was feeling protective around her; you could see it in his body posture—and Dr. Singh deliberately distracted the Cantrip agents when they got in her face and tried to intimidate her. And you know Singh."

"You think she was faking it?"

Leslie shook her head. "No. Not really. But both of the werewolves looked at photos of dead bodies and didn't bat an eyelash. Granted we didn't show the bad ones in full color, but the old police black-and-whites are pretty nasty."

"You think they've spent some time looking at dead bodies," Nick said. "You think they're killers."

She nodded. "Him, yes. He has that . . . that look. You have it. A lot of the armed forces guys have it. I think he could have killed us all and not given it another thought. As for her . . ." She frowned, trying to get a better handle on it. "Have you ever worked with Lee Jennings? The guy the Behavior Analysis Unit sends to interview the nasty guys in prison?"

Nick frowned. "Yes."

"He's pretty unremarkable. I like him a lot, and so does everyone else who's worked with him. And the reason they send him into the prisons with the scum of the earth and the crazies is because they like him, too. They fall all over themselves to give him whatever information he asks for."

Nick raised his chin and his face went still. "Right. She's like that?"

Leslie nodded. "Her husband didn't say more than two or three words, but he dominated the room. The only one not intimidated was Craig—and he just wasn't looking. I'd bet Charles Smith is an Alpha of some pack we don't know about."

"Intimidating."

She nodded again. "He was playing muscle, I think. But she didn't treat him that way." Why did she think that? "He came in late with coffee for all of us—she'd sent him out so she could explain to us how to make the matter easier for him."

"To keep everyone safe?"

Leslie shook her head. "She said so, but I got the distinct impression she was a lot more worried about him than she was any of us. It was the standard stuff—don't meet his eyes if you can help it. No aggressive moves. The only new thing was that we weren't supposed to try to touch her at all. I expected a wild-eyed maniac, and the man who came in was tight, controlled, and at ease. He looked like he conducted meetings with the federal government every day of his life."

"And that made you think he was running the show behind the scenes?"

"No. That's not all of it. Body language said she respected him and deferred to his judgment. She was in front, but he was more than just backup."

"So do we invite them in?"

"She pointed out that our killer took out werewolves. Taking out werewolves, I gather and surmise, is akin to taking out a SEAL team. This UNSUB has been hunting fae and coming out—as far as we know—unscathed. Do we have a choice?"

"The FBI has some fae on payroll. We have a choice. You met them and you're damn near the best agent I have for reading people. What do you think?"

Leslie sighed loudly. "I like her. I told you. And he is . . . competent— he's got that air. The one that says, 'I've seen a lot and made it out alive.'

They won't cost us anything, so the budget will be happy. But"—she held up a finger—"he's not going to take orders."

Nick nodded his head and did his finger-hand-talk thing for a good half minute before blowing out a breath of air. "There's a couple of people at the BAU who are familiar with the Big Game Hunter. I'll give them a call and see what the profilers say might happen to our killer if the media knows we have werewolves hunting him. You and Craig can pick up information on werewolves as you work with them. Let me think about implications for the rest of today, and if nothing strikes me as too stupid, I'll give you a go tomorrow."

5

After a hard day of being a tourist, Anna slept deeply in the bed on the other side of the bathroom wall. Charles put his forehead against his side of that wall for a long moment before he worked up his . . . "Courage" was not the right word. Fortitude.

After a deep breath, Charles stepped in front of the bathroom mirror. It was one of those full-length things that women used to use to make sure their ankles weren't showing below their skirts and now used to make sure, he assumed, that their underwear showed only when they wanted it to.

And he was trying to distract himself by looking at the mirror rather than looking at the image it held.

Charles couldn't see them if he turned his head to look behind himself, but in the mirror the spirits who haunted him were as clear, as three-dimensional, as they were when they were still alive. They had stayed away all day while he and Anna did the tourist thing, this evening when Anna took him on the silly haunted tour that had been a surprising amount of fun, and tonight when he had held her as she fell asleep.

As soon as she slept, they returned.

We see her, they said. *Does she see you? Does she know what you are? Murderer, killer, death bringer. We will show her and she'll run from you. But she can't run far enough to be safe.*

Hollow-eyed and cadaverously thin, they stared at him, meeting his eyes in a way that no one except Anna, his father, or his brother had dared to do in a very long time. The oldest ones morphed into something they had not been in life—their eyes black, their faces distorted until they hardly looked human. The three newest ones looked as they had the moment before he'd ended their lives. They stood so close to him that it was strange that he could not feel the heat of them—or the chill—at his back. Even so, it wasn't only his eyes that told him they were there.

Charles could smell them. Not the odor of rotting meat precisely, but something close, the sweet, sickly smell that some flowers produce to attract flies and other carrion-feeding bugs. The smell penetrated his skin. Like the ghosts in the mirror, the scent was a reflection, not the real thing.

And he heard them.

Why? they asked. *Why did you kill us?* He knew they weren't interested in the answers, not really.

The first time he'd seen them, when he'd first started this job for his father, he'd tried answering them, though he'd known better. He'd been certain that if he hit upon just the right thing to say, they would go away. But explaining things to the dead never works. They don't hear the way the living do and words have little effect. The questions were for him, but not for him to answer—and talking to them just gave them more strength.

Guilt attracted them. *His* guilt—it kept them from moving on to where they belonged. There should have been something else that could have been done for them. That there had not been didn't make him feel any differently about it.

They had been protecting a child and lost control of their anger. Charles knew, as any werewolf did, all about losing control. There had been a pedophile stalking children in the pack's territory, and they'd been sent out to hunt him down. That was exactly what they had done. Then they botched the job beyond repair. In another time, they'd have been punished, but not killed.

And now they haunted him. That Charles could not release them was a second burden to bear, a second debt he owed to them.

His grandfather—his mother's father—had taught him it was so, and his very long life had given him no reason to doubt it.

Dave Mason, the dead man nearest Charles, the last of the Minnesota wolves Charles had killed, opened his mouth and darted forward. Dave had been a good man. Not the brightest or the kindest, but a good man, a man of his word. He'd understood that Charles was only doing what was necessary. Dave wouldn't have wanted his ghost to torment anyone.

In the mirror Dave's cold, eager eyes met Charles's as his lamprey mouth attached to Charles's neck, cold and sharp, feeding on guilt. He disappeared from sight after a few minutes, but not from Charles's senses as, one by one, the ghosts behind him did the same, until Charles stood apparently alone in front of the mirror and felt his ghosts gain strength from him while they weakened him. They didn't touch him physically, not yet. But he knew that he wasn't thinking as clearly, wasn't able to trust his judgment anymore.

On the other side of the wall, Anna moved restlessly. Not awake, but aware.

He should close down his bond with her, again. He didn't think any of his ghosts could cross it and touch her, but he wasn't certain. He couldn't bear it if he caused her harm.

Equally, Charles couldn't bear to be separated from her again.

Anna's cell phone rang and she grumbled as she fumbled around the unfamiliar nightstand for it.

"Hello, this is Anna," she said, her voice husky with sleep.

He was too distracted to pay attention to the words of the person on the other end of the conversation. He listened to Anna, let her voice remind him that he hadn't driven her away, hadn't hurt her irreparably. Not yet.

"Right now?" A pause. "Sure. We're glad to be of assistance. Can you give me the address? No. Not necessary. There's Wi-Fi here so I have the Internet. Just wait for me to find a sheet of paper." She pulled something else off the table next to the bed—her purse, he thought from the sound of it. Charles looked away from the mirror.

"Okay. Have pen and paper. Shoot."

He couldn't go out and perform for the feds. Not like this. He would hurt someone, someone who didn't deserve it.

Use me, said Brother Wolf. *If I stay with Anna, it will be safe for everyone. I will not harm any of the people. I will keep her safe from them.*

Which "them"? Charles asked.

FBI, killers, the dead. All of them and any of them. She will be safe— and so will the others. I will not hurt them unless I have to. Can you say the same?

Charles almost smiled at the thought that Brother Wolf would be less dangerous than he, but at the moment it seemed to be true enough. Without another look in the mirror, he let the change take him: he would trust the wolf to keep her safe.

"**HOW LONG WILL** it take you to get here?" Leslie Fisher's voice was cool and professional, but her question had just a hint of urgency.

A young woman was missing from her condo, though she hadn't been gone long. Luckily, the policeman who'd gone to check it out had been briefed on their serial killer and thought it was a close enough match to the way other people had been taken to call in the FBI.

There was something wrong with Charles. It had been nagging at Anna since she woke, but she'd already answered the phone. It didn't feel urgent, just not good—so she decided to take care of the truly urgent matter first to get it out of the way. If it was their serial killer, they had a chance of getting to the girl before anything happened.

"How far is the apartment from the hotel we were at"—it was two in the morning—"yesterday morning?" Charles hadn't been in bed beside her, though she knew he was in the condo. She could feel him.

"Ten- or fifteen-minute walk. Something like that. The victim's apartment isn't too far from the Commons." Then Fisher clearly remembered that Anna and Charles weren't from Boston. "The Boston Common. The big park a couple of blocks from the hotel."

After a day of sightseeing, Anna could have told Fisher how big the Common was and approximately how many people were buried in it and all about the ducks that inspired a famous children's book.

Their condo was less than a five-minute run from the hotel, and she and Charles could always take a taxi if the place they needed to get to was too far.

"Less than fifteen minutes, then," Anna told her.

"Good," said Fisher. "We'd appreciate anything you can do. Assuming this is our UNSUB, based on previous cases, she's still alive and will be for a few more days."

"We'll do our best."

Anna hung up the phone and began dragging on her clothes. "Charles? Did you hear? There's a girl missing. Is Lizzie Beauclaire one of our werewolves? I don't remember her name from the Olde Towne Pack roster."

Not that I know of. It wasn't Charles who answered.

Anna paused, one foot off the ground as she'd been shoving it into a pant leg. Brother Wolf padded out of the bathroom, all three hundred pounds of fox-red fur, fangs, and claws. There were bigger werewolves, but not many. Her own wolf was closer to the two-hundred-pound mark—so was Bran's, for that matter.

"Well," she said slowly. The wrongness in their bond was fading, leaving behind the cool, thoughtful presence that was Brother Wolf. "I suppose it'll help save time if one of us is already wolf when we get there."

Charles is worried that he will do something bad, Brother Wolf told her. *We decided that it would be best if I take point tonight.* Brother Wolf had gotten better about speaking to her in words rather than images. She got the distinct impression that he looked upon it as baby talk, but it amused him anyway.

She resumed dressing while she considered his words. Of all the wolves she'd known over the past few years, none but Charles could let the wolf rule without disaster. The wolf part of a werewolf was . . . a ravaging beast, born to hunt and kill, protect the pack at all costs, and not much else. Brother Wolf was different from other werewolves' wolf spirits because Charles, born a werewolf, was different from other werewolves.

Different because of you, too, Brother Wolf told her.

"I suppose if you—both of you—think it's wise. You know better than I do. Let me know if there's some way I can help. But it does mean we aren't getting a taxi."

It no longer felt odd to talk to Charles and his wolf as if they were two separate people who shared the same skin, both of them beloved. She and her wolf nature were much more entwined, though she had the impression that they were still not as integrated as most werewolves were.

Brother Wolf butted up against her, knocking her over, and licked her face thoroughly. *Yes. No taxis for werewolves. Charles doesn't like driving in cars.* The werewolf stepped away and tilted his head, gold eyes gleaming with humor—whatever had Charles upset, it must not be too bad because his wolf wasn't worried.

I will take care of him. Brother Wolf's humor fled. *As your sister wolf took care of you when you needed her to defeat the Chicago wolves.*

"All right, then." Anna didn't know what to think of that because her wolf had helped her endure rape and torture. But in the optimism of the change in Charles yesterday, she decided to believe that Brother Wolf's intervention was a positive thing. Anna dried her face on her shirt tail and got up to finish dressing.

Shoes on, face washed, she looked up the address on her laptop. "We're in luck," she told him. "Only two miles from here."

THERE WERE PEOPLE out and about at two in the morning, but no one seemed to think it odd that she was running down the street with a three-hundred-pound werewolf. Might have been a touch of pack magic making people see a large dog—or not see them at all. Pack magic, she'd discovered, could be capricious, coming and going without any of the wolves calling for it specifically. Bran could direct it, as could Charles—but she had the feeling that pack magic mostly did what it chose to do.

The lack of interest they were spawning might also simply have been city survival skills on the part of their observers. Anna had grown up in Chicago. In a city, you don't look at anyone whose attention you don't want to draw. Who wants to have a big scary wolf decide you might be interesting?

Brother Wolf was on a leash, because Bran thought that the leash and collar made a lot of difference to the humans they ran into—and not much difference to the werewolf. The collar was store-bought from a big-box pet store and came with the cute plastic clasp designed to make sure someone's dog didn't get caught and choke to death. It meant that the collar wouldn't even slow a werewolf down before the plastic broke.

The name on the collar he wore was Brother Wolf. Bran had disapproved. He liked the names to be less truthful, more friendly and cute. Unusually, Charles's brother had told her, Charles had held out until his father gave in.

The address Leslie Fisher had provided led them to one of the skyscrapers, a tall but narrow edifice squeezed in between two even taller buildings. Anna would have picked it out even without the giant black numbers tastefully etched into the glass over the main door because it was the one with police cars parked in front of it.

No one looked at them when they entered the building, though there was a small group of officers huddled up in the foyer. A young man in a security uniform manned the desk; he looked upset.

On impulse, Anna walked over to him. "Excuse me. Were you on duty when the young woman went missing?" She waited for him to ask her for her credentials, but either he was too shocky or he'd just gotten used to answering any and all questions put to him.

"Lizzie," he said, his eyes drifting over her face, down to Brother Wolf and back up, as if not looking at the giant wolf in front of his desk might make the scary thing go away. "Her name is Lizzie. She came in about eight and I never saw her leave. Neither did the security tapes." He swallowed. Glanced down at Brother Wolf again.

"Who used the elevator after she came in?"

"Tim Hodge on the fifth floor. Sally Roe and her partner, Jenny, on the eighth. That is the biggest dog I've ever seen." He sounded a little apprehensive.

"And Lizzie is on the twelfth."

"That's right."

"How many people use the stairs?"

"Businesses on the first three floors," he answered, frowning at Brother Wolf. She could hear his heartbeat pick up as something instinctual kicked in to tell him that there was a big predator on the end of her leash. Though he continued talking, he took a step back. "A couple of the people on the fourth and fifth floor take the stairway down sometimes, but mostly everyone who lives here takes the elevator."

Brother Wolf took a step forward.

"And where is the stairway?" Anna asked, then hissed, "Stop that," to her mate. If it had been Charles, she would have been certain he was only teasing—the wolf was a different matter.

Brother Wolf turned his head toward her, his eyes half-veiled, and let his ears slack a little in a wolf smile. All of which didn't mean that he hadn't been interested in hunting the young man down—just that he *also* had enjoyed teasing her.

"Over there." The security guard pointed just beyond the police officers. "I'll have to buzz you in. For that, I'll need some ID."

"Do you have to buzz people out?"

He shook his head. "Against the fire code, I think."

The stairs would have been a better way to exit. The door was out of the way and didn't chime, as the elevator's doors did, to announce when someone was leaving. She'd take Brother Wolf up that way—if she could talk her way around the ID thing. She hadn't brought any with her, and wouldn't have used it if she had. She wouldn't lie with a false ID, and she had no intention of giving them any more personal information than she could help, not unless Bran told her differently.

"Do you have a card from Agent Fisher or Agent Goldstein of the FBI?" Anna asked.

He looked at the small collection of cards on the desk in front of him. "Agent Fisher. Yes."

"Why don't you buzz us in and call her. She called me in and I left in a hurry and forgot my purse and ID. She's expecting me."

He frowned at her.

"Really," Anna said dryly. "Woman with werewolf. It's hard to mistake us for anyone else."

The security guard's eyes widened and he took another good look at Brother Wolf—who slowly wagged his tail and kept his mouth closed. Apparently he'd decided not to torment the young man.

"I thought they'd be bigger," the security guard said, unexpectedly. "And . . . you know. Grayer."

"Less civilized, more slathering?" asked Anna with a smile. "Half-human, half-wolf, all monster?"

"Uhm." He gave a quick smile and kept a wary eye on Brother Wolf. "Can I plead the fifth on that? You'll still have to wait until I call for confirmation. If I don't know you, you don't get in without ID or an invitation."

"Did the police already ask you about the people who came in today?" Anna asked.

The guard nodded. "Everybody. Police, FBI, and possibly a dozen other agencies and people as far as I could tell. Starting with Lizzie's father."

"I don't need to repeat their work, then," Anna said.

He gave her a polite smile, picked up the phone, and called the number from a card resting on top of the desk. "This is Chris at the security desk downstairs. I have a woman and a werewolf down here."

"Send them up," said Leslie Fisher's voice. She sounded a good deal less calm than she had when she'd called Anna. She hung up without ceremony.

Chris the Security Guard nodded at Anna. "I'll buzz you through. How come you're taking the stairs? Twelve stories is a lot."

"He doesn't like elevators," Anna said. "And it sounds like, if she was kidnapped, maybe her assailant would have taken her down the stairway because you'd have noticed him in the elevator." She indicated the wolf with a tip of her head. "He's got a good nose. We'll check it out."

Chris looked at Brother Wolf with less fear and more interest. "It would be good," he said, "if he could find her fast."

Anna nodded. "We'll try."

BROTHER WOLF TROTTED up the stairs scenting the people who'd come this way. There were old scents—several people had dogs and someone had the *worst* cologne . . . and six or eight fresher scents. As he and Anna moved up at an even and steady pace, the other scents fell away, leaving just a few. He could smell the woman who cleaned here—she came up often—but there was another that overlaid it, fresher by days.

Brother Wolf pinned his ears and stopped, because Charles told him what he was smelling was unlikely.

"What?" asked Anna, then, more properly, *What?*

She came here on her own, without touching the floor. Brother Wolf knew his tone was grumpy, but he could not change what was just because it didn't make Charles happy. *Sliding against the wall about three feet from the floor. Charles says, "No."*

"Fair enough," said Anna, her voice soothing his ruffled fur. "Momentarily inexplicable evidence in an abduction that possibly involves fae or werewolves isn't surprising when you think about it." She put her hand on his head, between his ears. "Arguing with your senses at this point is useless—which is something Charles taught me. There will be an explanation. Let's see what her condo tells us."

More cheerfully—because she had taken his side over Charles's—Brother Wolf resumed the hunt.

They came, by and by, to the twelfth floor, where Anna held the door open for him. It wasn't difficult to locate the missing girl's condo, because, like the building itself, there were police and other people standing around just outside the door.

The woman from the FBI was there, her arms folded and her face set. In front of her was a delicately built man, taller than the FBI woman, but he appeared shorter because of his build. His hair was chestnut and grayed at the sides. Fae—Brother Wolf's nose could smell it. Some sort of water fae, maybe; he smelled like a freshwater lake at dawn.

He looked so very helpless, this fae, though there was no sense of timidity about him. Brother Wolf couldn't get a fix on how powerful he was, either. Brother Wolf was no expert on fae, though he'd met his share. But it seemed to him that the ability to hide from all of Brother Wolf's senses might mean the same thing among the fae as it did among the werewolves. Only Bran could hide what he was so well that Brother Wolf could not immediately discern his power.

"We are doing what we can," the FBI woman said. "We don't know if this case is related to the others—only that our serial killer has been killing fae for a number of years and abducts his prey in a manner similar to this. No one sees or hears anything—though the abduction site is well guarded or well populated."

"My daughter is only half-fae," said the man. "And until Officer Mooney, here, asked me, no one knew it. No one. There is no reason to suppose that your serial killer has my daughter before your forensic people go in to see what they can find. I was in there, and there is no sign of a struggle. We were meeting to celebrate her successful audition—she won a place in a top-flight ballet troupe—and she would not have stood me up. Not without calling to cancel. If there is no sign of a struggle, then she knew her kidnapper and let him get too close. She was a trained athlete and I saw to it she knew how to defend herself. I need to find her address book and you need to start down the line and send people to visit each and every person there while we wait for the kidnappers to call and demand a ransom. We are wasting time."

This one, thought Brother Wolf, was used to giving orders rather than following them. He might have been tempted to teach him better except for the smell of frantic worry and heartsick terror that the fae was covering with quiet orders.

"If it is our serial killer," said the FBI woman, sounding much more patient than she smelled, "then there will be nothing our forensic units can find, and it won't be anyone she knows. I have a—" Something caused her to look around just then. Probably the startled swearword one of the young cops said when she noticed Anna and Brother Wolf standing just outside of the stairwell.

The FBI woman—

Leslie Fisher, admonished Anna, because she had a thing about proper word-names.

To demonstrate that he knew perfectly well who he was talking about, Brother Wolf sent her a complicated impression of muted dominance, human, and a scent that was a combination of skin, hygiene products, and a family smell indicating that the FBI woman had a long-term relationship with a male and several not-adult children and two cats. He was showing off a little, because it took a lot of experience to separate a person's scent into so much detail.

Anna thunked him lightly on the head with her knuckles. "Behave," she told him sternly. But he felt her laughter.

"Here they are," said the FBI woman, *Leslie Fisher.* Her eyes slid over him twice. She blinked, then focused on the leash.

Anna smiled. "We use the collar and leash because it makes people feel safer," she explained. "That way no one does anything stupid."

The fae looked at Brother Wolf and reached for a sword on his hip that wasn't there—which seemed to discomfort him quite a bit. Brother

Wolf relayed that to Anna so that she would know that the fae saw them as a possible threat.

"Anna Smith and Charles Smith, I'd like to introduce you to Alistair Beauclaire, a partner at the legal firm of Beauclaire, Hutten, and Solis. He was to meet his daughter, Lizzie Beauclaire, age twenty-two, here at eleven p.m. for a late celebration. But sometime between when he talked to her at six p.m. and when he came at ten minutes before eleven, she went missing."

Though her tone was mild, her body language, the way her own hand moved so she could reach a weapon, and the spike in her pulse told Brother Wolf that the FBI woman had seen what he saw. She talked more than she'd had to in order to give everyone time to calm down. All of which made her altogether more of a person to him, because she was not anyone's victim and she was smart, Leslie Fisher of the FBI.

"Sir," said Anna, "we're here to help. In addition to his other victims, this killer has taken out three werewolves in Boston this summer."

The slender man let his eyes drift from Anna to Brother Wolf, and Brother Wolf resisted displaying his fangs because he'd promised Charles that he would take care of Anna. Provoking a fight with a fae might be entertaining, but it was *not* protecting Anna.

"You're both werewolves," said the fae.

Anna nodded. "Does she have a lot of people over?"

He shook his head. "She spends six to eight hours a day taking classes and rehearsing. Usually she'll meet her friends at a club or restaurant if they want to go out. Most of her friends are dancers, too, which means poor. I think it embarrasses her to live this upscale. Her mother lives in Florida with her stepfather, as do Lizzie's two younger half siblings."

"Good. That will help a lot. So who has been in the apartment tonight?"

Leslie raised her hand. "Me." Pointed to the fae. "He has." She looked around. "Hey, Moon. Mooney, are you still around?"

One of the police officers farther down the corridor stepped out from behind several others and raised his hand. "Right here," he said.

"If that's true, that'll really help when we go in to check who's been in there. But Charles needs to scent you all so he can discount your presence. He won't hurt you; just stand still."

Anna dropped the leash. Brother Wolf approached the policeman with his ears up and his tail wagging gently, and the man still stiffened and lost color. That was fine. Enjoyable, even. Not as much fun as if he'd run away, but Brother Wolf took his pleasure where he found it. Still, a quick sniff from several feet out was enough.

When he had the policeman's scent, he stopped by the fae—who kept a wary eye on him, but otherwise did not object. Interestingly, Leslie Fisher didn't flinch, either; only her rising pulse gave her fear away. He liked her better all the time.

He looked at his mate.

"Anyone else that we know has been in there tonight?" Anna asked.

"No," said Leslie. "As soon as I got here I sealed the room."

"If you'll let us in?" Anna nodded at the apartment's door.

Brother Wolf waited until they were closed in the apartment together before setting to work. Cross-scenting a room was old hat, but required no less concentration than the first time he'd done it—he just did a better job now. It was a matter of dismissing old or stale scents, then sorting through the ones he'd picked up in the hallway and seeing what was left.

The woman's scent he'd picked up in the hallway was the one he'd found in the stairwell. Outside of her father, once he left the main living space, there were no scents of anyone who had been there in the last six months. Only the woman's scent was in her bedroom.

She was a dancer, her father said, Charles told Brother Wolf. *Look at the closets. One for everyday clothing and for parties. The other filled with workout clothes and a few competition dresses. Ballroom competitions. I thought her father said she danced ballet.*

Brother Wolf considered it. *The first set of clothing is camouflage,* he offered. It was good that Charles had decided to participate instead of just observe. *The clothes in this one are a disguise to help her blend in and look like everyone else. They smell like perfume—she even hid her scent when she wore them. The second is who she really is. They smell like long hours working: like triumph and pain, blood and sweat.*

Brother Wolf grew more interested in her bedroom. She was as much the prey he hunted as the one who took her was. Maybe something he could learn about her would help in their search.

On the wall were some framed art photo prints of dancers, and eight of them were black-and-white photos set in a circle. Fred Astaire and Ginger Rogers were immortalized in a moment when Ginger was up in the air, a huge smile on her face, and Fred had a sly grin. Another black and white was of the scene from *Dirty Dancing* that caught the primary actors on hands and knees, staring hungrily at each other— though the tension of their pose told the observer that they were still in the midst of a dance. A number of other dancers he didn't know, mostly couples in a wide variety of dances from ballroom to tribal to modern. In the center of the circle of photos was a poster-sized image that dominated the room.

The photographer had caught a male dancer in mid-flight, stretched across the canvas in a graceful Y. His feet at the lower left-hand corner were slightly out of focus, giving the photo a sense of aliveness and making the stillness of the rest of it more profound. The dancer's left arm, farther from the viewer, was stretched out to the top right, and his right arm, nearer to the viewer, flung back to the top left corner. His head was bowed, the line of his body so pure and straight he might have been swinging from the rope of a pirate ship. His muscles were flexed and straining, yet somehow he managed to give the impression of being relaxed, at peace.

Unlike the others, it was in color, but just barely, as if someone had filled it with shades of brown. The loose white shirt he'd worn looked cream, his tights were taupe, and the backdrop came out a dark brown rather than black. A warm, beautiful image.

Rudolf Nureyev, supplied Charles.

"Brother Wolf," called Anna from somewhere nearby. "Charles? Could you come here for a moment? I think I smell something."

She was standing out in the hallway, next to the bathroom, a thoughtful look on her face.

"What do you smell?" she asked him, and when she did he came another step closer and caught it, too.

Terror, he answered—and tried again, closing his eyes to shut out other senses. *Blood. Her blood. And . . .* A low growl rose . . . *And his.*

She had fought her attacker, the little dancer had. It was only a small drop of blood, but it was enough.

He licked it—feeling the scent rise up as soon as his tongue touched it, breaking the magic of concealment that had tried to hide even so little of the man who had come here to do harm. A man, but not human, or not wholly human. The bitter flavor of magic in the blood made his tongue tingle. He would recognize this man when he smelled him again.

Half-blood fae, he told her.

"We probably should have left that blood for the FBI labs," said Anna, her tone a little rueful.

My hunt, Brother Wolf assured her, though Charles agreed with Anna. *My rules.* That last was as much for Charles as for Anna. He looked at the closed bathroom door. If he'd been stalking her, he might have waited in the bathroom. *Would you open the door so I can seek him there?*

She wrapped her hand in the tail of her shirt and opened it. At first he thought there was nothing to find, that the woman's attacker had awaited her somewhere else.

Then he caught a faint trace of excitement, something he felt almost more than scented—and a hint of something else that brought Charles to the fore, drawn by something he understood better than the wolf did: spirits.

Some homes had spirits and some did not, and neither he nor Charles knew why that was. Spirits weren't ghosts; they were the consciousness of things that Charles's da didn't believe were alive: trees and water, stones and earth. Houses and apartments—some of them, anyway.

This one was faint and shy, better for the shaman's son to deal with rather than the wolf.

Show me, said Charles to the spirit of the house. *Show me who waited here.*

The condo was new. It had not been a home for generations of children, so the spirit was weak. All it was able to give them was an impression of patience and largeness, so much larger than she whose home this was. Clean smelling—no, that was wrong; he smelled of cleaners. He carried a . . . something.

Something? Charles was patient with it. *A weapon?* Brother Wolf provided the smell of a gun, oil, powder, metal.

Swift negation and a response, an answer more sensory than in words: something soft, mostly textile, with only a hint of metal.

A bag, like a gym bag, Charles thought, picturing such a bag carefully in his head, and the spirit all but jumped for joy, providing more and more information about the bag. As if by naming it, Charles had pulled a cork out of the bottle of what the spirit knew.

He brought a bag, Brother Wolf told Anna—triumphantly, because he'd been right about the stairway. *A big canvas bag, and stuffed our missing woman inside. He carried her down the stairs, which is why I could only smell her along the walls.*

"He has no scent?" Anna asked, having caught something of what he'd found. Her voice sent the shy spirit fleeing.

He hid his scent with magic that feels something like fae magic, Charles told her.

Brother Wolf thought of the bitter taste that still lingered on his tongue from the kidnapper's blood. *It also feels like witch magic, black and blood-soaked.*

Charles agreed. *It feels less . . . civilized than the fae magic I'm familiar with.*

"Would a witch have been able to carry a full-grown woman down twelve flights of stairs?" Anna asked.

Maybe not directly, answered Charles after a moment of consideration, *but there are ways.*

"Early in the hunt," said Anna.

Exactly, agreed Charles.

"Who do we know who knows a lot about fae and their magic?" asked Anna. "Would Bran know?"

We have a better source, suggested Brother Wolf. *Her father is old and powerful.*

"He reached for a sword," Anna said. "Is that how you could tell he was old?"

Brother Wolf supplied the memory of the scent of creatures that were older than a few centuries, a light fragrance that grew richer.

Old, explained Charles.

And then they gave her what power smelled like among the fae, beginning with something weaker and increasing until Charles told her, *That is strength. But they are subtle creatures, the fae. They cannot add to their scent because they, for the most part, cannot smell it. However, when they conceal what they are, sometimes they can also obscure what we can smell about them. This one smells old, but he smells as weak as is possible for someone who still smells like fae.*

"So a fae will probably not smell more powerful or old than he is," said Anna, "but he might smell weaker. Like the way Bran enjoys hiding what he is."

Brother Wolf huffed out an affirmative sneeze. Charles added, *I think it might be a good thing to discuss this with Lizzie's father—when there are no humans present.*

"Discuss how powerful he is?" asked his mate, a corner of her mouth twitched up. She knew what Charles had meant—she had a silly sense of humor sometimes. Brother Wolf liked that about her. Charles, however, was in a more serious mood and treated her question as if she'd really meant it.

No. Discuss with him what kind of fae would fit the parameters we have been given for this serial killer.

Brother Wolf sneezed to let her know that he thought she was funny.

"DID YOU FIND something?" asked Leslie as Anna let Charles and herself out of the apartment.

Anna looked at the techie-type police officers who awaited them and wondered if it was the serial-killer angle—or something about the missing girl's father—that had brought out the big guns on a missing person's case where the victim had been gone for only a few hours.

"Yes," Anna said, answering the FBI agent's question. "Whoever took her is fae . . . or has some access to fae magic. He concealed himself in her bathroom and waited for her to come to him."

After gesturing the waiting forensic team into the condo, Leslie took out a small spiral notebook and began scribbling things down in it. She didn't look up when she said, "What else did you find?"

"He came up unobserved. A pure-blood fae could have come up looking like anyone else, probably someone who actually lives here," Anna told her. It was speculation, but that was what she'd have done if she could conceal herself the way the fae could. They had several variants of the "don't look at me" magic that were stronger than pack magic was, but glamour, the power that all fae shared, was more than that—a very strong illusion. "However he arrived, he left with his prey in a gym bag and carried her down the stairs."

Leslie looked up at that. "He carried her down? Twelve flights of stairs?"

"Without dragging her," Anna said, putting a finger on the hallway wall about the height that Brother Wolf had been tracing. If he had been carrying her with his arms hanging down . . . he was more than human tall. Anna didn't say that, though, just told Leslie the facts. "Our perpetrator doesn't leave a scent, so we were pretty confused at first."

She glanced at the missing woman's father, who stood at parade rest, his gaze on the floor. "Because he didn't leave a scent, it might have been someone who had been to the apartment before, someone she knew—but it didn't have that feel. He took her by surprise in the hall in front of the bathroom. She fought him—fought hard. There's a pretty good ding in the drywall next to the bathroom door. But she was no match."

He used a drug, Charles said. *I caught a hint of it in the bathroom.*

"What did the wolf just tell you?" asked Alistair Beauclaire. His voice must have been quite an asset in the courtroom, cool, even, and beautiful. If she had been human, without her senses to tell her better, she'd never have known that her words had hit him hard—he'd been hoping it was someone he could track down.

"The kidnapper drugged her." She looked at Charles. "Do you know what he gave her?"

Smelled like ketamine to me, said Charles. *But it isn't my area of specialty.*

She related his answer and caveat to their listeners while she thought about how to get Lizzie's father alone to discuss matters away from human ears.

"I am sorry we cannot be of more help," Anna said. "As you know, we have a stake in this—and no one wants another person dead. Perhaps if we knew more about the fae who took her or what exactly the killer was doing to his victims." She paused and said delicately, "Or is that 'killers'?"

Agent Fisher gave her an assessing look while Mooney, the only regular police officer left on scene, cleared his throat harshly. Beauclaire looked at her with interest.

Anna met his gaze and said with no particular emphasis, "We'll find him, but the more we know, the faster we can be." She turned back to the FBI agent and told her, "If you need to get in touch and my phone rings through, you might try Charles's." She rattled off the number, which had a Boston area code because Bran thought that advertising they were from Montana was a mistake.

Leslie Fisher's face grew speculative before it returned to neutral. She'd caught that Anna's slip had been on purpose, but she didn't comment out loud.

"You might as well go home," Fisher said. "If you think of anything else, give me or Agent Goldstein a call."

Anna locked their door and took the collar off Charles, laying both it and the leash on a small table against the wall.

"If her father is an old and powerful fae, why can't he find her?" Anna asked.

Perhaps his power doesn't lie in that direction, answered Brother Wolf. *Or there is something blocking him. I do not know a lot about fae magic, other than to say that no magic has answers for everything. It is a tool. A hammer is a good tool, but not useful for removing screws.*

"All right," she said. "I'll buy that." She pulled off her shoes and finger-combed her hair. She was tired. "Can you tell me what's wrong with Charles?"

Brother Wolf looked at her and said nothing.

"I didn't think so," she said. "Charles, how can I help if you don't let me in?"

You cannot help, Charles replied.

She sucked in a breath. "Did you just lie to me?" She wasn't sure, but it hadn't felt like the truth, either.

Brother Wolf looked away. *Charles will not let you help.*

"Fine," she said. "There. I lied to you, too." It wasn't fine, not even close to fine.

We should be human when the fae lord comes, Brother Wolf said, finally.

Anna didn't know what to say, so she didn't say anything. After a moment, Charles began changing back. It wouldn't take him long, five or ten minutes. The blood of a Flathead shaman meant that it took him a lot less time to change than any other wolf she'd met.

It hurt to change, hurt more when you did it back and forth in only a couple of hours—and Charles hadn't been in a good place when he'd started. Anna could feel the pain he was in—faintly, because he'd never let her feel it all if he could help it.

It was better to leave him alone for a few minutes. It was better to remove herself from the temptation of a real fight, especially when they could have visitors at any time. And they weren't back to square one, either. Their bond lay open between them, a testimony that he was better than he had been.

It was four in the morning. She debated showering and getting dressed—or brushing her teeth and going back to sleep. She didn't make it to the bathroom. The bed was still rumpled from when she'd left it earlier, and it was too inviting to resist.

She crawled under the blankets and buried her head in Charles's pillow. She felt more than heard when Charles came into the room. He paused by the bed and patted her rump lightly, and something inside her relaxed. "Don't get too comfortable, Sleeping Beauty," he rumbled teasingly, sounding like his old self. He might not be letting her help, but he was making progress just the same, despite his decision to retreat behind Brother Wolf earlier. "We'll have company sooner rather than later. You made the fae an obvious offer to give him information the FBI won't, and he won't wait until a polite time of day to come calling. I doubt he'll sleep much as long as his daughter's fate is uncertain—I wouldn't."

She waited until the shower started before pulling her head out from under the blankets. No. Charles wouldn't rest while a child of his was in danger. If he had children.

Female werewolves couldn't carry babies to term. The moon called and they changed to wolves, the violence of it too much for the forming child. She'd asked Samuel, who was a doctor, about staying in wolf form for the full term instead. He'd paled and shaken his head.

"The longer you stay a wolf, the less the human rules. If you stay wolf too long, there is no coming back."

"I'm an Omega," Anna had told him. "My wolf is different. We could try it."

"It always ends badly," her mate's brother had said roughly. "Don't, please, talk to Charles or Da about it. The last one was brutal. There was a woman . . . She managed to hide from Bran until it was too late. A werewolf isn't a wolf, Anna, who will care and protect its young. When we finally tracked her down, Charles had to kill her because there was nothing of humanity left, only a beast. He backtracked her to the cave where she'd established her den. She'd given birth, all right. And then she'd killed the baby."

His eyes had been raw and wild, so she'd changed the subject. But Anna had her own thoughts on the matter—Brother Wolf was no unthinking creature who would eat his young, and she was pretty sure her own wolf was gentler still. But there was no need for desperate measures yet.

The werewolves were out to the world now with no further need to hide. There were options for couples who could not have biological children for one reason or another that would work for werewolves as well.

Right now, with the public so ambivalent about werewolves, it would be difficult to try to use a surrogate to carry their child. But they could afford to wait awhile for public opinion to change.

"For public opinion to change about what?" asked Charles as he opened the door of the bathroom to let the steam roll out. He had a towel wrapped around his waist and was drying his long hair with another.

She didn't have to answer him because someone rang their doorbell. The fae was supposed to call them; she'd left Charles's number. Apparently he'd decided to drop in uninvited instead.

Anna hadn't undressed, so she ran her fingers through her hair and started toward the door. Charles moved in front of her and dropped the towel he held to the floor.

"No," he said.

She rolled her eyes, but said, "Fine. I'll wait for you."

He dressed quickly without apparently rushing while she watched him. Watching Charles dress and undress was one of her favorite things to do—better than wrapping and unwrapping Christmas presents. Werewolves were, as a whole, young, healthy, and muscled—which were attractive characteristics. But they all weren't Charles. His shoulders were wide and his dark skin had a silklike sheen that invited her fingers to touch. His long, black-as-midnight hair smelled—

"If you don't stop that," he said mildly, though he paused with his shirt just over his shoulders so she could see the way the smooth muscles of his back slid down into well-fitted jeans, "our gentleman caller might have to wait awhile longer."

Anna smiled and reached out to run a finger down his backbone. She pressed her face against his cotton T-shirt and inhaled. "I missed you," she confessed.

"Yes?" he said, his voice soft. It got even softer when he said, "I'm not fixed yet."

"Broken or whole," she told him, her voice dropping to a growl, "you're mine. Better not forget that again."

Charles laughed—a small, happy sound. "All right. I surrender. Just don't go after me with that rolling pin."

Anna tugged the shirt down and smoothed it. "Then don't do anything to deserve it." She smacked him lightly on the shoulder. "That's for disrespecting my grandmother's rolling pin."

He turned around to face her, wet hair in a tangled mess around his shoulders. Eyes serious, though his mouth was curved up, he said, "I would never disrespect your grandmother's rolling pin. Your old pack did everything in their power to turn you into a victim, and when that crazy wolf started for me, you still grabbed the rolling pin to defend me from him, even though you were terrified of him. I think it is the bravest thing I have ever seen. And possibly the only time anyone has tried to defend me since I reached adulthood."

He touched her nose, bent down—

The doorbell rang, an extended buzz, as if someone was getting impatient.

Eyes at half-mast, Charles looked at the front door the same way he would a grizzly or a raccoon that had interfered with his hunt.

"I love you, too," murmured Anna, though she found herself at least as grumpy about the interruption as Charles could possibly be. "Let's go see what Lizzie's father has to say."

The doorbell rang again.

Charles sucked in a breath of air, ran his fingers through his wet hair to get rid of the worst of the tangles, glanced in the mirror on the wall, and froze.

"Charles?"

His side of their bond slammed down so fast she couldn't help a faint gasp, but not so quickly that she didn't see that his motivation was singular and huge: he wanted to protect her. Charles didn't look

at her, and when the doorbell rang again, he stalked out of the bedroom.

She stood where he had, in front of the mirror, and tried to see what
it was that had disturbed him so much. Men's voices and a woman's
rushed past her ears. The mirror was beveled, set in a plain but well-
made frame, and in it she saw herself and a reflection of the walls of
the room behind her. There was an original oil painting of a mountain
on the wall to the right of her, next to the door to the bathroom.
Directly behind her, cream-colored lace curtains hung over the window, still dark with night's reign.

What had he seen that he wanted to protect her from?

By the time she got out to the living room, Alistair Beauclaire was
already inside the condo—and so were Special Agents Fisher and Goldstein.

"I thought," Beauclaire was saying, "it would save time to have us
all meet together and put all the cards on the table. My daughter's life
is more important than politics and secrets." It was, from a fae, a shocking move. Anna hadn't had much to do with fae, but even she knew
that they never gave a shred of information to anyone if they could
help it.

Beauclaire looked at Charles; he had to look up.

"I know who you are," the fae told Charles. "You just might have a
chance of finding her, but not if we're all tripping over the secrets we
cannot tell." He glanced over to pull the FBI agents into the conversation. "If you withhold something that would have allowed us to find
Elizabeth one minute sooner, you will regret it. We will talk this morning about things that outsiders do not know—trusting you to use this
to stop the killer."

Leslie's eyes tightened at the threat, but Goldstein absorbed it without a reaction, not even an increase in heartbeat: he just looked tired
and more frail than the last time Anna had seen him.

"I assure you," Goldstein told Beauclaire, "that it is our mission to see that your daughter is found quickly. If we didn't agree with you, we wouldn't be here. No matter what favors you called in."

Anna wondered how the FBI or Beauclaire had figured out where she and Charles were staying. The condo belonged to a small company that was wholly owned by a larger company, and so on ad infinitum. The whole thing was owned in turn by Aspen Creek, Inc., which was the Marrok.

Appearing unannounced was a power move, saying *You can't hide from us*. It seemed a little too aggressive for the FBI: she and Charles weren't suspects. Anna thought it was more likely that Beauclaire was responsible for the early-morning visit, looking to establish dominance with his unannounced invasion of their territory—claiming the point position on the hunt for his daughter. She could see what he was trying to do, but it wouldn't work on Charles, though it might make her mate more dangerous if he decided to take offense. Charles's public face was too good for her to read right now, which told her that he was feeling a whole lot of things he didn't want her to know about.

He'd closed their bond to protect her.

Anna tried to get mad about it, so she wouldn't have to be worried or hurt, but he was a dominant wolf and part of being dominant was taking care of what was his. His wife, his mate, headed that list. So Charles would protect her from whatever he thought would attack her through their connection.

But he had forgotten something along the way. He was hers. *Hers.* He was hurting himself to protect her and she was going to put a stop to it—but not now. Not in public. A good hunter is patient.

Charles glanced at Anna, and she narrowed her eyes to tell him that the anger he sensed from her was aimed at him. He raised an eyebrow and she raised her chin.

Redirecting his attention to the intruders, Charles soundlessly gestured everyone to the big sectional sofa in front of the TV. He pulled a hardwood chair away from the dining table for himself and set it to face them over the coffee table.

The FBI agents perched on the edge of the sofa. Goldstein appeared more tired than interested, but Leslie Fisher watched Charles intently, not looking him in the eyes, not challenging him, just cataloging. Such intent interest would have put Anna on edge except there was no heat in Leslie's gaze. It was more of an "observing the subject in his native habitat" than a "he's really hot" kind of thing.

Beauclaire, for his part, sank back in the soft material of the couch as if the thought that it would impede him should he have to move quickly had never occurred to him. *I'm not afraid of anyone here,* his body posture said. Charles's—relaxed, arms folded loosely, chin slightly tilted—said, *You're boring me; either fight and die—or back off.*

Anna grabbed another of the hardwood chairs and parked it next to Charles, then sat down. "All right," she said, to break the testosterone fest before it could really get going. "Who goes first?"

Charles looked at Beauclaire. "Do the fae know that there's been someone hunting them since the eighties?"

"We are here to share information," Beauclaire said, spreading his hand magnanimously. "I am happy to begin. Yes, of course we knew. But he's only been hunting the nobodies, the half-bloods, the solitary fae. No one with family to protect them. No one of real power." His voice was cool.

"No one worth putting themselves at risk for," said Charles.

Beauclaire gave Charles a polite look that was as clear as any adolescent raising his middle finger. "We are not pack. We are not all good friends. Mostly we are polite enemies. When a fae dies, if it is not one of power—who are valuable to us, just because there are so few left—if it is not someone who has family or allies with power, mostly other fae look upon that death with a sigh of relief. First, it was not they who died. Second, it didn't cause anyone else harm, and that fae is no longer free to make alliances with someone who might be an enemy." His voice deepened just a little on the last sentence.

"It bothers you," said Leslie.

Anna liked competent people. Not many humans were as good at reading others as the wolves were. Leslie was very good to be able to read Beauclaire so well.

Beauclaire looked at the agent, started to say something, hesitated, then said, "Yes, Agent Fisher, it bothers me that a killer was allowed to continue picking off those he chose for nearly half a century. Had *I* known of it, I *would* have done something—which was probably why I was not informed. A mistake I have taken steps to correct. What should have been is, in this case, superseded by what is: a killer who tortures his victims before he kills them has my daughter."

"Do you know who or what we are hunting, Mr. Beauclaire?" asked Goldstein. "Is it a fae?"

"Yes. I know what kind of fae could get into a building without leaving a scent trail that a werewolf could follow, and could hide so that people who walked past him could not discern that he was there."

"It is unusual," said Anna. "Most glamour doesn't work on scent."

"You can't hide what you don't perceive," agreed Beauclaire. "Most of the fae who could follow a scent as well as a werewolf were beast-minded—like the giant in 'Jack and the Beanstalk.' Those fae couldn't hide themselves from the cold-iron-carrying Christians who drove us from our homes—so they perished, most of them. But there are a few left who would be capable of perceiving and hiding their scents. Among those who have these abilities, the only one who would also be strong enough to carry my daughter out of her home in a satchel and be mistaken for someone carrying laundry is a horned lord."

Goldstein narrowed his eyes. "The old term for a man who was cuckolded? That's not what you mean."

"Horned," said Charles. "You mean antlered."

Beauclaire nodded. "Yes."

"Herne the Hunter," suggested Charles.

"Like Herne," agreed Beauclaire. "There were never many of them, less than a handful that I'm aware of. The last one on this side of the Atlantic was killed in 1981, hit by a car in Vermont. The driver thought he killed a very large deer, but the accident was witnessed by one of us who could see the fae inside the deer's skin. When no one was looking, we stole the body away."

"You think there is another one?" Leslie asked.

The fae nodded. "That is what the evidence suggests."

"If the killer is fae, then why didn't he start hunting fae victims before the fae came out?" Anna asked.

That the UNSUB was fae would explain why he was still active after so many years, why he could take down a werewolf without anyone noticing. But it didn't explain why he began targeting fae only after they admitted their existence.

"I am not the killer to know his motivations, Ms. *Smith*," said Beauclaire. He bit off the "Smith" to show that he knew what their last name really was—still jockeying for top dog in the room. "Coincidences do happen."

"Call me Anna," she told him in a friendly voice. "Most people do."

He stared at her a moment. Charles growled and the fae jerked his eyes off of hers, then frowned in irritation at losing the upper hand. But Anna could feel the whole atmosphere of the living room lighten up as the fight for dominance was lost and won.

Beauclaire gave a bow of his head to Charles, then smiled at Anna, and she thought that she'd never seen such a sad expression in her life. In that look she understood what he was doing and why—he thought his daughter was lost, she saw. He hadn't, not when they were at his daughter's apartment, but something—maybe that the killer was fae—

had changed his mind. He was hunting her killer now, not trying to save his daughter. Perhaps that was why he'd given in to Charles so easily.

"Coincidence," Beauclaire admitted, "is highly overrated. I have an alternative explanation about how a fae could not know what he was until he knew that there were such things as fae."

He glanced around the room, but Anna couldn't tell what he was looking for.

"In the height of the Victorian era," Beauclaire said finally, in a quiet, calm voice that belied what her nose told her, "when iron horses crossed and crisscrossed Europe, several things became obvious. There was no longer a place for the fae in the old world—and we were too few. From 1908 until just a few years ago, it was the policy of the Gray Lords, those who rule the fae, to find fae of scarce but useful types and force them to marry and interbreed with humans since humans breed so much more rapidly than we do."

Anna knew about that, but she hadn't realized how long it had gone on. From Leslie's face, Anna was pretty sure that the FBI agent hadn't known about the crossbreeding policy. That was interesting, because her face hadn't changed at all when Beauclaire had mentioned the Gray Lords, who were also a deep secret.

Goldstein might have been listening to the weather report for all the change in his face. There was no telling what he knew or didn't know about the fae.

"It was believed," continued Beauclaire, "that humans were of weaker bloodlines and the fae blood would prevail—and humans breed so very easily, even with the fae for a partner." He closed his eyes and drew in a deep breath. "The wisdom of these forced interbreedings is now being reexamined. Half-blood fae face many challenges. They, for the most part, are not accepted by the other fae. And too many of them exhibit . . . odd properties—birth defects are very high. Once fathered or mothered, a high percentage of the halflings were abandoned by their fae parent altogether, which left them to discover who and what they were on their own—to sometimes disastrous results. And a large number of the children have turned out to be entirely human."

Charles sat back. "Like your daughter?" he said in a soft voice.

"Like my daughter. The only thing she gets from me is my mother's love of dance—and she has to train hours every day to do what my mother did effortlessly." Beauclaire looked down, then back at Charles. "You are old, but not so old as your father. Maybe you can understand why I fought this dictate as hard as anything I've ever fought against. To deceive a human woman for the purpose of fathering a child upon her . . . it is dishonorable. Yes. And yet it gave me someone I care deeply about."

He drew in a breath and then looked Charles in the eye. It was not a challenge, more a way of showing how serious he was. "It is not wise," Beauclaire said, his voice clipped, and somewhere in the vowels Anna heard an accent not too far from Bran's when he was angered. "It is not wise to give something old and powerful something they care about. And I am very old." He looked at the FBI agents. "Even, possibly, older than your father. We haven't compared notes."

Leslie reacted to the idea that a werewolf could be older than an old fae—an immortal old fae. Goldstein just looked more tired, and maybe that was a reaction, too.

"Don't get the wrong idea," Anna told them. "The average life expectancy for someone from the time they are Changed and become a werewolf is about ten years."

"Eight," said Charles, sounding as weary as Goldstein looked. Anna knew her data had been correct last year. She reached out and touched his thigh, but he didn't look at her. Charles wasn't, she thought, totally involved with the proceedings. He kept glancing over the couch to the wall of windows beyond. She frowned, noting how, with the sky still dark outside, the window reflected the room back at them. He was seeing something in the reflection.

"Four out of ten of our halfling children survive to adulthood," Beauclaire was saying. "They are a favorite prey of other fae if they are not protected. My daughter is twenty-three in two weeks."

Anna glanced at Charles. He didn't appear to be listening, and whatever he was seeing in the window-mirrors was making him more and more remote.

"What kind of dancer is your daughter?" Anna asked suddenly. "I saw ballet shoes, but also ballroom costumes." She hadn't, not really, but Brother Wolf had and had kept her informed.

"Ballet," Lizzie's father said. "Ballet and modern. One of her friends is into ballroom dancing and she partnered with him for a while a couple of years back. Ballroom is for fun and ballet for serious, she told me." Beauclaire smiled at Anna. "When she was six, she dressed for Halloween as a fairy princess complete with wings. She was dancing around the room and I asked her why she wasn't flying. She stopped and told me quite earnestly that her wings were make-believe. That dancing was the closest she could do to flying. And she loved to fly."

It wasn't enough. Charles was still preoccupied.

Anna touched Charles's face and waited until he turned from the window. "Lizzie Beauclaire is not quite twenty-three. She loves to dance. And she's all alone with a monster who will torture and kill her if we don't find her soon. You are her best hope." She didn't add, "So suck it up and pay attention," but she trusted that he heard it in her voice.

Charles tilted his head, though his face was quiet. At least he wasn't looking in the windows anymore.

"Remember that," Anna told him fiercely as she dropped her hand. "You can't change the past, but this we can do. Beauclaire answered first; it's our turn. What do we know that would help the hunt?"

She met Charles's gaze and held it until he shifted his weight forward and gave a brief nod.

"The bodies that the police have been finding are cut up." Charles turned to the FBI agents. "I smelled black magic—blood magic—on the man who took Lizzie Beauclaire. That makes me think witches, and that those cuts on the victims might be significant. The fae have no use for blood magic."

"It doesn't work for us," said Beauclaire, but his voice was absentminded. He was watching Charles. Not looking him in the eye, not quite.

Goldstein said, "I have more details on that." He opened up his briefcase and handed Charles a thick file of photographs. "Most of the victims have shapes carved into their skin—we've been looking at the witchcraft or voodoo angle for the past ten years. But the witches willing to talk to us only say that it's not anything they know. Not voodoo or hoodoo. It's not runes. It's not hieroglyphs, nor any other symbolic language used by witches."

Charles opened up the folder and then spread the photos out on the coffee table. These were mostly blowups or close-ups, some in black and white, some in color. Names, dates, and numbers were written in white marking pen on the upper left corner. The photos documented symbols, ragged and dark around the edges. Some of the markings were ripped down the middle by angry slashes; others were distorted by degradation of the flesh they had been carved in.

"They lied to you," said Charles, bending over to get a closer look at one.

"Who?"

"The witches," said Beauclaire. He pulled one out of the mix, then set it back down quickly. He closed his eyes for a moment and when he opened them again they were hot with . . . rage or terror; Anna's nose wasn't sure which.

"The symbols witches use," Beauclaire told Goldstein in polite, formal tones, "follow family lines, for the most part. I can't, but the witches should have been able to tell you what family line these came from. There's something wrong with the way they're placed or the shape . . . In a very long life, I have seen many things. I do not perform blood magic, but I've seen it often enough."

Charles turned one of the photos to view it from a different angle and frowned. He took his phone out of his pocket and took a close-up of one of the photos. He hit a few more buttons and put the phone to his ear.

"Charles," said Bran.

"Ears might hear," warned Charles, telling his father that there was someone else in the room who could overhear their phone call. "I sent you a photo. Looks like witchcraft to me. What do you think?"

"I'll call you back," Bran said and hung up.

Goldstein rubbed his face tiredly. "We're supposed to be holding these back from the public," he said. "Can I ask that the photo won't hit the Internet or the news services?"

"You're safe," Anna reassured him. "We're calling in an expert opinion."

The phone rang before anyone could say anything. Charles put it on speaker as he answered it.

"Everyone can hear you now," he said.

There was a little pause before Bran spoke. "You need to get a witch to look at that. It appears to be something from the Irish clans to me, but it doesn't look quite right. Some of those symbols are nonsense and a few others are drawn wrong. It would be best if the witch could see the real thing, not just the photos. There's more to a spell than only the visual can tell you."

"Thanks," Charles said, hanging up without ceremony. "So, anyone know a local witch we can talk to?"

"I know a witch," said Leslie. "But she's in Florida."

Charles shook his head. "If we're going to bring someone up, I know a reliable one or two. Do you know any in Boston?" He looked at Beauclaire, who shook his head.

"I know of none who would help."

"If we find someone," Anna said, "could we get her in to see one of the bodies?"

"We can arrange it," said Leslie.

"All right, then, let's call the local Alpha and see if he has a witch who will cooperate with us."

Charles dialed and then gave Anna his phone. "He likes you better. You ask him."

"He's scared of me," Anna said, feeling a little smug.

"This is Owens."

"Isaac, this is Anna," she said. "We need a witch."

THE FBI AGENTS left to arrange a viewing for the witch, who wouldn't be available until ten in the morning. Beauclaire told them he was going to see if he could find anyone who might know if the horned lord who died in 1981 had left any half-blood children behind.

Anna waited until Charles had closed the door. "What do you see in the mirror?" she asked him.

He closed his eyes and did not turn to look at her.

"Charles?"

"There are things," he said slowly, "that are made better by talking them out. There are things that are given more power when you speak of them. These are of the second variety."

She thought about that for a moment and then went to him. The muscles of his back were tight when she touched them with her fingertips.

"It doesn't appear," she said slowly, "that being silent about whatever it is has helped, either." What kinds of things did he not like to talk about? Evil, she remembered. "Is it like a Harry Potter thing?"

He turned his head then. "A what?"

"A Harry Potter thing," she said again. "You know, don't say Voldemort's name because you might attract his attention?"

He considered it. "You mean the children's book."

"I have got to get you to watch more movies," she said. "You'd enjoy these. Yes, I mean the children's book."

He shook his head. "Not quite. Noticing some things make them more real. They are already real to me. If you notice them, they might become real to you as well, and that would not be good."

Suddenly she knew. Charles had told her once that he didn't speak his mother's name for fear that it would tie her to this world and not let her go on to the next. Ghosts, he'd told her, need to be mourned and then released. If you keep them with you, they become unhappy and tainted.

"Ghosts," she said, and he drew in a sharp breath and stepped away from her, closer to the window.

"Don't," he said sharply. She'd have snapped back at him if she hadn't remembered that when he'd closed down their bond he'd been worried about her.

"All right," she said slowly. "You feel better than before we came here, though. Right?" If he was getting better, he was dealing with it.

He had to think about that one before he answered her. "Yes. Not good, but better."

She wrapped her arms around his waist from behind and breathed him in. "I'll leave it alone if you promise me one thing."

"What's that?"

"If it starts getting worse again, you'll tell me—and you'll tell Bran."

"I can do that."

"All right." She brushed off the back of his shirt, as if there were some lint or something on it and not as though her hands were hungry for the warmth of his skin. "Sleep or breakfast?" she asked briskly. "We have two hours before the FBI picks us up and takes us to the morgue."

THE SMALL, SHEET-COVERED body on the table smelled of rotting flesh, salt, and fish. None of which managed to quite cover up the lingering scent of terror. From the size of the corpse, Anna thought he might have been seven or eight.

Anna had been Changed by rape both physical and metaphorical. She had served three years in a pack led by a madwoman, during which time death had become something to look forward to, an end to pain. Charles had changed all of that—and Anna appreciated the irony that the Marrok's Wolfkiller, arguably the most feared werewolf in the world, had made her safe and made her want to live.

Irony aside, Anna knew death. The morgue smelled of it, as well as a healthy dose of antiseptic, latex gloves, and body fluids. When they had entered the small viewing room, the scent of a little boy added itself to the mix, a boy who rightfully should be out playing with his friends and instead bore the unmistakable signs of autopsy.

Beside her, Brother Wolf growled, the sound low enough that she didn't think any of the humans heard it. He'd come as wolf—again. Anna dug her fingers through the fur of his neck and swallowed hard, trying to focus on something besides the little body on the table. Even worry about her mate was better than a dead child.

Charles promised that he'd let her know if it got worse—but he hadn't reopened the bond between them, not even wide enough that he could talk to her while he was in wolf shape.

"His family were supposed to pick him up today," said the man who'd let them in. He was dressed in scrubs that were clean and fresh—

either he was just beginning his day, or he'd changed for them. "When I explained to them that a werewolf had offered to look for clues we couldn't find, it was not difficult to persuade them to leave him here until tomorrow."

"You didn't tell his parents they were bringing me, too?" said the witch, who looked like she'd come right out of a 1970s sitcom—middle-aged, a little dumpy, a little rumpled, hair an improbable shade of red, and wearing clothes that didn't quite fit. "The werewolf is incidental and, I might add, begged the witch to come—and you didn't think to mention me?" The death threat in her voice did a fair job of removing any sense of comedy, though Anna couldn't help but think of Sleeping Beauty and the evil fairy who was offended because she wasn't invited.

Anna didn't like witches on the whole. They smelled of other people's pain and they liked causing problems. But even if this one hadn't been a witch, she doubted she'd have liked her.

Dr. Fuller—Anna had missed Leslie's introduction of their contact at the morgue while absorbing the smells of the place, but he wore a name tag—frowned. "He comes from a staunch Baptist family. Werewolves were a big stretch for them already. I didn't think they'd have taken to the idea of a witch at all well."

The witch smiled. "Probably not," she agreed cheerfully, just as if she hadn't taken offense a moment before.

Isaac had warned Anna that his witch of choice was a little unstable. He'd also told her that the witch wasn't all that powerful, so the harm she could do was minimal. He had another witch who worked upon occasion for his pack, but that one was secretive and a lot more dangerous. The witch here now, Caitlin (last name withheld), would tell them everything she found out, just to prove how much she knew. The other would keep it to herself for later use or just for her own amusement, which wouldn't do Lizzie any good at all.

"Tell them we appreciate their cooperation," said Heuter, the younger Cantrip agent, who had shown up as they were waiting for the witch in front of the building where the county morgue resided. He'd claimed that someone told him that they were going to visit the body, but from Leslie's attitude (polite but distant) it hadn't been her.

Goldstein had been called away to discuss the case with someone in the Boston Police Department, so Heuter's addition made them five. Had there been any more of them, they'd have had to leave the door to the small room open.

Dr. Fuller pulled back the sheet. "Jacob Mott, age eight. Water in his lungs tells us that he drowned. Joggers found him washed up on Castle Island early in the morning. His parents tell us that he did not have pierced ears, so the killer must have pierced both—though only the left ear was tagged. The tag is in evidence."

Anna let the words run in one ear and out the other. They were unimportant next to the small body laid out before them. Besides, Charles would remember every word—and she didn't want to.

Jacob had been in the water and the fishes had nibbled, though he wouldn't have cared at that point. Compared to what had been done to this boy, the fish were only a footnote. Death had nothing much to teach Anna, but dying . . . dying could be so hard. Jacob's dying had been very hard.

The witch reached out and touched the body with a lust Anna could smell even with her human nose.

"Ooh," she crooned, and the doctor's clinical recitation stumbled to a halt. "Didn't you make someone a lovely meal, child?" She put her face down on the boy's chest, and Anna wanted to grab her and rip her off. Anna folded her arms across her chest instead. No use ticking the witch off before they got what they needed from her. Jacob was past caring what the witch did.

"Someone's been a naughty girl," the witch said to herself as her fingers traced a series of symbols incised into the boy's thigh. She pulled her face away and began humming "It's a Small World" as her fingers continued to trace the marks on the body. "There's surely more on the back," she said, looking at the doctor.

Mutely he nodded, and she picked up the body and rolled Jacob on his face. She was strong, for all that she looked lumpy and dumpy, because she didn't have to struggle particularly. Dead bodies were, mostly, harder to move than live ones.

More on the back, the witch had said, and there were. More symbols and more marks of abuse. Anna swallowed hard.

"Before death," said the witch happily. "All of it was done before death. Someone harvested your pain and your ending, didn't they, little one? But they were sloppy, sloppy with it. Not professional, not at all." Her hands caressed the dead boy. "I recognize this. Bad Sally Reilly. She wasn't a very talented witch, was she? But she wrote a book and went on TV and wrote more books and became famous. Pretty, pretty Sally sold her services and then—poof, she went. Just like a witch who was bad and broke all the rules should."

"Sally Reilly carved these symbols?" asked Agent Fisher, her voice only a little sharp.

"Sally Reilly is dead. Twenty years or more dead, because she gave mundane people a way to do this." Caitlin bent down and licked the dead boy's skin, and Heuter drew in a harsh breath. "But they did it wrong and they didn't get it all, did they? They left all this lovely magic behind instead of eating it."

"Precious," murmured Anna.

The witch tilted her head. "What did you say?"

"You forgot the 'my precious,'" Anna said dryly. "If you want to act like a freaking nutcase, you have to do it right."

The witch lowered her eyelashes, flicked her hands at Anna, and said something that sounded almost like a sneeze. Brother Wolf bumped Anna aside, flexed a little as if he were absorbing a hit, and then hopped over the table, pushing the witch away from Jacob Mott's body and onto the floor. Neat and precise as a cat, he did it without touching Jacob at all, though he knocked Heuter and the doctor back a few paces.

Anna ran around the table so she could see what was going on, and so she saw Brother Wolf bare his ivory fangs at the witch—who immediately quit struggling.

"Charles has a grandmother who was a witch and a grandfather who was a shaman—on opposite sides of his lineage," Anna said calmly into the silence. "You're outmatched. Now, why don't you tell us everything you know about the markings?"

A low growl worked its way out of Brother Wolf's chest and she added, "Before he thinks too hard about whatever it was you tried to do to me." Anna wasn't sure if Brother Wolf was really playing along with her or if he truly wanted to kill the witch, but she'd use what she had. Though space was tight in the room, the other people present managed to crowd together with the table between them and Brother Wolf. It *might* have been the witch they were trying to get away from.

"The symbols inscribed are meant to increase the power of whoever is named in the ceremony," the witch Caitlin said, her voice somewhat higher and tighter than it had been. Sweat dripped down her forehead and into her eyes and she blinked it away.

"You know," Anna told her. "If you quit staring him in the eye, he won't be so likely to eat you." The witch turned to stare at Anna instead, and Brother Wolf increased the span of teeth he was showing and the threatening noise he was making. "Probably."

"So the symbols will increase a witch's power?" Leslie asked unexpectedly.

"Yes."

Brother Wolf snapped his teeth just short of Caitlin's nose and the witch shrieked, jumped, and struggled involuntarily before forcing herself limp.

"Werewolves," Anna said blandly, "can smell lies and half-truths, witch. I'd be very careful of what you say next. Now, answer Agent Fisher's question, please. Will the symbols increase a witch's power?"

Caitlin swallowed, her breathing rapid. "Yes—anyone's magic abilities. Fae, witch, sorcerer, wizard, mage. Anything. You can store it. For use later. To power a spell or some magic."

"What could you store it in?" Anna asked.

"Something dense. Metal or crystal. Most of us use something that can be worn or carried easily." She hesitated, looked at Brother Wolf's big teeth, and said, "But that's not what happened with this spell, specifically. This is designed to feed the magic of a fae."

"So this boy was marked by a witch," Heuter said.

Caitlin snorted despite her terror of Brother Wolf and answered Heuter as if he'd asked a question instead of making a statement. "She only *wishes* she were a witch."

"What do you mean?" Leslie's voice was cool, as if she questioned witches who were flat on their backs being threatened by werewolves every day.

"Some of the symbols are done wrong, and a couple of them are complete nonsense." The witch's voice was laced with contempt. "Sally's been gone since the late eighties. Maybe someone copied them wrong. A real witch would have been able to feel that they were off, and could have fine-tuned them on the spot. So someone's playing make-believe witch." Caitlin spoke as if the boy's life were less than nothing, that the worst thing the person carving on Jacob Mott had done was to get the symbols wrong.

"Tell us about Sally Reilly," Anna suggested. "If she's dead, what does she have to do with this?"

The witch set her jaw. "We don't talk to outsiders about her."

Brother Wolf gave her a little more fang to look at.

She swallowed.

"If it makes you feel better," Anna murmured, "we do know some witches who will tell us what we want to know."

"Fine," said Caitlin. "Sally Reilly figured out a way to let mundane people use our spells. If someone paid her enough, she'd teach them how to write the symbols. She'd give them a charm that, if they wore it while they worked the magic—usually only one specific spell— behaved for them as if they were a real witch. Like playing a tape recorder instead of a violin, she liked to say. It's been a long time since she was killed, and mostly people have lost either the symbols or the charms that allowed them to use the spell. This one was done wrong. It might have been drawn that way on purpose, though Sally had the reputation for delivering what she said she would. Probably they thought they had it memorized."

Caitlin smiled maliciously. "Spells don't like the wrong people using them; they tend to fight back when they can. Maybe in a couple of decades it will be wrong enough that they'll be cutting into someone and it will kill them all." Then she looked at Charles and stiffened. "I'm telling the truth," she said, sounding a little hysterical. "I'm telling the truth."

Muscles flexed in Brother Wolf's back and Anna thought it might be a good idea to get him off the witch before Caitlin really ticked him off—though part of her was happy to see that he was involved in the hunt again.

"She's cooperating, Charles," Anna told him. "Let's let her up before you scare her to death."

The werewolf snarled at Anna.

"Really," she told him, tapping him on the nose. "It's enough already. You aren't a cat. No playing with something you aren't going to eat." It wasn't the words she hoped to persuade him with; it was the calming touch.

Brother Wolf stepped almost delicately off the witch and watched with yellow eyes as the woman scrambled untidily to her feet.

"Better?" Anna asked, and then, without waiting for her to respond, continued with another question. "How do you know it's a she? The one who is trying to be a witch?"

Caitlin straightened her hair with shaky hands. "Witches strong enough to do this are women."

"You just said that whoever put these symbols on the boy wasn't a witch."

"Did I?"

Brother Wolf growled.

"I really wouldn't push him much more," Anna advised. "He's not very happy with you right now." Brother Wolf gave Anna an amused look and then went back to being scary.

The witch snorted archly. She reached out to touch Jacob's body again and stopped when Brother Wolf took a step closer, his eyes on her hand. She pulled it back and answered Anna's question. "Anyone could have drawn this and made it work. There's no reason but habit to assume it was a woman. I suppose that the rape means it was probably a man, doesn't it?"

"And it did work, even though some of the symbols are wrong?" It was Heuter who asked. Anna had been so focused on the witch and Brother Wolf that she had almost forgotten the others in the room.

"I can feel that it did," Caitlin said. "Not as well as if the symbols had been inscribed correctly, but yes."

"Which symbols are wrong? How would you have done this better?" Heuter's voice was a little too eager.

Caitlin gave him a cool gaze. She did psycho suburban housewife about as well as Anna had ever seen it done. "I am not here to instruct the FBI in witchcraft."

Leslie cleared her throat. "I'm Special Agent Fisher of the FBI. He's Agent Heuter of Cantrip."

"Cantrip," Caitlin snorted contemptuously. She took a card out of her purse and handed it to him. "If you have questions, you can call me at this number. But I'm not Sally Reilly, Agent Heuter. I don't intend to disappear, so I probably won't help you at all. And I'll charge you a lot for not doing so."

Brother Wolf sneezed, but Anna wasn't about to laugh because the witch was stepping toward the boy's body again.

"Is there anything else we should know about this?" asked Anna.

Caitlin looked at the table. "The sex isn't part of the ritual." She pursed her lips. "I don't know if that's useful."

"The killer keeps the victims alive for a while," Leslie said. "Seven days, usually. Sometimes a few more or less. Is that important?"

Caitlin frowned. "That's probably why the magic functioned, even though he screwed up. He cut the symbols in and left them to work—like a Crock-Pot, you know? Can't cook very fast at a low temperature, but give it enough time and it gets the job done." She huffed. "Maybe the sex is because he got bored waiting. If we're done here, I'd like to go. I have an appointment in half an hour."

Leslie handed her a card. "If you think of anything more, please call me."

"Sure," Caitlin said. Then she turned to Anna. "I'm going to tell Isaac what your wolf did to me." She smiled archly. "He's not going to be pleased with you."

"Tell him I'll buy him dinner at The Irish Wolfhound to make up for the offense," Anna suggested, holding the door open.

Caitlin looked disappointed at Anna's lack of reaction. "He's the Alpha of the Olde Towne Pack, and he owes me. You'll be sorry."

"You're going to be late for your appointment if you don't hurry," Anna told her.

The witch scowled, turned on her heel, and marched out the door. Before she was out of sight, Dr. Fuller had the boy's body back flat on the table and covered protectively. "That . . ." He sputtered a little, trying to keep his voice down.

"There are reasons we don't like witches much," Anna told him, when she was sure Caitlin was well out of earshot. "I know it's upsetting. But Jacob's killer has another victim right now. She's probably alive. And something the witch told us might help us find Lizzie Beauclaire."

She thinks the witches killed Sally Reilly.

Anna looked at Brother Wolf. Their mate bond was still as frozen as a Popsicle in Antarctica, but it was his voice in her head.

"You think differently," she said.

Shaman's eyes looked at her, Charles's eyes, then he closed them and shook himself, as if trying to shake off water after a dip in a lake. *I think that she gave a spell to a killer who didn't want her to talk. The witches wouldn't have been the only ones to want her dead.*

"Anna?" asked Leslie. "What's he saying to you?"

"Nothing we can prove just yet," Anna told her. "Though it might be interesting to see if Sally Reilly disappeared in one of the years that all of the bodies weren't found."

"We don't know anything about Sally Reilly," Leslie reminded her. "Let alone that she disappeared."

"Witchcraft and fae in the same case," said Heuter, sounding fascinated and a little excited.

In the small examination room with a dead little boy on the table, Anna found his excitement distasteful.

CHAPTER

7

"I don't think Fuller is going to let any more witches into his morgue in the near future," said Heuter as he bit into the piece of half-raw steak on his fork.

"That was the creepiest thing I ever saw," said Leslie, who was eating her salad and not looking at Heuter. Anna couldn't decide if she was a vegetarian or just didn't like watching someone eat raw meat. Maybe the visit to the morgue had something to do with it.

"The witch or Heuter's bloody steak?" asked Anna, taking the first nibble of her cheeseburger and deciding she approved. She'd ordered six cheeseburgers on two plates—all medium well. Yes, she preferred rare, though before she'd been Changed she liked very well-done. But she didn't eat raw meat in front of strangers.

"Heuter's eating habits are pretty creepy," Leslie said. "But I was talking about the witch. At least she told us some things we didn't know."

After they'd left the morgue, Leslie had called Goldstein with an update. From what Anna could tell, he'd been pretty excited because his voice had even sped up for a word or two. When she'd finished, Heuter recommended a restaurant with good food and outdoor tables where they could talk without having to fuss about Brother Wolf.

The waiter's eyebrows had risen when Anna ordered so much food. He'd protested when she put the plate with four burgers down for Brother Wolf, but had shut up when Leslie produced her badge and said, with a nod, "Werewolf."

There had been a quick switch in waitstaff, and the new waitress had asked if she could get Brother Wolf a bowl of water (yes)—or if he'd like something else to drink (no). Anna figured that waitress had just earned a pretty big tip. From the smile on the waitress's face, she figured so as well.

"That was wicked fun, how you yanked the witch's chain," Leslie told her. "Until then I hadn't realized she was just trying to freak us out."

"Umm," answered Anna, taking a bite to give herself time to think.

Brother Wolf looked up and focused on Anna. Okay, she was here to share information. Might as well do her job.

"She wasn't trying to freak you out," Anna told them. "Isaac told us she wasn't very powerful. She didn't have the control to keep up appearances in the presence of the death magic on the boy's body. I was trying to distract her, get her focused on me, so she'd tell us something instead of doing something dumb that was going to get her shot."

"Shot?" Heuter asked.

Anna smiled at him. "Guns are quite easy to smell. You should see about changing up the holster in the small of your back. You have to reach too far for it; it takes you too long. Try a shoulder holster or get some more practice." The bun had been toasted with real butter and the meat seared on charcoal. Anna ate a few fries to put off starting on the second burger.

"And you need to wait until you're sure you are going to draw before you reach," agreed Leslie. She smiled at Anna. "Cantrip doesn't require the same weapons training that we get at Quantico."

Something cold came and went in Heuter's face before he resumed his bland appearance. "Right. There's been some talk about changing that. I'm afraid most of the shooting I've done is with a rifle. My folks are from Texas and we have a place in upstate New York where we go hunting every year, too—hunting is a family ritual. But that witch . . ."

"Creepy," said Leslie with a nod. "I wish she had been faking it. Did either of you recognize the name she gave us? Sally Reilly?"

Anna shook her head. "No, but I think Charles did. I'll talk to him when he changes back and let you know."

Leslie frowned and started to say something, then glanced at Heuter and stuffed her mouth with salad instead.

"According to Wiki," said Heuter, reading from his phone, "in 1967, Sally Reilly wrote a book called *My Little Gray Story Book*." He looked up and grinned. "It was a play on the *My Little Red Story Book* series of readers in use in elementary schools. *My Little Gray Story Book* was an underground sensation, and when the second book, *A Witch's Primer*, hit the stands three years later, it hit the *New York Times* bestseller list. Sally Reilly was beautiful, shocking, and funny and became an instant, if small-time, celebrity. The books were less how-to books than here-is-my-life-as-a-witch books. She did a few talk shows, including *The Mike Douglas Show*, where she straightened some spoons bent by Uri Geller without touching them the day after the famous Israeli psychic appeared."

"Witches can't straighten spoons," said Anna involuntarily. Witches did things with living and once-living tissue—blood and bodies and stuff like that.

Heuter tipped his phone at her. "It's on Wiki."

"I've never heard of her," said Leslie. "I know about Uri and his spoon bending. Did something happen to her? The witch seemed pretty sure that she's dead, and Charles, according to Anna, thinks that she was a victim of our serial killer. What does Wiki say?"

"Wiki *doesn't* say," said Heuter. "Hold on."

"My dad talks about the sixties and seventies as a heyday of New Age thinking before the New Agers," Anna said. "Lots of free love and Wicca and magical thinking."

Heuter, still searching the Internet, nodded. "The Victorian era was the only thing that came close to it. Ouija boards, séances, games that tested whether people could read minds. Then, because everyone was doing it . . . it became less mysterious, less shadowy, and more . . . ridiculous. Interests changed."

"So maybe our Sally Reilly just disappeared from public view as the world gave a yawn," suggested Leslie. "Is this going to help our missing girl?"

Heuter didn't answer her question. "There are rumors of a third book she wrote and printed only a few copies of—*Elementary Magic*. When I get back to the office, I'll check our archives, see if we have it in the library. I should also be able to find out what happened to her, or if she's still around."

"The witch seemed awfully sure she was dead," said Anna. She hadn't been lying.

Heuter snorted and a scowl marred his handsome face. "That witch was . . . well. I wouldn't trust her to know which way was up."

"She gave us Sally Reilly," Anna pointed out.

"Which was more than we'd managed to get out of any of the other witches the FBI consulted with on this case," agreed Leslie.

Anna finished her last cheeseburger and retrieved Brother Wolf's empty plate, stacking them together on the table. She tried to see any way she and Charles could be of more help.

"Maybe if we went out to where Jacob's body was found, we might be able to find something more," she said slowly. "He was the last victim, before Lizzie?"

"Right," Leslie said. "Was he fae or werewolf—could you tell? Dr. Fuller said his parents were Baptist. That doesn't quite go with the whole supernatural thing."

Anna blinked at her a moment. She hadn't thought about that. Why had their killer reverted to killing humans again?

"Fae," said Heuter. "His father, Ian Mott, is listed in the fae database at Cantrip as full-blood fae and Jacob is clearly listed as half-fae. I ran the list of victims after we talked yesterday. Cantrip's database is far more extensive than the official one."

"Is it?" asked Anna; then she took a quick drink from her water glass to disguise any expression she might be showing. If Jacob Mott had been any sort of preternatural, she'd eat her hat. He hadn't smelled fae—and even half-bloods smell like fae. Wasn't it interesting he was listed as fae in Cantrip's database? Maybe the killer was finding his victims in the same database. Even so, shouldn't the fae who'd stolen Lizzie away be able to tell Jacob Mott hadn't been fae? She didn't really know if one fae could tell if another one was around, though she suspected it was so.

Charles was watching Heuter with sudden interest. How she could tell it was Charles and not Brother Wolf was . . . like how a mother of twins knew which one was which: less about the small details and more about instincts.

Heuter looked at Anna as if he'd forgotten she was there. "Oops," he said. "I don't suppose you can forget that."

"Don't want anyone filing paperwork to see if they are in that database of yours?" Leslie asked. "One of the fringe benefits to working with Cantrip or one of the other, smaller enforcement agencies in the government is that no one ever thinks to file on them with the Freedom of Information Act."

"You'd be surprised," said Hueter in a voice very nearly a whine. "The people who use FOIA do it extensively and well. Answering those requests is the job we give newbies—and that includes Important Senators' Sons, like yours truly, too." He grinned, showing that he didn't think that made him any more deserving of privilege than the rest of the newbies. "But not even the powers that be could keep me there for long. Information gathering about unknown werewolves is a lot more interesting." He looked at Anna. "Anna Latham of Chicago, musical prodigy. Left Northwestern University a couple of years short of a degree—much to the chagrin of the co-chair of Musical Studies, whom I talked to this morning, because he thought you'd become the next Yo-Yo Ma. No one seems to have heard from you since—except for your father, who was pretty short on conversation."

"My father is a lawyer," Anna half explained and half apologized. "He wouldn't say anything without a lot more information flowing his way. And probably a court order, though I wouldn't count on that."

"He wouldn't tell me your husband's name or where you live now—and the IRS is extremely uncooperative."

"Aren't they supposed to be?" Anna asked. "My husband and I came here to help; we did not come here to become names listed in your database—though we knew that you'd probably figure out who I was." He thought he'd pulled a rabbit out of the hat with his revelations about her real identity. She should have let him continue to pat himself on the back, and she knew it. Heuter was one of those people who liked being smarter than everyone else. He'd have been happier if she was mad or worried that he'd discovered who she was. But he was just a little too smug for Anna to be willing to indulge him.

"Where are you staying while you are here in Boston?" Heuter asked.

"Why are you worried about that?" returned Anna. Leslie, who knew where she and Charles were staying, was making steady inroads on the last of her salad. "I promise neither of us is going to go berserk and start killing people."

Heuter tapped his fingers lightly on the table. "I was raised to service," he said. "It's a family tradition. I believe in this country. I believe that innocents need protecting. I believe it is my calling to make sure that they are protected from people like you."

Heuter's voice was cool and controlled, even when he spoke the last bit. If Leslie hadn't drawn in a breath, Anna would have thought she'd misheard. Beside Anna, Brother Wolf stiffened, so she pulled herself together.

"That's funny," Anna said. "I'd have thought that terrorists and murderers would be more troublesome than me." As a comeback it was weak, but she was more worried about the silver bullets all Cantrip agents loaded their guns with. The gun that Heuter had almost pulled in the morgue. She couldn't really remember now exactly when he'd tried to go for it. He'd been so slow and clumsy that he hadn't managed to pull it before Brother Wolf had Caitlin down and contained on the floor. Had he started for it before Brother Wolf jumped, so that he could aim it at the witch? Or had he been too slow and by the time he could have gotten it out, it was already obvious that Brother Wolf wasn't going to hurt the witch?

If he had fired his gun back in the morgue, he might have killed Charles. Her hand reached out and touched her mate, to reassure herself that he was okay.

"Heuter," said Leslie sharply. "That was uncalled for."

He gave the FBI agent a tight smile and put some money on the table. "I'm due back in the office. I'll leave you to your afternoon of fruitless explorations."

Leslie waited until he was gone and then shook her head. "Trippers," she said.

"Trippers?" asked Anna.

"What the boss calls Cantrip agents." Leslie took a sip of her iced tea. "Just when you think that they are actually by golly professionals, they pull some weird stunt like that." She looked at Anna thoughtfully. "I'm not going to blow rainbows and happy faces at you and say that there aren't people worried about werewolves and the fae. We probably have some agents in the FBI who are pretty freaked-out by you or by people like Beauclaire. But at the very least they are professional enough not to go ape all over you when all you're trying to do is help us catch a freaking serial killer."

THEY TOOK A taxi to Castle Island where Jacob's body had evidently washed up, leaving Leslie's car in the parking garage next to the morgue. There was apparently parking at the Island, but it was the middle of summer and Leslie didn't like to waste time trying to find a place to park.

Anna's doubts about traveling by taxi with Brother Wolf proved to be unfounded. Their taxi driver had a big mutt at home, he told them, who was a Great Dane crossed with a dinosaur. Once he found out that Anna had never been to Boston before, he gave her a complete rundown on the island that hadn't really been an island since the 1930s. His stories included a ghostly tale of an escaped prisoner that somehow resulted in a haunting and a wandering yarn about how Edgar Allan Poe's army service at Fort Independence had led him to place his story "The Cask of Amontillado" at the fort.

"Wicked," Anna told him when they got out of the car and she handed him a tip.

He laughed and gave her a high five. "Frickin' wicked yourself. You'll be a native in no time."

"Don't you believe it," Leslie told her half jokingly. "Native Bostonians are the ones who've been here since the Revolutionary War—all others are interlopers, no matter how welcome."

The ocean air was refreshingly brisk as Leslie led the way down the cement walk that paralleled the ocean on the harbor side of the island. It wasn't crowded, not really—there had been plenty of places to park—but there were a number of people out enjoying the sun. The tall granite block walls of Fort Independence dominated the landscape, which was mostly grass with a few bushes and moderate-sized trees.

"Jacob wasn't here long before he was discovered," Leslie said. "Not a lot of places to hide a body around here and—as you can see—there are a lot of people this time of year. The harbor breeze keeps the temperatures to a reasonable level and the fishing is supposed to be pretty good."

"Do you think he was dropped in the harbor by boat?"

"That's the theory. Too many people around to drop him off unseen, and the ME says the body was in the water for at least a full day. Jacob was found a number of days ago. I suspect that if there was something we missed initially, it's too late now."

"Probably this is useless," agreed Anna. "But I'm not clear on what else we can do right now that is more helpful."

There were all sorts of people out and about—joggers, dog walkers, people watchers. The sound of kids yelling in the distance competed with airplanes from the airport across the harbor and seabirds.

They were passed by a woman with a Pekingese coming the other way. Her little dog hit the end of his leash and started barking hoarsely at Brother Wolf.

"He's perfectly friendly," his owner said. "Now stand down, Peter." To his owner's obvious embarrassment, the dog growled, keeping himself between the werewolves and his owner in a brave but misguided attempt to protect her, until they were long past.

"Peter," said Anna, smiling involuntarily. "Peter and the Wolf."

"Is that reaction usual?" Leslie asked.

"Most dogs have troubles with us at first," Anna admitted; then she smiled. "He was all of ten pounds, wasn't he? Pretty brave of him when you think of it. After insults have been exchanged it usually works out fine. Cats . . . cats don't like us. And they don't adjust, ever." She grinned at Leslie. "Just like Cantrip agents, I expect."

"Heuter is just one man," Leslie pointed out. "Hard to judge all of Cantrip by one man."

"I don't know about that," Anna said. "Who else would join an agency like Cantrip except for people who are afraid of the dark?"

"People who need jobs?" Leslie suggested dryly. "Cantrip takes a lot of Quantico graduates who don't get on with the FBI. As a job, Cantrip is less time-consuming than the FBI or Homeland Security, and it pays better than most police departments. It's less dangerous, too—because they don't actually do anything but collect information."

"Not yet," Anna said affably. "My father says that government unchecked is like a snowball; you can always count on it getting bigger and gathering more power." She walked a few paces. "Heuter was going to shoot someone in the morgue. If he could have gotten the shot off before it became obvious Charles wasn't going to hurt anyone, he'd have shot Charles. If you hadn't been there, he would have done it. I thought at the time he was going to go for the witch, but I've changed my mind. Cantrip carries weapons loaded with silver bullets."

"Mine is, too," admitted Leslie, sounding sheepish.

"Good for you," Anna told her. "You didn't even think about drawing, though."

"I don't know why not. I really should have."

"Charles did what you wanted to," Anna suggested. "Got the witch's hands off that poor boy. She was preparing to feed off him, and Charles stopped it."

"Feed?"

"Suck up the residual magic the killers left behind."

"That doesn't sound appetizing. Sounds necrophilic."

"Mmm," agreed Anna. "But you and I are not witches."

Leslie stared out in the harbor for a moment, then smiled. "I suppose that was it. I wanted to smack her, and your Charles did it for me."

There was a monument up ahead that looked something like the Washington Monument in miniature—or, since they were in Boston, like the Bunker Hill Monument. It was a tall, sea-battered, narrow-sided rectangle that lifted to the sky and ended in a point. On the ocean side of the path were some wharfs with a few people fishing from them.

"Still, Heuter . . ." Anna said. "You know Senator Heuter's views on werewolves, right? He's one of the proponents of that bill to include us as an endangered species."

Leslie frowned. "Endangered species?"

"And therefore not citizens," Anna said. "I don't suppose it would be of as much interest to you as it is to us werewolves. He also wants to RFID tag us as if we were pets who might go astray."

"RFID?"

"That one hasn't made it into a bill yet," Anna said. "But it's been in a couple of his speeches."

"That wouldn't be constitutional," said Leslie.

"It would if we were an endangered species." Anna looked at Brother Wolf. "I'd like to see someone try to put a radio control collar on Charles. It might be fun to watch on YouTube."

He gave her a look.

Anna raised the hand that wasn't holding the leash. "I'm not saying I'd do it. I'd just pay money to watch someone try."

Leslie gave her a thoughtful look as she stopped. "I thought that you were mismatched when I first met you two. But you aren't, are you?"

"No," Anna agreed. "I'm the only one who knows when he's teasing."

"If you say so," said Leslie, amused.

Anna looked around. "Is this where Jacob was found?"

"Over here."

Between the sidewalk and the sea stood a two-rail decorative pipe fence that the salt water had colored green and rust. Beyond that, a short rocky shoreline edged in green sea grasses gave way to a bit of water and a wall of worn wooden poles stuck side by side like soldiers keeping the waves off the land. Leslie pointed to a small patch of dirt between the wharf wall and the wooden poles.

Jacob would have been sheltered a little from the weather. Anna bent down a little closer than she needed to when she unclipped Charles's leash, and she breathed in his familiar scent to comfort herself. He waited until she stood up before he hopped over the fence and down to the strip of land below. Anna made no attempt to follow.

Leslie gave her a searching glance. "He can scent things better in wolf form than you can in human?"

"Yes. But he's also better at this than I am." Anna didn't feel a bit defensive about it. He'd taught her a lot, but . . . "He has a lot more experience than I do. Scents don't come with a label—this is the villain; here is a lady with a dog; here is a police officer and that sticky-sweet-and-sour-milk smell is someone's old banana ice cream cone. Charles can pick out what he's smelling better than I can, and date them, too, usually."

Brother Wolf trotted down to the isolated bit of dirt that Leslie had pointed out and then followed it toward them with his nose on the ground.

A jogger approached them and stopped, jogging in place. "Your dog should be on a leash," he said in politely disapproving tones. "It's the rules. There are lots of kids here and a big dog like that might scare someone."

"Werewolf," said Anna blandly, just to see what he would do.

He stopped jogging and looked, his jaw dropping. "Shit," he said. "You're kidding me."

"It's a werewolf," said Leslie.

"It's red. Aren't werewolves supposed to be black or gray?"

"Werewolves can be whatever color," Anna told him.

He bent down, stretching his legs and breathing deeply. "It's beautiful. Hey, that's where they found that little boy, isn't it? I saw the police tape out here a couple of days ago. Are you with the police?"

"FBI." Leslie gave him a sharp look. "You run here all the time?"

"When I'm off duty," he admitted. "I'm a fireman. Missed the fuss, though."

"You get a lot of things washing up here?"

"Yes, ma'am. Lotsa. New stuff every day, but we keep it picked up pretty well. His is the only body I know about, but I've only been running here a couple of years." He stared at Charles, who happily wasn't paying any attention. "FBI. You've got it looking for clues."

"*He* is," said Anna, getting tired of the "it."

The jogger wasn't disconcerted by her correction. "He work for the FBI?"

"No. Strictly volunteer," Anna told him.

"Wicked," he said approvingly. "Wait until I tell the guys I saw a werewolf. He mind if I take a photo?"

"Not at all," Anna told him.

He popped his phone out of a pouch on his belt and stood still long enough to snap a photo. "Cool. The guys are not going to believe this." He looked at the photo and frowned. "They're going to say that I took a photo of a big dog."

"Charles," Anna called. "Can we get a smile?"

Charles turned and gave her a look.

"Public relations," she suggested.

He turned his gold eyes to the jogger and then dropped his jaw in a wolfish smile that displayed fangs too large for any dog ever born.

The man swallowed. "Werewolf," he whispered, and then, remembering what he was doing, he snapped another photo. "Thanks, man . . . wolf. Thanks. They won't laugh at that." He glanced at Anna and Leslie and started jogging backward down the path. "Hey, good luck. I hope you get the guy."

"We do, too," Leslie assured him.

He turned back to watch them a couple of more times before he sped up and headed off the island.

"Doing a little PR?" Leslie asked.

"Never hurts," agreed Anna absently. "It's kind of my job." She'd been watching the jogger and he'd just passed a familiar figure. Goldstein saw her watching and waved.

"I texted Agent Goldstein and told him where we'd be," said Leslie.

Anna nodded. "Charles doesn't seem to be finding anything. I suspect I've just wasted your time."

"A lot of my work is like that," said Leslie.

Agent Goldstein sauntered up. "Find anything?"

"No," Anna told him. "Charles?"

Charles trotted up and started to change, right in front of them. Right in front of anyone who happened to look over and see what he was doing. It wasn't like him.

"What do we do, Mrs. Smith?" asked Goldstein quite calmly.

"Stay quiet and don't touch, okay? This really hurts and touching him makes it worse."

Anna glanced around, but no one else seemed to be paying much attention. That might be sheer dumb luck, or it might be something that Charles was doing.

"Remember, please, don't look into his eyes." There were a couple of meaty pops and Leslie winced.

"Yep. That hurts," Anna agreed. "This is why, if you're around a recently changed werewolf—either direction—you walk softly for a while. Pain makes the best of us pretty cranky."

"Does this mean he found out something?" Leslie asked.

"I don't know," Anna replied. "Either that—or he decided it was a good day to give a few Bostonians a heart attack."

"It's not as bad as it is in the movies," said Goldstein, sounding philosophical. "There's no liquid or clear oozing jelly, for one thing."

"Ick," said Anna. "Though if you move at just the wrong time, it can get bloody."

Leslie turned away and swallowed.

"Just kidding," Anna said. "Mostly."

"Still," Goldstein continued. "I can see why no one has agreed to change in front of the camera."

"That whole changing naked thing that most of us have to do makes it awkward, too," Anna told him. It wasn't easy to watch, even for her. Mostly, it was the empathy—you didn't have to be a werewolf to watch joints and bones changing and feel the ache in your own flesh in sympathy. And then there was the weirdness of watching things that should only be on the inside of a body show up on the outside. "You'd have to have a cable network like HBO. And we're trying to make people forget that we're monsters—this is kind of an unpleasant reminder."

"I thought it took longer than this," Goldstein said, as Charles became mostly human.

Leslie was scared, but holding it together. Goldstein looked like he was ready to fall asleep.

"For most of us, it does," she agreed. "Alpha wolves tend to be faster, and they can change more often. Charles is faster than most Alphas. We think it's for the same reason that he can wear clothes when he changes—he's got magic users on both sides of his parentage." They didn't need to know that he was the only werewolf born.

"For a secretive werewolf," observed Goldstein, "you are awfully happy to talk."

"The unknown is scary," Anna told him. "My orders were to come here, help you where we could—and try to make werewolves look good, to the FBI and to the public. How I carry it out is up to me. Hard to be friends with someone you think is scary."

"Your husband is scary—wolf or human," said Leslie.

Anna nodded her head. "He has to be. Regardless, Charles is one of the good guys."

Charles had changed completely back to human, and was wearing jeans, dark leather lace-up boots, and a plain gray tee. He stood up, eyes closed and muscles tight as he worked through the last debilitating cramps of the change. He flexed his fingers a couple of times, then looked straight at Anna.

"Call Isaac. Tell him we need a boat and his other witch." His voice was gravelly.

"Okay."

He looked at Leslie. "Call your medical examiner. See if we can get some hair from Jacob. Skin would work, but hair would be easier on the rest of us."

"I'll have to tell him why."

Charles raised a challenging brow. "I'll tell you why, and you can come up with a good lie. One of the little water spirits told me that the boy was taken from an island and dropped into the harbor. She made sure he came to rest here, which was useful to us, but I think she did it because she didn't want the black magic to linger in her water. That kind of magic can attract some nasty things. It occurred to me that if his body still had enough magical residue to get Caitlin the witch all excited, then his death site might still have enough for a real witch to locate it—if she has a bit of Jacob to orient with."

"Water spirits?" said Leslie, sounding dumbfounded.

"That's his shaman heritage, not a werewolf talent," Anna told her. "I can't see them, either."

"I know the ME from my stint in Boston a few years back," said Goldstein after a moment of silence. "I'll talk to him. Maybe do a bit of blackmail if it comes down to it. And we can get a boat."

Charles shook his head. "No witch I know would be caught dead on an official boat with the FBI. It'll have to be one of Isaac's people."

"I'll call Isaac—and then Beauclaire," said Anna. "If we have a chance at finding his daughter, he'll want to know."

"Witches and fairies don't get along," Charles warned her.

"If his daughter's fate rests in the hands of a witch, Beauclaire will bring her flowers and kiss her feet," Anna told him with absolute certainty. "Besides, if we run into this horned lord, it might not be a bad idea to have a big bad fairy on your side—and the way he's dropping information without worrying about it either means he's crazy—or he's a really big bad fairy."

Charles looked at her, then tipped his head. "I trust your judgment."

Anna looked at Leslie. "But let's leave Cantrip out of it, okay? We'll have werewolves, witches, and fae—we don't need a hostile and frightened man who is as likely to take out allies as enemies."

"Besides, Heuter is a jerk," Leslie said. "And I don't know about you, but I don't want to be stuck on a boat with him."

"Exactly."

CHARLES DIDN'T LIKE the ocean.

He liked boating even less and despised the way the life jacket restricted his movement. The *Daciana*, the thirty-foot boat they were going out on, might be designed for offshore ocean fishing, but the center-console fishing boats like this one had never felt like they were really big enough to handle ocean weather.

The boat was barely big enough to hold all of them: he and Anna, the two FBI agents, Malcolm (the owner of the boat), Isaac (who insisted on coming), Beauclaire, and Isaac's witch (who was late). If they found Lizzie, they might have to tie her to the bow or make her swim for it. The only thing that would have made it worse was if the boat were handled by someone other than a wolf—it wasn't only the witch who would have balked at a police or federal boat.

"Charles," said his mate, coming up behind him where he stood alone in the bow, which was somewhat isolated from the rest of the little boat. Malcolm and Isaac were muttering about courses and fiddling with the instruments packed in under the little central raised deck that provided the only protected area of the boat. Everyone else had chosen to wait on the docks until the witch arrived.

He'd heard Anna approach, felt the slight sway of the boat. It had been easier to be with her when he was in wolf form. Brother Wolf was not torn; he knew that they could protect her from anything—but his wolf was like that: confident. Charles was not so sanguine.

The taint of the ghosts he carried was beginning to wear on him. One day soon Anna would look into his eyes and see the evil within him. He wished he could have stayed in his wolf shape, but talking to Anna without opening the bond between them was too difficult. And he couldn't open the bond for fear that the ghosts might use it to get to Anna. There were stories about that, about ghosts that killed all of the people close to the man who carried them.

It was easier to be wolf than human because their evil could not touch Brother Wolf. The wolf felt no guilt, because guilt was a human emotion.

Anna touched his shoulder. Charles didn't turn to his mate, because he couldn't face her while he was thinking of the evil he carried inside of him. Instead he looked over the starboard side of the bow and out on the water where the sun was setting in streaks of azure, silver, and faint gold. "It'll be dark before we get out on the harbor."

Anna made a sound of agreement. "I know this is not the time, but, watching you brood over here, it occurs to me that you have evidently forgotten something and I think I'd better remind you. I should have reminded you this morning."

He did turn to her then. Like him, she was staring off into the distance, her shoulder brushing his like the wings of a butterfly.

"What's that?"

"You are mine." She didn't look at him but her hand closed possessively over his on the rail of the boat. Her voice was soft and without emphasis; not even werewolf ears would have heard her ten feet away. "Your ghosts cannot have you, Charles. So exorcize them before I have to." The last was a clear order, sharp as a shard of ice.

Brother Wolf grunted in satisfaction. He liked it when their mate got possessive and asserted her rights over him. So did Charles.

"Go ahead and smirk," she said, seriously, though her body was relaxed against him. "Just keep it in mind. Maybe you don't have to fight all of your battles alone."

"I'll remember your words," he told her with returned seriousness, though he pictured Anna taking her grandmother's rolling pin after the ghosts who haunted him, and it made him want to . . . smirk again.

"That's better," she told him smugly. "No more brooding."

And she was right.

The boat swayed a bit as both Isaac and Malcolm moved suddenly and there was a zing of expectation in the air.

"About time you got here, woman," Isaac called out in tones of real affection.

Startled, Charles looked over to see a woman walking down the pier to where their boat was docked. She was taller than average, taller than Isaac, who had vaulted up off the boat to trot down the pier to greet her. He kissed her, leaning into it, lingering.

"He's sleeping with the witch he told us was too devious to be trusted to gather information from Jacob's body?" said Anna, sounding disgruntled.

Charles laughed and pulled her closer so he could put his chin on top of her head. "Gutsy," he said. "But he's forgotten the first rule of the men's locker room."

"What's that?"

"Don't stick your . . ." He didn't need to be crude, so he corrected himself. "Don't screw with crazy, no matter how pretty it is."

She snorted. "You don't know her."

"I know witches," he said. "They are all crazy."

"What about Moira?"

Moira was the white witch who was on the Emerald City Pack's payroll. Anna had met her a couple of years ago and they had become fast friends.

"Except for the blind ones," Charles allowed.

They watched as Isaac introduced his witch to the FBI agents as Hally Smith. She wasn't beautiful, but she was striking with dark coloring, a long, elegant nose, and a wide, generous mouth.

Isaac helped her down into the boat. To Charles, she stank of black magic as she neared and he wondered how Isaac stood it. Moira, Anna's friend, was a white witch. She generally smelled of the herbs, spices, and magic of her gift. Hally reeked of death, old blood, and ghosts.

The witch looked at Charles as if she could read his mind, which he knew damned well she couldn't.

"Well," she said in a low, husky voice. "I've heard so much about you, Charles—"

Isaac made a noise in his throat and she smiled.

"Charles *Smith*. Look, we even share a last name. How delightful."

"Her last name really is Smith," Isaac told him.

"Convenient," said Anna. "People will think you're lying even when you aren't."

"But not you," said the witch, and Charles fought the desire to grab his mate and set her behind him where he could protect her better. "You and your kind can tell if I'm lying."

"Only if you aren't a good liar," said Anna, half apologetically and half honestly. Being a good liar might keep a young wolf like Anna from discovering a lie, but an old wolf like Charles could almost always tell.

Anna continued to clarify matters. "If you believe your own lies or if telling lies doesn't bother you, we can be deceived. In fact, we're even easier to fool because so many of us assume we're infallible. I, personally, am always careful not to underestimate how well people lie."

"I'll keep that in mind." Hally smiled and accepted a life jacket from Isaac, then handed him her satchel, a waterproof canvas backpack, to hold while she put it on. There was an unspoken arrogance about the act that set Brother Wolf on edge: Isaac was neither her mate nor her servant whose service was to be taken for granted. She snapped the vest on over her serviceable wool sweater.

"Are you planning on lying?" asked Leslie Fisher with interest. Anna gave her a quick look and then glanced up at Charles. He let her see that it didn't bother him, and she relaxed.

Hally's smile deepened. "I don't know yet. Isaac said you'd have some of Jacob's body for me?"

Goldstein took the seat next to Leslie's with his back next to the stern of the boat. He pulled out a Baggie from his life jacket pocket that contained a two-inch square of skin and a pinch of dark hair and handed it to Hally, who took it with the enthusiasm of a child being given a lollipop.

"Splendid," she said. "It would probably be best to wait until we are out in the harbor before I start to do magic. All I will get is distance and a direction, not the closest route there. It won't last forever, so I'd rather wait until we're somewhere it will do us the most good. Isaac filled me in"—she looked at Charles—"and promised me recompense."

She hadn't been cheap. If it weren't for the time factor, he could have had Moira and Tom fly out from Seattle for considerably less expense.

"Ten thousand," Charles agreed.

Leslie whistled. "No wonder we don't consult with witches much."

"You pay for the best," said Hally smugly. "Shall we set sail?"

"Motor," Anna said, pointing at the stern. "No sails."

CHAPTER

8

Charles kept a close watch from the bow as Malcolm threaded the *Daciana* around boats and other assorted obstacles with all the sailing skill of a pirate and a cheery rendition of "The Mary Ellen Carter," a song about men reclaiming a sunken ship, whistled off-key. If Bran had been with them, doubtless he'd have joined in the song. Charles's da loved impromptu concerts, especially with people who sang—or whistled—Stan Rogers songs, though considering the boat's passengers, "The Witch of the Westmoreland" might have been more appropriate.

The rise and fall of the ocean made Charles's stomach roil—another reason he didn't like boats. Anna was kneeling on the bow as far forward as she could, with her face in the wind and a peaceful expression that made Brother Wolf want to kiss her feet and other places—if only he wouldn't have thrown up the moment he bent over.

"Gets me, too," said Isaac, coming up from the rear of the boat. He braced himself on the wall of the console and talked in a voice nicely calculated to carry just over the noise of the engine, but not so loudly that anyone else was likely to hear. "Once I throw up, I'm okay." Then he raised his voice. "But I'm the Alpha of the Olde Towne Pack, damn it, and I can't afford to upchuck in front of a bunch of strangers. They might find bits of that annoying salesman I ate last night."

Charles scowled at him. "Thanks for the visual."

Isaac threw his head back and laughed. "You're all right, man. Malcolm says he's headed to a spot that he thinks is pretty much a clear shot to most of the islands. There are also lots of abandoned warehouses along the shoreline, thanks to the crumbling of the fisheries around here. Lots of places to hold and torture people without anyone hearing. You really see Indian spirits and talk to them?"

"Spirits," corrected Charles. "Nothing Indian about them other than we believe they exist and most of you white-eyes don't. Yes."

Isaac cackled. "I can't believe you just called me a white-eye. Better than a pale-face, I suppose, but it just seems so *Bonanza*." His face softened. "My granddad, he could see ghosts. When he was really old, he would rock in this old, dark wood rocking chair and tell us kids about the murderer who haunted the house he grew up in and tried to make his life hell when he was too young to read and write."

"Ghosts are different from spirits," Charles said. *Yes,* howled the ones who haunted him, *tell him about your ghosts, make us a little more real every time you speak of us, every time you see us or think about us. Tell him that ghosts of people you kill can come back and kill the ones you love if you are dumb enough or too clueless to figure out how to set them free.*

Charles had to wait a moment before he could continue, and disguised it as his motion sickness from the boat ride by swallowing heavily. "The spirits I see are more . . . a way for nature to talk to those with the eyes to see and the ears to hear. They never were human. I don't see ghosts"—*Liar!* cackled one in his ear—"not the way your granddad did, but I've met a couple of people who do. Not an easy gift."

"My granddad, he was a tough old bird. I'd guess he was tough even when he was five years old and faced down a haunt no one else could see." Isaac grinned. The sun was down now and his teeth gleamed in the light of the waxing moon. It was two days until full moon. "Tough like me."

Tough and stupid, thought Charles with a sigh. "You are sleeping with the witch?"

Isaac smiled whitely. "Yessir. And she makes me breakfast in bed, too."

Charles liked this young, tough Alpha, so he wanted to warn him. "Black witches are untrustworthy lovers."

"I get that," Isaac said. He shook his shoulders to loosen them. "I'm a werewolf; I can't afford to be delicate—but I could never fall for a woman who tortures kittens to make love potions, even if she doesn't do it around me. She's just scratching an itch and I'm enjoying it while it lasts—and I'm clear with her that's all it is."

"Women hear what men say," Anna said without turning around. "That doesn't mean they believe them. A witch isn't anyone to screw with, Isaac, and they get as possessive as any other woman. You're beautiful, strong, and powerful—she's not going to let that go easily."

"Are you trying to steal my man?" Hally didn't seem to have any of the trouble the rest of them did moving about the bouncing boat. And she was good at sneaking around because Charles hadn't noticed that she'd gotten up from her seat to round the opposite side of the console. She still had her satchel—and was holding the Baggie next to her face as if it held a rose instead of a piece of dead boy's skin.

Anna kept a hand on the railing and rolled to sit with only one hip on the ledge at the bow so she could face the witch. His mate smiled one of her big, generous smiles. "No. Just warning him about sleeping with dangerous things. Tigers are rare treasures—and they will eat you and not give it a second thought."

The witch preened, her ire sliding away. His Anna was so good at managing people—him included. It was a good thing that the witch was looking at Anna and not Isaac, because Isaac had clearly heard what Anna had said, too. And when an Omega talked, the wolf listened no matter what the man thought. Isaac looked like he'd been slapped.

"Tigers need to be wary around wolves," Charles said, to keep her from looking Isaac's way.

Hally narrowed her eyes. She reminded him more of a snake than a tiger—they were beautiful, too, beautiful and cold survivors, killing with poison rather than fang or claw.

"You are sticking your nose into places they don't belong, wolf," she said, as if she thought he ought to be worried about her.

Hally had overstepped, and so Brother Wolf met her eyes and let her see that they had killed more powerful witches than she was—and that it wouldn't bother them to do it again.

She swallowed and stepped back, stumbling when a wave threw her off balance.

"You scratch whatever itches you choose," Charles told her, his voice cold and quiet. "Enjoy yourself. But at the end of the day, you remember that Isaac belongs to my father—and to me. He is necessary to us as you are not. You will leave him unharmed or I will hunt you down and destroy you."

She hissed at him like a cat. When he just stared at her, Hally scrambled ungracefully around the far side of the console, out of his line of sight.

Isaac was watching him, his eyes bright gold. And then he tilted his jaw, exposing his throat. Charles lunged forward and nipped him lightly before releasing him.

From the back of the boat Beauclaire watched them with inhuman eyes, and Brother Wolf wanted to teach the fae man respect the way he'd just put the witch in her place. The moon urged, the ghosts in his head howled . . . and Charles took a half step away from the gunwale railing.

"You made yourself an enemy," Isaac said, his voice quiet and soft, distracting Brother Wolf. Beauclaire dropped his eyes at last and the moment was gone.

"She is a black witch," Charles said, equally quietly. "We have always been enemies. For right now, we are aimed at the same target; that is all. If your target is pleasure and you're sure that's what hers is, too, that's fine. Just remember—a black witch doesn't love anything but power."

Isaac swallowed and looked away. "White witches are just food for the rest. Hally had a sister who died when she was sixteen because she refused to take the black route to power. A big, bad wicked witch ate her down."

Charles nodded. "You can admire the survivor—but Hally *did* survive. She'll make sure she *always* survives. You better make sure that the same is true of you."

The little boat slowed; the engines quieted. The sky was inky except for the silver moon and the thin ribbon of cloud that crossed between them and her.

"Here," said Malcolm unnecessarily.

The witch took her satchel and the Baggie Goldstein had given her and climbed up the aluminum ladder to the fishing platform above the console. It was the best place to do it—a flat open surface on a crowded boat—but Charles was sure that the witch knew and enjoyed the fact that the height put her onstage and made the rest of them her audience.

Standing on the top of the ladder, Hally took a small rug out of her pack and laid it out flat. While she was snapping it into place, Charles caught a glimpse of circles and symbols and realized that she'd woven into the rug the protections that a witch would normally have used chalk for. It was a clever thing, something that would save her time and trouble—and also work admirably well on a boat in the rain.

Kneeling on the rug, she took out four or five small pottery jars and set them up as if their placement was important. She did the same with eight silver candlesticks holding dark-colored candles—probably black candles, but some witches worked with red. She adjusted and moved things around for a while. At last she set a tall candle in the center of her work.

"Light," the witch said, in an ordinary voice a half beat before the candles lit themselves despite the salt-sea air. The flames on the wicks burned steady and true though the wind whipped the strands of hair that had worked their way out of his braid. Magic. Her voice hadn't been the trigger, just a distraction or embellishment. The smoke told his nose what Charles already surmised—there was human blood worked into the candles she burned.

The way witches cast spells differed from one witch to the next depending upon a lot of things: their family background, who their teachers had been—and a little of their own personalities. This one was a wiggler and moaner, but she did it with all the grace of a talented belly dancer, and her moans were both musical and mesmerizing. Charles felt her magic rain down upon their little boat and found himself agreeing with Isaac's assessment: she was a power.

It made him wish that he'd called the white witch Moira after all. Hally didn't scare him, but his paranoia didn't like being in the middle of the ocean on a boat with his mate with a world-class witch who would—as Anna had helpfully pointed out earlier—as soon kill them as not. He intensely disliked being in someone else's power.

If we jumped up there, she'd scream and fall in the water, Brother Wolf assured him, because he didn't like being in her power, either. *Or we could just kill her and save her the trouble of drowning.*

Hally put the contents of the Baggie in a small ivory-colored pot shaped like a toad with big black cartoon eyes, its back open as if it had been made to hold a candle or a small plant. It fit into the palm of her hand. She pulled a vial out of her bag, pulled a cork stopper out with her teeth, and poured the liquid into the pot. By the smell, Charles knew it was brandy, and not the good stuff. Annie Green Springs, Everclear, or rubbing alcohol would have probably done just as well.

Storing the empty vial back in her pack, she held the pot over the flame of the middle candle with both hands and continued her melodic chanting. After a few moments, she slid her hands away and the pot hung over the candle without moving. She sat back on her heels and lifted her face so that the moon caressed her English-pale skin and slid down her hands, which were shaking feverishly about three inches from the pot. Theatrics designed to hide which were the important bits, in case another witch was watching.

Charles started to turn away from the show, but the corner of his eye caught something and he froze. A shadow thicker than steam slid out of the mouth of the frog. It sank to the rug and grew even thicker and darker, filling the space between the witch and the candles. He glanced around at the others, but no one looked worried or excited so he supposed he—and Beauclaire, who was slowly rising to his feet—were the only ones who saw the shadow.

In the middle of her music, at the height of her dance, the witch stilled and said, *"Darkness."*

The candles and every one of the boat's lights went out.

Malcolm swore, dove for his console, and frantically played with the switches. He put a foot on the first rung of the ladder, presumably to go up and confront the witch for meddling with his boat.

Malcolm was under Charles's protection, so Charles shoved past Isaac (still watching the witch instead of Malcolm), trusting that the Alpha wolf would have enough presence of mind not to fall overboard. He caught Malcolm by the shoulder when he was two rungs up, pulling him back to the deck. Interrupting a witch was not a good idea for anyone who wanted to survive long. Malcolm wrenched himself free of the unfamiliar hold and snarled. The noise cut off as soon as he saw who it was who'd manhandled him.

A dim light began to glow on the top of the fishing platform, distracting both of them.

"What in . . ."

In Hell, thought Charles, as the light resolved itself into the three-dimensional shape of an eight-year-old boy.

The smell of the black magic made Charles's earlier seasickness rise with a vengeance, and he moved as far from the center of the boat as he could get. Anna's cold hand closed on his. She was shaking. Not with fear. Not his Anna. No, she was shaking with rage.

"Tell me this was necessary," she said.

"No," Charles answered. He knew Anna didn't mean the witch; she meant the method the witch had chosen. Directional spells were easy. He didn't do them himself, but he had watched them cast. Calling a ghost as a compass was a major spell, a show-off spell, and entirely unnecessary.

"Tell me she doesn't get to keep him."

"She won't get to keep him," Charles told her. He was no witch, but his grandfather had taught him a thing or two. He might not be able to get rid of his own ghosts because he had to somehow fix himself first, but Jacob Mott, held by black magic, would be no trouble.

"All right," Anna said, her voice tight, trusting him to keep his word.

"Jacob, I invoke thee," the witch said, her voice like honey rising over the wind and slap of wave. "Jacob, I conjure thee. Jacob, I name thee. Do thou my will."

The boy's figure, glowing with silvery moonlight, stood with his back to her, his head bowed, reluctance in every line of his body. But

Charles could see his face—and there was no expression at all upon it, and his eyes glowed red as fire.

"Where did they kill you, Jacob Mott? Where did they sacrifice your mortal being?"

The boy lifted his head, looked south and east, and pointed.

"I can't run without lights," Malcolm said. "It's illegal, for one thing. And I don't want to get caught with candles made with human blood. I don't mind fines, but jail isn't going to happen."

"My magic needs darkness," said the witch in a midnight voice.

Beauclaire got out of his seat and touched the rail of the boat. The lights came back on and the witch turned to glare at him.

"Your magic *is* darkness," said the fae repressively. "The rest is cheap theatrics."

The witch ignored him and put her hands on the shoulders of the boy, caressing him in a not-motherly fashion.

"Thanks," said Isaac to the fae.

Malcolm, his face tight—he had to stand directly under the taint of black magic in order to run the boat—turned the *Daciana*. When the direction the boy was indicating lined up with the point of the bow, Isaac said, "That's good," and the *Daciana* steadied on course.

Malcolm got busy with his charts and then called out loud enough that people who were not werewolves or fae could hear him over the engine and waves, "Looks like we're headed to Long, Georges, or Gallops Island."

"What do you think?" Isaac asked; then to the rest of them he said, "Malcolm makes his living hauling anyone who will pay him out fishing or exploring. He's been doing it for thirty-five years and he knows the harbor as well as anyone living."

"Could be any of them, I suppose. Georges has a lot of people during the day, which would make me nervous if I was trying to keep live prisoners."

"What about Long Island?" asked Leslie. "It's accessible by car, too, right?"

"Right." Malcolm was quiet. "Long Island has the public health facilities, and people who live and work there every day. But there are lots of places no one goes. Places for someone to hide people in, more than either Georges or Gallops. Those old hospital buildings have tunnels going from one to another. There are a few empty buildings—the old concert hall, the chapel, and a couple associated with the old hospital. Fort Strong is falling down and full of good hidey-holes. The old Alpha had me lead a couple of full-moon hunts out there. We hunted Gallops, too—ought to do some more there because there are rabbits doing a lot of damage. As long as no one notices the boats, it would be cool. We don't have to hunt quiet there 'cause it's been quarantined for the past decade. Gallops has old military buildings full of asbestos and there's no money to clean it."

"Our UNSUB knows a lot about the local area," Anna noted.

"Always seemed that way to me, too," agreed Goldstein, who had gotten up and worked his way around the boat until he could get a better look at the dead boy who guided their trip. "He does that in most of his hunting grounds—uses the territory more like a native than a traveler."

Goldstein stopped and frowned up at the softly glowing boy.

"Is he a ghost?" he asked.

Anna looked at Charles and everyone else followed suit.

The witch looked at him, too, and smiled.

Charles ignored her and did his best to answer. "Not his soul; that's gone on. She couldn't have touched it." He believed that, believed that the only person who could destroy or taint a soul was the person whose soul it was, even though his ghosts were laughing as he spoke. *You tainted us,* they told him. *You stole our life and tainted us.*

He continued, stoically ignoring the voices of the dead. "A ghost is the little left-behind bits, collected together. Memories held in buildings or things—and here by flesh and hair."

"It's not really the boy?" asked Leslie Fisher, and from the tone of her voice, if he said yes, she would have shot Hally without a second thought.

"No. More like a sweater that he wore and discarded," Charles told her. The red eyes, he was pretty sure, were caused by some aspect of the witch's magic.

Leslie looked at him, and he thought that if she looked at her children that way, they would squirm. Then she nodded her head and made her way to the rear of the boat—and sat next to Beauclaire instead of the backward-facing seats behind the console that would have left her back to the witch. He didn't blame her.

After a while, Malcolm said, "It's not Long Island or Georges. We're either going to Gallops or someplace along the coastline."

"It's not the coast," said the witch, lifting her face to the night sky. "Don't you feel it? It's glorious. They must be amateurs to leave such a feast behind unconsumed." She smiled, and it was a terrible smile because it made her look so sweet and young—and the cause of the smile was the death of Jacob Mott and others before him.

"It is too bad that so many of us, so many witches, are afraid of water," Hally said to Charles. "Otherwise we'd have known about this a long time ago. They've used this more than just this season."

The Hunter had hit Boston twice, Charles remembered.

"If this were springtime, we'd have trouble accessing Gallops," said Malcolm. "As it is, there are some docks that are still usable. I'll take us around."

"We know where we're going," said Charles to the witch. "Release the boy."

"I thought he was just a collection of memories," she murmured. "Just an old sweater discarded when Jacob died."

Charles jumped to the top of the railing of the fishing platform and bent his knees, balancing with the sudden lurch the force of his jump had caused and then settling more comfortably as the rise and fall of the boat steadied to the ocean's hand.

He caught the witch's eyes and, bringing Brother Wolf and all of his power to the fore, said, "Let him go."

She obeyed before she thought, his sudden appearance and the force of his order dictating her actions. She dismissed the ghost with a flick of her power. Then her jaw dropped in outrage, and magic gathered around her.

"Don't," said Charles before she could complete whatever mischief came to mind. "You won't like what happens."

He hopped down beside her and picked up the little frog pot. The sickly magic residue tried to crawl onto his fingers, but flinched back from Brother Wolf's presence at the last moment. His instinct said that whatever ties the contents of the pot had to Jacob were gone, used up—and that was good enough for him. He tossed the frog out over the side of the boat, making sure that it spun upside down and scattered its contents as it fell.

She hissed and flung something that slid off him like water. Charles shook his head.

"Do you think I would have survived this long if some hastily constructed spell could harm me?" It wasn't a lie. He was just asking her a question. If her answer was the wrong one, it was not his fault. Half of his reputation rested on stories people told about him. He'd been lucky. He wore some protections, and being a werewolf was another kind of protection, but no one was invulnerable. The secret of being safe from magic was to make people think it was useless to attack him by that method.

Charles swung back over the platform railing and landed lightly on the deck below. He took a seat on one of the benches that served as bait containers near the bow, and his mate scooted over and sat on his lap.

Anna kissed his jawline and he felt the ghosts' predatory rumblings. *Closer, bring her closer,* they said, cackling. *We shall eat her and share her among us.*

Mine, answered Brother Wolf. He tightened his arms around her when Charles would have sent her to safety. But Brother Wolf held her and stared at the moon, who sang serenely to him.

CHARLES JUMPED OUT with one of the dock lines as soon as the boat was near. The wooden platform felt sturdy under his boots and the cleat he tied his line off to looked new. He asked Malcolm about it as the others disembarked.

"The parks department comes out and they need somewhere to tie up their boats, don't they?" asked Malcolm rhetorically. "So they keep the dock up."

"Stick together," said Charles. "Malcolm, your job is to keep our FBI agents safe."

Leslie drew in a breath, but Goldstein held up a hand. "You and I can't see in the dark if our flashlights give out. There's a moon out right now, but given the clouds in the sky, that could change. We are slower and more vulnerable than they are—and if this is the killing ground, then someone might be here to guard their latest victim."

Leslie pulled out her gun, checked to make sure it was loaded, and then put it back in her shoulder holster.

"If you can manage without flashlights," Charles told them, "it will help the rest of us keep our night vision. But don't risk a broken ankle. I don't know how well you can see—we wolves can see just fine in the dark; most witches have a trick or two—" He glanced at Beauclaire.

The fae nodded. "I can see fine."

"So it's up to you. If you use the flashlights, please try not to shine them in our eyes."

"I have a question," said Leslie. "If you can see in the dark, why did Malcolm say he needed lights to find the island?"

"Because I'm not taking a boat that has parts not working into waters that aren't safe," Malcolm said. "There are some pretty nasty places around here if you don't know where you are, and her spell killed all of my instrumentation lights—GPS, depth finders, the whole kit and caboodle."

The witch smiled at them all. "Are you still talking?"

Isaac touched her shoulder. "Lead the way, Hally."

The fae followed Isaac and his witch, her pale skin standing out in the darkness like a candle in the night. The FBI agents followed the witch with Malcolm trailing them. That left Charles and Anna to take the rear guard.

Castle Island had been parklike with carefully planted trees and bushes. Gallops was more like a jungle. Not quite as dense as the temperate rain forest near Seattle, but the undergrowth could have used a machete or two to clear it out. Perforce they followed paths that had once been sidewalks or narrow roads before nature had started to reclaim them. Mostly they walked uphill—from what he'd seen on the water, the whole island was mostly one long, narrow hill. It wasn't very big, less than forty acres, he thought. It wouldn't take them long to find the place where Jacob had been killed, as long as the witch was telling the truth—that she could feel it.

Anna pointed out the cornerstone of a house and what was undoubtedly originally a planted hedge of roses that had gone wild. He pointed out some poison ivy and a pair of curious rabbits who weren't at all scared of them. Any hunt on this island would be boring if they were hunting rabbits.

The whole thing stank of black magic. If he'd been trying to find the center on his own, he'd have had to crisscross the whole island and hope he'd stumble into it.

As much as he hated to admit it, the witch had been right. Only amateurs would leave this much power residue behind. After they were done here, he'd have to talk to his father about how to clean it up. This much tainted power was more troublesome than asbestos—people would get sick here and die from colds. They would scratch themselves on a thornbush and die from the resultant infection. They would kill themselves from a despair they would never otherwise have felt.

This much residue would also attract dark things—and in the ocean there were some very bad things who might decide to come ashore for the kind of invitation the island was sending out. And the worst part was that there were more places like this, everywhere the killers had struck over the years.

Sally Reilly, Caitlin the witch had said when she identified the marks the killers left on their victims. It made sense. He hadn't ever met Sally, but his father had made a point of attending one of her "demonstrations" and had come back shaking his head and sent Charles out to do research. Back then it had been more foot and phone work than computer work. After talking to her father (her mother was dead), some old friends, and a couple of witches, he'd returned to Bran with a report.

Sally wasn't a hack or an amateur, but rather a skilled witch. She'd broken with her family and decided to turn the heat up—maybe cause another witch hunt. A hunt that she intended to protect herself from by money she gained while she was busy convincing the television-watching public that witches were real.

He'd told Bran that they needed to stop her—and then she'd quit trying to publicize witches. Instead, she'd started charging rich people large fortunes for her work. She'd disappeared altogether sometime in the early 1990s, but he'd always supposed that she had retired, until Caitlin the witch had been so utterly convinced that Sally Reilly was dead.

It would have been just like Sally to do something like agree to work up a spell that would leave a residue like this, one with incorrect symbols, maybe—while she charged them through the nose for it, thinking them fools who intended to kill chickens or goats.

Had *they* killed her? The timing was right. And if they'd paid a witch for a spell to let them feed from people they killed, they'd have felt the need to get rid of her, since she was a witness they wouldn't have wanted. And serial killers didn't stay free and killing for this many years without being smart enough to take care of witnesses.

Charles let his hand linger on Anna's back. She wore a sweater and a light jacket, but he pretended he could feel the heat of her through the clothing that covered her.

Brother Wolf wanted her off this island and somewhere far away from killers who hunted werewolves and left no scent behind for them to discover. But Charles knew better. To try to encase his Anna in Bubble Wrap would be to kill the woman who protected him with her grandmother's marble rolling pin. She was the woman he fell in love with.

Then why are you hiding your ghosts from her? Brother Wolf said.

Because I am afraid, Charles answered his brother, as he would have answered no one else. He had lived a very long time, and only since he gained Anna had he learned to fear. He'd discovered that he had never been brave before—just indifferent. She had taught him that to be brave, you have to fear losing something. *I am afraid I will lose her. That they will take her from me—or that I will drive her away when she sees what I really am.*

Beauclaire had addressed that. Charles couldn't remember the fae's exact words, but he felt them. People as old and powerful as he should never be given someone to love.

For Anna he would destroy the world.

ANNA FELT CHARLES more than heard him, even though he'd taken his hand off her back and let her go ahead. She could hear the others walking in front of her, but Charles was a silent, reassuring presence behind.

She could smell the wrongness in the air and it made her wolf nervous. It felt like something was watching them, as if the wrongness had an intelligence—and it didn't help to remember that at least one of the people they were hunting could hide from their senses.

Anna fought the urge to turn around, to take Charles's hand or slide under his arm and let his presence drive away the wrongness. Once, she would have, but now she had the uneasy feeling that he might back away as he almost had when she sat on his lap in the boat, before Brother Wolf had taken over.

Maybe he was just tired of her. She had been telling everyone that there was something wrong with him . . . but Bran knew his son and thought the problem was her. Bran was smart and perceptive; she ought to have considered that he was right.

Charles was old. He'd seen and experienced so much—next to him she was just a child. His wolf had chosen her without consulting Charles at all. Maybe he'd have preferred someone who knew more. Someone beautiful and clever who . . .

"Anna?" said Charles. "What's wrong? Are you crying?" He moved in front of her and stopped, forcing her to stop walking, too.

She opened her mouth and his fingers touched her wet cheeks.

"Anna," he said, his body going still. "Call on your wolf."

"You should have someone stronger," she told him miserably.

"Someone who could help you when you need it, instead of getting sent home because I can't endure what you have to do. If I weren't Omega, if I were dominant like Sage, I could have helped you."

"There is no one stronger," Charles told her. "It's the taint from the black magic. Call your wolf."

"You don't want me anymore," she whispered. And once the words were out she knew they were true. He would say the things that he thought she wanted to hear because he was a kind man. But they would be lies. The truth was in the way he closed down the bond between them so she wouldn't hear things that would hurt her. Charles was a dominant wolf and dominant wolves were driven to protect those weaker than themselves. And he saw her as so much weaker.

"I love you," he told her. "Now, call your wolf."

She ignored his order—he knew better than to give her orders. He said he loved her; it sounded like the truth. But he was old and clever and Anna knew that, when push came to shove, he could lie and make anyone believe it. Knew it because he lied to her now—and it sounded like the truth.

"I'm sorry," she told him. "I'll go away—"

And suddenly her back was against a tree and his face was a hairbreadth from hers. His long hot body was pressed against her from her knees to her chest—he'd have to bend to do that. He was a lot taller than her, though she wasn't short.

Anna shuddered as the warmth of his body started to penetrate the cold that had swallowed hers. Charles waited like a hunter, waited for her to wiggle and see that she was truly trapped. Waited while she caught her breath. Waited until she looked into his eyes.

Then he snarled at her. *"You are not leaving me."*

It was an order, and she didn't have to follow anyone's orders. That was part of being Omega instead of a regular werewolf—who might have had a snowball's chance in hell of being a proper mate.

"You need someone stronger," Anna told him again. "So you wouldn't have to hide when you're hurt. So you could trust your mate to take care of herself and help, damn it, instead of having to protect me from whatever you are hiding." She hated crying. Tears were weaknesses that could be exploited and they never solved a damned thing. Sobs gathered in her chest like a rushing tide and she needed to get away from him before she broke.

Instead of fighting his grip, she tried to slide out of it. "I need to go," she said to his chest. "I need—"

His mouth closed over hers, hot and hungry, warming her mouth as his body warmed her body.

"Me," Charles said, his voice dark and gravelly as if it had traveled up from the bottom of the earth, his eyes a bright gold. "You need me."

He kissed her again, his hands roaming from her jaw down her neck and shoulders. His hips pressed forward, and he released her mouth as he slid his body up until his sex pressed, hard and full, against hers. She jerked involuntarily, and he laughed in the same deep way that he had spoken. She growled at him, wolf to wolf.

"There you are, there you are," he said. "Are you just going to let me do this alone?"

He was talking too much when he should be feeling. She curled one leg up until the angle of their hips was better, climbing his body until she could bite down on his collarbone. He drew in his breath at the pain and she released him. Now his attention was on her instead of on making words, so she could be gentler. She licked the wound she'd made, feeling it heal under her tongue as she cleaned the iron-rich blood from his skin. She lunged upward and this time she caught the tendon in his neck gently, and his gasp had nothing to do pain.

She wiggled her hips, rubbing the seam of her jeans on him as she absorbed the heady smell that was her mate when he was aroused. She wanted to smell it better so she slipped down and rested her open mouth against his hardness, letting her hot breath caress him through his jeans. It had been so long since they'd touched.

His scent grew stronger: musk and forest, salt and bitter, with an indescribably delicious edge of sweetness.

"Anna," he said, a little desperately. "Isaac, Malcolm, and probably that damned fae can hear us."

She opened her mouth and bit—not hard, just enough to shut him up and to let him know that pushing her away was not an option.

Charles made a noise that might have been a laugh, but all she heard was the surrender in it, and then he let her knock him onto his back in the damp soil of the island and unzip his jeans until she could get to him. Once she had his bare skin in her hands, the frantic need lessened, partly assuaged by the clear evidence that he wanted her as much as she wanted him.

His skin was so soft to sheathe something so hard. She licked him delicately, loving the taste of him now seasoned by the ocean's salt. She loved him in all of his flavors, loved the noises he made as she pleasured him, loved the catch in his breath and the jerkiness of his movements— he who was always graceful.

She swallowed him down, claiming him, man and wolf, in the most basic way possible.

"I am yours," he said, a finger under her chin dislodging her claim. "And you"—he moved his hands under her shoulders and pulled until she was all the way on top—"are mine."

Her jeans were in the way so he rolled her to the side and stripped her shoes, pants, and underwear off in three quick motions. He pulled her back on top with hands that were more urgent than gentle and slid inside her.

She closed her eyes and absorbed the feel of the slow burn, the slick pressure and warm friction that meant he was hers. Then he grabbed her hips and asked, so she moved—and quit thinking altogether.

Limp and well loved, Anna panted on top of Charles. As the last tingles died down, she started to think again instead of just feel.

"Did we," she whispered, feeling the blush start at her toes and travel all the way out to her ears. "Did we really make love while everyone was listening? Right out in the open? When there might be a bad guy we can't see or hear watching?" She might have squeaked the last word.

Underneath her, Charles laughed, his belly bouncing her up and down. He felt resilient and relaxed, like a cat bathing in the sun. "All I was trying to do was get you to call up your wolf so she could fight off the black magic that was making you doubt yourself." He paused and the relaxation faded. "Making you doubt me." He rubbed her back. "I made you doubt me."

Anna tucked her head in the hollow of his shoulder and closed her eyes, but hiding didn't work. After a minute, she laughed helplessly. "There is no saving it, is there? We might as well go face the music."

Anna sat up and lifted her head to scent the air. All she smelled was green growing things, Charles, sex, and the ocean air. "The wrongness is gone," she told him.

He frowned and closed his eyes, breathing in deeply. "From here," he said. "Not from the whole island. That's interesting." Then he looked up at her and smiled. "I think we'd better pull ourselves back together. They're waiting for us."

Anna stood up and he handed her his T-shirt. She cleaned up as best she could, handed him back his shirt, and then climbed back into her clothes. He was faster, since he had only to zip his jeans. She was brushing the dirt off one of her socks when he took the shirt and pressed it against a tree.

She watched him as she put on a shoe and started dusting off another shoe.

Charles murmured to the tree in what she was pretty sure was his native speech—which he very seldom used. He and Bran were the only ones left who spoke it as his mother's band of people had used it, a variant of the Flathead tongue. It made him feel sad and alone to use it, he told her once, and he and his father communicated quite nicely in English, Welsh, or any number of other languages.

Clothed and shod, she ran her fingers through her hair to dislodge leaves, grass, mud, and whatever creepy crawlies might have come to rest there. Charles went down to one knee and pressed the shirt into the ground . . . which ate it.

He murmured one more phrase and came back to his feet. He saw her watching him and smiled, his face more open than she'd seen it in a long time. "I wasn't going to put it back on," he explained. "And leaving something like that lying around when we're traveling with a witch is just not smart. The apple tree will absorb it eventually and guard it until she does."

"Are you done yet?" called Isaac.

Charles tilted his head and called back, "I suppose that's why they call you the five-minute wonder."

Anna could feel her eyes round and her mouth drop open. "I can't believe you just said that." She paused and reconsidered. "I am so telling Samuel you said that."

Charles smiled, kissed her gently, and said, "Samuel won't believe you." Then he took her by the hand and started off in the others' wake.

As they climbed, scrambling over broken cement, rocks, and bits of assorted underbrush, Anna had too much time to think about the show they'd just put on.

It had been her fault.

Charles had been trying to raise her wolf—because apparently the black magic had been affecting her. She cringed away from the self-pitying stupidity she'd allowed herself to wallow in. Talking hadn't worked to pull her out of it, so he'd kissed her, and her wolf had risen up to shrug off the effects of the magic, just like he'd thought she would. And then her wolf had changed the game.

Anna remembered distinctly that he'd warned her that they had an audience—and she'd totally ignored him. That was bad enough. To do it when there was a distinct chance that they were going to run into the bad guys was the height of stupidity.

"Anna," said Charles. "Stop brooding."

"That was really dumb," she said without looking at him. "My fault.

I'm sorry. We could have been attacked by the killers." She threw up her hands. "We might as well have set up cameras and invited everyone to watch. And now we're going to have to go meet up with our audience and explain ourselves."

He stopped abruptly and jerked her to a halt beside him with a hand on her wrist. It startled her with its hint of violence—Charles was never out of control.

"If you think that it was dumb, unnecessary, and your fault," he said in a husky voice, "then you weren't paying attention." He kissed her again, his mouth demanding her response, his body hot against hers.

Charles smelled like home, warm and right. She knew she should pull back, knew that this was more distraction they couldn't afford, but she was so hungry for him—not just for sex, but for the simple touches, the absolute certainty of knowing she was welcome to pet and tease and laugh. Anna sank into him and gave as good as she got.

They were both breathless when he pulled back.

"When we get back tonight, we will talk," he told her. "I just learned something."

"That my wolf is shameless," she muttered, though she couldn't pull away.

He laughed, damn him. More of a huff than a chuckle, but she knew amusement when she heard it.

She'd thrown him down in the middle of a hunt when there were a herd of people listening in. All the werewolves, he'd reminded her—and Beauclaire, who was here to find his daughter, not to listen to her make out in the woods. And now, to show that she hadn't learned her lesson, all she wanted to do was take up that last kiss where it had left off.

"No help for it," Anna muttered. "Time to face the music."

"Shame is . . . not a very productive emotion," Charles told her.

There was a funny little pause when he tilted his head to look at her face and then away. "Brother Wolf liked claiming you in front of the others so that there will be no question who you belong to. While I . . . *I* regret your embarrassment but otherwise agree with Brother Wolf."

Anna stared at him incredulously. If there was a more private man in the world than her husband, she hadn't met him.

"As for the other . . ." Charles grinned rather fiercely at her and raised his voice. "Isaac, go on ahead; we'll follow."

"You're the man," Isaac called back.

"We'll trail them closely," Charles said. "If something happens, we'll be right there—but if we wait until there are more interesting things about than we are, they won't give you a hard time." He didn't need to say that no one would give him a hard time.

"Thanks," Anna said, not knowing how else to respond.

He put his hand on her shoulder as they started back up the trail. While they hiked, there was none of the reluctance to touch her that had characterized him for the past few months. He kept a hand on whatever part of her was closest to him.

CHARLES HAD TRIED to open their bond and call up her wolf to defeat the black magic and hadn't been able to. Brother Wolf had panicked because Charles had somehow messed up their bond—and then Anna threatened to leave them and Charles had panicked, too. If she hadn't allowed them to make love to her, to reestablish their claim, things might have gotten . . . interesting, in the same way that a grizzly attack is interesting. Because neither he nor Brother Wolf was capable of letting her go.

It had been something of a revelation.

The bottom line was that he was a selfish creature, Charles decided more cheerfully than he'd been about anything in a long time. He guided Anna around a hole in the ground with a subtle push of his hand on her hip. She probably had seen the hole, but it pleased him to take care of her in such a small way. He was willing to pay any price to keep her safe . . . any price except for losing her.

When they got back to the condo he would tell her about the ghosts who threatened to kill all that he loved unless he could find the key to releasing them. It was a risk—but quite clearly, he had damaged their mate bond by trying to do this alone—and that was worth any risk to fix. He'd see if, between the two of them, they could mend what he'd broken—and if not, he'd call his da.

If this trip had done nothing else, it had given him distance from the unrelenting grimness that his life had become since the were-wolves had revealed themselves to the public. He'd been so focused on duty, on need, and on just getting the job done that he'd lost perspective.

Honor, duty, and love. He would not sacrifice Anna for his father and all the other werewolves in existence. Given a choice, he chose love.

That meant he had to find a way to deal with the ghosts—or quit being his father's hatchet man. It wasn't the result his father had been hoping for from this trip, but Charles couldn't help that. He would not lose Anna even if it meant they went to war with the human population.

The decision left him feeling oddly peaceful, if more than a little selfish.

"We found it," Isaac called.

Charles started jogging and Anna stayed by his side—just where she belonged.

The place where the others awaited them had once been a yard with a small house or storage shed, maybe ten feet by fifteen, in the center. The wooden part of the structure was long gone, but the granite foundation blocks were still in situ. The eyebolt that was driven into one of the blocks might have been original, but the chain and cuffs attached to it were bright and shiny new.

Beauclaire was standing in the center of the foundation, his eyes closed and his lips moving. Charles was pretty sure he was working some magic, but with the feel of the blood magic that had already been done here clogging his senses, he couldn't tell.

Along the perimeter of the clearing, Malcolm trailed after the FBI agents, who were busily using their flashlights to examine the ground for clues or a trail.

"We'll have to come back in daylight with a team," Goldstein said, and there was a hard edge to his voice. "We shouldn't be tromping around here at night; we're going to miss or destroy clues."

"You aren't going to get Beauclaire to leave without his daughter," said Leslie. Then she glanced back at the werewolf behind them and stepped a little closer to Goldstein.

Charles took a good look at Malcolm himself. "Malcolm," he said sharply.

The bearded werewolf looked up. "You told me to watch them."

Isaac had been in a low-voiced conversation with his witch, but when Charles spoke he looked over, too.

"Malcolm?" he asked, his voice too gentle.

The other wolf sighed and drifted a little farther away from the FBI agents, but also shifted his body language from stalker to bodyguard. Charles wasn't sure that the humans could consciously read body language well enough to tell the difference, but their hindbrains could. As soon as Malcolm started to behave himself, Leslie's shoulders relaxed and she quit patting her thigh with her right hand.

Isaac left the witch kneeling beside the chains, her fingers tracing spells that left little red glowing lines behind them.

"Hally says that there were ten or twelve people killed here over a period of years," he told Charles. "She says that she'll gather some of her apprentices and they'll put the island to rights after the police have gathered their evidence. She's doing what she can now. We don't want a herd of armed people in a place that has such a strong dark magic residue—the words 'accidental shootings' don't even begin to cover the disasters that could spring up."

"Good," said Charles. That was one less thing for him to worry about. "Any sign of Lizzie?"

"Not right here. No one alive but us and some rabbits within hearing range, and there aren't any trails into or out of this place. I can't smell anyone but us in the vicinity. Maybe if I were in wolf form, I could do better."

"We'll all change to hunt for the girl—except Malcolm, if he can help it," Charles said.

"I can help it." Malcolm sounded a little put out to be left behind.

"We need you to be able to take us back to the mainland in a hurry when we find Lizzie," Charles explained. "She's going to need medical attention as soon as possible. It's not just guard duty."

"You believe Lizzie is here," Beauclaire said sharply, leaving off his spell casting. "Can you smell her? Do you have proof?"

Charles waved his hand at the stone. "They have used this place to kill all of their local victims once they are through with them. Do you think that they found a better place than this isolated and quarantined island to keep their victims while they are still alive?"

The fae stared at him, his face hungry. "How do you propose finding her? If she were here, I would be able to find her. But my magic doesn't tell me anything. It hasn't from the beginning." His voice dropped to a whisper. "I thought it meant that she was dead."

"I know a few ways to stymie fae magic," said the witch without pausing in whatever she was doing to the granite stone. "The Irish and German witches are well-known for their ability to disrupt your kind of power, one way or another, and Caitlin told me that this guy got his rune spell from an Irish witch. There's a dozen ways to make charms that I know, some more effective than others."

Beauclaire looked at her, face taut with hope. "There are," he said. "There are indeed."

Isaac started stripping off his clothes and so did Anna. Charles moved until he stood between them in answer to a small fit of territoriality and unfounded jealousy. Brother Wolf was feeling possessive tonight.

Not bothering to take off his jeans, he began his change. It was harder this time because he'd been changing a lot today, and the last time he'd pushed for speed. His shift was slower and it hurt more, leaving him with the dull ache in his bones that told him he would pay for the next change back to human. If he could, he'd wait until they got back to their condo before attempting it.

He still managed the full change before the others and was shaking the tingles and cramps out of his muscles when Isaac staggered to his feet, a wolf of medium height and a gold coat that reminded Charles of Bran's mate, Leah. Anna was still changing.

Charles left the others to recover and started to explore the ground with his nose. Like the FBI agents, he concentrated his efforts along the edge of the clearing. He found nothing on his first pass or his second and was starting a third—Beauclaire pacing attentively by his side, a hand on the long knife he wore in a sheath on his belt, a knife Charles didn't remember seeing on the boat—when Anna called him over with a couple of demanding yips.

He took his time, casting around where Anna stood, but he scented nothing, not even the ubiquitous rabbits and mice. She whined at him when he lifted his head and he tried again. The second time he lifted his head, she yipped and started trailing something he couldn't smell.

Frustrated at his inability to perceive what she had, doubly frustrated because if he hadn't messed up their bond somehow, she could have told him what she found, Charles stalked after her with Isaac and Beauclaire following. Probably because he was so annoyed, it took him about fifteen feet to figure it out.

Nothing. He smelled *nothing*.

As if something that disguised scent had trailed by here many times, he smelled absolutely nothing. His mate was very smart. He touched his nose to hers to let her know he understood. She smiled at him, her tongue lolling happily between sharp white fangs.

"Wait," said the witch.

Charles stopped and looked at her.

"Isaac said that you won't be able to see or hear this fae you are chasing."

Charles gave Isaac a dark look. He'd told Isaac what they were hunting when he'd called him for help tonight. That information had not been for general distribution, and the Alpha wolf had known it.

"Peace," the witch said. "Isaac only told me because I was putting myself at risk in coming here, and he knows that I do not talk. This fae has been eating the essences of the people who died here, and that Isaac did not need to tell me. I talked to Caitlin about the nature of the magic they were using. So. I can give you some of that power and it will recognize the fae—sympathetic magic, wolf, like to like. There is enough to give it to only one of you."

Charles flattened his ears at Isaac when that wolf would have stepped up. If there was a risk, it was for Charles to take—of them all he was the one with the best chance of taking on the enemy.

He trotted over to the witch and waited for a lot of smoke and dramatic gestures and dancing. Instead she simply bent until her face was level with his and blew on him.

He coughed and then choked and gagged at the smell. It hurt, too. Like getting stung by a thousand bees at once or leaping from a car onto asphalt that shredded the skin off of him—both of which he'd done before. But that wasn't the worst of it. It felt like used motor oil had been poured over his body and clung there, smelly and greasy.

Brother Wolf growled and hung his head low, his ears pinned. Isaac whined and took a step forward, as if he might try to get between Charles and the witch. The ghosts inside of him began howling and laughing. Then Anna brushed up against Charles, silencing the voices inside with a radiant peace, the gift of the Omega, that let him regain control.

Only then did the witch move. She stood up and dusted her hands briskly. "My apologies. I didn't know that it would affect you so adversely. It will stay on you until dawn dispels it—and likely it will only be enough for a quick warning, so pay attention."

Calmer now, if not more comfortable, Charles nodded his thanks it was not her fault that it hurt, or that it made him long to go jump in the ocean to clean the oily filth of it off his fur. Or that she gave him orders, because Isaac hadn't taught her any better. The spell, if it worked as she said it would, allowed them a chance if they ran into the fae. For that, he could forgive her a great deal.

Hally the witch stood before him unafraid—and so fragile in her humanity.

She could not help being a witch any more than he could help being a werewolf. Both of them born to their *otherness*. Isaac was right that most white witches died while still very young, unable to defend themselves from their blood-magic-using kin. She had, within the limits of what she was, been very helpful—and he would remember it.

THE WOLVES AND the fae left the others behind to the dubious safety of the little clearing, and the guardianship of Malcolm and the witch.

Charles let the other wolves take the lead, as his nose was not at its best under the burden of the spell the witch had used. They traveled slowly because it was more difficult to follow no scent than it was to trail any given odor.

Isaac picked up on what they were doing after a few hundred feet and his nose was better than Anna's, but Anna caught him once when he'd taken a false trail. Eventually their noses led them to a door rough-set in cement that seemed to be attached to the side of the hill. Charles ran uphill to the top of the cement where it was capped by a crude roof, about two feet by three feet. A possible entrance or exit if they needed it, he thought, but better if they went through the door.

The door, when he ran back down to study it, looked as if it had been purchased used and rehung on new hinges. It was locked with a steel bolt lock latch. Steel wasn't as damaging to fae, he'd been told, as iron, but it would still resist any magic Beauclaire could bring to bear.

The fae had evidently had the same thought. He stood up from where he'd been scrounging in the bushes with a big hunk of stone in one hand. He muttered a few words until the stone glowed mud green and then chucked it at the door. It hit with a bang more reminiscent of a grenade than a rock and shattered into dust, leaving a good-sized dent in the door. Neither the lock nor the latch survived the encounter. The doorknob was aluminum and didn't seem to give Beauclaire any trouble opening it.

Inside it was pitch-black, but even so Charles could tell that it was far deeper than the two-foot-by-three-foot roof would have indicated. Someone had burrowed into the side of the hill. All of this he sensed from the way the chamber echoed, not from anything he could see. Even a wolf needed some light to see by.

The air smelled fresh, so there was either another entrance or some sort of ventilation. Charles couldn't smell anything dangerous, but, under the circumstances, he wasn't willing to trust his nose alone to warn him of danger.

The fae lord solved the light problem by throwing a ball of glowing magic through the doorway and into the darkness within. It stopped before it hit the dirt floor, hovering about three feet off the ground six or eight feet ahead of them, lighting a space that looked as if it had begun life as the basement of a large building—maybe part of an old military building. A large number of the islands in Boston Harbor had had military installations at one time or another over the last four hundred years.

"Who's there?" whispered a slurred voice as they stood just past the entryway. It was such a soft voice, coming from an empty room— all of them froze in place.

"Help me, please." Her voice was so quiet a human would never have heard her. The effect on Beauclaire was electric.

"Lizzie!" he thundered, poised to run, head cocked trying to figure out where her voice came from. The room didn't have any doors, was barren of everything except a scattering of debris. It obviously did not hold Lizzie Beauclaire.

"Papa?" Her voice didn't get stronger; it sounded querulous and hopeless.

Isaac had been cautiously exploring the dark edges of the room, and he made a soft grunt to attract their attention. Behind a pile of rotted timbers, pipes, and broken granite blocks, what Charles had thought was just a dark shadow or more debris turned out to be a narrow cement stairway with holes and rusted metal fittings where there would once have been a handrail. One side, the side with the rusty fittings, ran along the wall of the room; the other was open.

Beauclaire, his light leading the way, scrambled down the stairs and left the rest to follow. Not the smartest idea in the world, thought Charles—but he understood. If it had been someone who belonged to him below, he'd have lost no time in getting to her, either.

The fae's ball of light revealed a room nearly half as big as the one above with a doorway on the far wall. The door was long gone and one of the uprights of the doorframe had tipped over and lay on the floor. Beauclaire stopped momentarily at the foot of the stairs: Lizzie had quit making noise. When he started forward again, his initial rush had slowed, and he moved cautiously, aiming for the open doorway because the subbasement was obviously empty.

Only it wasn't.

Charles paused, still six or eight steps from the bottom of the stairs. There was a scattering of fine gold sparks, like a constellation in miniature. "Pay attention," the witch had said.

He might not have, might not have noticed them if they hadn't moved. But once he did, they did a pretty good job of telling Charles a little something about the fae they were stalking.

The horned lord, if that was what it was, was big. The ceiling of the subbasement was nine, maybe ten feet high, and the little sparks started right at the top and took up a fair chunk of the corner of the room it stood in. He didn't get any details, but he knew it was there.

Charles wished he'd thought to ask Beauclaire what the horned lord looked like in its original shape. Even knowing whether it stood on two legs or four would have been useful. As it was, he was hoping for two—a four-legged creature that was big enough to brush the ceiling would be nearly elephant-sized.

Anna had stopped when he did, her stillness alert and watchful. Charles turned his head and nipped her shoulder lightly. When she looked at him he directed her toward Beauclaire, who was already halfway across the room.

The fae should have backup—and Anna didn't have a whole lot of experience in combat. Fighting something that she couldn't see wasn't the best way for her to gain more.

She gave him a puzzled look and then trotted off after the fae, while Charles continued more slowly down the last few stairs behind her.

Isaac, aware that something was going on, stopped at the bottom and waited for Anna, then Charles, to go past him.

Charles bided his time, watching the hidden fae, trying to use the sparks to infer what it was doing. When Anna and Beauclaire passed it, it moved. Charles gathered himself, but the hidden creature stopped before it got close to Anna—the top part of it moving with a dizzy swirl of sparks.

He imagined that it had finally noticed the pair of werewolves, he and Isaac, focused on where it stood, though it should be invisible and had turned its head to watch them.

After a moment, the top part of the creature bent down and shook itself at him like an irritated moose—it was definitely paying attention to Isaac and him. Rather than jump from above and find himself impaled, Charles crept cautiously down the stairs until he stood just in front of Isaac, letting the other wolf see from his body language just where the enemy stood.

Isaac sank down into a crouch and took a couple of gliding leaps away, separating so that they could attack from different directions and also would be two targets instead of one.

There was an abrupt crash from the doorway that Anna and Beauclaire had disappeared into, and then came the broken sound of a woman sobbing. The mostly invisible fae moved again, swinging its head toward the noise, Charles thought. Then Anna appeared in the opening, and the fae rushed her.

But it wasn't as fast as Charles. He aimed low, relative to the size of the creature he was attacking, about three feet up. From the way it moved he was pretty sure it was bipedal—and that meant tendons. He hit something that felt like the front of a moose's hock and changed his bite mid-attack, letting his momentum pull him around so that his fangs cut through the joint horizontally as his body swung around until he was behind the creature. Then he set his jaw like a bulldog and hung on, digging into bone while he tore at the horned lord with his claws, reaching upward to see if he could find an important part to damage.

The fae creature howled, a wild, piercing whistling sound that was an odd combination of elk bugle and stallion scream, and when it did, air moved through the subbasement like a sea-fed storm hitting shore. Something that felt like a club hit him in the shoulder, and then Isaac leapt into the fray, striking higher than Charles had, perhaps hoping to knock it over. Beneath Charles, the fae creature swayed, but it didn't go down as Isaac found something to set his fangs into. His head rocked in a motion that told Charles he'd scored a chunk of muscle rather than bone. He was tearing it while he held on with front claws and raked with his hind legs like a cat.

Charles's back legs were on the ground and he used them to shift his weight, preparing to find something more fragile than the thick bone he had, no matter that it gave him a good solid hold. It was too thick to break with his jaws and he needed to incapacitate it so it couldn't get to Anna.

The creature screamed again and ripped Isaac free, tossing him all the way across the room and into the cement wall. Watching how it handled Isaac told Charles that the horned lord had hands of some sort—and was seriously strong, stronger than a werewolf.

Free of distraction, the creature turned its attention back to Charles. It pounded twice more at him, but awkwardly, as if it couldn't quite get to him. Then it lifted the leg Charles had grabbed and something hit him in the shoulder again, a fair hit that loosened his grip. Before he could regain his hold or drop it, the horned lord kicked his hock against the back wall.

Charles dropped to the floor. For a moment he was helpless, the wind knocked out of him, but before the creature could do anything about it, a black dynamo dove over Charles like a whirlwind.

Anna didn't bother trying anything fancy. She just ran, back and forth and in dizzying circles. When she hit something she sliced at it, but kept going. Distracting it.

Charles staggered to his feet and launched himself at the creature again. This time, dizzy from hitting the wall and then the floor, he had no idea what he hit—all he knew, all Brother Wolf knew, was that they had to protect their mate. But luck favored him and he got a clean hit. It was flesh and bone beneath his fangs and he sank his claws in deep.

He didn't know when Beauclaire joined the fight. Just suddenly he was there, his face icy and more beautiful and inhuman than Charles remembered it. He was taller, too, and thinner, and he fought with a knife in one hand and magic in the other. He was quick and tough, fighting blind, but he scored again and again with the knife—and when he used his magic, Charles couldn't tell what Beauclaire did, but the horned lord felt it and shuddered underneath his fangs.

Charles was pretty sure that it was the magic that turned the tide. As soon as Beauclaire attacked him with it, the horned lord quit fighting to win and started fighting to get away.

The fae beast that Charles clung to screamed, this time a raw, drum-deep sound that hurt his ears, and threw itself on the floor, rolling as if it were on fire, first one way, then the other. Charles hung on for two rolls, but fell off on the third. Beauclaire, having neither fang nor claw, lay motionless on the ground after the first roll.

Free of his attackers, the creature made for the stairs—and Charles got a good look at what they'd been fighting, because whatever it was that kept it invisible had quit working. Its antlers were huge. He thought at first that they were shaped like a caribou's, but it must have been a trick of shadows because they started . . . glowing faintly with an icy white light, and they were the horns of a deer—a huge ancient deer.

It had a silvery coat that whitened as it staggered upward—and Charles realized he'd been mistaken earlier because it had four legs, long and delicate looking. Black blood disappeared even as he watched, absorbed by the silvery coat of a great white stag taller by a hand or more than any moose he'd ever seen.

Brother Wolf wanted to chase it down and kill it because they wouldn't be safe until it was dead. Charles agreed, but decided that since one of his shoulders was out of joint or broken, having one were-wolf go after a creature that was healing as it retreated faster than a werewolf could was stupid. Especially when it had nearly defeated three werewolves and a tough fae already. He wondered if the horned lord, a half-blood, was really that tough, or if his borrowed magic made him that way. Either way, Charles wasn't going after him, no matter what Brother Wolf wanted.

He wasn't going to leave his Anna defenseless.

Brother Wolf roared his frustrated rage and took what satisfaction he could when the stag leapt up the last five or six stairs, staggering at the top when its left rear leg, still healing, didn't support its weight.

When it was out of sight, Charles turned to survey the fallen. Isaac was still on the ground, but he'd rolled to a sphinxlike pose and blinked a little stupidly at Charles. If he wasn't dead, he'd heal soon. Beauclaire was on one hand and his knees, trying to regain his feet with limited success—but everything seemed to be moving all right except for an obviously broken wrist. Anna . . . Anna was crouched next to Lizzie Beauclaire and crooning to her, or as close to a croon as a wolf could get.

The girl . . . He'd seen photos of her on her wall and she'd been beautiful. Now scabby wounds decorated her forehead and cheeks, all of the skin he could see. She was wearing her father's shirt, but was obviously naked underneath it, and her formerly flawless skin was cov-ered with sigils and bruises—just as Jacob's body had been. On a living, breathing person it was even worse, because she was also covered with a miasma of black magic that he could see—like a fog of invisibly small fleas. Lizzie blinked at him with drugged eyes and moved backward, stopping abruptly with a little gasp because something hurt.

They'd broken her knee. Shattered it, if he was any judge—and he was. It was deliberate—and he wondered if she, a trained athlete, had been a little tougher than they expected. Her feet were bruised and bloody, as though she had broken free and gone running through the rocky terrain barefoot. She'd have had no chance of really escaping, not unless she could call upon the merfolk—and he doubted that. They tended to be standoffish or aggressive, even with their own kind.

Lizzie was clearly in no shape to walk. She'd have to be carried out, and, looking at the others, Charles knew he would have to do it. With a broken wrist, her father wasn't going to be able to, and Anna was still too new of a werewolf to change back and forth this quickly. Isaac was dazed and confused, and pretty new as well. He'd been Changed about the same time as Anna, as Charles recalled, only a few years ago. So Charles was just going to have to manage one more shift to human right this minute.

It hurt. He'd forgotten how badly it hurt to change when something was wrong. He was old and changing would help heal any injury that wasn't caused by silver—but the change healed the same way salt water kept wounds from getting infected: accompanied by a lot of pain.

Charles didn't cry out. He didn't howl and scare the poor little dancer who had wrapped herself around Anna as if the werewolf were a stuffed puppy. Sweat poured off his body even before he should have been human enough to sweat. And then he became human, kneeling in the dust-covered cement, wearing a red T-shirt soaked with sweat and his blue jeans, which—he noted with a hint of amusement—were old-style button fly.

It took Charles a couple of tries to get to his feet, and even then, his hands were still shaking. But the shoulder must have only been dislocated, because that injury the change had healed completely, other than a lingering soreness.

When he and Anna got back to their condo, he was going to have to sleep for a week. He looked around to do triage, with the idea of getting everyone up the stairs and on their way to the boat before the horned lord came back to finish them.

Charles left Lizzie Beauclaire with Anna for a few minutes more and walked over to crouch in front of Isaac.

"Hey," he said. "Are you with us?"

The wolf just panted, not focusing.

"I'm going to touch you," Charles told him in a tone that brooked no opposition: dominant wolf to less dominant wolf. "To see if there's anything that needs mending. You won't like it—but you will let me do it. Growls are acceptable. Biting is not."

After a quick exam, during which Isaac growled a lot, Charles was pretty certain that, though there had probably been other damage initially, the Boston Alpha had healed most of it. What was left were a lot of sore spots and a humdinger of a concussion that would work itself out in a few hours with adequate food. Charles hoped that Malcolm had more in his bait boxes than squid, chum, and worms—though protein was protein.

Charles stood up and looked around again.

Beauclaire had managed to get to his feet and walk unsteadily to his daughter. He sat down on the ground a foot or so from her and reached out to touch her hair with a light hand. She flinched and he started to sing to her in Welsh.

Ar lan y môr mae lilis gwynion
Ar lan y môr mae 'nghariad inne

He had a good voice. Not spectacular, as Charles would have expected from a fae of rank and power (and the fae who'd fought beside Charles this night obviously had power), but good pitch and sweet-toned, though that was somewhat affected by the unshed tears in his voice. Another song might have suited Beauclaire's range better, and this particular song wasn't among Charles's favorites. He preferred those that had a story, powerful imagery, or at least better poetry.

Charles took a step forward and, though Beauclaire didn't look up or quit singing, Charles felt the fae's attention center on him. It felt like the attention of a rattlesnake just before it strikes.

" 'Beside the Sea,' indeed," Charles said softly, watching Beauclaire's body language.

The fae lord quit singing and looked up. Charles saw that he'd read him aright. Beauclaire was ready to defend his daughter against anyone who got too close. Like Isaac, he'd taken quite a beating on the unforgiving stone, and he looked a little dazed—something Charles hadn't noticed in his first assessment. Being wounded made the fae all the more dangerous. The long knife had reappeared in his good hand and it looked very sharp.

"Ar lan y môr," sang Charles, and watched Beauclaire stand down just a little, so he sang a few more lines for him. "All right. Allies, remember? We need to get everyone on the boat. Maybe have Isaac's witch do something for your daughter so the black magic doesn't eat her—I don't know if you can see it, but I can. We need to fix your wrist."

Beauclaire shut his eyes and banished his knife. Magic, Charles thought, or quick hands. The fae nodded, then winced and grimaced. "Right." His speaking voice was less steady than his singing voice had been. "We need to get her to safety in case the horned lord comes back. I can't carry her."

"I can, if you let me," offered Charles. If necessary, he'd pull the same sort of dominance on Beauclaire that he had on Isaac. But Beauclaire wasn't a wolf. It might work for a second, but it might also get Charles knifed in the back when he wasn't paying attention to Beauclaire. Better to get real cooperation.

"Her knee," Beauclaire said.

"I know. I see it. It's going to hurt no matter how we do this. But this island isn't that big. It shouldn't take us long."

Beauclaire looked up and gave him a half smile. "First we have to stand up and go up the stairs."

"Yes," agreed Charles.

"It could be waiting for us up there."

Charles started to agree, but Brother Wolf spoke up. The old wolf might not know horned lords, but he knew prey, and Charles trusted his judgment. "The white stag is long gone."

Beauclaire froze. "You saw it? As a white stag?"

Charles nodded. "When we fought it, it wasn't in that form." He'd had time to think about it. Charles knew what he'd touched and it had been vaguely human shaped with legs like the hind legs of a moose. "But it ran up the stairs and turned into a stag—just as its invisibility ran out."

"It didn't run out," Beauclaire said. "He dropped the glamour on purpose. Why didn't you follow it?"

"I wasn't in any shape to take it on by myself," said Charles, gesturing around to the fallen. "Even with allies, we might not have been able to defeat it had it not decided to run. And I wasn't going to leave you injured and vulnerable."

Anna snorted. She knew him, knew who he wouldn't leave vulnerable.

Beauclaire bowed his head and smiled. "I should have known that Bran's son would be too hardheaded to be led by his nose by any magic—even by the white stag. Had you chased it, you would have continued, never stopping, never catching up until your legs were but bloody stumps or you died."

Charles looked at him. "Thanks for the warning."

Beauclaire laughed. "Bran's son, no one can guard against the white stag—and knowing what he is and hunting him anyway is very dangerous. Even more dangerous than hunting in ignorance. If the white stag walked past me two weeks ago, I would not have been compelled to go after him. But if I had seen him tonight, after hunting him since he stole my daughter away—I would have followed him, power that I am, until one of us was dead."

"I thought fae were immortal," said Charles. "At least those who can refer to themselves as 'power that I am.'"

Beauclaire started to say something, but broke off as Charles held up a hand.

There was a scuffing sound above them. Someone was upstairs.

"Isaac?" It was Malcolm.

"We're down here," called Charles, relaxing, though Brother Wolf was upset with them. They were supposed to stay safe where he had left them.

Malcolm, the witch, and the FBI came charging to the rescue, bringing more noise and chaos with them than four people should have been able to manage. Goldstein and Leslie Fisher took over, and Charles, tired, aching in every bone of his body, let them.

Leslie stripped out of her knee-length waterproof jacket and helped Beauclaire wrap it around his daughter. The witch dug through her satchel and muttered unpleasant things. Finally she found a Baggie of salt, made them take the coat and Beauclaire's shirt back off the girl, and dusted Lizzie from head to toe in salt.

Brutal but effective. The black magic dissipated—but the salt burned in her open wounds. She cried, but seemed to be too deeply under the influence of whatever her kidnappers had fed her to make too much noise. Charles smelled ketamine and something else.

"We could have thrown her in the ocean and fished her back out," Hally told them. "But the cold wouldn't have done her any good. Better leave the salt on. A half hour should be long enough, but longer won't hurt. It'll also stave off infection."

They bundled Lizzie back up and Charles picked her up, to her evident distress, even with whatever drugs they'd given her in her system. She hadn't been in their hands long—a little more than a full day—but she'd been tortured and who knew what else. Males were not anything she wanted to deal with.

But Anna couldn't change back, and Leslie, though in good shape, was human, and not capable of carrying Lizzie all the way back to the boat.

Charles tried singing to her, the same song her father had been singing. Beauclaire—and Malcolm—joined in, and the music seemed to help.

Goldstein had used a stick and a strip off the bottom of his cotton dress shirt to splint Beauclaire's wrist. And when they started up the stairs, he wedged a shoulder under the fae's arm and helped steady him, having evidently decided Beauclaire would be his personal responsibility. Beauclaire shot Charles the ghost of an amused look, and let himself be helped—possibly a little more than he really needed.

Isaac was obviously in pain, panting with stress, but he got to his feet and followed, Malcolm walking steadily beside him. Charles kept a close eye on them for a while—wolves could be a little unpredictable when a more dominant wolf was injured. It was a good time to eliminate the dominant and take his place. It didn't usually happen when an even more dominant wolf like Charles was around to keep the peace and protect the pack, but better to be safe. Happily, Malcolm seemed honestly concerned about his Alpha.

Anna ranged, sometimes walking beside Charles, but mostly trotting in a wide circle around them, looking for danger. Leslie took rear guard, her gun out and ready to shoot. Hally walked in front of them, leading the way as she mostly ignored them all.

They staggered and stumbled, wounded but triumphant, singing the old Welsh folk song "Ar Lan y Môr." And if there was something odd about returning from battle singing about lilies, rosemary, rocks, and—for some reason he'd never fathomed—eggs, of all things, by the sea, well, then the three of them made it sound pretty good and only he and Beauclaire knew Welsh.

CHAPTER

10

On the boat, Charles stretched out his legs and tried to ignore the lingering ache of that last change. Anna had tried sitting several different places, but the human seats were too narrow and the wrong shape. The ledges she'd used on the way over were slick, and instead of using her claws to dig into the fiberglass, she slid around with the motion of the sea. Finally she'd heaved a huge sigh and curled up by his feet on the deck.

Beauclaire had forbidden any questioning of his daughter until she'd seen a doctor. Goldstein and Isaac had elected to stay behind until the various agencies summoned arrived on the island. Malcolm told them that he'd decided Beauclaire and the wolves might need rescuing when he heard a boat leaving the island. Charles felt safe enough making the assumption that the horned lord they'd fought had left in that boat. Which would mean that very little danger remained—but it was good that Isaac had stayed anyway, just to make sure everything was okay.

Charles rather suspected that Isaac had decided to put off the boat trip until he felt better, though he'd felt good enough to change back to human. Hally was staying with Isaac to make sure that the residual magic didn't get a grip on any of the forensic people who were going to go over the island with a fine-tooth comb.

So the boat was a lot emptier on the way back than it had been on the way over.

Leslie left Beauclaire in the back half of the boat to sit beside Charles.

"She's in pretty rough shape," she said, sitting precisely on the edge of the seat. "There will be an ambulance waiting for us at the *Daciana*'s regular berth."

The FBI agent looked a little less than professional, wrapped in a blanket from the boat, her hair windblown. Like Charles and Anna, she'd been up for a little more than twenty-four hours. Lack of sleep and lack of the subtle makeup that had worn off sometime while running around the island added years to her face.

It intrigued Charles that she chose to sit next to him with so many seats available.

"You aren't afraid of me?" he asked.

Leslie closed her eyes. "Too tired to be afraid of anything. Besides, if you could see my husband, you'd understand that it takes a lot to scare me."

That sparked his curiosity. "How is that?"

"Linebacker for the LSU Tigers for three years in college," she said without opening her eyes. "Hurt his shoulder his senior year or he'd have gone pro. He's six-five and two hundred forty-two pounds. None of it is fat, not even now. He teaches second grade." She looked at him. "What are you smiling about?"

Charles opened his eyes wide. "Nothing, ma'am."

She smiled a little. "Jude says he loves the kids better than he ever did football. But he coaches the local high school team anyway."

"You didn't come over here to tell me about your husband," he said.

"No." Leslie looked at him and then away. "How old are you?"

"Older than I look," Charles said. "A lot older."

She nodded. "I've asked around about you. We have some were-wolves who talk to the FBI. They tell me that you're a detective for all the wolves. You come in and solve crimes."

He wondered if that was all they'd told her—and thought it probably was. He didn't respond because he didn't know if agreeing with her was more of a lie than disagreeing with her would be.

"And you know a lot about this world that we're just learning about. We got Lizzie out of their hands because you knew to bring in witches—and because that witch was scared enough of you to behave herself."

That was fair enough. He waited for her to get to the point.

"Lizzie says that there were three of them," Leslie told him. "Two young men and an old man. One of the young men called the old guy 'uncle' before he was shut up. The old man made the cuts on her skin. Both of the young men raped her first, 'while she was still pretty.' They told her the old man preferred women after they were broken."

He'd hoped that they had gotten to her soon enough to spare her that, but he'd been pretty sure they hadn't.

"I thought Beauclaire had refused to have her questioned," Charles said. He'd heard Lizzie talking, but Leslie didn't need to know just how good his hearing was.

"I didn't ask her a question. She just talked. Told me she wants them caught and caged so they can't do anything to anyone else. Tough woman. She fell asleep mid-word—and I think her father had something to do with that. Can the fae send people to sleep?"

"I am not an expert in fae magic," Charles said carefully.

She turned her head and nodded. "You are very good at skirting the truth." Leslie sighed. "You are an experienced detective and you met the enemy. What are your impressions?"

"I've only met the one," Charles said. But her request for information was fair—and he wanted the perpetrators caught. "The fae is definitely the junior member of the group, even though he's probably the only one with magic—and he's the reason they can take on fae and werewolves."

"What makes you think so?"

"He's not a hunter," Charles told her. "He's a stag—he's not a predator, no matter how tough or deadly he is." Herne the Hunter notwithstanding, Brother Wolf knew that the fae they'd fought with was prey. Maybe Herne was more huntsman and less deer, but this one . . . This one ran from his foes. He was not a hunter; he was a tool of the real hunters.

"You think he's a victim?"

Charles snorted. "No. He's no angel—but he'd never go out hunting victims. He might rape and kill someone who came too close to him—but he wouldn't hunt. That's predatory behavior. Doesn't mean he's not dangerous. Most years, moose kill more people in Canada than grizzlies do. Moose, though, generally don't trail people with the intention of killing them like a grizzly will."

"All right," Leslie said. "We have a moose, not a bear. What else?"

He reflected on the fight. The horned lord fought instinctively instead of strategically, seemingly incapable of focusing on more than one attacker at a time. "That fae isn't smart. If he has a day job—and I'd guess that he does—" Charles tried to verbalize the instincts that allowed a dominant wolf to control his pack. "If you are going to keep someone that dangerous under control, you don't let him start thinking that he's too valuable. You don't support him just because he's useful in your hunt. He has to go support himself."

"Okay."

Leslie sounded doubtful and Charles shrugged. "It might be different if our family of killers didn't come from money—then they'd find some other way to make sure he knew he was subordinate."

"They come from money?"

"This much traveling, this many years—if you were looking for a group of poor people, you'd have found them. Money makes a lot of things easier. Murder is just one of them. And they had to have money to be able to afford Sally Reilly."

"Fair enough. Our profilers figured that the Big Game Hunter was well-to-do about fifteen years ago. You were going to speculate about a job."

"Right. He's not bright, and because of that his *other* nature is going to be difficult to conceal."

"'Other' as in fae?"

Charles nodded. "Yes. So he'll be a box boy at a grocery store or a stocking clerk. Maybe a janitor or handyman. He'd be very strong. Dockworker, if you still have them here."

"Would people remember him?"

"Is he scary, do you mean? Like your husband?" Charles shook his head, following Brother Wolf's instincts. "I don't think so. I think people are going to feel sorry for him. Otherwise he'd be in jail. Scared people generally run or attack. If someone ever attacked this one, he'd kill them. If he went around killing people in the open like that, he'd be in jail or dead."

"All right," Leslie said. "We'll see what we can do with that. Run it by our profilers and see if they agree."

THE CONDO WASN'T home, but it felt welcoming all the same. Charles pulled some steaks out of the fridge and cut them up in bite-sized chunks. One of them he set down on the floor for Anna and the other he ate standing up. His human teeth weren't really sharp enough for the raw meat, but he persevered and was rewarded as the aches and pains gradually settled down as the energy from the food entered his system.

He watched his mate eat with a satisfaction that had never faded since he'd met her, half-starved and wild-eyed. Brother Wolf never forgot how thin she had been, and he would get pushy if he thought Anna wasn't eating enough.

When she was finished eating, she changed back to human.

It always made Charles restless when she changed, seeing her hurting and knowing that there was nothing he could do to help. He paced back and forth a couple of times, then sat down and turned on the TV, idly flipping through channels until Anna, human again, took the controller out of his hand and turned the TV off.

"Bed," she said. "Or you're going to be married to a zombie."

He'd intended to talk with her, he remembered, to tell her about his ghosts. But neither of them was in shape for talk.

Charles looked at her and said in his most serious voice, "I don't think werewolves can become zombies."

"Trust me," she said in a passable zombie voice. "Another ten minutes and I will eat your brains."

He pulled her down onto his lap. "I think I'll chance it."

She sighed as if annoyed, though his nose told him she liked being in his embrace. "So, *can* you do this without an audience? Is that what's been bothering you these past few months? All I needed to do was invite the pack into our bedroom? You should have told me."

He laughed. *She* made him laugh. "I don't know. Let's find out."

A RATHER LONG while later, Anna stretched and then flopped comfortably next to him. "Urr, brains," she said.

"Go to sleep," Charles growled, pulling her closer.

"I warned you," she said. "You didn't let me sleep." She yawned widely and said regretfully, "And now I have no choice but to eat your brains."

"Obviously," he said. "You need more exercise before you go to sleep." He rolled onto his back. "I suppose I'll just have to be a good mate and help you with that."

She crawled on top of him, naked and warm and soft, smelling like a miracle that had saved him from a lifetime of aloneness.

"I wouldn't want you to strain anything," Anna told him. "Why don't you just lie back and think of England."

His mouth caught the nearest of her body parts—the soft inside of her elbow—and gave it a light nip. "England is the furthest thing from my mind."

She settled down on top of him, taking him inside her, and he quit talking altogether. Her eyes were blue, her wolf's eyes, when she came for him for the second time that night.

Flushed and joyous, Anna bent down and nipped his ear. "No audience necessary, I see."

"Move," Charles told her.

She laughed again, her eyes still moonlit azure—but she moved.

THEY SLEPT IN.

Charles woke up first and watched her face in the late-morning light. It was peaceful and pleased Brother Wolf even though the moon was waxing nearly full and the urge to hunt always ran strong in his bones at that time. Contentment was still something new for Charles, something he'd never experienced in all his long life before he'd met Anna.

"I've been thinking about the killers," Anna said without opening her eyes. "Three people is a pack."

Charles waited for her to continue.

She sat up with a snap. In a voice filled with hushed excitement she said, "The fae—he's the soldier, the bottom of the pecking order. Doing as he's told, when he's told to do it. The old guy, he's the one who started this. He's the Alpha."

"Mmm," Charles said, when it appeared she needed his agreement. The hunting moon might not be stirring Brother Wolf, as long as he had Anna in his bed, but apparently Anna was feeling it pretty strongly.

"Who is the second young one?" she asked. "Do you think he's the obedient second? Loyal, dedicated? Or is he the Alpha in training, waiting until the old man is too old to control the pack so he can kill him and take over?"

"Neither of us is a trained profiler," he felt obliged to point out.

She bounced in the bed, her brown eyes glittering with excitement. "Now that Lizzie is rescued, all we have to do is solve the rest."

"As they have been trying to do for longer than you've been alive," he told her dryly.

"Yes," she said, "but they didn't have you and me on the case."

They had a TV now, and satellite—mostly so Anna could watch her detective shows. She was enjoying this. Charles . . . He supposed he was enjoying it, too. More now that the innocents were safe, in the hospital or the morgue.

"Motive," she said in the same voice he imagined Archimedes might have said, "Eureka!" in his bath all those years ago.

"Doesn't work the same way in serial-killer cases as it does in most murders," he said. "Serial killers are addicted to the hunt and they aren't capable of stopping, most of them. Their lives are controlled by the kill."

"He's tagging his victims," Anna said. "What does that say?"

"These are less than human," said Charles, repeating what they both knew. "Animals I have killed."

"Right. Animals that he has killed. He's claiming the kill with that tag." She frowned. "Aren't serial killers supposed to try to step into the investigation? To watch people struggle and fail to solve the case—or to control the case better?"

"I've heard that," Charles agreed. "For some kinds of killers."

She grinned at him.

"All of which the FBI knows better than we do," he said. "We've probably helped the case as much as we can until someone else is taken."

Anna sobered. "It's too bad we weren't able to hurt the horned lord worse than we did. He was mostly healed by the time he hit the top of the stairs—did you notice? The police don't have a chance against him."

"We'll stay here for a while. Leslie and Goldstein seemed to be sensible people. They'll call us in if they need us."

She tilted her head and asked, "What does Brother Wolf say about all of this?"

"That these hunters didn't get what they want; we stole their prey. They're going to be hungry and even more dangerous. On the other hand, I, Charles, say that we ought to eat something, as it is long past morning and we missed breakfast and are in danger of missing lunch— and Brother Wolf is pleased to concur."

"You are always trying to feed me," she accused him without heat as she got out of bed.

"No, that's Brother Wolf." Charles smiled. "I'll cook."

CHARLES HAD MEANT to talk to her about his ghosts over breakfast, because he'd been tired last night, and then he'd been distracted. But something she had said nagged at him.

"Charles?" Anna asked patiently.

"Sorry," he told her. "Thinking."

"Do you want some more bacon, or should I put it in the fridge for later?"

There were four pieces left. He took two and ate them. Then he took the other two and held them up to her mouth. "You need more protein."

She rolled her eyes, but ate them anyway.

"I need to look something up on the Internet," he said. "Can you get the dishes?"

"You cooked; I'll clean," she said.

He took his laptop into the spare bedroom where there was a small writing desk. It was slower than his desktop at home and the screen was too small to let him pull up as many images at a time as he liked to—and the Internet connection here was not too fast, either. He growled in frustration as his fingers flew over the keyboard, as if by moving faster he could coax the machine to greater effort.

He started out with the legitimate things he had access to—Goldstein had sent him a file on the case, as he had promised—and then dug deeper. These killers, these UNSUBS, they had money—had power. Anna was right: they would not be able to stay out of the investigation.

At some point Anna brought him a pizza—though he hadn't noticed her ordering it. A little later she came in to tap him on the shoulder.

"You, Isaac, and I have been invited to a celebration for Lizzie's safe return," she told him.

"I'm waiting for two phone calls," Charles said.

"This would be an excellent time for some PR with the Boston Police Department—which is important for the Olde Towne Pack. Isaac told me they've had some issues this year."

He rolled his seat back from the desk and looked at his mate. She looked a little antsy and her brown eyes glowed slightly, highlighted with her wolf's light blue.

It was dark outside, which meant she'd been cooped up in here for hours with nothing to do but watch TV. And it was close to the full moon. It wasn't fair to make her sit around any longer.

"This may be a wild-goose chase, but I'm on to something and I'd like to finish it up," he told her. "Would you agree to letting Isaac be your escort?" Brother Wolf didn't like it, but Charles didn't want to smother her. He might be finished in five minutes—or twelve hours. And Isaac was a good fighter; Charles had seen it last night. He'd been outmatched in sheer size and strength and hampered by not being able to see their opponent, but he'd fought smart.

"I don't need a bodyguard," said Anna, not fooled for a moment by Charles calling Isaac an escort, but Charles hadn't expected to get away with it. "We're going somewhere that will be filled with cops and FBI agents and werewolves. It should be pretty safe. And isn't an Alpha above being a bodyguard?"

"Humor me," said Charles.

She sighed heavily—then ruined it with a sly grin. "I told Isaac to come pick me up—and that you were going to make him responsible for my health and well-being."

"If you knew what I was going to say, why did you come in here and bother me?" He growled with mock annoyance.

Anna laughed. "I'm going to go change."

"Let me know when you leave," he said, already caught up in his work again. Where had he been before she interrupted him?

When he next emerged, she was gone.

"HE LETS YOU out alone?" Isaac, without Charles to put him on edge, was more relaxed than Anna had thought, but also more pushy.

"I'm with you. Besides, werewolf here," she told him with a thumb to her chest. "Not exactly a frail princess in need of rescuing."

"That's not what I heard about you," Isaac said. "I asked about you.

Omega. I was informed by my second that we should be honored that you were visiting our city. We should bring you gifts and see if we can get you to abandon your pack and join ours. When I pointed out that that meant Charles would come, too—and displace me—I was told that the blessing of having an Omega in the pack would outweigh even putting up with Charles."

Anna laughed. "Old wolves. Think they know everything."

"And then he wonders why I don't ask him more questions," Isaac agreed. "So do it."

Anna looked at him just as a raindrop hit her nose. The clouds had been threatening and the air smelled wet, but that was the first drop. "Do what?"

"'That voodoo that you do,'" Isaac said. At her expression he turned to walk backward so she could get the full effect of his eye roll and comic exaggeration. "What? You don't know Adam Ant?"

"'A thrill a day keeps the chill away,'" she sang, then said dryly, "Not his best song. You want me to what? Zap you with my awesome cosmic super Omega powers?"

"That's what I said." Isaac turned so he was walking beside her once more. "Only my request sounded cool, and yours sounds like it belongs on Saturday morning cartoons."

"They are more of an anti-superpower," Anna explained as the first few drops of water became a more steady rainfall. "If I were in a comic book, *I'd* be the lone stupid girl in a team of awesome, powerfully charged males. Like Sue, Invisible Girl—who was invisible in so many ways—in the Fantastic Four. Which should have been called the Fantastic Three and the Cute and Clueless Girl Who Runs Around Getting into Trouble and Being Rescued."

Isaac grinned, his expression lighter, that edge that Alphas always carried with them softened. "Not even Jessica Alba could save Sue from being wimpy."

Anna sighed in a misery-shared way. "I *like* superhero movies. Still, it was better than *Catwoman*—and *Catwoman* had much better material to draw from."

"So are you going to whammy me?" Isaac asked again.

She waved and did something fluttery with her fingers in her best stage magician manner, though she'd already hit him while he was quoting from "That Voodoo." She contorted her face and made funny gobbling sounds, then said, in the perfectly serious voice she'd picked up from Charles, "Consider yourself whammied."

They strode along companionably for a block. "I don't feel whammied," he said.

"What do you feel?" she asked.

Isaac took three more steps before he stiffened and stopped. "I haven't been drunk since I was changed," he whispered. "What did you do to me?"

"You aren't drunk. Not impaired physically or mentally," Anna told him.

He bowed his head, working his hands; then he turned and started walking backward again, facing her. Anna followed, keeping a sharp eye out for things he might back into or over. She wondered if Isaac did this all the time—and, if so, how he avoided getting photos in the paper with captions like "Local Alpha Trips over Child" or "Wolf Versus Street Sign, Street Sign Wins."

"I'm myself again," he said, his face almost slack with wonder. "It's just me in here." He tapped his forehead. "One night before the full moon and I don't want to hunt or sink my teeth into anything." He blinked rapidly and turned back around again so she couldn't see his face anymore. After a moment he said, "It's like the wolf is gone." There was a hint of worry in his voice.

"No," Anna answered. "Just . . . at peace. You could start changing right now if you wanted to."

"Before God, it is no wonder my second was salivating at the thought of you," Isaac said. "Do you worry about being kidnapped?" His voice altered just a little. "I heard that Charles rescued you from an abusive situation." He glanced over at her, his eyes glowing light yellow. The other effect of being Omega was that dominant wolves tended to be overly protective of her.

She nodded her head. "Charles saved me. My first pack turned me and kept me under their thumb. One of their old ones was crazy and her mate thought I could keep her sane. When Charles got through dealing with them, he taught me how to rescue myself." Charles had helped her regain confidence in herself. But no matter how competent she was at protecting herself, Anna knew what ultimately kept her safe from wolf packs who wanted an Omega of their own. "If someone tries to kidnap me, Charles will hunt them down. Do you know very many wolves who would be willing to face that?"

"The Marrok's bogeyman?" asked Isaac with a snort. "No." He paused a moment. "Especially if they've ever seen him fight. Hally told me that he wouldn't be able to see that fae—just know when he was around. But Charles fought like he could, like he knew exactly where it was. And I've never seen anyone—not werewolf, not vampire, not anyone—move that fast."

"His gift," Anna agreed. His bane. Maybe if he hadn't been such a good fighter, his father would have sent someone else to maintain order among his packs. But that wasn't for public discussion. She needed to change subjects.

"So where are we going?" A diner would be perfect—just a little worn-down, with cracked Naugahyde seats and scuffed-up, bad-imitation wood-grain Formica tables, where coffee was served to every-one in white cups and all of the meals were cooked in unhealthy grease: a cop's hangout, the cliché of every cop film or novel.

"When Goldstein called me, I offered to host the party at The Irish Wolfhound," Isaac told her. "The pub owned by our pack. There's a big room for parties."

Anna couldn't help being a little disappointed. "I was hoping for a diner."

Isaac laughed. "The food's better at the Wolfhound, and we're less likely to have uninvited guests." Amusement died from his face, and the smile he gave Anna was tight and unhappy. "As I told you, there are members of our law enforcement community who dislike us and would love to provoke a fight under the cover of too much drink. This way it's just the people who are working on this case—and most of them are way too ecstatic about Lizzie's rescue to be fussy about how it was done."

"It seems like a lot of celebrating, when we didn't catch the killers," Anna said.

Isaac nodded. "It's like when I was in high school. My junior year our football team just had this . . . synergy. The year before, the year after, they were good. But that year, they not only had the players; they had the *team*. No one even scored against them until the last game of the season. The other team scored a field goal in the fourth quarter— and the stands erupted. You'd have thought they won the game instead of losing by thirty-odd points. What they *had* done was what no one else had managed to do."

"I see," Anna said.

Isaac's white teeth flashed. "We didn't win this one," he said. "But we didn't lose, either."

"You weren't on that football team, were you?" There had been something in his voice and the way he referred to his high school team as "they."

"Nope. I was the little geek the football team halfback liked to shove into gym lockers for fun when the team captain wasn't around to keep him in line. Sometimes, when I'm feeling particularly mean, I'd love to meet Jody Weaver again and have him try to shove me in a locker now."

Anna laughed . . . paused, because she didn't know football, but she had a father and brother who were football fanatics. "I know that name. Jody Weaver. He's a big deal, right?"

Isaac nodded. "Went on to get rich and famous—and he's still a bastard. Proving once and for all that life is not fair."

"Speaking of not fair," Anna said, "have you heard anything about Lizzie? I called Leslie earlier, but all she knew was that she was listed as stable and that they already had her in the operating room for her knee."

Isaac shook his head. "You know more than I do. I left a message on Beauclaire's phone and invited him over tonight. I suspect he won't be leaving the hospital."

"Were there any clues to be had on the island?" Anna already knew that the forensic people hadn't found much from her earlier conversation with Leslie. But there was a possibility that Isaac or his witch might have found something they hadn't talked to the authorities about.

Isaac shook his head. "No. It was like they knew the island would be searched by werewolves—the whole prison area had been doused with ammonia. They found a few personal effects, enough to determine that Jacob, Otten, and a couple of the other victims had been kept there."

"If they had known we were coming, they'd have moved Lizzie," Anna said.

Isaac nodded. "Right. I suppose it was in preparation for a worst-case scenario. They've been killing werewolves. They don't want *us* to figure out who they are."

Isaac's explanation made sense. He was probably right. And if he wasn't, they'd figure it out when the bastards were caught.

THE RAIN WAS pouring down when they reached the pub. Irish pubs in Boston, Anna had noticed, were sort of like pizza parlors in Chicago: there were a lot of them and most of them served pretty good food.

Just inside the door lurked a life-sized, wooden Irish wolfhound. It was, Anna judged, only a little smaller in height than Charles, but about a quarter as broad. Around his neck was a sign that read WEL-COME FRIEND.

Isaac waved one hand at the hostess and, with his other hand at the small of Anna's back, directed her to a rough-sawn wooden stair-case. At the top of the stairs, just past the restrooms, was a door marked PRIVATE PARTY.

Through the door was a big room with four trestle tables with chairs and benches mixed in, filled with people, most of whom Anna didn't know. Celtic music filtered in through speakers in the ceiling, and there were pitchers of beer and water on all the tables.

A waitress came in through a door in the back of the room. She put her fingers to her mouth and whistled. Anna had plugged her ears as soon as the girl's fingers touched her lips, and the piercing noise still hurt. She could pick out the werewolves, because they were the ones with grimaces on their faces. She recognized Malcolm, of course, but there were three others in the room, too.

Quiet descended.

"All right, gents and ladies all. There's beer and water on the table and we'll keep the pitchers full until nine p.m. If you want something different to drink, our Isaac says he'll cover it, too—" She broke off, interrupted by cheers. Isaac bowed, and nodded for the waitress to continue. "Again until nine, after that your food and drink comes out of your pocket. We'll be coming around for orders for food. Our specialty is bangers and mash, but we have a great stew tonight and the fish and chips are to die for. Enjoy!"

She retreated through the door at her back to another smattering of applause, and two young men and a middle-aged woman came in through the same door and started to take orders.

Anna looked around. There were maybe thirty people in the room—if seven were werewolves, that meant that there were twenty-three police officers. Which seemed like a lot until she laid eyes on Leslie. The FBI agent was sitting beside a giant of a man who looked as though he could do his share of shoving people into lockers. He made two or maybe even three of Leslie and, while she talked to a pair of plainclothes police officers, he kept a big hand on the back of her neck. This must be the football-playing husband Leslie had talked about.

If everyone had brought a date, the numbers made more sense. She caught sight of one of the two Cantrip agents, the one who was not Heuter. His name had started with a *P*. Patrick . . . Patrick Morris. He was talking to Goldstein. So it wasn't just police officers here. She decided to avoid him if possible, just in case he shared Heuter's views on werewolves.

Leslie looked up, saw Anna, and waved her over. In the two hours that followed, Anna found herself shuffled around from one table to another, answering questions about being a werewolf. In a quiet moment, she pointed out, rather grumpily, to Leslie that there were six other werewolves—Isaac and his five pack mates—in the room. So why was everyone asking her questions?

"All the wolves are answering questions," Leslie replied. "But you're easier to talk to—women aren't as threatening as men." She thought about it. "Most women, anyway—I know a few that would scare any person with a modicum of sense. But you're approachable. And you are going away soon. So if they offend you, they don't have to live with the consequences."

So Anna explained, over and over, that werewolves could control themselves when they ran as wolves—though they tended to be hot-tempered. Yes, all werewolves had to change during the full moon, but most of them could change whenever they wished it. Yes, silver could kill a werewolf—so could beheading or a number of other things. (Bran thought it important that the public not perceive werewolves as invulnerable.) No, most of the werewolves that she knew were staunch Christians and none of them that she knew of worshipped Satan. Once, she recited a few biblical verses to prove that she could do so. She'd have been more exasperated about that one, but there *were* things out there that couldn't quote scripture (not that she told them that).

"Your husband's a werewolf, right?" said one young man as she walked by his table.

"That's right," she told him.

"You ever have sex as wolves? Is it different from normal sex? Do you like it better?" He grinned hugely and took a swig from his glass, obviously thinking he'd gotten one over on her. But Anna had been raised in a household of men—her father, her brother, and all of her brother's friends who thought of her as a little sister. He'd had a lot of friends.

"You ever have sex with your mother?" she asked casually. "Was it better than with your girlfriend or did you prefer it with your boyfriend or your pet rat?"

His jaw dropped open and the guy nearest him slapped him on the head and told him, "And that is why you are never going to get a date, Chuck. You see a pretty girl and the things your mama taught you about politeness and all the IQ points you can't count on your fingers to keep track of just leave your head—and then you are compelled to open your mouth. Women are *not* impressed by crudeness." He looked at Anna. "He apologizes for being a dumbass. He'll feel really bad about it in about four hours when he starts to sober up. He's really a good cop and not usually—" He looked at the offending man and sighed. "Well, okay. There's a reason he doesn't date much."

"How did you know I had a pet rat?" said Chuck in a tone filled with awe. He was really drunk and had probably missed the point of everything anyone else had said in the last few minutes: everything except, evidently, the rat.

Several of his buddies laughed and gave him a hard time.

Anna smiled; she couldn't help it—he sounded about six years old. "I can smell him." And that started another round of questions.

It wasn't exactly a fun evening—Anna felt like she'd spent most of her time walking a tightrope. But it was better than being stuck in the condo while Charles buried himself in electronics. And it wasn't all bad. She enjoyed meeting Leslie's husband, who was funny and smart— and offered to stuff Chuck in a wastebasket. The fish and chips were superb and so was the stew.

Eventually the fascination with werewolves seemed to wear off and Anna found a quiet table in a corner where she could relax and watch everyone.

The crude Chuck's friend saw her and came over to apologize again. "He knows he's stupid when he drinks, so he usually doesn't. It was just a bad day today, you know? The last call we took before coming here was a domestic abuse call—some lady's boyfriend beat her up and then started in on her toddler. Chuck has a little boy he hasn't seen since his ex-wife moved to California, and he took it pretty hard."

"I have bad days, too," Anna told him. "I understand. Don't worry about it."

Chuck's friend nodded and wandered off.

She closed her eyes for a minute. She was a little short on sleep thanks to Charles, and it made her eyes dry.

Someone came over and sat on the chair opposite her. Anna opened her eyes to see Beauclaire pouring himself a glass of beer.

"Isaac said he invited you," she told him. "But we were pretty sure you weren't coming."

"Lizzie's out of the operating room," he told her, sipping his beer as if it were fine wine. "Her mother and stepfather are there—and Lizzie will be drugged and sleeping until tomorrow." He took a bigger sip. "Her mother thinks it is my fault that she was taken. As I agree with her, it was difficult to defend myself, and so I retreated here."

Anna shook her head. "Never accept the blame for what evil people do. We are all responsible for our own actions." She was lecturing him, so she stopped. "Sorry. Hang around with Bran too long, and see if you don't start passing around the Marrok's advice as if he were Confucius. How is Lizzie doing?"

"Her knee was crushed." He looked at the wall behind Anna where there was a very nice print of an Irish castle. "They might repair it enough so she can walk, but dancing is definitely out."

"I'm so sorry," Anna said.

"She's alive, right?" Beauclaire said, and took a long, slow drink. "The things they carved in her skin . . . In time, the surgeons might be able to get rid of them, they think. Until then, every time she looks in a mirror she'll have the reminder of what she went through." He paused. "She knows she'll never dance again. It broke her."

"Maybe not," said Leslie. She sat down beside Anna on the dark brown bench seat and put her purse on the table. "Someone gave something to me, a long time ago—and I've never used it. I think mostly because I was afraid. What if I'd tried to use it and it failed?"

She opened her purse, dug down until she found her wallet, and slipped a plain white card out, handing it to Beauclaire. It looked like a business card to Anna, but instead of a name, the word GIFT was typed in the center of the card.

Beauclaire took it and rubbed his fingers across it, and a faint smile crossed his face. "And how did you get this?"

Leslie looked uncomfortable—almost embarrassed. "It's real, right?"

He nodded, still playing with the card. "It's real, all right."

She took a deep breath. "It happened like this," she said, and spun a tale of monsters who ate children and childhood dreams—including Leslie's puppy—and a fierce old woman who knew a little of the fae, and about a debt owed and a bargain made.

"You can use it to fix your daughter's knee?" Leslie asked.

Beauclaire shook his head and handed the card back to Leslie. "No. But I'll remember you offered—and I'll give you some advice, if you don't mind. The fae who gave that to you did it with the best of intentions. For all that we do not reproduce, we tend to be a very long-lived people. Treasach was very old, and powerful, too. But death comes for us all, eventually, and it came to him."

Leslie tucked the card away and rubbed her eyes with the edge of her finger so her makeup wouldn't run. "I don't know why I'm feeling this way. It's stupid. I met him once, for less than ten minutes . . . and . . . I won't forget him."

"No," agreed Beauclaire gravely. "Treasach was a marvel. Poet, fighter, joyful companion, and there are no more of his like to be found. None of us will forget him. Fae magic, though, sometimes has a mind of its own. That was given to you to resolve a debt. He intended it to be a gift and a blessing, but his death means that his will no longer binds that bit of magic. Use it or not, as you wish—but use it for a small thing, or for something that equals the grief of a good man who could not spare a child the pain of her puppy's fate. If you remember his exact words, use it for that—by his words and by the debt this magic is tamed. Go beyond those things with your wish, and it will cause havoc of an unpleasant kind."

"Do you have healers?" Anna asked.

"Healing is among the great magics and we have very few healers left among us—and most of them are even less trustworthy than Treasach's gift would be." He took a drink of his beer and nodded to Leslie. "My daughter will walk again, but she will not dance. It is the way of mortals. They fling themselves at life and emerge broken."

"She survived," said Anna. "She's tough. She fought them every step of the way. She'll make it."

Beauclaire nodded politely. "Some mortals do. Some of them make it just fine when horrible things happen to them. Some of them . . ." He shook his head and took another sip of his beer and then said with quiet savagery, "Sometimes broken people stay broken." He looked at her. "Why am I telling you all of this?"

Anna shrugged. "People talk to me." She didn't know what else to say, so she followed her impulse. "I've been where Lizzie is, brutalized and terrified. Someone rescued me before my captors were able to kill me. Next to that . . . losing something she loves is tragic. But she doesn't seem to be the kind who will think that she would be better off dead—not in the long run."

Beauclaire looked at his glass. "I'm sorry to hear that you had to be rescued."

She shrugged again. "That which does not destroy us makes us stronger, right?" It came out sounding flippant, so she added, "I knew a woman when I was in school. She was smart, a talented musician, and hardworking. She came to college and found out that those weren't enough to make her a first violin, or even a second—and she tried to kill herself because she had to sit with the third violins. It was the first real disappointment she'd ever had in her life and she didn't know how to deal with it. Those of us who live in the real world and survive horrible things, we emerge stronger and ready to face tomorrow. Lizzie will be okay."

Beauclaire frowned at her. He looked away and then said, "You might visit her and tell her that."

She didn't want to. She wasn't a counselor and she didn't like talking about what had happened to her to strangers—though it hadn't stopped her tonight, had it? Anna was okay because Charles found her and taught her to be strong. Lizzie would have to find her own strength, and Anna didn't know how to tell her where to find it.

"I'll see what I can do," she promised reluctantly. She was exhausted from being on display, and from thinking about things she'd tried to put behind her. "If you'll excuse me, I think I'll go visit the ladies' room."

She left Leslie talking to the fae and let herself out of the banquet room. Away from the noise and the room full of mostly strangers, Anna felt better. She'd use the restroom, eat the food she'd ordered, and go home.

When she came out of the restroom, she wasn't pleased to see that Agent Heuter was leaning against the wall next to the door. There was no one left in the restaurant proper—it must have closed at ten. So she and Heuter were alone in the hallway next to the entrance for the room where the party was still going strong.

"So you are the heroine of the day," he said.

Something in his voice didn't track and she frowned at him. "Not really, no. If you'll excuse me?"

But he stepped in front of her. "No. I don't think so. Not today."

And someone who wasn't there grabbed her from behind and sent her to sleep.

CHAPTER

11

Anna woke with a sickly sweet taste in her mouth that spread into her nose and up through her sinuses, deadening anything else her nose might tell her.

Nausea and a rotten headache vied with the silver collar and high-silver-content, medieval-style cuffs and chains for the honors of the most miserable distractions. Anna tried to remember what had happened that had left her chained up like someone's extreme BDSM fantasy in a human-sized cage that hung in a large empty room. It was dark, and she was alone.

She'd been talking to Heuter, who'd been acting weird. And then . . . jeez. Had they really chloroformed her? Decades-long killing spree, witch's magic, rare old scary fae bloodlines—and they used chloroform. Several times, if her vague memories of waking up in the backseat of a car were accurate.

That just seemed so . . . mundane.

She rose to her hands and knees—and that was as far as the chains would let her go. She let the burn of the silver and the desperate need to upchuck her dinner keep her from panic as she tried to think around the headache for a plan of attack.

Lizzie had been raped within hours of when they took her. It was almost the first thing that they had done. And that was the thought that made Anna throw up.

As delicious as the food in Isaac's Irish pub had been, it didn't taste very good the second time around. She managed to get most of it out of the cage, but enough lingered on her hair—for some reason having her hands cuffed and chained had impeded her ability to keep her hair out of her mouth—and had spattered on the edge of the floor that it added to her misery.

And then she wondered if she was as alone in the room as she had thought. She hadn't been able to see or smell the fae who'd been guarding Lizzie's prison on the island. Panic threatened and she forced it down because it wouldn't do her any good.

Charles would be looking for her by now. But when she tried their bond, it was closed as tight as it ever had been. Didn't he know she was missing? Isaac would tell him right away. But what if Isaac didn't know? What if Heuter told him that Anna had decided to go back to the condo on her own? But that didn't make sense, because Isaac would be able to tell Heuter was lying—and Heuter knew that. He'd have to stay as far out of the way as he could so he didn't give himself away to the werewolves.

So why hadn't Charles opened the bond between them?

There was noise outside the cavernous room and Anna crouched low, trying to quiet her breathing and slow down her pounding heart so she could hear through the closed doors and the walls. They were talking pretty loudly so it wasn't too hard to get most of it.

". . . pretty one. I like the women and the pretty ones best."

"I thought you had decided you were a superhero, Bulldog?" Heuter's voice was mocking.

"It pays well," the stranger said. "Better than janitorial work. Never got a blow job for cleaning a floor; got one for saving that hooker from her pimp. This one we got now is pretty. Isn't she pretty?"

"Not as pretty as the one you let get away," said Heuter.

"Not my fault. Not my fault. That big wolf—he was going to kill me." There was an edge of hysteria in the man's voice and an odd cadence to his speech pattern. "You never said they'd have a monster with them. Killing werewolves isn't hard. I killed all of them Uncle Travis sent me. Why is that one so hard to kill?"

"The witch did something," said Heuter. "Used some kind of magic so the wolf could see you, and it must have made him stronger. The girl we got tonight is his wife."

"He's going to be so mad at me." He sounded scared.

Heuter headed it off at the pass. "He has to find us first. This will be the last one for the year, and then we'll move on."

"I get her first," said the man who wasn't Heuter. Anna was pretty sure that Heuter was not the fae—surely Beauclaire would have been able to tell if he had been. She decided that the other man must be the fae. Neither of them sounded old, and Lizzie had told them that one man was older—and if Anna decided one of the speakers was the fae, no unseen person could be watching her from the shadows.

"I get her first because that wolf hurt me. I get to hurt her. I'm going to take her until she understands who's boss. I'm—"

He continued in that vein, working himself into a frenzy as he used fouler and fouler language to describe her fate in ugly detail. Anna deliberately tuned him out. She'd learned how to do that shortly after she'd been Changed and there had been no Charles to save her from the crazy bastards in the broken Chicago pack.

She couldn't feel Charles. He was going to be too late, and that would destroy him. She tugged on the chains, but they'd held werewolves before and there was no way she could break them. Blowing on her hands to ease the burn, she thought about how Isaac had said that his wolf Otten had been waiting for a chance and the killers hadn't given him one.

She couldn't afford to wait—she had to make her own chance. Because Anna had been a victim once upon a time, and she was damned sure never going to be one again.

Despite her determination, she was scared. Her chances weren't good—these men had managed to kill a lot of people, werewolves and fae, some of them considerably more experienced at protecting themselves than she was.

The sick, acrid smell of her terror burned out the last of the chloroform from her nose and she grabbed her fear, the lingering pain of the headache, and the ache that was seeping into her muscles from the silver. She pitted it all against the metal cuffs that held her—neck, wrists, and ankles—and called on the change.

These were not a pack of werewolves; they were human and fae. Raping Anna when she was a wolf was an entirely different proposition from doing the same to her when she didn't have freakishly sharp teeth and claws that would be a credit to any cougar on the planet.

The change always hurt. Always. And she'd long ago learned to use the pain to bully her way through the freaky feeling of her bones stretching and bunching, of muscles growing and teeth sharpening that was so much more intolerable than mere pain.

This time the change was worse than usual.

Her throat buckled under the pressure of the silver collar. Then it rehealed and buckled again, trapped inside a metal band that was too small to contain it. She thought she'd just stymied her kidnappers by killing herself when something in the more-fragile mechanism of the lock finally broke, sending a piece of metal flying. The collar fell away from her, hitting the floor and bits of chain with a harsh clank.

Sucking in air like a bellows, she still had to hold on to her thoughts and make her arms that were becoming her front legs move at just the right time while her hands were still hands but after her arms had slightly reshaped in order to get out of the wrist manacles. Her wrists bled and she panted, trying to keep quiet, as she dragged herself free of the two-inch-wide silver bands that imprisoned her. She didn't worry about the cuffs on her ankles because they were wider and the wolf would just step out of them.

She waited, but there was no pause in the conversation outside. Either they were too involved to notice, they expected her to be making some noise, or their ears were too human to hear through the walls the way she could hear them.

She lay spent for a moment—then realized that moment was dragging on into the next without any further change happening. Dangerous to stay half-shifted, though some of the most dominant wolves could do it for a while. She scrambled for a way to continue the change, but her body was exhausted, shaking with the need for food and . . .

They had doped her up with something. Mostly werewolves were immune to drugs and alcohol. Their metabolism just ran through it too fast, but they had given her something, probably a whole lot of something. GHB or Rohypnol, maybe—or some sedative designed to keep her passive. It had been no match for the adrenaline surge that the thought of being helpless in the hands of rapists and murderers had brought—but it had stalled out her shift.

Pain came in waves, because her body wasn't meant to be caught between for this long. Fluids, clear, pink, and bright red, began to leak onto the floor of the cage. She reached out for Charles and found the moon instead.

Tomorrow would come the night of the full moon, when her song was too strong to resist, but tonight she was waxing and full of strength that she lent to her daughter who asked. With a painful jerkiness that scraped chain and manacles loudly on the bottom of the cage as her muscles flexed and tore and reshaped themselves, Anna restarted her change.

CHARLES WAS DEEP into his work. Brother Wolf loved the hunt even when it was on computers instead of in flesh and blood. Both of them could smell their prey, weak and quivering just out of their reach. So the first knock on the door elicited no more than a growl of annoyance.

It was Brother Wolf who noticed something was wrong the second time the knock came. Even buried in the endgame of his hunt, his senses were still on alert, and they told Brother Wolf that the smart FBI lady, the smart FBI man who tried very hard to be underestimated, the fae whose daughter had been hurt, and the local Alpha were knocking on his door—and they were all supposed to be with his mate, who was not here.

Anna. Charles reached for her, but he couldn't touch her through their bond, not even through their pack bond. With his help, his ghosts had well and truly isolated him.

Enraged and terrified for Anna in equal measures, he opened the door knowing his eyes were showing Brother Wolf. "Where's Anna?" he growled.

Isaac was supposed to make sure no one hurt her while Charles worked. The temptation to blame the Olde Towne Alpha rose and was banished. Anna was Charles's; she was his to protect and he had failed. Brother Wolf wanted to charge into the night and kill until they found her; Charles held him back with the knowledge that there were better ways to find Anna faster—and that blood would flow when he did.

"We were hoping you could tell us," Isaac said. "She went to the ladies' room and never came back. You two are mated, right? Can you tell where she is?"

Charles tried again. Right there and then, with the others still standing in the doorway, he tried again to open up the bonds he'd closed to protect her.

Nothing. He tried harder, tried until it hurt worse than the change. He growled and tried again—and felt the ghosts who haunted him howl in triumph. He turned and walked almost blindly until he stared into the big mirror in the bedroom. The ghosts were unrecognizable, having melted into one creature with fifty mouths and twenty hands that were busily tying the ribbon of his bond into knots.

We can kill her no matter how you try to protect her, it told him, its voices high and vicious. *Your fault, your fault we died, your fault she dies.* One voice started laughing, and then the others continued until there was an unholy cacophony in his head.

There was a drip of blood leaking out of Charles's nose and the whites of his eyes were pink from broken blood vessels—it made his yellow eyes look particularly bizarre.

"Did you try to track her?" he asked Isaac, as Charles continued to stare into the mirror, his voice so low and rough he didn't recognize it as his own. He stuffed his rage into a small icy place and promised it release if it would let him work right now. He would be cold and controlled until he found where they had stashed his Anna—and then he'd take them down into small, bite-sized chunks.

"Yes," the Olde Towne Alpha said. Charles turned away from the mirror to find Isaac watching him warily from the relative safety of the living room as he continued to explain. "I trailed her into the ladies' room and out again. Then she walked about two feet the wrong way if she intended to go back into the party—which she did, because she'd ordered another round of fish and chips according to the waitress who delivered it—and then her scent trail just ends. Like Otten's did."

Isaac must be a good tracker. It was unusual for a wolf that new to be able to trail that well, even in wolf form. No matter how good he was, Charles was better.

The computer hadn't confirmed his guesses yet, but he was only waiting for the final nail. He considered going after the people he had decided were behind the killings—but if he was wrong, it meant Anna would stay in her kidnappers' hands while he chased down the wrong trail. And then there was the problem that the people he was looking at had nearly Bran's resources and he would need—

"What's wrong with him?" Leslie asked in a quiet voice that none-theless interrupted his thoughts. "Why is he bleeding like that? Do you see his eyes? They weren't like that when he opened the door."

"I don't have a clue," Isaac said in a calm voice. "Look, you two, you don't stand a chance if he loses it. You stay out here, back, out of the way—keep your guns out and watch. If he looks like he is headed your way, just shoot—and make sure your shot counts. If he's the wolf I think he is, he'd rather be dead than have you become collateral damage. And if he's far enough gone that he's taking out civilians, he's not going to be much help to Anna anyway."

"Civilians?" said the male FBI officer, sounding offended. Brother Wolf might have known his name, if he had cared. But his mate was missing and he cared for nothing and no one except for that.

Isaac ignored him—maybe he'd fallen for that tired, worn-looking mien, but Brother Wolf knew better. He recognized a fellow predator in the male FBI agent, even though Goldstein—the name rose up when he called for it—Goldstein was no threat to anything Charles cared about.

"Humans are civilians here," said Charles. To himself he sounded calm. "And you might listen to Isaac, though I don't think I'm far enough gone to hurt our allies. Isaac, I should be able to find her—but I'm not going to be able to use our link tonight." His throat shut down as Brother Wolf fought to the surface in a panic at Charles's admission.

Anna was missing. Anna was in the hands of the people who'd hurt the little dancer. His Anna who'd already survived so much—he'd sworn nothing like that would ever happen to her again when she was theirs. And they had failed, Brother Wolf and Charles, two souls sharing one skin . . . They had failed their mate.

Charles convinced Brother Wolf that they had a better chance of finding Anna in man-shape rather than as wolf, but it took more willpower than he knew he had to do it.

"He can't find her?" Leslie asked.

"I told you it wasn't a sure thing," Isaac told her. "The mating bond is a very personal thing."

Isaac was doing a good job of keeping his Alpha nature tamped down; his voice was soft and nonthreatening. Brother Wolf liked Isaac, but just now would not be a good time to interest him in proving who was more dominant. People got killed in fights like that—and Brother Wolf was craving violence just now.

"You also said if it didn't work, we might be in serious trouble," said the tough little dancer's fae father. "Because there isn't a person in this city more dangerous than a wolf whose mate is in danger. Are we in serious trouble?"

Yes, thought Charles. He needed to do something urgent—but Brother Wolf's rage was clouding his thoughts. He needed to get to his computer and confirm—

"I don't want those bastards to get Anna," Leslie said. "If Charles can't find her, what about my wish? You said it was dangerous to use except in specific or small ways. But I lost a puppy—and now we're trying to find another one."

Charles narrowed his eyes at her. "What wish?"

Beauclaire ignored him, staring at Leslie with something approaching delight. "Clever," he said. "Oh, that is a clever way to look at it."

"A fae man left me a gift when I was a child," Leslie said to Charles, and she remembered not to look him in the eyes. "To make up for not being there to rescue my puppy, I think. I've never used it—and our expert in fae magic says that I need to be careful with it. But that sounds like a fair exchange to me." She looked at Beauclaire.

Gravely, he nodded. "I think that might be right."

She opened her purse and took out her wallet, and Charles could smell the magic from where he stood. Fae magic strong enough to make him sneeze, powerful enough to give him hope. She pulled out a little white card from her billfold. "I'm not exactly sure how to do this."

"Magic follows intention," said Charles, and Beauclaire gave him a sharp look. "Tell it what you want—and tear up the card to seal the deal."

"Since when did the Marrok's son become an expert in fae magic?" asked Beauclaire—and Charles saw Goldstein look very bland. It was "the Marrok's son" that had done it. Goldstein had heard that term before and now wanted to know what it meant.

"Since when did the fae give up information on the werewolves?" countered Charles silkily. Anna was missing: he didn't care what Goldstein found out. But the fae would do very nicely to sate Brother Wolf's desire to tear into flesh until it bled. Beauclaire, Brother Wolf decided, would be a worthy opponent, and once he killed something, maybe he could think clearly again.

Beauclaire took a cautious step back and Isaac eased between them. "You don't want to do anything rash, Charles," he cautioned. "We're all on the same team here."

"I wish—" said Leslie, drawing Charles's attention away from the fae. "I wish . . ." She looked at Charles. "One lost puppy for another— but Anna is yours as Toby was mine. So I wish that as I lost my puppy, my dog that I loved, that Charles should find his lost wolf." She tore the card in half and the magic . . . did something.

Charles's phone rang before he could figure out what the magic had done. Its sudden blaring ringtone that wasn't the song it sang when Anna called him irritated Brother Wolf, who pulled it out of their pocket and crushed it to make it stop.

Everyone in the condo quit breathing—and Charles realized that his ability to speak coherently had apparently given them a false sense of safety.

"How long until it works?" he asked Beauclaire in a soft, soft voice.

The fae sighed. "We don't even know it will work, werewolf. Something happened, but it wasn't my magic in that card. Treasach tended toward subtle magic that snuck up behind you."

Another cell phone rang and Charles growled. Isaac pulled out his phone and started to hit the off button, but paused. "Four-zero-six is the Montana area code, right?"

He answered the phone before Charles replied, and clear as day Charles's father's voice came out of the speaker of Isaac's phone.

"I have a feeling that my son is in a bad place," Bran said. "And I have made a habit of not ignoring my feelings—especially when neither he nor Anna are answering their phones."

Isaac gave Charles a nervous glance. "That's right. Charles is here and Anna's been taken by the murdering bastards we've been chasing. We have the FBI here, the two who've been working with us. And Beauclaire is present as well, the fae whose daughter we rescued yesterday."

It was a very good rundown of what was happening, Charles thought.

"Why isn't Charles chasing down Anna?"

Brother Wolf growled.

"That's not helpful, Charles," Bran said.

"He says he can't contact her."

There was a very long pause and then his father said quietly, "Charles. Is it the same thing that was bothering you before you went to Boston?"

Charles couldn't answer, wasn't human enough to answer. He turned around and stalked to the far side of the room. If he hadn't killed them, hadn't executed those wolves in Minnesota, he'd have been able to find Anna before she got hurt.

"Before Boston . . ." said Isaac and his voice trailed off. "Oh, I know what you did before Boston, Charles. This could get messy," he said to the others, suddenly decisive. "I think we can work something out, but it might be better if you people, who are a little too easy to hurt, are out of the way. Would you mind waiting in the hall?"

"You have something to talk about that you don't want us to hear," said Goldstein. "You don't have to lie. We'll go wait."

"I never lie to the cops or the FBI," Isaac said. He was being truthful, Charles noted somewhat absently. "Things might get pretty bad before they get better and I don't want you hurt."

Isaac didn't say anything to Beauclaire, but the fae said, "I think I'll wait outside with the others. He'll be easier without me here."

There was a quiet click as his front door was shut and another as Isaac threw the dead bolt.

"All right," Isaac said, and it took a moment for Charles to realize he was talking to Bran. "It's just Charles and me—though Beauclaire hears just fine. He might be able to hear every word we say."

"Acceptable," said Charles's da crisply. "Beauclaire is trustworthy—and he owes us a debt, if you've rescued his daughter."

Trust Da to know Beauclaire.

"Fine," said Isaac. "So am I reading this right and there's something about that fu—" He caught himself, probably remembering someone warning him not to swear around Bran. Charles's father was old, and though he could swear with the best of them (usually in Welsh) he generally preferred to avoid it. He could get pretty scary with underlings who had foul mouths. Isaac continued with slightly milder adjectives. "Screwed-up thing in Minnesota that Charles got stuck with that is somehow interfering with his bond with Anna?"

"I don't know," said Bran. "Charles, is that what the problem is?"

Charles didn't know Isaac well, and talking in front of him was akin to dancing naked in public. But if his father could figure out a way to help—and if he couldn't, then no one could—then he would have stripped off his clothes and run naked down Congress Street in downtown Boston at lunch hour just to get a chance to talk with him.

"They've broken the link," Charles said.

"Who has?" asked Bran.

"The ghosts of the people I've killed who should have lived." He turned to look at his father, but all he saw was Isaac holding his cell phone open.

He smiled grimly at Isaac, who took a step back, and spoke to him. "Another man would probably have a mental breakdown—and blame all sorts of psychoses. But my grandfather was a shaman and he gave me the gift that allows me to see the ghosts of those I've wronged."

"So they are haunting you," Isaac said, his face quiet.

Charles hadn't expected the Alpha to get in his face and call him a liar—Charles was the Marrok's hatchet man, after all. But the simple belief he saw made him remember that Isaac's grandfather could see ghosts, too.

"And they are haunting me," he said, Brother Wolf standing down a little from immediate attack. Brother Wolf approved of Isaac, as long as the other wolf didn't get too pushy.

"Tell him why," Bran said into the silence. His voice was odd, as it got when he was following an impulse he didn't understand. The truth was, Charles got his ability to deal with magic from both halves of his heritage—but it sometimes bothered Bran when magic spoke to him, probably because *Bran's* mother had made the Wicked Witch of the West look like Cinderella's fairy godmother.

"Because my guilt holds them here," Charles answered Isaac,

because Bran thought it might be important. "They should be off wherever dead people go, but I'm holding them here because I can't let them go."

"You feel guilty about what?" Isaac asked, sounding honestly bewildered. "We all know about Minnesota—no one gossips like us Alphas. Three wolves killed some old pedophile, half ate him, and then left him for the civilians to find—and it was some ten-year-old kid who found him. Probably, taking into account what the gossip says and the police reports I saw, the ten-year-old was the kid the old guy was after. The damned fools probably made so much noise fighting over the body that the kid came to investigate. At least they had the sense to run instead of killing the kid, but I think they racked up enough stupidity to register on the Top Five Dumbass Moves list for the next ten years or so."

Charles hadn't known that it had been the child who found the body. His father had told him that his job was to go find out if they had killed the man and left him for humans to find—and, if so, execute them. Brother Wolf had forced their confession—dominant wolves can do that if they are more dominant enough—and then carried out his Alpha's orders.

"Poor boy," murmured Bran. "No one told me it was the boy who found him." Someone, Charles knew, would contact the boy's family and make sure he got counseling. His parents would think it some sort of victim's organization or something. It was one of the jobs Charles used to handle or oversee.

"You feel guilty for executing them," Isaac said, dragging Charles's attention back to him. "I get that. But I don't get why you should. Were they crying like babies? Because that really sucks when they do that. Was it Robert, their Alpha? I heard that garbage he was passing around. Their victim was a bastard who deserved to die. Fine. If they were sure he was guilty, kill him somewhere quietly and get rid of the body. If you ask me, I'd have executed their Alpha, too, for being incompetent enough to let them get so out of control that they left him for civilians to find."

"Had this happened before we came out," Charles said, "I could have let them live."

"Could you?" Isaac said. He shook his head. "If they had been in my pack, I'd have killed them. Now, ten years ago, whenever."

Charles read the truth of that in Isaac's voice.

"It didn't matter to them that the guy was dirt," Isaac said. "If they were after a righteous kill, they wouldn't have eaten him. If they hadn't been hunting in a pack, they probably wouldn't have killed him, either. They were dumbasses. They were out of control. And you can't have dumbass out-of-control werewolves. Not now. Not ever. And it was their Alpha's job to make sure they weren't dumbasses. I know better than to send a pack out hunting when we don't want a bloody mess to result, and I haven't been a werewolf half as long as Robert has been Alpha of his pack. And he couldn't accept the blame—oh no. They were the good guys; he wasn't going to kill the good guys—because he knows it was his fault they needed to be killed in the first place. So Bran must send you out to kill them. I bet that f—" He cast a panicked glance at the phone and bit his lip and finished more quietly, "I bet he said all the right things, all the polite things, and still made you feel like a murderer, right? He did it because he knows it's his fault and he can't admit it to himself so he's looking for someone to blame. And they all know, we all know, that right now we werewolves cannot afford headlines like we've been seeing in Minnesota."

It was truth as Isaac felt it. And it sounded right. Maybe he'd been listening too hard to Robert and not thinking clearly.

Charles took a deep breath. "Anna knows how people work," he said. "She'd have seen it, too. But I don't bring Anna with me anymore."

"It makes sense, though, right?" Isaac said.

"If you weren't already worn-down with the killing," said Bran heavily, "you would have recognized the truth yourself. If I weren't so busy trying to justify something that has less to do with justice than expedience, I would have seen it, too. Just because it was necessary, doesn't mean that it wasn't the right answer anyway."

"One of the wolves had been a wolf for less than two years," Charles said.

"Too bad for them," said Isaac. "They chose to give in to the wolf at the wrong time. They chose to hang out with idiots. They chose to act as they did. They chose their own death and you were just the delivery system."

"I think," said Bran, "that the Minnesota pack needs a different Alpha."

"Agreed," said Isaac.

"Charles," said Bran. "Where is Anna?"

He pointed southwest, unaware until he did so of how accurate a fix he had on her. "Ten miles that direction." He couldn't tell anything else, couldn't touch her mind, but he knew where she was.

"Find her," his father told him. "And take these people down. Avoid killing them if you can—remind your wolf that jail is a much worse sentence than death. If we can help take them down with minimal violence, that would be good."

"Yes," agreed Charles, though his da had already disconnected.

"Are you all right?" asked Isaac.

Charles gave him a shallow bow of respect, one dominant wolf to another. "Better." Not fixed, not anywhere near normal, but he couldn't find it in him to care one way or the other, because now he could find Anna. "I have a lock on her. What's ten miles in that direction?"

"Islington, Dedham, Westwood. Milton, maybe. I know my way around here by road, not as the crow flies. We'll have to consult a map to be sure—and how certain are you of the ten miles?"

"It's close to that," Charles said. He considered just getting into a car and following his link, but it would probably be faster if he knew where he was going. "As the crow flies" directions had some serious issues in a day of fences and roads. Especially when he was pretty sure that he could figure out exactly where she was before they left the condo. He hadn't wasted his time today. "Why don't you let the rest of them back in and join me at my computer?"

He needed the moment it would take Isaac to assemble the others. Charles was shaking, and dominant enough not to want anyone to see. She was alive. It would be enough for the moment.

He sat down at the table and found that his computer had finished the task he'd set for it. He heard them file in but he didn't turn around. He didn't want to risk meeting anyone's eye unexpectedly until he had Anna safe.

"Anna is a nut for police procedurals," he told them as he resized a window so he could see if he'd made any progress. "This morning she observed that serial killers often like to insinuate themselves into the investigations. I initially dismissed it—because you would have noticed something like that after this many years, right?"

"We looked," Goldstein said. "There was no sign of anything."

His script had done its job and he was in through the firewalls—it always was good to have friends on the inside. He could talk and hack at the same time, and maybe it would keep the feds from figuring out where he was. It would probably help that none of them had worked for the IRS—and that the back door he'd gotten in through was low on graphics and high on code.

"I decided that maybe the initial killer, the old one, maybe he wasn't that kind of psycho. But the new guy might be—the mysterious third man. So I went back ten years. And I ran a list of the names of everyone involved in the case for all those years. There were two people who showed up more than three times."

"I assure you, I am not a serial killer," said Goldstein dryly.

"I was pretty sure it wasn't you," Charles agreed. "You want to catch him so badly I can smell it. So I took a look at the other guy first."

Goldstein drew in a sharp breath. "You can't be serious."

Goldstein had been involved in a number of the investigations, and he would know who else had been there with him.

"Someone was present for six of the last ten years," Charles continued. "Giving an interview to the newspaper or the TV news. Helping out at the call center. Assigned as liaison to someone—and once I lucked out and found his photo on the front page paper of where one of the bodies turned up. I was able to confirm that he has been in the right town at the right time for nine of the last ten years in a job that usually moves people around. The other year, when he was assigned halfway across the country, he was on a mysterious vacation at the time of the killings. So I went looking into his background. Called in a few favors. Hacked a few databases. Called a couple of police officers and a retired minister."

"Who is it?" asked Beauclaire, an eager bite to his voice.

Charles hit a button and a photo of Cantrip's poster boy came up on half his screen, leaving him to file through records on the other. "According to a former nanny, the good senator was obsessed that his son be a manly man—Texas-style. And when the six-year-old Les Heuter was discovered playing with his mother's makeup, he was bundled up and sent to spend some manly time with the senator's older brother, the Vietnam War vet and avid hunter Travis Heuter, who lived and still lives in Vermont. Travis Heuter also has houses and properties in a number of the cities where the Big Game Hunter's killing sprees have taken place, as well as a good dozen in places that haven't had killings. In the few places our killer has been active and Travis Heuter doesn't own property, his family owns property or one of his three companies has condos or apartments. He's a little bit crazy, is Travis, so the

Heuter family doesn't let him appear at public functions or on TV because he might not be politically correct in his views."

"Heuter." Goldstein spoke with the barest shadow of Brother Wolf's desire to destroy the killer in his voice.

"A senator's son. This is going to be a nightmare of political pressures," Leslie said. "My boss is going to love it."

Charles couldn't tell if she was being sarcastic or not—probably because she didn't know, either.

"And the nail on the coffin is this—Travis and Senator Dwight Heuter had a younger sister, Helena. In 1981, when she was sixteen, she turned up pregnant—raped, she claimed. She moved in with her big brother and then committed suicide a couple of years later, leaving Travis in charge of her half-blood boy. A retired teacher I talked to told me that the boy was 'different,' not precisely slow or autistic, but definitely odd, with a tendency toward violence. His name is Benedict Heuter and he finds menial jobs, according to the IRS"—this had been the last little bit he'd needed to tie it all up in a bow—"and for the last five years he's been doing janitorial work or maintenance, moving every year or so."

Charles backed out of the IRS database and closed his doorway. Then he slid into a chunk of Darknet—a separate little space of the Internet unseen by search engines and mostly engineered by hackers who'd abandoned the Internet for most of their more questionable pursuits—and pulled up a list of properties from Travis Heuter's tax records, something he'd copied over during an earlier excursion into the IRS database.

"I don't think you're supposed to be able to get at that information," said Leslie.

"Don't look," said Goldstein, peering over Charles's shoulder. "We don't know anything about illegal hacking." He whistled cheerily. "Travis Heuter owns half the world."

Charles searched for Massachusetts and found an address.

"Not that one," murmured Isaac. "That's downtown. You want ten miles southwest of here. Not that one—that's way up north. There. Dedham. One of my college girlfriends kept a horse out there and that's about the right direction and distance."

Charles didn't want to be wrong, so he committed that address to memory, but kept going through the records until his search jumped back to the beginning. It was Dedham or they'd have to follow the bond. Either way, Heuter was done.

Weighing time lost investigating versus lost time, Charles took a moment to look up the address on another Darknet site that specialized in property records official and unofficial—the Darknet was a rather tedious mix of conspiracy theorists, brilliant black hats, and OCD record keepers. Travis Heuter's Dedham property was a largish two-story farmhouse with a barn on four-point-two acres that had sold five years ago for close to a million dollars. Charles printed the house plans and the county record of the last survey of the land, folded them, and shoved them into his pocket.

"One of my pack has a van waiting for us outside," Isaac said. "Shall we go?"

Focused on Anna, Charles had forgotten that they would need a car to get there. It was probably best that he not drive.

CHAPTER

12

Anna was panting with the pain of shifting, and her muscles shook at random for what she told herself was the same reason. She felt weaker than she'd ever been while in wolf form and she smelled wrong, too. Sick or drugged, maybe.

The other man, the one who was not Les Heuter, was still ranting in the other room about what he would do to her in very explicit language . . . which meant that either her shift had been Charles-fast or he had been talking for fifteen or twenty minutes. She was betting on the latter.

Heuter encouraged the other man, whose name evidently was Benedict, adding ugly details or making fun of him, whatever it took to goad him to new heights. Heuter probably thought that she was cowering in the cage listening.

"Do you remember what we did to that girl in Texas?" Heuter asked.

"The one with the butterfly tattoo?"

"Not that one; the tall one—"

Anna came to her feet and shook like she was throwing water off her fur in an attempt to get her muscles working—and so she would not look as though she was cowering in her cage, afraid of them before they'd even done anything to her. She did her best to tune them out, turn them into background noise like an unpleasant song on the radio.

She needed something else to focus on.

Her night vision as a human was pretty good. In her wolf form, it was even better. Her cage hung about two feet off of a polished floor that looked more out of place than the cage itself did in the big open room. There was a lingering scent of horses to tell her that this had originally been a barn, but someone had repurposed it into a dance studio. On the far end of the room, on the short wall, a bench held a couple of pairs of slip-on shoes and what looked like a . . . belly-dancing coin belt.

Next to the bench, one corner of the barn was closed off and a sign that read OFFICE hung on the door. A wall of mirrors spanned the long side of the barn, mirrors that reflected her image, still looking like she was terrified. A long brass bar, placed about three feet up and running the length of the mirrored surface, clinched the deal. She was imprisoned in a cage hanging from the rafters of a dance studio. No dungeon or dank hidden basement for her. When she was performing regularly, she used to have nightmares about being imprisoned on a stage where she would be able to get out only if she played "Mary Had a Little Lamb" backward, which should have been easy but someone had replaced her cello strings with violin strings. A cage in a dance studio was better than that, right? Honest terror instead of frustrated embarrassment.

She had to get out of here.

But, in the meantime, she needed to do something about the frightened-looking werewolf reflected in the big mirror.

She stood up straighter and pricked her ears, and the mirror-Anna appeared slightly less pathetic. She didn't quite manage scary—Charles could do that without even trying—but at least she didn't look so scared. She was a werewolf. She was not a victim.

Seeing that they had brought her to a barn-turned–dance studio, Anna wondered if there was any connection to Lizzie. Maybe she had danced or taught here. Maybe this was how the killers had found her. Or maybe Beauclaire and his daughter were simply on Cantrip's mysterious and sometimes inaccurate list of fae and others living in the United States—a list Heuter would have access to. But if there *was* a link between Lizzie and this dance studio, there was a slight chance that Charles could make the connection and find her.

Because he had to know she was gone by now. If he hadn't contacted her through their bond, then he couldn't. He'd have to find another way. And the dance studio might lead him here . . . in a couple of months or so.

And now she looked pathetic again. There was a sharp smacking sound—like someone getting slapped in the face. A second smack, and the background noise of the men fantasizing about torture and rape stopped abruptly.

"You know what I told you." An old man's voice, a little quavery but still powerful, spoke in almost-soft tones that reminded Anna of Bran when he got really angry. "You keep using those words and you're going to forget and use them in public. Then you'll lose your nice job and find yourself out in the streets begging for bread because I'm not going to feed you. No child of my house will be useless and living off the dole."

Someone said, "Yessir," in an almost whisper.

"Those words are for trash," the old man continued. "For lowborn scum. Your father might have been scum, but your mother was a good girl and her blood should be stronger. You shame her when you speak that way."

The old man's voice changed a little, as if he'd moved, but also sharpened. "And you. Les, what do you think you're doing? Do you think I don't know where he gets it? You think you're so damned smart, but you are nothing. Nothing. Too stupid for the FBI, too pansy-ass for the military. You like to forget who is in charge here, or what our mission is and what it means. Distraction is not useful; you know how hard he has to work to seem just like everyone else. You want him to get caught? How far would you get trying to destroy the creatures who are taking over this land of ours without Benedict? Are you trying to ruin us?"

"No, sir." Heuter's voice was subdued, but there was venom lurking below the meek tones. "Sorry, Uncle Travis."

"You aren't a kid anymore," the old man said sternly, apparently missing the undercurrents in the younger man's attitude. "Start acting like it. What are we doing here?"

"Saving our country." Heuter's voice strengthened, almost military-style—and he was telling the truth. "Making our country safe for her citizens by taking out the trash and doing the things that our government is too liberal, too soft, to do."

Anna couldn't fathom it. She remembered his little speech at their lunch yesterday; he'd been telling the truth as he believed it then—and though she'd thought him unlikable, she'd also felt a certain respect for him.

She should have remembered Bran's law: zealots are one-trick ponies. They love nothing so much as their own cause. Don't get in their way without expecting to be hurt. She'd always thought Bran had been talking about himself—but she knew better, even if he didn't. Bran was driven, but he loved his sons and he loved his pack. He was not a one-trick pony.

"Do you remember the little girl that we hung by her braid while we—" The lust in Heuter's voice as he'd urged the unseen Benedict on to a greater frenzy was more real than the sincere speech he'd given her at the lunch table.

Heuter wasn't a zealot, either, she decided. He only said he was protecting America from monsters to make himself believe that he was in the right as he satisfied his lust for power over others, his desire to cause other people pain and suffering. Murder and rape were his real cause; keeping America safe was only an excuse.

"Can I have her first, Uncle Travis?" Benedict asked. "I like the girls better. And her husband hurt me. Can I have her first?"

"That's better, boy," the older man said. "You keep your language polite. Let's go take a look at her before we decide anything. We'll have a while to play before you get to feed on her death. There will be time enough for everything."

He sounded like he was talking about going fishing instead of torturing and killing someone. The door near her cage opened and the old man turned on the light as they all walked in.

Hail, hail, the gang's all here, she thought as she got her first good look at her captors.

Even knowing what she did, Les Heuter still looked sort of all-American, like the kind of guy who helped little old ladies cross the street. The other young man, Benedict Heuter . . . he was big. Taller than Charles and maybe fifty pounds heavier, and Charles wasn't a beanpole. There was something wrong with his eyes and he smelled like a deer in rut. She found it uncomfortable to meet his eyes—and she could stare down Bran. It had nothing to do with dominance and everything to do with the madness in his face.

The features were different, but Benedict's expression, the thoughts that lurked behind his eyes, were classic Justin, the crazy werewolf who'd Changed her and . . . done all the other things that no one else had particularly wanted to do to an Omega wolf. Not long after she and Charles met, Charles had killed Justin. But even years later, she had nightmares about Justin's eyes.

Because Benedict made her so uneasy, she turned her attention to the other stranger in the mix. Clearly related by blood to both of the younger two, the old man—Uncle Travis, that was what Heuter had called him—showed her what Heuter would look like in forty years, assuming he didn't die under her fangs as she hoped. Age had not so much bent this man as clarified him. Heuter still looked a little soft around the edges; it was what gave him his wholesome appearance. This man was all rawhide and leather.

Even in his mid-sixties or early seventies, he was good-looking, with bright blue eyes unfaded by the years and sharp, clean features that might have been spectacular when he was young but had been solidified by a sense of strength and determination. If Anna thought that the strength of character in his face was slightly mad—well, she was in a better place than most to make that judgment.

He moved like there was muscle under his skin despite his age. And from the body language of the others, she knew that here was the Alpha wolf. He ruled by fiat, by strength of character, and by their understanding that it was this one who kept them safe and gave them direction—and would kill them if he needed to.

The body language she observed when the older man wasn't looking at his minions also told her that Heuter chafed at his secondary position: he was ready to take over at the first sign of weakness. It had been in his voice, too. The old man should have known, and that he didn't, signaled to Anna that he was weakening and would not rule here much longer.

"Let's have a look at you, darling," the old man crooned as he came up to the cage, seemingly unfazed by her change to wolf. "Black as pitch and ice blue eyes. I've never seen a wolf with blue eyes before."

She had to fight not to back away. Close up, he smelled of pipe tobacco. Charles sometimes smelled like that after he performed one of the ceremonies his grandfather had taught him.

Charles didn't do one often, but she'd learned to see the signs. He'd get restless for a few days. Then he'd head off to the woods on his own—or haul her off with him—to find a place to burn tobacco and sing to the spirits in his mother's tongue.

Sometimes he'd tell her what he was doing; sometimes he wouldn't. She didn't ask him about the rocks he'd bring in or the small bits of cloth he'd set on top of them during certain seasons of the year. He'd told her once that some things were to be shared, and others were not—and that was good enough for her.

But Charles's tobacco scent had come to be comforting. She resented the old man for ruining it.

"Uncle Travis, she's a wolf." Benedict's voice was a whine better suited to a teenager arguing for a later curfew than the grown man he was. Anna was sure by now there was something wrong with him, something more than his being a sociopathic—or was that psychopathic?—serial killer. "She's no good as a wolf. I don't like old men or boys, but I can do them. I won't do a wolf—that's just sick."

"Hush," said the old man. "They can't stay wolves forever. Tomorrow's the full moon; she can stay a wolf through that, but then she'll have to change back when the moon sets."

He was wrong. As long as she didn't mind losing herself to the wolf, she could stay in wolf shape indefinitely, but he sounded very confident. Maybe Cantrip's databases had inaccurate information about more than simply who was and was not fae.

"I can't wait until tomorrow," said Heuter.

"You're not a werewolf," Benedict said. "You don't need the full moon to do anything."

"No, I don't care about the moon." Heuter smiled. "I can't wait to see that smug bastard lose it because we have his wife and he can't find her."

"You aren't going anywhere near him," Uncle Travis snapped irritably. "Don't be stupid. You'll get cocky and he'll smell it on you. Smell her on you, maybe." He didn't take his attention off Anna, so he didn't see the resentment that flashed and disappeared on Heuter's face.

Anna didn't have Charles's memory for information, but she was pretty sure that Heuter was nearly thirty. That was old to be taking orders issued as if he were a child. Werewolves had to follow their Alpha's orders that way, though. They followed them or they were killed. Maybe it was the same kind of thing for Heuter? Maybe his uncle read him better than she did, and the threat of death was enough to keep him in line.

"You look so meek in there," Uncle Travis said—and it took a moment for Anna to process that he was talking to her because he'd switched from talking to Heuter without altering his voice or his body posture. "Are you afraid, princess? You should be. Your kind is trying to take over the world. You don't fool me with the 'we're good guys' spin-doctoring. I know a predator when I see one. It's just like the gays. Just like the gooks and the spics and the dagos. Trying to turn this country into a cesspool."

Gooks were . . . Vietnamese, right? Score one for her high school history class, because she'd never actually heard that one out loud before. Spics were Hispanic. She had no idea who the dagos were. Her racist vocabulary obviously needed work. What would a racist call werewolves? Wargs? She kind of liked that one, but suspected that racist bastards didn't read Tolkien. Or if they did, she didn't want to know about it.

"But we're here to stop you," Uncle Travis said, then smiled seductively—and he was handsome enough that she would bet that a lot of women had followed that smile into a bedroom. "And for payment, all we ask is that we have a little fun along the way—right, boys?"

"Yes," said the big man. "Yes, fun."

It was weird hearing the simplemindedness in his speaking voice and smelling his lust. In her experience—and she'd volunteered in high school with a group that specialized in free babysitting for parents with autistic or special-needs kids—most people who were mentally disabled were pretty sweet as long as their parents hadn't totally spoiled them.

Benedict was not sweet, and he was something a lot more deviant than a spoiled brat. Listening to him and smelling his need gave him an oddly pedophilic vibe. It made her feel filthy by association.

Anna wondered if there had always been something wrong with Benedict, or if Uncle Travis had turned him into this . . . twisted soul.

"Look at her, Uncle Travis," said Heuter. "She's just staring. Is she too scared to fight? Or maybe she thinks she can get away, that she can fight us and win. Maybe she's not scared of a bunch of mere humans."

"No snarls or raging," agreed Uncle Travis. "Might mean she's already given up. Maybe we won't wait until she's human. She's not half as big as that last one was, and he didn't give us any trouble." He put his face near the cage, as if by accident, but she could smell his excitement. He was taunting her, trying to get her to attack. "We took that one apart, piece by piece, until the creature that was left was a mewling, broken thing. We put him down out of pity when we were done with him."

Otten hadn't been trained by Charles, Anna reminded herself firmly. Let success make them careless. She relaxed her ears and changed her posture until the glimpse she saw of the black wolf in the mirror showed a beast who was scared and alone, who knew there was no way her mate could find her—as if the reminder of what had happened to Otten had been enough to steal her confidence.

She had to remind herself firmly that she was only acting hopeless and afraid. That she was not a victim, that she would prevail over them.

Uncle Travis sneered. "Pathetic. But they all are eventually."

"I don't mind pathetic," said Benedict earnestly. "As long as they are pretty. And human. I don't screw animals. Screwing animals is bad."

But Anna noticed that he didn't get any closer to the cage than he had to. His scent was . . . uneasy. Charles had hurt him when they fought and now he didn't want to get too near her.

Uncle Travis ignored Benedict, studying Anna as though she were a puzzle. "I don't think we'll wait. Get the bang stick and the muzzle. We'll put her out again and get the chains back on her."

Uncle Travis didn't specify whom he was ordering around, but Benedict strode off to do his bidding while Heuter never even moved.

Bang stick. A bang stick was a long pole with a firearm that could fire bullets at sharks underwater. She'd seen one on some *National Geographic* show on TV. She'd been rooting for the sharks.

Benedict went into the office in the far corner of the barn and came out with a seven- or eight-foot-long stick with what looked like a hypodermic taped on the end with duct tape. It wasn't a bang stick—but it looked like one had inspired its creation.

Anna rocked back warily. She had no intention of being unconscious again if she could help it. Drugs might not work right on werewolves, but enough drugs could knock her out for a few minutes. She didn't want to be helpless with these men.

ISAAC WAS PRETTY surprised that the high-and-mighty Lord of the Elves didn't get how scared he should be right now, stuck as they all were in a car with Charles while Charles's mate was in the hands of a bunch of serial killers.

That the FBI agents didn't get it, either, was a tribute to the hellacious fine poker face Charles had on, but Isaac would have thought that the fae, being so much older and wiser in song and story, would have better instincts. He should know that the Marrok's Wolfkiller was about to lose it and lots of people were going to die.

Of course, Isaac had gotten the distinct impression that Beauclaire was a tough, tough bastard last night when they'd fought the horned lord together. Attacking an invisible monster with nothing more than a long knife was all sorts of gutsy and maybe a little crazy—though the fae was still alive, which might mean that he hadn't been as crazy as all that. Not that either of them, Isaac or Beauclaire, had done a tithe of the damage the bogeyman of the werewolves had managed. Isaac had been impressed even when he thought that Charles must have been able to see the monster, but Hally had disabused him of that notion.

"He might have seen a flicker," she had told him as they waited for the cops and officials to do their cleanup bit on Gallops Island. "But it's been nearly a week since they killed Jacob. Magic goes fast when you waste it the way these guys do. Like to like, the magic released by Jacob's death would have lit up a little, enough to tell him that there was something in the room, especially if it were a little dark, but not enough to see what it was."

And Charles had attacked as if he knew exactly where he was aiming. Fast. Freaking fast and powerful. Isaac had heard the thunk as the other wolf had landed on the beast, had watched him hang on after the creature had rolled over on him a couple of times. By that time Isaac's clock had been rung but good, so all he remembered were bits and pieces of the end of the fight—but it was enough to wow him.

Isaac had been in his share of fights, both before and after his Change. He knew without arrogance that he was damned good, and five years of karate before he'd been Changed inspired by the desire to never let anyone throw him into a locker again—had proved useful in his job as Alpha. But if he ever went in a ring against Charles, he might as well roll over and show his throat before the first round of hostilities began. No wonder the Marrok used Charles as his cleanup man. Who was going to stand up to that?

Isaac drove the van because when Horatio, the wolf who owned the van—Horatio was not his real name, but he wanted to be an actor and his grasp of Shakespeare was really good, so the nickname stuck—got a good look at Charles's set face, he'd tossed Isaac the keys. Then he'd suggested that he could stop by Isaac's house sometime in the morning to pick up the van if they didn't really need him to come along. He'd waited to make sure that Isaac wouldn't order him to drive, but looked extremely relieved when Isaac gave him the nod. Horatio had more common sense in his little finger than anyone in this van had in his whole body—including Isaac.

Horatio was a good fighter, though. He might have been handy when they ran into the bad guys. Isaac glanced over his shoulder at Charles, who was playing intently with the phone he'd taken from Isaac. Beauclaire was sitting in the far backseat, so maybe he wasn't so oblivious to Charles's state after all. The Marrok's Wolfkiller kept his body turned in the exact direction of their goal. Probably they didn't need Horatio. Probably they didn't need anyone except Charles.

And Horatio would have insisted on driving if he'd come; it was his van, after all. Charles had chosen to give Agent Fisher the shotgun seat—which might have been old-fashioned manners; old wolves did things like that. It was unlikely that he'd done it so he could screw with Isaac by sitting behind him, even if that was the end result. The black cloud of intensity Charles shed made Isaac all sorts of jumpy and would have had Horatio, who was much more high-strung, driving like a six-year-old trying to throw a bowling ball.

It was late, maybe one in the morning, and traffic was correspondingly light so Isaac punched it a little. Not so fast that the cops would feel like it was imperative to pull him over, but not so slow that the wolf in the backseat would decide to take over.

It was a delicate balance. Horatio didn't have any kind of GPS navigation in his old van, but Agent Fisher used her phone to imitate one. They decided that I-93 would be the fastest way there, even though it was a farther distance than taking the back roads.

"Pull over," said Charles, his voice rough.

Isaac wasn't going to argue with him. So he eased the van to a stop on the shoulder of the road.

Charles hopped out, patted the side of the car, and said, "Go on out to the address I gave you. I'm going to run the direct path and I should beat you there."

It wasn't until then that Isaac realized Charles had begun changing to wolf. Isaac couldn't speak—except to swear at the worst bits—while he changed, and Charles could have a regular conversation, or something pretty close to it. Damn. When he grew up, he wanted to be like Charles.

Charles shut the door and took off into the darkness, still on two legs, but his gait was an odd leaping glide, neither human nor lupine. Funny, Isaac mused, how being a werewolf had made him complacent, made him think he knew all there was about being a wolf.

He pulled back onto the interstate and asked, "How long until we get there?"

"Fifteen, twenty minutes," Leslie said. "He thinks he can beat us?"

These weren't Isaac's usual stomping grounds, but he had a fair idea of geography—and a pretty good idea of how fast a ticked-off werewolf was. He mentally added 10 percent more speed just because it was Charles and said, "I think he can, too."

CHARLES WASN'T SURE if this was a good idea or not, but Brother Wolf was done with riding in a car when he had four good feet and Anna needed them. He changed the rest of the way as he ran, which wasn't his favorite way to do it, but he managed.

Isaac's phone, which Charles had left on the seat of the van, had suggested that he could cut through some woods, a few cemeteries and golf courses, and end up where he wanted to be. He didn't expect it to be quite that simple—which was a good thing. Fences, waterways, and houses kept him from a direct path, but he managed. As he got closer, his link to Anna sharpened. He still couldn't talk to her, but he could feel her pain and fear—and that made him flatten out and run even harder.

He narrowly missed being hit by a Subaru Outback on a narrow highway, left it stopped dead with the sour smell of burnt rubber and the driver asking his companion, "Did you see that? What was that thing?" Only as he approached the house did he slow down.

She wasn't hurting anymore.

And now that he could think instead of panic, he knew what Anna had done. Who knew better what a shift felt like than another werewolf? She was smart, his mate. The wolf was tougher than the human and better able to defend herself, so she'd shifted to her lupine form.

She didn't need immediate rescuing; she wasn't hurting now, so he could take a moment. Brother Wolf was all for finding where they had her and killing everyone involved. Charles was okay with the last half, but thought that resting until he wasn't breathing like a steam engine would make it more possible. He dropped to the ground under a bunch of lilac bushes near a sign that read WESTWOOD DANCE STUDIO: ESTAB-LISHED 2006.

Charles would go in when he was at his best, not panting like a greyhound after a race. Brother Wolf wasn't happy, but he had learned that sometimes his human half was wiser—and sometimes not.

High above him, the moon sang. Tomorrow she would be full and there would be no ignoring her. Tonight she kept him company as he rose to go hunt down those who would harm his mate.

BENEDICT SHOVED THE stick at Anna in a quick, jerky motion designed to fool the eye. Charles occasionally sparred with Asil using

Chinese *qiang*, and they used the same sort of movements, twirling the spears and making the ends bob around.

Maybe if she'd been human, it would have worked.

Instead Anna dodged, then grabbed the end just behind the hypodermic when the stick pushed past her. She twisted her head while she clamped her teeth on it.

If it had been a human holding the spear, she'd have pulled it from Benedict's hands. If she had been a real wolf, she couldn't have damaged it. But, though she was small for a werewolf, she was huge for a wolf and stronger than a wolf her size would have been. The end snapped and the hypodermic fell at her feet.

She had a weapon—just let them try to get it out of the cage while she was in her wolf skin. And when she was human, she could use it. She smiled at the old man, letting her tongue loll out at him. Take that.

I am not anyone's victim, not anymore.

Benedict dropped the stick and jumped back—and she smelled fear. She showed her teeth to him and growled, just a little. A taunt.

Uncle Travis took four big strides to reach Benedict and slapped him hard in the face with the flat of his hand. "Stop that. Stop that. She is an abomination, but we have killed abominations before. She's a prisoner and weak—you are a Heuter. We don't cower before disease-ridden monsters."

Benedict started to say something, then stiffened and raised his head. "He's coming."

"Who's coming?" asked Travis.

Benedict changed without answering. Between one breath and the next he became something . . . fantastical.

Anna expected him to be ugly in his fae form, for the outside to represent the inside, but she should have known better. She'd seen the white stag.

A wide rack of antlers, snow-white and silver tipped, rose like a crown from his head—which was not quite human. The eyes were right and the mouth, but the rest of the face was sharper, elongated in an oddly graceful manner.

There was such beauty in the odd symmetry of his features, a beauty not hurt at all by his silver skin. No. Not his skin, though that was pale as well. His whole upper body, face included, was covered with a short, silvery white fur that caught the light and sparkled. His hair was three or four shades of gray and it cascaded through and over the base of his antlers and lay over his hugely muscled shoulders in locks, like drips of melted wax.

He was huge. He wouldn't have been able to stand in a normal house. If Uncle Travis was six feet tall, and she thought he was near that, then Benedict was twice that, not including his horns.

His clothes had melted away—and it occurred to Anna that he probably hadn't changed at all, just lost his hold on the glamour that all fae could use to look human. But his shoulders, chest, and belly were covered with silvery armor that reminded her of an armadillo's covering. It wasn't clothing, but part of his skin.

From the chest downward the pelt of silver hair grew longer, thicker, and curled like the pelt of a buffalo. It covered his hips and left his genitalia peeking through here and there. His legs were built like the back legs of a buffalo or deer—though the size looked more like the giraffe she'd seen at the Brookfield Zoo when she was a kid.

At his . . . hocks or knees, the fur darkened to steel gray and grew longer, like the hair—feathers, her horse-crazy friend from third grade had insisted they call it—on the bottom of a Clydesdale's legs.

He stood on a pair of two-toed hooves, like a moose. He bent his head back, his nose rising toward the ceiling and his antlers exaggerating the movement, and raised one foot up nervously, before setting it down and lowering his head again. He rocked from one hoof to the other, making hollow noises on the wooden floor and leaving marks on the polished surface.

"He's just scared," said Heuter, in the lazy Texas drawl he seemed to drop and pick up again without notice. "There's no one out there. They are clueless."

Anna hadn't heard a car drive up and couldn't smell anything different, though the door was closed and she couldn't get a good scent-fix on anything outside of the barn anyway. Still, she suspected that Les Heuter was right. She knew that no one was looking at Heuter for the killings.

Benedict tossed his head and let loose with the challenging roar she'd heard before. Nothing answered him but the distant sounds of rushing cars and wind trailing through leaves.

But Anna sensed it, too. A feeling of impending doom, like standing on railroad tracks and feeling the rails begin to vibrate before she could hear the train. It took her a moment to realize what that feeling was: she'd been so sure he couldn't find her.

He didn't come through the door. He crashed through the walls like a battering ram. Old two-by-twelve timbers bent open before him like leaves of grass and dripped off him as toothpicks and twigs. His eyes caught hers, swept the room, and then focused on Benedict.

The red wolf's head lowered and he sank down just a little and growled, a sound so deep that the floor of her cage vibrated.

The horned lord shook his great antlers and bellowed, charging forward, in spite of the terror Anna could smell. Charles waited, then moved just enough to get out of his way. The fae's hooves slipped on the hard, slick floor and he hit the mirror, cracking it, before he managed to stop.

"Les, get my Glock," snapped Uncle Travis. "It's still loaded with silver bullets."

Heuter had pulled his own gun, but, obedient to his uncle still, he ran for the office. It meant that he wouldn't shoot Charles yet, but the respite wouldn't last long.

Anna couldn't do anything, stuck in the cage. Charles had many strengths, but he was even more adversely affected by silver than most werewolves. She couldn't let them shoot him.

She had to do something. Anna shoved her head through the silver-coated bars and fought to get free, digging her claws into the wooden bottom of the cage for leverage. She was smaller than most werewolves, so maybe she could force her way out—or maybe the bars would yield to her need to protect her mate. The silver burned even through her thick coat of hair, but she ignored it and kept struggling as she watched her mate battle with the monstrous fae.

Charles leapt as Benedict swept past, landing momentarily on the horned lord's back, and then Charles kept right on going for a dozen strides before turning to face his prey again. It happened so fast that Charles had already stopped before blood started gushing from the long tear down the side of Benedict's neck. Arterial blood, black with oxygen, it sprayed a little as it pumped out.

Heuter had reached the office and Anna felt the bars give against her shoulders. She lunged again, harder. Uncle Travis grabbed the remnants of the bang stick and, swinging it like a baseball bat, he hit her in the face, slamming the side of her head into the bars and wrenching her neck.

Mindful of Charles's battle, not wanting to distract him, Anna didn't make a sound, just kept struggling.

Charles crossed the room in the same zigzag motion she'd seen him use when hunting moose. He didn't look like he was moving very fast—but he crossed the space in record time. This time he sliced the horned lord's face open with his fangs.

The cut on the side of Benedict's neck had already quit bleeding;

he healed that quickly. But fully half of his silvery body was crimson with gore. He staggered and reached both hands to his face. Charles had taken out one eye entirely and sliced though the fae's nose.

It took the fight out of Benedict—Anna could see how that would be; she was pretty sure that something in her nose was broken, and it hurt, blurring her vision and sending weakness shivering through her muscles. Then Heuter came out of the office with a second gun, and she quit caring about anything except getting out so she could keep them from shooting Charles. The bars had moved that last time, before Travis hit her; she *knew* it.

Anna wiggled with all of her might, and the floor gave a little beneath the claws of her back feet. It was too little, too late. The red wolf prowled slowly forward about fifteen feet from Benedict, giving Heuter the perfect shot.

Heuter stopped, fumbled the second gun before putting it in his holster. The fumble made him rush his shot to make up for it and he squeezed the trigger just after Charles lunged.

The sound pulled the old man's attention from the fight. "Les! Get your scrawny ass over here and give me my gun. You can't hit the broad side of a barn. Get a move on. My grandfather was faster than you when he was eighty-six."

Instead of trying for a second shot Heuter ran back toward Travis— proving to Anna that he was no Alpha wolf, whatever he thought he should be.

The bars gave a little bit more and she was sliding forward—and Travis hit her again, in exactly the same spot on her nose where he'd hit her the first time.

CHARLES KNEW HE was winning. He didn't know why Benedict Heuter wasn't going invisible; maybe he was too panicked to do it. Charles wouldn't complain. The horned lord healed faster than a werewolf, but he couldn't replace blood, not unless he was a lot more powerful than he seemed. Blood loss was slowing the fae down, making him clumsier.

There were things that would have made this better. The floor was too slippery—it was a dance floor and he could smell the wax on it. It bothered the fae more than it did him, though, so it wasn't really a major problem as long as he didn't miscalculate. He'd also rather not have two other villains loose and running around with silver-loaded guns while he fought the fae, but they were human and Brother Wolf's instincts were to discount them as a threat. The other thing he knew was that, winning or not, he had to keep his attention on the fae. Slower, clumsier—but he was fast enough and deadly with those antlers. He'd scored once on Charles's shoulder when he'd gone for the fae's throat, and it burned. The tips of those antlers didn't just look silver; they were silver.

The second rule of any drawn-out fight was to demoralize your opponent. The fae had started out scared of him. The strike to Benedict Heuter's face wasn't anything near fatal, but losing an eye was scary—and creatures with antlers and hooves were prone to panic. Fight or flight instinct, the scientists said. Wolves were all fight, and creatures like Benedict were all flight. Panic made people stupid, and since Benedict was already not all that bright from what Charles could tell, panicking him could only make things better.

Of course, the first rule in any kind of fighting was not to get into a long-drawn-out confrontation in the first place. Charles started to sprint forward again when there was a crack of a pistol. The bullet didn't hit him so he ignored it and continued his line of attack. But the small pained sound that Anna made almost immediately afterward was another thing entirely.

He looked over to see Anna half in and half out of the cage, her nose dripping blood, and Travis Heuter standing beside the cage with an extra-long, extra-thick pool cue that had been chewed up on one end. Anna jerked herself back into the cage, where all they could do was poke at her—and something hit him like a freight train in the ribs.

Ignoring the pain, he caught the horned lord's leg, just above his hock, and his fangs severed the big tendon and the smaller muscle there. In a human this would be the Achilles tendon, and slicing it rendered the fae's leg useless.

Benedict tried to put his leg down and fell when it collapsed under him. Charles slid under the antlers and closed his teeth on the horned lord's neck.

Benedict was beaten. Helpless.

He had raped Lizzie Beauclaire and doubtless dozens of others, probably killed as well. Brother Wolf thought he needed to be killed. Charles hesitated.

A car pulled up in a squeal of brakes and rubber and Charles recognized the sound of the van Isaac was driving. The cavalry was here, the horned lord subdued. Killing him to save Anna was unnecessary.

There was something wrong with Benedict's ability to reason, possibly wrong enough to make him not responsible for his actions. Had he been born into a different family, maybe he wouldn't have spent his adulthood killing people. He'd given up the fight, lying still beneath Charles and waiting for the final, killing strike just as deer or elk sometimes did. He was harmless. Imprisoned in bars of steel, he'd hurt no one.

On the island, Charles had decided that he would no longer kill for political expediency, because it had put Anna in danger by interfering with his mate bond. Brother Wolf and he were in agreement: this was not a political kill. This one would have hurt their mate, had killed the wolves under their protection—and had hurt the brave little dancer. Brother Wolf knew what should happen to those who broke the laws: justice.

Charles sank his teeth in deep and then gave a sharp jerk, popping the bones of Benedict's neck apart. The fae spasmed briefly as life left and death entered, and then Charles's prey was nothing but meat. It felt right and proper, and something inside him settled with the meting out of justice. This was what he was, the avenger for Benedict Heuter's victims. This was his answer to the ghosts who had haunted him.

Why had he killed them? Because it was just that they pay for the harm they had done. Warmth flooded his flesh as the cold fingers of the dead left. He was free of them—as they were free of him.

Something warned him, instincts or the sound of a finger pulling a trigger, and he moved instantly. He heard a gun go off and something hit Benedict, almost where Charles had been a moment before. That was a second shot that had missed: someone was a lousy shot.

Charles moved again, leaving the bulk of the horned lord's body between him and the guns, before turning to see that both Travis and Les had guns out, impossible to see who had shot at him. But Travis's gun was aimed at Anna.

"This is the FBI. Drop your weapons," Goldstein shouted from the open door next to the hole Charles had put in the wall. He and Leslie both had their guns drawn, too. There was no sign of Isaac or Beauclaire—Charles assumed they were rounding the building to see if they could enter from the back. "Drop your weapons or I'll shoot."

"Don't be hasty, Agent Goldstein," said Travis. He had his gun in a steady two-handed grip. "This gun is loaded with silver. I shoot her in the head and she dies. I know that no one wants that."

Charles stood frozen, his breath still. He was too far away. It would take him three leaps to get to Travis—and that was two leaps too many.

Les Heuter had raised his hands over his head—but he hadn't let go of his gun.

"Les Heuter, Travis Heuter, drop your weapons," said Goldstein. "This is over."

No one moved.

Charles growled.

"Drop your weapons," said Goldstein, and then he gave in to what must have been years of frustration and pushed it too hard. "You are done. We know who you are and you are going down. Make this easy on everyone."

"You drop your weapon," Travis screamed. "You fucking drop yours. You are *nothing*. Nothing but the impotent tool of a liberal government too weak to serve its people and protect them from these freaks." It sounded oddly like a memorized speech, like some of the phrases Charles Manson's little harem had spouted. Maybe Travis Heuter had said it so often he didn't have to think about it anymore. "You drop *your* weapon, or I'll shoot her now and move on to you."

Goldstein and Leslie were focused on Travis. They missed Les, missed the odd expression on his face that changed from desperation to satisfaction. They didn't see him change his grip on his gun, drop down on one knee, and fire almost in the same single motion. Charles had seen it, but there was nothing he could do without risking Travis shooting Anna, and he wouldn't do that.

"Get down. Get down now," shouted Goldstein, but Les Heuter was already on the ground. "Flat on your face and lock your hands behind your head."

Les had already done it before Goldstein had gotten out a word. The human's reactions were too slow. Now Les was harmless and killing him would be more difficult. Had Charles had a gun at that moment, he would have killed Les anyway, because although Heuter had shot his uncle, it hadn't stopped Travis Heuter from pulling the trigger. Travis Heuter, with a bullet hole right in the center of his forehead, had still managed to squeeze off a shot before he died.

Anna had collapsed in a heap on the bottom of the cage.

He'd hit her in the thigh and her blood pooled around her like a red blanket. Her nose was bent and swollen; Travis had broken something when he'd hit her with the stick.

"It wasn't my fault," said Heuter. "It was my uncle. He made us do it. He was crazy."

Anna whined, and Charles quit hearing Les Heuter try to blame the dead for his crimes.

Charles wrenched the doors of the cage apart with his bare hands, not even realizing that he'd become human again until it registered that he had opposable thumbs to grip the skin-burning silver. He'd never been able to change that quickly before.

And he stank of fae magic. He jerked his eyes to Beauclaire, and the old fae, standing in the doorway next to Isaac, gave him a nod. Later, Charles would wonder at that; he didn't know that there was a way for a fae to affect the change of a werewolf.

But Anna was hurt and there was no time to worry about what Beauclaire was right now. No time for the blind panic he felt or the way he wanted to tear into Travis Heuter's dead body. He had to make sure that Anna would survive.

". . . stop the bleeding until we can get an ambulance out."

Charles growled because Goldstein had come too close to his injured mate. But Isaac stepped in before Charles was driven to act.

"Leave him alone; you don't want to be anywhere near them right now." Smart wolf, that Isaac. Too young or not, Bran had been right to leave him in power. Charles would have killed anyone who got too close.

Threat to his helpless mate averted, Charles mostly ignored the words going on behind his back as he checked Anna over with gentle thoroughness.

"Why is he wearing deerskin and beads?" "Shut up and stay there until we get some cops in to read you your rights." "I mean, he's Native American but how are we going to explain—"

When Charles changed without thinking, when he changed from wolf to human too fast, sometimes his clothes forgot what century he was supposed to be in. The soft deerskin felt comforting and familiar as he touched Anna's poor nose. She licked his fingers nervously because he was hurting her.

First, the bleeding.

He reached down and ripped Travis's sleeve off his arm, ignoring the squawk from the feds as he did so. But Anna growled when the makeshift bandage came close to her, so he dropped it. It made sense that she wouldn't want his scent on her, but Charles's buckskins wouldn't work, leather not being absorbent at all.

"I need—" He didn't get the words all the way out before Isaac said, "Catch," and tossed him one of the huge first aid kits all of the packs kept in their cars on Bran's orders. Just because you could heal fast didn't mean you could heal fast enough, the Marrok liked to say.

Charles banished his da's words, wishing the ghosts of them didn't linger in his ears. There was no reason to panic. She was bleeding freely, but the bullet had gone right through and was embedded in the floor, and there was no sign of arterial bleeding. But Brother Wolf wouldn't be happy until she was well.

Once he had the bullet wound under control, he took a second good look at Anna's head.

He bent down to touch his lips to her ears and asked her, "I can do it now, or you can wait until later. Their drugs don't help much and they'll have to rebreak . . ."

Now. Her voice was clear as a bell in his head—and he realized that their bond was open and strong.

For a moment he was breathless. When had that happened? When he'd accepted his role as justice once more? Accepted that there were other answers than death—but that death was the proper and fitting one? Or had it been when he'd seen blood and known that Travis had managed to hurt her even with her mate so close, when guilt and right and wrong had become only words next to the reality of his mate's wound?

But Anna was hurt and there would be time to figure out what had happened later.

He used their bond to soak up her pain and take as much of it into himself as he could. Then he set the bone of her nose back where it needed to go before the werewolf's ability to mend quickly made it heal crooked. She didn't flinch, though he knew he couldn't take all the pain from her.

Stop that, Anna scolded him. *You don't need to hurt because I do.*

But I do, Charles replied, more honestly than he intended. *I failed to keep you safe.*

She huffed a laugh. *You taught me to keep myself safe—a much better gift for your mate, I think. If you had not found me, I would have killed them all. But you came—and that is another, second gift. That you would come, even though I could have protected myself.*

She was confident and it pleased him. So he didn't think about the three experienced, tough wolves these men had killed at their leisure. Let her feel safe. So he didn't argue with her about it, just ran gentle fingers through the ruff of her fur.

The ghosts are gone, she pronounced with regal certainty, and was asleep before he could answer her.

But he did anyway. "Yes."

13

When Charles was a boy, every fall his grandfather had taken his people and met up with other bands of Indians, most of them fellow Flatheads, Tunaha, or other Salish bands, but sometimes a few Shoshone with whom they were friendly would travel with them. They would ride their horses east to hunt buffalo and prepare for the coming winter.

He was no longer a boy, and traveling east was not a treat anymore, not when it meant that he and his mate were back in a big city instead of settled into his home in the mountains of Montana. Three months had passed since he'd killed Benedict Heuter, and they had come back for his cousin's sensational trial. Boston was beautiful this time of year—the trees showing off their fall colors. But the air still smelled of car exhaust and too many people.

He had testified; Anna had testified; the FBI had testified. Lizzie Beauclaire on crutches with her knee in a brace, and the scars that the Heuters had left her with, had testified. She might, with enough surgeries, be able to walk without crutches again, but dancing was out of the question. Her scars could be reduced, but for the rest of her life she would bear the Heuters' marks as reminders every time she looked in a mirror.

When the prosecution was done presenting its case, the defense began.

They'd spent the last week guiding the jury through the hell that had been Les Heuter's childhood. It had almost been enough to engage Charles's sympathy. Almost.

But then, Charles had been there, had seen the calculation on Les Heuter's face when he shot his uncle. He'd been planning this defense, planning on blaming his ills on the dead. His uncle had been wrong; Les Heuter was smart.

Heuter sat in front of the court, neatly groomed in slacks, shirt, and tie. Nothing too expensive. Nothing too brightly colored. They'd done something with his hair and the clothing that made him look younger than he was. He explained to the jury, the reporters, and the audience in the courtroom what it was like living with a crazy man who'd made him come help him clean up the country—apparently Travis Heuter's name for the torture and rape of his victims—when he was ten years old.

"My cousin Benedict was a little older than me," he told them. "He was a good kid, tried to keep the old man off my back. Took a few beatings for me." He blinked back tears and, when that didn't work, wiped his eyes.

Maybe the tears were genuine, but Charles thought that they were just too perfect, a strong man's single tear to create sympathy rather than real tears, which could have been seen as weakness of character. Les Heuter had hidden what he was for more than two decades; playing a role for the jury didn't seem to be much of a stretch.

"When Benedict was eleven, he had a violent episode. For about two months he was crazy. Tried to stab my uncle, beat me up, and . . ." A careful look down, a faint blush. "It was like a deer or elk going into rut. My uncle tried beating it out of him, tried drugs, but nothing worked. So the old man called in a famous witch. She showed us what he was, what he must have instinctively hidden. He looked like a normal boy—I guess the fae can do that, can look like everyone else—but he was a monster. He had these horns, like a deer, and cloven hooves. And he was a lot bigger than any boy his age should be, six feet then, near enough.

"My aunt had been raped by a stranger when she was sixteen. That was the first time we realized that she'd been raped by a monster."

His lawyer let the noise rise in the courtroom and start to fall down before he asked another question. "What did your uncle do?"

"He paid the witch a boatload of money and she provided him with the means to keep Benedict's ruts under control. She gave him a charm to wear. She told him if he carved these symbols on an animal or two a month or so before the rut came to Benedict, it would stop them. She'd intended for us to sacrifice animals, but"—here a grimace of distaste—"the old man discovered that people worked better. But now the witch knew about us, and we had to get rid of her. My uncle killed her and left her on the front lawn of one of her relatives."

It was a masterful performance, and Heuter managed to keep the same persona under a fierce cross-examination, managed to keep the monster that had helped to rape, torture, and kill people for nearly two decades completely out of sight.

His father was nearly as brilliant. When his wife had died, he'd abandoned his son to be raised by his older brother because he was too busy with public office, too consumed by grief. He'd thought that the boy would be better off in the hands of family than being raised by someone who was paid to do it. He had, he informed the jury, decided to resign from his position in the US Senate.

"It is too little, too late," he told them with remorse that was effective because it was obviously genuine. "But I cannot continue in the job that cost my son so dearly."

And throughout the defense's case, the Heuters' slick team of lawyers subtly reminded the jury and the people in the courtroom that they had been killing fae and werewolves. That Les Heuter thought that he was protecting people.

When Heuter told how his uncle portrayed the werewolves as terrifying beasts, his lawyer presented photographs of the pedophile slain by the Minnesota werewolves. He was careful to mention that the man had been a pedophile, careful to say that the Minnesota authorities were satisfied that those involved had been dealt with appropriately, *very* careful to say that these were examples of the kinds of things that Travis Heuter had shown his nephew.

And, Charles was certain, no one on the jury heard any of what the defense attorney said; they only looked at the pictures. They showed photos of Benedict Heuter's dead body. The body itself had disappeared a few hours after it had been taken to the morgue, but the photos remained. The photos showed a monster, covered in blood and gore, none of the grace that had been the fae's in life visible in his death. One photo showed the bones of Benedict Heuter's neck, crushed and pulled apart though they were as big as the apple someone had used, rather gruesomely, for a comparison.

Though the biggest monster in the room was sitting in the defendant's chair, Charles was sure that the only monsters the jury saw were Benedict Heuter—and the werewolf who had killed him.

THEY WAITED FOR the verdict in Beauclaire's office, he and Anna, Lizzie, Beauclaire, his ex-wife and her current husband. Charles wished that they could have accepted Isaac's offer of a good meal instead—but Beauclaire had been insistent in that polite-but-willing-to-draw-a-sword-to-get-his-way kind of manner that some of the oldest fae had. Charles was pretty sure that it was Anna's presence he wanted, and that he wanted her to be with Lizzie when Heuter was sentenced.

Because the lawyer surely knew, as Charles knew, that it would be a light sentence. The defense attorneys had earned their pay. They couldn't erase all of the bodies that the Heuters had left behind, but they had done their best.

Beauclaire's office smelled empty. The wall-to-wall bookshelves were clean and vacant. He was retiring. Officially outed as fae, his firm felt that it was in their best interest, and the interest of their clients, that he cease practicing. He didn't seem too upset about it.

Charles's nose told him that the rest of the firm were mostly fae— and that there were a lot of taped-up boxes in the hallway. Maybe they were planning on closing the firm altogether, reinventing themselves and going on. One of those gift/curse things about a long life. He'd "retired" and started anew a few times himself.

They played pinochle, a slightly different version than either he or Anna knew, but that was, generally speaking, true of pinochle any-where. It kept them busy while they waited and kept the tension at a low sizzle.

There was no love lost between Lizzie's parents, though they were frighteningly polite to each other. Her stepfather ignored the tension admirably and seemed to have decided it was his job to keep Lizzie entertained.

When the call came that the jury had handed in a verdict, after only four hours of deliberation, they threw in their hands with a sigh of relief.

THE JUDGE WAS a gray-haired woman with rounded features and eyes that were more comfortable with a smile than a frown. She had avoided looking at Charles, Anna, or Isaac during the trial—and she had quietly stationed a guard between her and the witness stand when any of the werewolves or fae, including Lizzie, had been questioned. Her voice was slow and patient as she listed the names for which murder charges had been lodged against Les Heuter. It took a long time. When she finished, she said, "How do you find the defendant?"

The foreman of the jury swallowed a little nervously, glanced at Charles, cleared his throat, and said, "We find the defendant innocent of all charges."

The courtroom was silent for a long breath.

Then Alistair Beauclaire stood, his face expressionless, but rage in every other part of his body. He looked at the members of the jury, then at the judge. Without a change of expression, he turned and stalked out of the courtroom. Only when he was gone did the room explode into noise.

Les exchanged exuberant hugs with his lawyers and his father. Beside Charles, Anna let out a low growl at the sight.

"We need to get Lizzie out of here," Charles told her. "This is going to be a zoo."

He stood up as he said it and used his body to clear a pathway for Beauclaire's daughter and her mother and stepfather while Anna shepherded them out. Several reporters came up and shouted questions, but they backed off when Charles bared his teeth at them—or maybe it was his eyes, because he knew that Brother Wolf had turned them to gold.

"I expected he'd get off lightly," Lizzie's mother said, her teeth chattering as if the brisk autumn air was below freezing—rage, Charles judged. "I thought he'd be convicted on a lesser charge. I never dreamed they'd just let him go."

Her husband had an arm around Lizzie, who looked dazed.

"He's free," she said in a bewildered voice. "They knew. They knew what he did. Not just to me but to all those people—and they just let him go."

Charles kept half of his attention on Heuter, who was speaking to a crowd of reporters on the courthouse steps, maybe fifty feet away. His body language and face conveyed a man who was sincerely remorseful for the deeds his uncle had made him do. It made Brother Wolf snarl. Heuter's father, the senator from Texas, stood behind him with a hand on his shoulder. If either of them had seen Lizzie's mother's face, they'd have been hiring bodyguards. If she'd had a gun in her hand, she'd have used it.

Charles understood the sentiment.

"They played up the strangeness of the fae and the werewolves and used it to scare the jury into acquittal," said Lizzie's stepfather, sounding as shocked as Lizzie. Then he looked Charles in the eye, though he'd been warned by Beauclaire not to do so. "Travis and Benedict won't hurt anyone else—and people will be watching Les if I have to hire them myself. He'll make a mistake and we'll send him back to jail."

"You might consider investigating the jurors, too," suggested Anna in a cold voice that didn't hide her fury. "The good senator has more than enough money to bribe a few people if necessary."

Lizzie's stepfather turned to Lizzie and his voice softened. "Let's get you home, sweetheart. You'll probably have to give an interview to get rid of the reporters, but my attorney or your dad can set that up."

"Trust Alistair not to be here when we need him," muttered Lizzie's mother. But she said it without venom. Then she said, "Okay, I know that's not fair. He knows you're safe with us, honey. And he probably was worried he'd kill Heuter if he had to look at him, running around free as a bird. And much as I wish he could do that, it would cause more problems than it solved. He always missed the days when he could kill anyone who bothered him."

Anna put her hand on Charles's arm. "Do you hear that?" she asked so urgently that everyone turned to look at her.

Charles didn't hear anything over the crowds of people, honking cars, and carriage-horse hooves.

Anna glanced around, standing on her toes to see over people's heads. There was still a crowd on the steps and hordes of reporters because serial killer plus senator's son equaled Big Story. Charles looked around, too—and then realized that he couldn't see any carriage horses.

He never saw when they appeared, or where they came from, but suddenly they were just there. After a few minutes, other people saw them, too, and fell silent. Traffic stopped. Les Heuter and his reporter were still wrapped up in his statement full of lies for the national news, but Senator Heuter was facing the street and put his hand on his son's shoulder.

Fifty-nine black horses stood motionless on the roadway in front of the courthouse. They were tall and slender, like thoroughbred race-horses, except their manes and tails were fuller—absurdly so. Silver chains were woven through their manes, and on the chains were silver bells.

Charles knew horses. There was no way fifty-nine horses would stand still, with neither a flick of an ear nor a twitch of their tails.

Their saddles were white—old-fashioned saddles with high cantles and pommels, almost like a western saddle without a horn. The saddle blankets were silver. None of them wore bridles.

Every horse bore a rider dressed in black with silver trim, as motionless as their horses. Their pants were loose-fitting, made of some lightweight fabric; their shirts were tunics embroidered with silver thread, the pattern of the stitching different for each rider. This one had flowers, this one stars, the other ivy leaves. Charles knew that there was magic at work because he could not discern a single face, though none of them wore a mask.

Just when the spell of their arrival started to thin, when people in the crowd started to whisper, they parted. The horses backed up and around to form two lines facing each other, and through this passage a white horse cantered slowly. As with the other horses, he wore no bridle—but this horse had no saddle, either. Just black chains strung through his mane and tail, covered in silver bells that jingled sweetly in time to the horse's steady movement.

On the horse was a man dressed in silver and white. In his right hand he held a silver short sword, in his left a sprig of a plant, blue green leaves, and small yellow blooms. Rue.

The white horse stopped at the foot of the stairs and Charles noticed two things. First, the horse had bright blue eyes that caught his and studied him coolly before the horse moved on to stare at Lizzie. Second, that the horse's rider was Lizzie's father.

"I told them," he said in a clear, carrying voice, "that they should not give someone as old and powerful as I a daughter to love. That it would end badly."

His horse shifted, raising one front leg and pawing at the air before replacing it exactly where it had been.

"Now we shall all live with the consequences."

The white horse rose on his hind legs, not rearing. This was a precise, slow levade, as balanced and graceful as any ballet movement.

"What was done today was not justice. This man raped and tortured my daughter. When he was finished, he would have killed her. But you all see us as monsters—so frightened of the dark that you cannot see truly your own monsters among you. Very well. You have made it clear that we and our children are not citizens of this country, that we are separate. And that we will receive a separate justice that has little to do with the lovely lady who holds the balanced scales—and has every-thing to do with your fear."

The horse came down to rest on all four feet again.

"You have made your choice. And we will all live with the conse-quences. Most of us. Most of us will live with the consequences."

The white horse started forward again, up the cement stairs. His silver-shod hooves clicked as he walked and Alistair Beauclaire crum-bled the rue in his left hand and scattered it as they walked, leaving behind a trail of leaves that was too thick for the small sprig he had started with. The last of it fell from his hands as the horse stopped in front of Les Heuter.

Charles tried to move at last—but found he could do nothing except breathe.

"It is not meet that my daughter's attacker should live," Beauclaire said. He raised his sword and swung, scarcely slowing as metal met flesh and won. He beheaded Les Heuter in front of the television camera—and then spoke into it.

"For two hundred years I have been bound by my oath that I would not use my powers for personal gain, nor for the gain of my people. In return we would be allowed to come here and live in quiet harmony in a place unbound by iron."

He didn't say whom he'd sworn his oath to, though Charles rather thought it didn't matter. For one such as this fae, an oath sworn to a child was as valid as an oath sworn to a king or the pope.

Tipping his bloody blade toward the body on the ground, Beau-claire said, quietly, "The time of that oath is past, broken by this man and by those who freed him without regard to justice. I reclaim my magic for me and for my people. Our day begins anew."

Then he raised the dripping sword up toward the sky and announced harshly, "We, the fae, declare ourselves free of the laws of the United

States of America. We do not recognize them. They have no authority over us. From this moment forward we are our own sovereign nation, claiming as our own those lands ceded to us. We will treat with you, as one hostile nation treats with another, until such time as it seems us good to do elsewise. I, Alistair Beauclaire, once and again Gwyn ap Lugh, Prince of the Gray Lords, do so determine. All will abide my wishes."

The white horse raised his front feet and spun, bounding down the stairs and back through the path the other riders had made for him. As the white horse ran, a white mist rose behind him, covering them all for a moment before dissipating, taking with it all the fae.

Senator Heuter dropped to his knees to mourn his son.

THE MARROK LET himself into his son's house. Charles had flown home the night before—all the way from Boston. He'd decided to quit taking commercial flights until security no longer required him to watch others pat down his mate. Bran couldn't argue with his logic, but they had arrived late and gone straight home. Bran had tried to let them sleep in, but the need to make sure they were safe had overridden his sense of courtesy.

He walked soundlessly down the hall to the bedroom.

Charles lay on the bed with Anna sprawled bonelessly on top of him, her hair covering her face. Bran smiled, pleased that his son was happy. No matter what else was wrong, and he was very afraid that a lot was going to be wrong in very short order thanks to the unexpected move by the usually cautious fae, the knowledge that Charles was going to be all right was satisfying. In that moment, watching his son sleep, he understood Beauclaire's actions entirely.

Charles's eyes slit open, bright gold.

"Sleep for a little while, Brother Wolf," Bran murmured very softly. "I'll keep watch until you wake."

"**THE FAE HAVE** retreated to their reservations," Da said as he served Anna pancakes. His da liked to make pancakes for breakfast, but the deer-shaped ones were a new thing. Charles tried not to analyze his father when he could avoid it.

"What about the humans?" Anna asked. "The reservation bureaucracy?" She didn't seem bothered by the pancakes.

He'd woken up after flying from Boston to Montana to find his da cooking breakfast for them: sausage and pancakes shaped like deer. It wasn't just any deer, either—they looked like Bambi from the Disney cartoon. Charles didn't want to know how his father had managed that.

Charles preferred his deer to taste like meat and his pancakes to look like pancakes. Brother Wolf thought he was too picky. Brother Wolf was probably right.

"The humans were driven out and the gates closed against them. Army helicopters sent to surveil the area can't seem to find the reservations to fly over them."

Charles snorted. "Typical fae stuff."

"They've approached me," Da said.

Charles put down his fork. Anna, being Anna, took the spatula out of his da's hand and tugged him down to sit with them. She didn't say anything, just piled up some pancakes on a plate, poured maple syrup over them, and handed them to his da.

"What did they say?" asked Charles.

"They apologized for the disruption their actions will have on our ability to integrate with human society." He ate a bite of pancake and closed his eyes. "They thanked me for my son's help in the matter of Les Heuter."

"The fae thanked you?" asked Charles. The fae didn't thank anyone, nor was it wise to thank the fae: it put you in their power.

His father nodded. "Then they asked me to meet with them to discuss matters of diplomacy."

"What did you say?"

His father smiled briefly, ate another bite of pancake. "I told them I'd consider it. I don't intend to let them force me into following their lead."

Anna held up her glass of orange juice in a formal toast. "To interesting times," she said.

His da leaned over and kissed her forehead.

Charles smiled and took a bite of his deer pancake. It tasted just fine.